THE CHAMELEON

Also by Sugar Rautbord

SWEET REVENGE
GIRLS IN HIGH PLACES (co-authored)

THE CHAMELEON

SUGAR RAUTBORD

WARNER BOOKS

A Time Warner Company

The majority of events and characters in this book are fictitious. Certain real locations, public figures, and historical events are mentioned; I used literary license with these people, places, and events to bring *The Chameleon* to life. All other characters, places, and events are totally imaginary.

Warner Books, Inc., 1271 Avenue of the Americas, New York, NY 10020

Visit our Web site at www.warnerbooks.com

 A Time Warner Company

Printed in the United States of America

First Printing: May 1999

10 9 8 7 6 5 4 3 2 1

Library of Congress Cataloging-in-Publication Data

Rautbord, Sugar.
    The chameleon / Sugar Rautbord.
      p. cm.
    ISBN 0-446-52187-6
    I. Title.
  PS3568.A827C48   1999
  813'.54—dc21   98-37558
                                                               CIP

To all the chameleons—the women who've had
the courage to change.

Acknowledgments

I wish to thank all the people at Marshall Field's who whirled me through the revolving doors and ushered me into their vast archives of social and fashion history. A special nod to retail wizard Michael Francis, window dresser superstar Jamie Becker, and store historian Homer Sharp, who was there when Coco Chanel herself swept into the store and young Vincent Minnelli was designing windows.

Thank you to my friends at Warner Books, especially Caryn Karmatz Rudy and Maureen Egen, and my stalwart cohorts Marcy Posner, Leigh Ann Hirschman, and Susan Leon.

My gratitude to the Chicago Historical Society and to Time Warner's Gerald Levin and Nan Miller for access to historical material from 1924 to 1970 or until my memory kicked in.

A salute to Jacques Leviant, Anne Roosevelt, Christopher Ogden, Maureen Smith, Bill Bartholomay, Kevin Johnson, Virginia Smiley, Audrey Pass, Patricia Tracy, John Remington, and all the wonderful people who helped me sort the facts and find my voice.

Always thank you to Shelley Wanger, the Arnold Jurdems, Miriam Schwartz, Roy Zurkowski, Audrey Gruss, Juanita Jordan, Gigi Mahon, Lane Davis, Bill Zwecker, Karen Patterson and Michael Rautbord for being there.

Change your hair, change your politics, change your tax bracket. Reinvent yourselves, my dear, or the world will pass you by. Keep changing and when one door shuts you'll turn the knob and open another.

—Virginia George

You know how it is, when you look back on your life, you hardly recognize the person you once were. Like a snake shedding skins.

—Jacqueline Kennedy Onassis

THE CHAMELEON

Prologue

I have learned to confront misfortune even when it swallowed me whole.
I adapt to surroundings. I do not cave in to odds.
I instinctively know when it is time to change.
I reinvent myself when necessary.
I am a chameleon.

—*Claire Harrison Grant*

She spoke in the low-pitched, cultured voice that was her trademark. The voice conjured up all the best places—private white beaches with big striped umbrellas, candlelit dinners in foreign embassies, highballs in old WASPy clubs—but its power lay in the instant intimacy it created, as if the focus of her attention was more fascinating to her at that moment than any world leader or lover she had ever known. Now the attention of the famous Claire Harrison Duccio Lefkowitz Grant was leveled at the eleven men who would decide her future.

She ignored the crowd in the chamber and the whirring television cameras as she answered their questions, one by one. When they brought up her past, she braced herself for the barrage of words that would echo off the hearing room's turn-of-the-century chandelier. Her stories, tossed up like an unsolvable puzzle that would fall down around her in a thousand pieces, rearranged to support their version of her history. She volleyed back with a practiced smile, the one she had cultivated for fifty years, the one that calmed her and belied any fear she was feeling. How often she had relied on this slight lift of her lips when she was in danger.

She lowered her voice an octave, as if she were inviting them into her private rooms, where each man's special interests would be listened to with all the flattery they deserved. There was a kind, maternal quality to her voice now. It had taken her years to get it just right, to have just this kind of effect on people.

Her listeners, wearing good-on-television red neckties, leaned forward to hear her better. This group of men, their brass nameplates arranged in front of them like giant place cards at one of Claire's famous dinners, were there to untangle the rumors that swirled around Claire from the facts. It was whispered that her celebrated stamp collection was a personal portrait gallery of all the great men she had known and that she kept her latest late husband's ashes in a green jar on her kitchen counter between the allspice and the oregano. Odd fodder for this stony lineup of middle-aged senators. She was seated at the green felt-covered table across from and several feet below their bench, wearing the same serene look that had stared out at them from dozens of magazines, her fingers gracefully interlaced. Her violet eyes pierced the dim room and seemed to beam directly upon each one of them, the currents of warmth in her soft irises rendering her unexpectedly vulnerable. Despite the acreage of years she had covered, most of it squarely in the public eye, Claire was remarkably handsome. She had opted not to change her face with cosmetic surgery. Most of her cronies, stalwart surgical pioneers, looked like they'd been hurled through wind tunnels at breakneck speeds. Claire had chosen to do her changing from within.

The sun emerged from behind a cloud and shone through the heavy wooden blinds, backlighting Claire like in a forties film noir. The kind she and Lefty used to cast. One of those romantic mysteries she could imagine she was starring in today. Would the heroine outwit the villain? Would the lady get her own microphone at the U.N.?

Claire inhaled deeply and adjusted her skirt length with only a slight movement of her leg. A subtle hitch. No hands. A trick she had learned from the image-conscious duchess of Windsor and mastered years ago when Claire realized she also would be on continuous public display. Everything that had been useful in her life she had learned early on in her unorthodox upbringing.

She drummed her fingers on the table and turned her head to survey the room. Why was it so difficult for these men to realize that the accomplished woman sitting in front of them was light-years away from that shy teenager photographed at Eleanor Roosevelt's elbow, or the notorious mankiller wrapped in a Christian Dior gown on the cover of *Look*?

Claire brightened when she saw the wild halo of apple-red curls and mouthed "I'm glad you're here" to her daughter. The earnest face suddenly put all her ambitions in perspective. This had been her hardest-fought battle, more bitter than any she'd fought with the powerful men who had crossed their swords with hers.

The men in her life. Fenwick Grant had called Claire a magnificent castle with no central heating. Fulco Duccio had called her the most expensive courtesan on the continent and many cruder things. Lefty Lefkowitz had said his beloved Claire was the most understanding wife in the world, whose skillful nursing had given him two more wonderful years. She had been called many other, less flattering, things, including murderess. Great luck and great tragedy had touched her, yet no one held the key to the castle that was Claire. She smiled now at the management of this carefully constructed facade, even as she thought of the men she had loved, and the one among them who had surely been the love of her life. As she thought of him now, of the touch of his elegant hands on her flesh, she involuntarily raised a hand to her lips and there was genuine excitement in her eyes.

Perhaps they would make her the ambassador. She believed with all her heart that she was singularly prepared for this role. After all, she had survived an avalanche of a life.

Not so bad for a girl who had come from humble origins.

Chapter One

Humble Origins

Many who arrive at the top are found to have very simple backgrounds.

—*Eleanor Roosevelt*

Violet Organ was in a pickle. It wasn't enough that Leland Organ had saddled her with a plainly ugly last name. He had abandoned her at the worst of times. She hadn't been able to keep anything down except Frango mints for the last two days. Her young husband had suddenly developed traveling feet and bolted six months earlier to see the Pyramids, leaving her, Hyde Park, his job as a geography teacher, and a growing bump now the size of a world globe in Violet's belly. She was feeling so queasy she almost hadn't made it out of bed this morning, but if she missed one more day of work, she'd get her pink slip for sure.

"Hurry up," Slim called to her friend. "We don't want to be trampled to death on the train by all these last-minute shoppers. Procrastinators!"

Talk about waiting until the last minute, Violet thought. She supposed not going to the doctor to check on her symptoms was her own form of procrastination. There was hardly any mistaking them now. But then there was the expense of a doctor, which she couldn't afford, not to mention the embarrassment of it all. Part of her had preferred not to think about her predicament, hoping it would just go away like the January white sales. She let Miss Slim wrangle her to the train door.

"I'm doomed," Violet Organ murmured. "It's probably too late for me." Could a healthy twenty-two-year-old be stricken with liver disease? Wouldn't that be better than having a baby? People were sent to sanatoriums out West where they recovered, weren't they? Or was that for some other disease? She was confused. She'd been feeling so light-headed since she'd awakened at dawn. How could she possibly work all day on her feet and take care of a child with only eighteen dollars in the bank? She could barely take care of herself. And how would she explain the sudden appearance of a baby? Did Marshall Field's Department Store believe in the stork? Violet sighed. Nineteen twenty-three was ending on a very low note.

When her belly had first started to swell a few months ago, she thought it might be an ulcer or a gallstone, her menstrual cycle being as erratic as her charming but peripatetic spouse. But as the bump in her belly was now swollen to the size of a pocketbook, even someone as naive as she could no longer deny the obvious. A baby born to a poor salesgirl whose husband was missing was utterly unthinkable. She hadn't dared to confide in anyone, not even Slim. She couldn't let anyone see how ill she was, or how desperate. Violet couldn't afford to lose her job at Marshall Field's this close to Christmas, not when there were a hundred girls in line anxious for the chance to work at the finest store in America, whose employees proudly felt a cut above anyone who worked anyplace else. By half starving herself and small-boned to begin with, she had put on only fourteen pounds. What if there were medical bills? What if she lost her Christmas bonus, her employee benefits, and all of the lovely friends she'd made in the two years she'd been there? They were becoming like family to her. Especially since Leland Organ had up and left. If only she could go to the store's Lost and Found on the third floor and find him, her "missing Organ," as Slim cheekily referred to Violet's aberrant husband.

She steadied herself as the Illinois Central train rounded its last

big curve. Why, Marshall Field's *was* her family now. Who else
was there? Her beautiful violet eyes brimmed over with tears. She
quickly dabbed at them with a gloved fist as the train pulled into
the black tunnel. Soon there would be the bright artificial lights
of the early morning hustle in the Randolph Street station with
its wake-up smells of freshly brewed coffee, warmed-over stale
popcorn, and roasted chestnuts. At this hour, everyone would be
headed in the same direction. To work.

And Violet was a good worker. She enjoyed her job in the
world's most luxurious store among the cashmere, couture, fine
china, and antique silver. She didn't even mind catering to the
rich, famous, and fussy. The store was like an enchanted fairy land
inviting the shopper as well as the lookers who couldn't afford
more than a thimble and thread or a purchase or two at the ribbon counter.

Some people came to Chicago just for the chance to window-
shop or daydream at Marshall Field's. Spotlighted display tables
were set with gleaming silver centerpieces brimming over with
freshly cut flowers, Waterford crystal, and Limoges china on
fine linen, the napkins folded as if company were coming to
dinner. Sometimes a flush customer would point to the whole
ensemble and say, "That's exactly what I want. I'll take the
whole table." The affluent carriage trade pushed through the revolving doors to shop for everything for their homes, their
births, their debuts, weddings, and, in the case of one or two ancient North Side matrons, their own burial gowns. Often the
younger society bunch would leave messages for one another at
the elegant emporium's message center, or preferably with
Charley Pritzlaff, the doorman, as they considered Field's their
private club. And although they tipped him from time to time,
it was hardly enough to compensate Charley for remembering
that Miss Donnelley was having her fitting at three on Five and
Miss Armstrong was lunching in the Narcissus Room at her
usual table if Miss Armour and Miss Smith cared to join her,

and didn't their hats look grand. Field's employees were required to be psychiatrists, confidants, fashion consultants, and
always in polite good humor.

"Hurry up, Violet," Slim said, scooping Violet Organ's elbow
into her steady hand like a forklift moving merchandise at Field's
warehouse. "Salesladies must be alert at their posts before the customers come barging in."

Thank goodness Miss Slim, Violet's best friend from the store,
was with her. They always referred to each other as "Miss Slim"
or "Miss Violet" in the store, as company policy dictated. She
didn't think she could have gone the distance by herself. It wasn't
as if Violet were looking for a sympathy slot—just a warm, safe
place to lie down and sleep. Perhaps for the rest of the winter. She
yawned wearily. How dreamy it would be to curl up in one of
the magnificent four-poster beds on the eighth floor, tucked in
with the finest French linens threaded with Egyptian cotton for
luxurious sleeping, as the catalog said, with mattresses so cushy
they would cradle her to sleep. Wouldn't that be nice! She fluttered her thick lashes as Slim dragged her past the newsboy.

Violet's vision was so blurry that all she could make out was
The Chicago Tribune, December 23, 1923. Only two more shopping
days until Christmas. The store would be packed with a sea of
people carrying parcels and good cheer, bundled up in, mufflers
and mittens, happily shopping for or with their families. She wasn't
feeling up to selling and chatting with her customers today. She
was feeling nauseated. A feeling-sorry-for-herself tear slipped
down, a dark eyelash falling on her porcelain cheek. She felt as if
she were going to crack just like the translucent Spode teacup
she'd dropped last week during a dizzy spell and then had been
charged for.

"Just lift your little feet, Violet. Don't worry, I'll push you
along."

Slim raised one of her eyebrows, which were tricky little art
deco deals, almost works of art, plucked and penciled into chic

arches. Slim was Ladies' Finery and Furs. Sixth floor. She was going to Paris as soon as she'd saved the money. Miss Slim had been married once for five days, at which time her handsome new husband had been called off to the Great War and was killed. Having only enjoyed the honeymoon and never the little let-downs of marriage, Miss Slim, who smoked cigarettes, wore lip rouge, and shook her sassy Clara Bow haircut whenever she was making a point, was the dressing-room authority on sex and "l'amour," as she called it, in her eternal devotion to things French. She adored all conversations related to the wonderful madness of romance and passion. Miss Slim always referred to her husband as her "war wound," since his World War I death had wounded her forever. With her short, straight band of bangs and ear-length bob, she was the epitome of the stylish salesgirl with just a smack of roaring twenties flapper.

By contrast, Violet, dreamy-eyed and reticent with her long, wavy hair held back in pins, all of it now tucked under a perky cloche, always looked as if she had just stepped out of the last century and was befuddled to find herself in this one.

Both Violet and Slim shivered as they moved out of the cocoon of the walkway tunnel and up the Illinois Central stairs, outdoors and into a blast of arctic air at the corner of Randolph and Michigan Avenue. The Windy City suddenly lived up to its reputation as a tornadolike gust blew an assortment of men's hats off their heads: bowlers, derbies, and fedoras whirling up, off and into the direction of State Street. The wind whipped through the working ladies' thin cloth coats, sending their shoulders to their ears as if they could shrug off the cold.

"Boy, if only that gentleman from Minneapolis had bought me that sable coat I sold him for his cow wife yesterday." Slim's lament froze in midair. She tucked her chin into her squirrel collar to prevent the cold wind from needling her lungs. "The two of us could have fit into it comfortably together. Why, it was so enormous—"

"I feel warmish." Violet was the color of those white silk bed sheets sold on Eight. Sweat beads were forming at her temples despite the terrific cold.

"Oh my dear, you're clammy." Miss Wren emerged from the shelter of Pete's newsstand and closed in on the left flank. She'd been waiting for them under the portico of the Chicago Public Library where the small oil-can fire had momentarily taken the chill off her bones. The apple-cheeked Miss Wren sturdily lifted Violet's other elbow so that her tiny feet needn't bother to touch the sidewalk, just as they'd been doing every day this past week.

"She's getting heavier," Miss Wren said behind Violet's ears.

"Don't be ridiculous. The girl looks like a scarecrow! Did you get my movie magazine?"

Miss Wren shoved the fan magazine across Violet's chest. She had just purchased the latest crossword puzzle book and a copy of *Collier's* for herself. As she slipped the copy of *Silent Screen* with a mournful Zasu Pitts on the cover over to Slim, she was struck by Violet's pallor. Miss Wren was suddenly reminded of her own poor mother, who had recently passed away.

"I tell you it's serious. She's too young to look so tired."

At that moment Violet winced and placed her hands on her right side. She apologetically explained, "Gas."

"Appendicitis." Miss Slim decided, blowing her frozen words over to Miss Wren.

"Gallstones." Miss Wren returned the volley.

Twins! Violet thought to herself in sudden horror. For months she had been hoping to hear the missing Mr. Organ's key turn in the door of their one-room Kenwood flat and announce that he was back for good to care for her and teach geography instead of traipsing the globe like a bespectacled Ulysses. Now she was seized with the terrible notion that he had brought her something more than the colorful souvenirs and native dolls from South America on his last trip home. What if it were something truly terrible, like syphilis? She had no idea exactly where Leland had been on his adventures; she had simply indulged his wanderlust, hoping it was just a thirst that time would quench. But if theirs was to be the Lost Generation, why did her husband have to take it literally? The pain that gripped her was double anything she had felt before. Why, if she had gone to a doctor, his diagnosis would have been "Stupid, stupid, stupid!"

"Sex." Violet blushed. How improper the whole business was. No, she didn't care if Mr. Organ ever came home.

"Divorce." Violet Organ whispered the forbidden words into the wind. She wondered how Marshall Field's Department Store would respond to the very unorthodox act of having one of its salesladies behave like the society folk to whom they were supposed to cater.

Violet thought it was so unfair that it was perfectly all right for her to sell Mrs. Hollingsworth an extravagant trousseau for her third marriage to some polo-playing playboy, but heaven help an abandoned, pregnant salesgirl thinking of legally leaving her "gone far and away" spouse—especially if she worked in a store that sold family values every bit as much as silver place settings, diamond chokers, chocolate truffles, school clothes, and shoes for the entire family.

"Archaeologist my foot!" Her words angrily assaulted the icy air as she thought back to his only postcard. He'd run off to join the excavators of the newly discovered King Tutankhamen's tomb the way an impulsive child might run off to join the circus. "He's just a geography teacher with a shovel."

"Uhhhhh!" A piercing pain shot through Violet's tummy like an eel weaving its way through her insides.

"Ohhhhh!" Miss Slim said, echoing the same sound, only in enchantment. The trio stopped in their tracks and stood wide-eyed in front of the big Christmas window.

Pain was pushed aside as Miss Slim, Miss Wren, and even the teary-eyed Violet fell under the spell of Fraser's greatest glory. Arthur Fraser, with his staff of twenty display artists, painters, carpenters, plaster molders, and electricians, created his windows like meticulously crafted stage sets. The sixty-foot window was breathtaking with its Noel magic and fashions of the hour. The two ladies balanced Violet between them as she pressed her nose against the window. It was too cold to snow outside, but inside the enchanted store window fake snow was softly falling, miraculously visible from two tall French windows that sheltered a stylishly decorated art deco living room. Inside, a happy family was gathered in front of a cozy fire. A mother mannequin wearing a Vionnet velvet evening gown and a father mannequin sporting a satin-collared smoking jacket were enjoying the magic with their two eager, round-faced mannequin children, a boy and a girl, while the doggy mannequin and the starched-white-aproned, crisp-capped maid mannequin looked on approvingly as she held out a tray of cheese puffs. A stern-faced nanny mannequin rocked her miniature mannequin charge, snug and warm in its Italian hand-crafted cradle, available in Infants' Goods on Four. All the holiday gawkers gathered outside oohed and aahed into the frosty air, creating ice balloons with their breath.

The details in Field's windows were artfully impeccable, but that was why thousands of people poured into Chicago to see the spectacular displays. In the center of the window scene, a pyramid of presents encircled an elegant twelve-foot Christmas tree lit by flickering candles. But the real stars of the "Window Show," decked out in red velvet with white satin trim and gold braiding, were the robust Mr. and Mrs. Santa Claus who were sitting down with the Field's family to Christmas cider and yummy gourmet treats.

"Uhhhh!" Another piercing pain shot through Violet, turning her into a skinny question mark. "I think I'm going to expire." Violet started to fold.

"Get her into the store!" Slim snapped.

"Why?" Miss Wren asked but did as she was told.

"Because nobody's ever died in Marshall Field's!"

"Oh dear, I'd hate for Violet to be the first," said Miss Wren.

"Nonsense! Christmas is no time for tragedy." And with that, the Misses Wren and Slim waltzed in the door of the employees' entrance, the airborne Violet Organ between them, up the main aisles wreathed in holly, mistletoe, ribbons, and tinsel, to a lovely little creche with the baby Jesus and the barnyard animals gathered in the manger that greeted them as they clocked in for work.

"Going up!" Homer Jackson, the impressively uniformed elevator operator, smiled broadly, courteously greeting the regular shop girls on their way to their posts.

Violet clenched her teeth to keep from screaming. The store smells of evergreens, fresh chocolates, brass polish, and rich perfumes accosted her nostrils, and she closed her eyes, ready to swoon in a dizzy vapor. The store was already full of anxious holiday shoppers. Somehow she thought if she could just get to her counter in Finer Dresses on Five, everything would be all right.

"Second floor. Linens. The Elizzzzabethan Roooom," Homer sang. He ran his elevator like a streetcar conductor, calling out the most interesting stops and sights along the way. His routine never varied. Whether he was running his Otis car for customers or employees, he let everyone know where the goods were.

Homer pulled open the heavy iron door to reveal the Marshall Field's Choral Society hitting a crescendo in "Away in a Manger."

"Oh dear! Violet looks like she's been hit by a train."

"Let's get her to the first aid room."

"Or the waiting room."

"Homer, hurry! Can't you make this an express?" Slim was panicked.

"Company rules." Homer sighed. "Gotta stop at every floor." Once again, he pulled the ornate iron door open. "Third floor. Booooks—Staaaamps!"

"Ohhhhh." A sharp stab in her lower back caused Violet to wince in pain.

"Fourth floor. Tooooys, stuffed animals, Weeeedgwood china, and don't forget to visit the Young People's Theater."

Two surprised shoppers opted not to enter Homer's elevator. One of them pointed to a small rivulet puddling on the floor between Violet's ankle-strap pumps.

"Fifth floor."

"Enough of the sight-seeing. We're getting out now!" Miss Wren announced. Violet's floor at last.

The pocketbook had just performed a somersault in Violet's stomach. Homer stopped the elevator perfectly level with the Fine Dress Department and the two women hurried Violet Organ out. Just in time. Violet's stomach performed one more aerobic maneuver. She let out a shriek that rattled the fine china off the shelves on the third floor, announcing the arrival of a wailing baby.

"It's a girl!" Miss Slim announced.

"Thank heavens—it's *not* a gallstone," Miss Wren fanned Violet with her *Collier's.*

"Claire Organ!" Slim shouted out the first French name she could think of, thus christening Violet's daughter amidst the pearl necklaces, silk lingerie, high-fashion shoes, and women's fancy custom apparel directly beneath Louis Comfort Tiffany's grand mosaic dome.

"Boil some water!" A customer scurried through the aisles on rubber soles.

"Marshall Field's has just given birth to a baby girl!"

Miss Slim pulled on a long pair of white opera gloves from the fake display arms on the counter and helped pull the child into the commotion on Field's fifth floor. One sales clerk rushed over with a monogrammed motor blanket while Miss Wren seized the scissors used for wrapping gifts.

"I'll cut the cord!" Miss Slim called out as gaily as if she were cutting a holiday ribbon.

Miss Wren took it upon herself to scurry down the back stairs to Four, where she purloined a bassinet, two swaddling blankets, and, just for good measure, a silver rattle. After all, it wasn't every day a Christmas baby was born at Marshall Field's Department Store. As soon as she turned the corner on her return sprint, she saw Miss Slim kneeling on the floor, proudly holding the loveliest, tiniest babe in her bloodied evening gloves and showing her to an astonished Violet Organ.

"Oh joy!" Mrs. Winterbotham clasped her hands together and waddled closer for a better look, the nodding minks wrapped around her neck as a stole still in possession of their eyes and noses. "Imagine being born in this great store and having all of these wonderful layette doodads and imported baby things at one's fingertips."

The nurse and doctor from First Aid on Seven bundled Violet and baby off the floor and onto a stretcher, carrying the new mother away as if she had the bubonic plague. Mrs. Winterbotham hurried off to telephone her husband, who was the editor of the *Tribune,* to tell him of the wonderful miracle that had happened on the fifth floor of Field's.

"Henry," his wife puffed into the phone, her voice carrying the news as rapidly as one of her husband's wire services. "A mother and child born practically in the manger display. Why Henry, right in sight of the stuffed barnyard animals and women wearing jewels and garments as splendid as the Three Kings, this child was born! And to a working girl! Henry, a simple working woman whose husband is missing. Well, I don't know. In Egypt I think. Oh Henry, what if it's the Holy Land? Henry, it's a story!" Indeed. It was the *Tribune*'s front-page Christmas Eve story, Field's being the *Tribune*'s biggest advertiser and all.

In her febrile state, it was Violet Organ's true belief that fate revealed her daughter's destiny that December day. The new mother somehow felt it was auspicious of great things to come that her dimpled daughter was born in the midst of luxury, even if it was only a warehouse of other people's luxuries. After all, it wasn't as if Claire had been born on the eighth floor among the toasters and vacuum cleaners.

It was the article in the *Tribune* that saved Violet from being fired on the eve of Christmas 1923, when the not easily amused store manager, Mr. Trost, treated Violet to her own private inquisition in the bleak maternity ward of Cook County Hospital.

"Where is the father?" he demanded to know.

"Wandering the desert."

"Missing in action."

"Dead." Miss Violet, Miss Slim, and Miss Wren answered in unison.

To the next question they silently established an order of protocol.

"Oh she's married, all right. They had a church wedding eighteen months ago. I was there." Slim was the authority on romance.

"Legally married." Wren was practical as she handed over the marriage certificate.

"It's just that he's excavating King Tut's tomb," Violet apologized.

"He doesn't know about the baby," Miss Slim added helpfully. She didn't know, so how could he, she thought to herself. How could Violet have been so duplicitous or so dumb? Either way this baby was going to be too much for Violet to handle on her own. Why, Violet could barely fend for herself! They'd just all have to knuckle down, pull up their socks, and pull together to be a family for the poor child.

When the nurse excitedly arrived carrying the freshly powdered infant and a late edition of the paper, Mr. Trost had to admit it would be bad policy to fire the mother of what the *Tribune* heralded as "Field's Littlest Christmas Miracle." The caption ran under a photo of an expensively swaddled Claire cradled by Violet, wearing a quilted satin bed jacket, her long, wavy tresses flowing past her shoulders like Lillian Gish's. The two salesgirls, whom the article described as the infant's aunties from the Field's family, were gathered around the mother and child bearing gifts from First Floor State Street and Baby Goods on Four. Mr. Trost was later promoted for his good public-relations sense.

Slim read aloud from the paper. " 'The young lady appeared promptly at nine-twenty a.m. Field's newest accessory weighs seven and a half pounds, has sapphire blue eyes, a button nose, and a little figure that could model any fancy infant ensemble."

"Five toes and five fingers on each little hand and foot." Miss Wren beamed broadly.

" 'Customers,' " Slim continued reading the story, " 'actually registered to buy gifts for the new baby from the store's vast collection of antique silver baby cups, christening gowns, warm woolen flannels, and English baby prams.

" 'Marshall Field's special events coordinator, one B. Cunningham, said, "You can't say that Field's doesn't deliver!" and presented the baby's mother, Mrs. Leland Organ, the wife of a prominent archaeologist' "—Slim rolled her eyes as she read on—" 'with a two-volume leather-bound boxed set of Lewis Carroll's *Alice's Adventures in Wonderland* and *Through the Looking-Glass*. What a lucky little girl!' "

All the women's eyes were tearfully focused on the child, who was noisily sucking air around her. What would become of her? They looked at one another conspiratorially and nodded. They would see to it. The child would be safe in their collective bosom.

"We'll all be little Claire's aunties," Miss Wren announced, making a mental list of all the practical things they would need. She clucked happily at the thought of reading to their baby.

"I'll teach her French and dress her in Paris couture." Miss Slim could hardly wait. Maybe the war widow hadn't been denied a child after all.

"We'll love her." Violet grazed her finger against her baby's dewy cheek.

And "their baby" she became. The three women and Claire had somehow bonded amidst the bloody opera gloves and the excitement of a new birth, all in the spirit of Christmas. It was tacitly understood at this moment that they had become a family for a variety of reasons. Each of the lonely women had room to spare in her heart, room Claire would fill for all their lifetimes.

Chapter Two

Elevators and Escalators

Being a Modern Heroine, she realized that no Gallant Knight
would come Riding to her Rescue—even if that could have done
any good. No, she must do her own Rescuing. So she set about
studying ways and means of Achieving her Purpose. She thought
of this and she thought of that and at last she heard about the
Lanchere Beauty Salon on the Fifth Floor at Field's.
—From "How She Triumphed,"
Fashions of the Hour, *Spring 1934*

Claire peered her curly head from behind Miss Slim's hip, holding on to her hem, and smiled shyly at Sally Pettibone, who was
being fitted for her traveling trousseau. The Perils of Pauline
paled in comparison to the Adventures of Claire at Marshall
Field's. For the precocious second-grader, school was only a pro-
logue to the encyclopedia's worth of experiences to be sampled
daily at the store.

"Come here, my little darling. You've got chocolate on your
smocking." Miss Slim scolded her favorite confection as she
rubbed the gooey stuff off Claire's chin and the front of her dress.

"You've stopped off at the candy kitchen again, haven't you?"

Claire nodded. It was part of her everyday routine. Instead of
coming home to cookies and milk in the family kitchen, seven-
and-a-half-year-old Claire simply took the Illinois Central train
downtown, accompanied by the seamstress Mme. Celine if one of
the Field's delivery men couldn't pick her up and deliver her di-

rectly to the store. There were sure to be a dozen deliveries a day to Hyde Park anyway for the fleet of russet brown trucks all bearing the Field's insignia, carrying washing machines, coffee tables, bedding, and party dresses. When the Bret Harte Public School let out at three o'clock, all Claire had to do was dial the telephone exchange "State 1000," and one of the uniformed drivers would be quietly dispatched to bring the child back "home" to Field's. There the after-school treats offered in the candy kitchen, with its bubbling copper kettles emitting inviting aromas of melting chocolate, mint, and vanilla, were infinitely tastier than anything her schoolmates were snacking on at home.

"I think I prefer the blue Schiaparelli but I don't want this silly design on just one sleeve! It's rather lopsided, don't you think?" Sally Pettibone pouted. She pointed her perky nose in the air so high she appeared to be snubbing her own shoulder.

"It's very Paris that way. Schiap says fashion is art and art isn't always symmetrical, but we will do whatever you like, Miss Pettibone," Slim fawned. If the silly girl insisted, they could cover the beaded abstraction of a woman's face, although it would be a fashion sacrilege. Slim was just grateful that the new fiancé hadn't been wiped out in the Crash. So what if a Lake Forest debutante thought she knew more than the current Parisian queen of fashion? The pretty blond with the marcelled waves was nearly eighteen and already impossible. But with a mother and three younger sisters all determined to be in the height of fashion from morning to night, they were a salesgirl's gold mine. And since many of Slim's clients had disappeared after Black Thursday two years ago when the stock market collapsed, any customer with cash was king.

"A jeweled eye on one sleeve simply won't work anyplace but in Paris and we are only spending two weeks of our honeymoon there and where else will they know it's a real Schiaparelli and be impressed? Do they know about Schiaparelli in London and don't I have to wear tweeds there? Abra Tipps says I do and she should know. She didn't come back to Miss Porter's last year because she married that old duke."

"Ah, Miss Pettibone. Where love is concerned, age doesn't matter." Miss Slim sighed aloud. Nor do looks, Slim thought to herself, having seen the *Tribune's* society page photos of Sally Pettibone and her Labrador-eared fiancé.

"Imagine having to call your husband Duke," the girl went on, nodding at a curious Claire, whose long skinny legs were twisted around one another like a pretzel. "Sounds like something you'd name a Great Dane, doesn't it? Oh, could you call up to Field's Travel for me and get tickets for the best plays—and Miss Slim, ask Violet to step in. She has such taste, don't you know. Ouch! And tell this seamstress not to prick me. I know I have a small waist but a girl simply has to have an inch to breathe."

"*Mais oui,* Miss Pettibone." Miss Slim bowed out of the fitting room backwards, running her next sentences together. "Your figure is blessedly divine. You could wear anything better than the French mannequins they showed this ensemble on. It's terribly smart on you. Madame Celine, please be careful with the pins. You mustn't stick the customers. Pansy, we'll have a cup of tea in here, please. Claire, remember your posture. No man wants to marry a slouch." Slim pushed Claire aside and hurried along to find the long-sleeved Charles James gown, decidedly more subtle than Schiaparelli's winking, surreal design.

"Pretty girl," Violet said to Slim as they collided in the hallway.

"Yeah," mumbled Slim. "Too bad she's got her mother's arms, thick as fence posts."

Claire skipped out of the fitting room and gave her mother a quick peck on the cheek as she turned the corner.

"Why on earth is Slim looking for a husband for a seven-year-old?" Sally Pettibone whispered to her mother. "Unless she's a midget. She's not a midget, is she?" She pulled off the priceless dress with such disregard she tore the basting stitches.

"A fatherless midget? God would never be so cruel." In Millicent Pettibone's own mind, she had a heart.

Claire knew she'd have a better time in the Costume Shop on Four, where she could try on every outfit from Guinevere to Robin Hood. This was her current favorite place to play and pretend, but today for a change she might pop into the Young People's Theater where trained dogs commandeered from a traveling circus were performing this September afternoon. The entertainment was bound to be better than the frantic grown-up theatrics in the dressing rooms of Custom Designs and Finer Dresses.

"Afternoon, Homer."

"Good afternoon to you, Miss Claire." A grinning Homer opened the elevator door wide for his best passenger. "Elevator"—or something closely approximating it—had been her first word.

"And which magical land am I taking you to today?" he asked, pulling the iron gate shut. Homer was the wide-eyed child's guide to the diverse selection of worlds that were all gathered under one roof. Each time he stopped the elevator it was as if Claire were entering an entirely new land. Endlessly curious and fiercely independent (as long as she stayed within the confines of the store), Claire didn't need fairy tales or children's games to entice her imagination. She had the store catalog to dream on and all of Marshall Field's to explore, just like a little Gulliver. With its gossip, activity, and fancy goods from all over the world, Field's was like a giant playhouse, an enchanted land of make-believe, and hadn't Auntie Wren observed just the other night that having a vivid imagination was essential for a child to bloom in the modern world?

Smoothing her school frock and wiping the ubiquitous chocolate off her mouth with the back of her hand, she pushed her chin out and looked straight ahead, mimicking the customers' elevator etiquette.

"To the dogs, please," she directed. Sometimes Claire sat on Homer's lap, but she was feeling grown-up today.

"Homer, is it true men don't marry women who slouch?"

"Who told you that?"

"Just kinda heard it in the dressing room."

"Then gotta be true."

Claire squared her little shoulders.

This morning at the first show-and-tell of the school year when the other children were bragging what their fathers did for a living, Claire had fibbed. She held everyone's attention regaling the class with stories about her father's store, Marshall Field's, and since every child in her class had on some article of clothing from the store or slept in a bed purchased there, Claire's classmates were green with envy. No way was anyone going to feel sorry for her just because her real father was missing an organ or something like Auntie Slim said, and would never be able to come home again. Claire's teachers had long ago given up checking on this child's stories, as so many "aunties" appeared for parents' nights that no one could keep track, and she was always being whisked away after school by a French-speaking "governess" or a uniformed man from Marshall Field's. It was simply easier for Claire's teachers to believe "chauffeur" over simple delivery man and "nanny" over immigrant seamstress.

Claire turned to look up at the two ladies in the back of Homer's elevator who were in a noisy discussion directly over Claire's head.

"That was Eleanor Roosevelt!"

"How could you tell?"

"From the newsreels, of course. The woman's a marvel. She just finished a whistle-stop tour of the western states and she's still got energy to shop!"

"Roosevelt will defeat Hoover, won't he?"

"Well, I certainly hope so. If somebody doesn't fix this terrible economy, Horace will make me cancel my Field's charge!"

"I had no idea she was so tall. Or toothy."

"Hush. She's going to be our next first lady. Horace is in Democratic politics, you know, so I can introduce myself." The woman reached into her purse to pull out a ROOSEVELT FOR PRESIDENT badge and pinned it on her silk dress.

Claire fell in with the Roosevelt ladies and got off with them on the first floor. She had never seen an "almost first lady" before. Maybe it was something interesting she could use for show-and-tell.

There was a small flurry of activity going on at the tobacco counter, where Miss Wren was pinch-hitting for a pal. Two imposing women in floppy hats rimmed with battered flowers and accompanied by a burly fireplug of a man were the subject of a fair amount of stares.

Claire stood behind the counter with Miss Wren and watched as Eleanor Roosevelt, her companion, Lorena Hickok, and her solidly built bodyguard, Earl Miller, all held up elegant cigarette holders and pretended to be smoking.

"Don't you think Franklin will like this one? It's very presidential."

"He isn't the president yet."

"Don't you want him to win? Think positively, Eleanor."

"Hick, you know that isn't the life I want to be living now." She signaled to Miss Wren that she'd take the medium-sized holder.

The stocky woman placed her hand over Eleanor's. "History calls, my dear."

As Eleanor looked at her friend's hand covering hers, she caught sight of the most beautiful pair of violet blue eyes staring up at her. Claire held her gaze and smiled.

"Are you employed here, young lady? You know I have become quite an authority on child labor." When she spoke teasingly to the child, she opened her mouth wide, displaying a crowd of teeth.

"No, but I practically live here," Claire said. "Are you going to be the president's wife?"

Eleanor laughed. "Why, I am already Governor Roosevelt's wife and we don't know if he'll be president or not. That will be for all of you to decide."

"He's got my vote, Mrs. Roosevelt," Miss Wren gushed as she wrapped the black enamel cigarette holder in Field's dark green paper emblazoned with the Fields' family crest.

"Now I should like to see some knitting needles," Eleanor said in her peculiar, singsongy voice. Claire thought it was the greatest sound she'd ever heard, like a cappella singing in church. "Perhaps one of you will show us the way."

Claire shot from behind the counter and took the two ladies' hands, walking snugly in between them as she led them over to the sewing counter, where Miss Wren displayed the finest silver needles and sold Mrs. Roosevelt two sets. "I'll take these with me. The rest of the things, will you please send them over to the Drake Hotel? We're stopping there overnight," Eleanor said. "Now, let's take a quick look at their vacuums, but I don't want to see any Hoovers." She drew out the "o"s like an owl and her two escorts chortled at her little joke right on cue.

"We better get upstairs to the ballroom, darling." Hick said, slipping her arm through Eleanor's. "The Junior League awaits." They marched to the elevator bank with Claire two steps behind.

Miss Wren tossed off her apron and smoothed her hair with the palms of her hands.

"I'm going on my break now, Mary Lou. Cover for me, won't you?" Too shy to ride in the same elevator as Mrs. Roosevelt, Miss Wren waited patiently for a second car to take her upstairs to hear the candidate's wife speak. Twenty-eight minutes later, awed by the eloquence and integrity of the speech, Miss Wren vowed then and there to become one of Eleanor's "Rainbow Flyers," a group of grass-tramplers going door to door to bring out women voters for FDR. Sitting in the back of the room with all the employees, little Claire was mesmerized not by the content of the speech, but by Mrs. Roosevelt's richly aristocratic manner of talking. She mimicked Eleanor's accent for a week, not stopping until she could startle shop girls into looking up in expectation of seeing Mrs. Roosevelt herself, and delighting in the smile that came when they discovered it was only their mascot, Claire.

"Claire dear, could you come into the parlor please?" Violet's voice was hesitant. When Claire appeared in the little sitting room clutching her favorite teddy bear, she found Auntie Wren collapsed in a fatigued armchair patched with floral fabric squares, soaking her bunions. Her mother had her own shoes off and was rubbing her arches.

"Store feet." Auntie Wren smiled wearily as she curled her aching toes in the steaming hot water.

Claire instantly recognized the familiar medicinal smell of Dr. Scholl's healing foot powders permeating the sitting room suite shared by Claire, Violet, and the Aunties at the Windermere Hotel.

They lived in this dignified but affordable establishment for ladylike widows, well-bred women in "reduced circumstances," and working girls looking for respectability. No transients were ever allowed in this residential hotel, and very few men ventured beyond the comfortably decorated lobby and homey Americana-style dining room with its antique convex mirrors topped by proud eagles. The Field's ladies, as they were referred to, enjoyed a small kitchenette in their apartment, allowing them to economize by eating in. The Misses Slim, Wren, and Violet had their own single rooms in this warren of doors, all ending up in the tiny sitting room. Just as they had vowed seven years earlier, they had come together to raise little Claire, and had been certain—until today—that they'd been doing a first-rate job of it.

"Yes, our Field's feet have had quite a workout. I must have run ten miles today. No really, I was all over the store. But standing on them for eight hours is just as bad, why . . ." Auntie Wren said nervously, delaying the conversation. She knew what was coming.

"Wren." Violet said in the stern maternal tone she had developed of late. "Come here, Claire." She extended a slender arm to her daughter, who climbed right into her lap along with her bear.

"It's time we had a little talk. I've had another call from your school. The principal says you've been telling everyone again that Mr. Marshall Field is your father."

Claire's mouth moved to one side of her face.

"I thought we had settled all this before." As soft as Violet's voice was, it had all the rumblings of thunder. She disliked being a disciplinarian but it was a role she grudgingly played for the good of her child.

"While I'm sure Mr. Field would love having you for a daughter—if he knew you—the fact remains that he is not your father. And people don't like being surprised by extra children."

Claire's eyes were filling with tears. She rubbed one away, pretending that Dr. Scholl's therapeutic steam, overwhelming with its heavy smell of wintergreens and curatives, was irritating them.

"You can't just wish something up and make it so."

"Yes, but if he knew me, really knew me, he'd probably want to be my father."

"Unfortunately, dearest, it doesn't work that way." Violet fought back her own tears.

"The fact remains you don't have a father. You have three mothers who love you. That should be enough. You don't need a father and you're not going to have one no matter how much you pretend."

"She could, Vi. One of us could suddenly marry and then adopt—"

"Hush, Wren." Violet had even begun disciplining her store sisters, assuming the head position in their little family. She was still bitter about Leland Organ leaving her and forcing her to become resilient and independent. The truth of her situation had

hit her hard. After he left her for King Tut, there had been a series of other "mistresses," or so his occasional postcards had suggested, and how could she compete with women who had names
like Hatshepsut and Nefertiti? Without a return address, Violet
had had no way of contacting him to let him know he'd become
a father. Out of desperation, she'd finally cabled him the news
through an archaeological society at the university. She never
heard from him again. It had taken all these years, but he was
now as dead to her as the crusty bones he excavated. Violet composed herself and, turning to her daughter, addressed her gently.

"You know dear, in the lion family . . ."

"They call it a pride," Claire corrected her, sniffling. She had
been to the Field Museum of Natural History with Auntie Wren
many times.

"Yes, of course. In the pride of lions, sometimes the father lion
leaves after the little cub is born."

"Where does he go?"

"Out." Slim slinked in the front door slightly tipsy, aiming her
cocktail hat at the side table.

"He goes hunting, or exploring, or sometimes he just moves
on."

"Does he ever come back?" There was utter silence in the little
room.

"Not after eight years," Slim answered. "And who'd want a
necrophiliac around anyway?"

Violet cast narrowed eyes in Slim's direction—her own
patented subtle warning to back off.

"We're an all-girl family?"

"Well, yes. And a very brave one. We defend one another like
lionesses and take care of each other. There's love and safety here."
Violet believed the words as she said them. She cradled her child's
cheek and stroked her hair.

"And will there never be a daddy?" Claire whispered into her
mother's breast.

"Someday you'll have a man of your very own. And you won't have to borrow someone else's."

Violet reached into her needlepoint basket and pulled out a packet.

"Claire," she said softly. "These postcards are from your father. Picture postcards from different places. I was going to give them to you when you were older. That's all there is of him. You may have them now if you like."

Claire slipped off her mother's lap, dropping her stuffed bear to the floor with a thud.

"Would you like to sleep with me tonight?" Auntie Wren popped out of her chair. "I'll even read to you from *Little Women*." Wren was relieved the discussion was over. She hated any kind of unpleasantness. Claire was looking a bit peaked. Perhaps she should give the child a thimbleful of Lydia Pinkham's Tonic.

Claire darted a glance around their meager apartment, so different from the vast luxuries at Field's, or the doll-like homes of her school friends with one mother and one father to match. She sighed, untying the ribbon holding the packet together, and fanned through the postcards with the cramped copybook handwriting on one side. Her eyes were drawn to the exotic, decorative stamps. She rubbed her finger over a stamp of a green sphinx sitting under a blue sky and rifled through the pile. All the other stamps were colorful and interesting, too.

"Now give me your word that you'll stop making up these stories, Claire."

"I promise," Claire said as she followed Auntie Wren across the hall, still clutching her postcards.

"I wonder if we've been unfair to Claire." Violet fretted after she and Slim were alone. An inverted letter V appeared on her brow as her face pinched in worry.

"Don't be a goose. She's not pining away for a father. You're overreacting." She sneered at the memory of Leland Organ. "Claire's only exercising her imagination. Marshall Field, indeed!

Clever girl, already setting her sights high. Show me what's the harm in that?" Slim kicked off her size five shoes and dumped her pedicured feet into the lukewarm footbath. She was pleased that her beige pumps with black toe-caps were perfect copies of the pair that a slinky, black-veiled Marlene Dietrich had worn as Shanghai Lil.

"Yes." Violet quietly inhaled her words. "But perhaps we've let her down."

"Oh, Violet, don't be such a wilted bunch of grapes." Slim raised both arms in the air, setting off a ringing of cow bells from the clanging charms on her bracelets. "Love is what the child needs and what she gets."

"Yes, but the stability of a proper family . . ."

"Proper family! Do you think that just because they're rich your supposedly stable customers are from proper families? Half of them keep a Vuitton bag packed just so they'll be ready to move into the next North Shore husband's house." Slim sloppily added some hot water from the kettle into the foot soak.

"But there is no head at our dinner table. We don't even have a dining room."

"Nonsense, lovey. Who's to say Claire isn't better off with three mothers than with a parent of each sex like salt and pepper shakers? And you and I are the two best mothers I know of." Standing, she blew a kiss in Violet's direction and tripped off on her wet feet to her own room across the hall. "I'll knock on Wren's door and look in on Claire and kiss her good night for you, too. The same God that gives us cramps once a month gave women the capacity to love. Love is all she needs. *L'amour.* It's all any of us needs!"

In a way, Violet mused, the store almost made up for whatever deficiencies existed in Claire's upbringing. In addition to the financially blessed from Chicago and the rest of the nation, the store played host to a wide variety of intellectually influential visitors.

Authors flocked to the Book Department on Three to lecture

or read aloud from their works. Everyone from Aldous Huxley reading from *Point Counter Point* to one Walter Greenwood, author of *Love on the Dole*, passed through its wood-paneled rooms, and held young Claire enthralled. F. Scott Fitzgerald, Ernest Hemingway, Cornelia Otis Skinner—each had shaken Claire's hand and ignited her imagination. Even just one afternoon spent in their orbit gave Claire an education that could rival that of her mother's customers' daughters, being educated and "finished" at the socially acceptable Foxcroft School or Miss Porter's.

Early on, the very young Claire would lie for hours in the book section listening to the parade of cultivated voices, her tiny elbows resting on the Oriental rug in the room that smelled of leather-bound books and musty antique maps, soaking up the rich knowledge as effortlessly as one of the sponges from the Bath Shop on Two. As she grew bigger, Claire would sit in an overstuffed leather armchair, her knees pulled to her chin, memorizing whole passages and imitating the mannerisms of the literary elite. Indeed, her gift for mimicry was becoming an inexpensive hilarious entertainment for her little family; her invocation of Greta Garbo was unparalleled by any comedian of the day.

Stacked on one wall of the book section were scores of magazines from Paris and London that showcased the English nobleman's domain and the French lady's chic. *English Country Life, French Vogue, Gun Collector,* and *Esquire* were Claire's Hans Christian Andersen. The prince that she encountered here was not a magic fairy-tale prince turned into a frog by a wicked witch, but rather the prince of Wales, sartorially splendid in a creamy double-breasted jacket and an ascot of blue silk foulard, casually watching a tennis match on the island of Nassau. Certainly, her mother would have been disappointed to know that her high-spirited daughter was combing the periodicals for a male lion—any lion—to head their comfortable little den. And so sometimes Claire fantasized about the single Prince Edward marrying Violet or one of the Aunties. But the Field's salespeople told the child there wasn't a chance in a million the prince would marry an American, especially a shop girl, so she continued her search for a suitable stepfather elsewhere.

More than two years had passed since her mother had given her Leland's postcards. Determined to make something positive out of something sour—and an itinerant invisible daddy was the pits—the day after the "postcard presentation" Wren hustled Claire into one of the most elegant and elite rooms in the store, the Stamp Department. With its brass chandeliers and revolving glass and polished walnut vitrines full of philatelic treasures, the stamp section was one of the finest in the world. Claire was immediately drawn to the faces of kings, queens, and adventurers emblazoned in miniature on the one-inch squares. Now the ten-year-old possessed a collection of her own representing over thirty countries in her burgundy bound book.

Claire's after-school Field's jaunts almost always included a browse through the quiet, green-carpeted room's inventory of eagerly anticipated new arrivals. Her days were also filled with chatty visits with the twenty-four operators who ran the store's telephone switchboard, a busy place handling up to forty thousand calls a day, or with a dizzying extracurricular schedule of "lessons." These might take Claire from the gourmet kitchen, where she learned how to whip up deviled eggs and chicken pot pie, to the knitting studio, where she joined a large roomful of women receiving instruction in the hand arts—embroidery and needlepoint, and learning just enough fancywork to knit her mother and each one of the Aunties a scarf and pair of mittens for a Depression Christmas when money was tight but the holiday spirit soared.

There had also been the obligatory waltz and fox trot lessons during Miss Slim's tenure as the hostess of the ballroom dancing classes offered on Six and, owing to the two years Wren had spent in Fine Antiques, Claire knew the defining differences between a Louis XIV and a Queen Anne chair and could easily distinguish a Sheraton piece of furniture from a Hepplewhite or a Chippendale.

Today Claire breathlessly raced through the store's south rotunda, leaving skid marks on the marble, on her way to Six, where Amelia Earhart was going to be hawking her luggage and sports line at four o'clock. Claire never missed a "personal appearance" if she could help it, but this wasn't just a designer dropping by. This was the world's most famous female aviator, an adventuress. *Fashions of the Hour* had described the collection as "what the active woman wants," however, at this moment in the spring of 1934, the aviatrix who'd achieved fame as the first woman to cross the Atlantic by air and for her daring cross-country solo flights was standing awkwardly on the sixth-floor Field's Sports-Room, amidst racks and stacks of her signature sportswear and suitcases. She financed some of her flights by endorsing cigarettes, and now she had added these articles of apparel.

Claire studied her latest heroine for a full half hour as Amelia amiably talked to the curious customers who stood around her gawking in an informal half-circle. With Earhart's spotlessly clean face, short, tousled hair, and clear, buffed fingernails, Claire thought how different she looked from the powdered and permed salesladies she encountered daily at the store, ladies who seemed to spend all their time getting *other* people ready to go places. This straightforward woman with her suntanned face and gap-toothed grin looked like she'd gone everywhere she'd ever wanted to and couldn't be bothered with fussy feminine adornments. She clearly lit up when she talked about her travels and setting her compass herself to embark on a singular adventure. Amelia's husband wasn't missing or dead, either. He was a real man, handsome and with a mustache, happily posed in the picture Amelia Earhart carried in her wallet— Amelia, her husband, George, and her Lockheed Electra—that she was now showing to the approving ladies around her.

The child stood wide-eyed, listening to Amelia describe her experiences in the air and her many landings in exotic locales.

Claire inched forward for a better look at the pair of wings pinned to the woman's shoulder, which kept catching the light, shining like a silvery bird as she spoke. There was a special quality of independence about Amelia Earhart, a radiant aura of standing on her own, that Claire was drawn to. Suddenly ten-year-old Claire was convinced she had to know more of the real world beyond State and Wabash and under the Tiffany dome. She wanted to be just like Amelia.

She studied Earhart's shoes to see if there was any indication of "traveling feet," the "condition" the Aunties claimed Leland Organ suffered from and which had caused him to abandon her even before he got the chance to meet her. "Dromomania" was how Miss Wren referred to his intense desire to wander, diagnosing it with its Greek clinical name, rendering the condition both medical and probably hereditary. Claire suddenly had an alarming notion. What if she had inherited the wandering virus from him? Just as quickly, she relaxed. After listening to Amelia Earhart, she thought maybe an adventurer's life would be rather exciting.

"And when you fly around the world, Miss Earhart, will you be going alone?" Claire spoke out for the first time, pushing her way to the front.

"I shall be taking a navigator."

"What's a navigator?"

Amelia Earhart thought for a moment. "Well, he's someone who's very good at geography."

Suddenly Claire did something she had never done before. She picked out a small, round overnight case from the neatly arranged suitcases and asked the saleswoman to "just charge it, please." Amelia graciously autographed the luggage tag for the precocious child. Claire knew, she simply knew, she'd need this luggage, she had never been surer of anything. She was going places.

"How could you!"

"With money being so tight and all?"

Three perfectly manicured Lanchere index fingers were shaking menacingly at a woeful Claire in the chintz-covered parlor.

"We're still in a depression."

"Well, now they're calling it a recession, Slim." Miss Wren was a total Roosevelt follower.

"Rich people are out of work!"

"Rich people are going back to work!"

"Why, Mr. Harry Davis, who owned his own store, is now selling sweaters and socks in the Men's Shop!"

"Last week two people jumped over the railings on Seven and Ten! S-U-I-C-I-D-E-S." Wren spelled it out over Claire's head. "Right under the Tiffany dome."

"And you go out and buy a traveling case like you were sailing first class to Paris on the *Homeric*!"

"Forty-eight dollars and fifty cents. That's food for us for three months, you know." Violet had tallied up what the overnight case cost in groceries. "In one grand gesture you've jeopardized our budget, Claire," Violet admonished.

"Who do you think you are, young lady—Shirley Temple?" Slim's red mouth was the only visible feature on her face. Imported French cold cream was smeared everywhere but her lips.

Claire thought she looked like Al Jolson in *The Jazz Singer*. She was turning into a giant mouth before her eyes. The day was turning into a nightmare.

"*Mon Dieu. Mon Dieu.*" Slim slapped her hands to her face as if she were going to beat the vanishing cream into her pores.

"'Charge it. Just charge it.' That's what little Miss Field said to the salesgirl. Like she was Queen Mary." Miss Wren was clucking like a hen with a nervous condition, her chest puffing up like a pouter pigeon's. "We've *spoiled* her!"

Claire couldn't help it. Big tears rolled down her wide cheeks and her shoulders were heaving up and down as the rest of her shook like a leaf. She had done something more terrible than murder. She had hurt her mother and aunties. She had damaged the small financial fortunes of her female family.

"Just today Miss Wren was laid off and is only going to work part time on commission."

"We weren't going to tell you." Miss Wren's finger was an inch from Claire's tear-streaked nose. "But if you're old enough to pretend to have a Marshall Field's charge account, Little Miss Marker, you're old enough to know just how bad things are!" The yellow canary in the brass cage from the Pet Shop on Four was in a nervous twitter. The sitting-room bird had never been exposed to raised voices before.

"That silly suitcase is going back tomorrow!"

"Today!"

Claire looked stricken.

"Now here," Violet said, extending a monogrammed handkerchief. "Blow."

"What we all wouldn't give for a good cry." Auntie Slim slumped into a side chair.

The frightened ladies were venting their own fear and frustration over their plight and the ongoing Depression, which still crippled the nation, even more than they were angered over Claire's impetuous purchase. The up-and-down escalator they had been riding for years had them all worried sick. And now there was Wren's news that she would no longer be a salaried worker at the store. How would they get by, and which one of them would be next?

"Go to your room, young lady."

Violet watched the small figure with the long skinny legs disappear down the hall. Claire's bedroom was a shoe box of a room crammed with dolls and stuffed dogs from the store, many of them wearing bandages or slings, as Claire had been pretending to be a veterinarian the previous week. The ceiling, painted a powdery sky blue with cumulus clouds airily floating overhead, was crafted by the talented window-display artists who adored

Claire and her aunties. If the talented fellows couldn't make the ladies' lives easier, at least they could make life prettier.

Violet sighed quietly, sinking down into the Sheraton reproduction armchair and picking up her needlepoint.

"And please rewrap the suitcase so you can return it in the morning," she called after her daughter. She waited until she heard the door shut. It was better if they discussed their situation out of Claire's earshot. She was, after all, only a child. They had already railed at Claire like a chorus of cranky witches. But what else could they do?

"Wren dear, could you hand me the ledger, please?"

"Yes," Miss Wren responded, rushing to retrieve Violet's household accounting records from the bookshelves sagging under the weight of Claire's autographed first editions. Over the years, Violet had blossomed into a quiet but stalwart force to be reckoned with, someone who recognized what had to be done and simply did it with very little fuss. The others had shifted places and knew to fall in behind.

"These layoffs that were issued today were cruel and heartless!" Miss Wren tried to keep herself from collapsing into tears. Her top-heavy frame emitted an audible shudder.

"It's un-American!" Wren protested, wondering if she should dash off a note to Eleanor Roosevelt.

"How can Marshall Field's lay off twelve hundred employees— four hundred from retail alone—and still unveil the most expensive escalators in the world at the same time?" Miss Slim wiped all the cream off her face.

"Will Westinghouse's people-moving conveyances replace human beings?"

"Yes, and those escalators are moving real people right out of the store. Loyal employees who have served the company their whole lives. It's just too terrible!"

Miss Slim dabbed furiously at her naked lashes while Miss Wren pondered what she should write to Mrs. Roosevelt.

To Miss Wren, the most curious part of the whole fallen economy was that there was always a segment willing and able to pay
for the fanciest dresses, the most expensive Georgian silver, or to
take advantage of the many personal services offered by the store.
But she had also noticed how some people lost a lot, earned back
a little, lost more, and juggled their finances, making them erratic Field's customers. All except for Miss Violet's ever-loyal
clients, who curiously continued to be regulars. But even if Violet
was turning out to be a retail wonder, her stalwarts were not numerous enough to stave off the store's losses, now nearing eight
million dollars, a fortune in anybody's book, and claiming in its
wake more than a thousand jobs, including her own. Was it any
wonder the ladies had gone to pieces over a suitcase?

Slim streaked in and out of their little kitchen, leaving with
only an empty mug. Miss Wren took it for granted she was going
to fill it to the brim with the imported French brandy she kept in
her lingerie drawer. Courvoisier, a gift from a gentleman friend.
Luckily for Slim, Prohibition had been abolished.

When Violet Organ tiptoed past the women into Claire's tiny
room to tuck her child in for the night, she overheard Claire's
prayers. The little girl was kneeling by her bed, which had been
done up by the window-display boys—"Uncle" Vincent with his
theatrical imagination was Claire's favorite—exactly like little
Gloria Vanderbilt's from a *Vogue* pictorial, with a papier-mâché
gold crown and yards of flowing pink chiffon. Two carved birds
covered in peacock plumes guarded the bedposts. The grandness
of the bed contrasted sharply with the closet-sized room with its
threadbare carpet. Claire's head was bowed and her small hands
folded on the pink cotton-nubbed bedspread.

"And, dear Lord, please help Mother and the Aunties get very,
very rich so they never have to worry about money and never have
to be cross again. Please, God, I think some money now would
change everything, cross my heart. Please bless us all and
Marshall Field so he won't need to lay any more of us off. Oh—

and God, bless Amelia Earhart and while you're at it, bless her navigator, too. Amen."

As Violet tiptoed out of the room she silently vowed that Claire would have every opportunity Field's offered to live a life free from money worries. Her mouth tightened in resolve. She'd just see to it.

Chapter Three

The First Man

Many young girls have a strange audacity blended with their instinctive delicacy.

—Oliver Wendell Holmes

Honestly, Violet, what do you keep in that book? Blackmail, I suppose, from the way you guard the little sucker." Slim saucily sported a knockoff of Schiaparelli's "Mad Cap" perched on her head, looking like a chic Peter Pan. "Here, let me see." She grabbed for the metal-clasped ledger over their corner table at Trader Vic's.

"Oh no. Never. If it's blackmail, why would I let anyone have a look for free?" Violet laughed and raised her lovely violet eyes.

Unlike Miss Slim's brows, still penciled and darkened into an art deco look, Violet's feathery eyebrows were naturally arched high over deeply set eyes, the color of which jumped out at you like a train light coming out of a deep tunnel. It was an oddity in a face that was placidly calm and, while pretty, subdued to the point of plainness. Violet's one vanity of late, for she spent nothing on herself, was a good but inexpensive toilet water that smelled vaguely of violets to complement the occasional bunch of silk violets she pinned to her left shoulder or at the throat of her basic black dress. It was her uniform, and her customers were comforted and unthreatened by the familiarity of it.

Violet instinctively understood the importance of not being competitive with her clients, many of whom had insecurities as high as the Wrigley Building or as tall as the Tribune Tower.

"Look, I had Madame Celine knock off one of the new Chanel suits. Pretty snappy work for a Hungarian passing for a Parisian, eh?" Slim winked and twirled the pink-and-aqua paper umbrella around in her Blue Lagoon. "You should get one." She slid a cherry down her throat and pulled the stem in the same move. "Gracious, Violet, I don't know how you can stand to wear the same thing day in and day out like a prison inmate or . . ."

"Or a Foxcroft girl." Violet's laugh was soft and bell-like as she unconsciously tugged at her uniform's other accessory, the wedding band that still encircled her slim finger. She'd continued to wear her ring even after all these years, not because it was valuable or had any stones in it (then surely she would have hocked it), but because it allowed the customers she waited upon and who relied on her almost neurotically to count on her married-lady expertise. The simple gold-plated ring held no sentimental value for her whatsoever, but just by wearing it she emitted a sense of propriety and correctness, as if the narrow band were a passport to some women's club whose doors only married ladies could enter. After all, what female in her right mind would feel comfortable purchasing a racy peignoir from an old maid? Violet dispensed advice to her lovelorn customers that only a worldly woman with years of marital experience might share.

So what if she gathered most of this domestic wisdom from dressing-room gossip and the popular women's magazines that Slim read aloud from nightly? The customer didn't know the real truth, because in reality the customer didn't want to know about any unpleasantness when she entered the perfect world of the Store. Salesladies' dilemmas were not to be hung out on hangers like skirt and sweater sets. But the customers' dilemmas—now that was another story. Dear Miss Violet could be depended upon to know which transparent negligee might patch up an argument, or what second set of china would be just right for the couple who had smashed the bridal set during their first quarrel, and she was even willing to travel obligingly out to Lake Forest in the evening on the train to hold a certain plate up next to the dining room wall for color coordination. She could be counted on to pick out just the right hat for divorce court or the reconciliation lunch that followed when everybody made up. And, above all, she could be counted on for her discretion.

Violet was breathless in the perfection of her craft. It was her soft, seemingly unaggressive way with people that allowed her to be promoted as others were laid off. That, of course, coupled with her ability actually to close a sale. And if some poor missy's misfortunes were her gain, she simply couldn't worry about it. She had Claire and her own little family to think about. It had been nearly a year since Miss Wren had gone on part time. Claire and the Aunties depended on Violet as never before, and she had risen heroically to their call of distress.

Violet had, in fact, just been promoted to head the Bridal Salon, which had been enlarged to include the Trousseau Shop and Debutantes' Dresses. Now she was doing the whole shebang: launching the deb, then dressing the bride, her bridesmaids, the mothers; planning the honeymoon and the appropriate trousseau; as well as bringing the Catering Department into all the related entertaining, including food and flowers. The Stationery Section for invitations, calling cards, and thank-you notes, was added to her full-range services. While some said Violet planned an event from soup to nuts, in reality she was in on it from the first dress for the first date to the "I now pronounce you man and wife" ceremony. She bumped Claire up from Crayolas to calligraphy so her little girl could assist in the arrangements that often kept Violet at her desk until midnight. She kept lists of ministers, priests, and rabbis; and for those hurry-up second and third marriages, she had the home phone numbers of "sympathetic" judges arranged in alphabetical order. Of course, she also served as mediator in any argument between the future mother-in-laws, taking the position that "Field's has always done it this way." That was usually enough to settle a quarrel in Violet's quiet, diplomatic way.

"Let's have another round." Slim sighed and sipped the last of her Blue Lagoon. The tropical drinks at Trader Vic's in the Palmer House looked like punch in frosted glasses with floating fruit but packed quite a wallop.

"No, we have spent our limit," Violet replied firmly, exercising a self-control her customers at Field's fortunately lacked. To be sure, while some of these women's husbands had survived the 1929 stock market crash, others, like the Pettibones, had lost money in the mini-crash of 1933, turning the spending habits of Mrs. So-and-So and Such-and-Such upside down, killing the golden goose but not the appetite. Many of these society matrons, anxious to keep up appearances and launch their daughters in splendid style and then marry them off grandly, turned to Violet, relying on her taste and talent for finding bargains and then burying the bills for months on end.

These were the important records Slim referred to that Violet kept in her leather ledger, the thick green book of secrets that lay between them on the teak table. Certain pages were folded back at the corner as if the book were actually a collection of poetry with favorite passages marked for rereading instead of the Social Register's lineup of deadbeat ladies who hadn't paid their bills. Even the Pettibones were on Violet's list. And the rumor in the salon was that Mr. Pettibone, fed up with his wife's spending, was sending Mrs. Pettibone to Reno right after the holidays for a divorce.

But rumors held little interest for Violet, and, catty Slim's speculations to the contrary, her ledger had nothing to do with anything so crude as blackmail, social or otherwise. At first, Violet had extended the ladylike IOUs out of her own natural kindness, her worldview generous enough to look upon her customers as an extended sisterhood that, too, had been set adrift on the sea of the Great Depression, never mind that her own little family was clinging to a rowboat while her clients were holding on for dear life to their trim but tired-looking cruisers. But once the layoffs began, it had suddenly dawned on a toughened and wizened Violet that if she were to continue to lay her job on the line every day with each new IOU, there would have to be something in it for her. Or for Claire, to be exact. The memory of her daughter's plaintive bedtime plea still haunted her to the extent that nothing had become more important to Violet than providing for Claire's future. Never mind, as Slim liked to remind Violet, that Claire was already eleven years old and had never had contact with a single man, unless you counted the elevator man or the permanently single boys who did the windows. When the time came, her daughter's gender-sheltered life would not matter. Like a lace-trimmed version of Al Capone, Violet was waiting for just the right moment to start calling in her chips. Her "blue chips." Just as she had planned.

Unaware of her mother's well-laid plans, Claire was out exploring the opposite sex for herself.

From time to time she would slip into the persona of a daughter waiting for her "father," pretending to shop for shirts and ties and other manly accoutrements, just so she could browse through the Men's Shop and soak up the smells and textures that never entered her daily reality. In the company of women was where she spent all her time and acquired all her opinions. This, on the other hand, was a whole new geography. Claire would run her fingers across the handsome pipes in their upright stands on the counter and inhale the smoky, acrid smells of fresh tobacco just released from their pouches. She would roll a Havana cigar in her fingers under her nose before sneaking it back into its solid wood humidor and revel in its pungent intensity, which, along with the scents of sandalwood soap, tweed jackets, and leather shoes, deodorized the lavender whiff of her female world.

Longing for a father was making Claire man-crazy. At first, she walked down the aisles of argyle socks and rows of shirts with collars called cutaway, button down, polo, or yacht as if she were an explorer in darkest Africa. As Claire grew accustomed to the terrain, she grew bold enough to touch, lightly at first, the rich roughness of a herringbone coat, buttons of leather, buckskin gloves, and silk foulard mufflers.

This was a foreign world of sport and humor, hunting caps and green-felt table covers for cards and poker chips, brass spittoons and walking sticks with real animals like serpents or horses on their handles. Sometimes Claire felt like a boar or a wild tiger would charge at her from a darkened wood-racked aisle of Wellington boots or safari gear. Sometimes she imagined she was stalking them.

She viewed the "male" as a special animal whose natural habitats were places of glamour to her: boardrooms, golf courses, and mahogany-paneled men's clubs, all of which were suggested in the shop's masculine decor; and she viewed herself as a predatory huntress in the little girl's game she played there. But the wild animals were never her prey. She was after the big game of the great white hunter himself.

A father, she decided, was what was needed to complete her otherwise happy world. And so Claire's quest for the perfect man had begun.

Miss Wren was a wreck. She was demonstrating a fly-fishing rod so eagerly that she snared a lady's veil right off the woman's emerald blue hat. It was freezing on Field's first floor early this frosty morning, the temperature comfortable for the fur-clad customers on their side of the counter, but nippy for the salesgirls standing on their side. As the day rolled on, the mass of humanity moving through the Corinthian-columned and marbled main floor would warm her up, but for now, even after three hot cocoas, Wren was catching a chill and, worse, could be fired at any minute without a sale.

The fish weren't biting at her hook, baited with Christmas stocking stuffers from the special Mistletoe Shop featuring fancy gifts for last-minute shoppers. Everything from boxed and wrapped sugar cookies in the shape of Christmas trees dusted with green and red sugar crystals to priceless pear-shaped pearls was available in this windowpaned enclosed section, where Santa's helpers served hot toddies and gingerbread to the mostly gentleman shoppers looking for that perfect last-minute present without having to leave the first floor and their car conveniently valeted outside, engine still running.

Miss Wren had almost sold the antique gold filigree and amethyst earrings to a couple from Cleveland. Mrs. Winterbotham had stopped in to say hello and happy holidays and sip a hot toddy, but hadn't purchased the Moroccan leather desk set she'd been looking at for her husband. Wren had wasted another forty-five minutes with a distinguished-looking gentleman who left his fingerprints all over a splendid pearl and diamond choker, examining it with a jeweler's glass before he confessed he used to be the head jeweler at C. D. Peacock and was now out of work. He congratulated Wren on her fine pieces and purchased forty-five cents' worth of red and green jelly beans. She had earned only a dollar twenty-five in commissions by the time Claire whizzed by and kissed her hello on her way to French class, part of a new regime of language lessons given to the Fancy Dress buyers that Miss Slim had managed to enroll her in. Claire was spending her Christmas holiday assisting at the store, of course.

Wren had just lost a sale to a young executive who decided right on the spot to take his wife to Bermuda for the holidays instead of giving her a diamond and ruby eternity ring when a tall, matronly woman coughed in front of her. It was an attention-getting kind of cough.

Wren sneezed for real. Her sniffles were turning into a whopper of a cold. She sized up the customer to see if she was worth catching pneumonia for. After years of counter experience, Wren identified her as a woman who was probably pre-Depression grand but was now just a "window-shopper." She sighed and patted her red nose, which, despite its congestion, was still able to sniff out the musky odor of mothballs. It was as if the clothes in the woman's wardrobe had been in the family forever, like heirlooms.

Looker, not buyer, Wren thought. By then, only the threat of a Christmas without any gifts at all was making her fight her cold and stay on the job. She eyed one of the hot toddies, shivered, and pulled her sweater closer to her clavicle.

"Can you help me with a very special Christmas selection, please." The dowdy matron's tone was clipped and condescending. It was evident she was from the aristocracy, monied or nonmonied. It was also obvious that she wasn't from Chicago.

Miss Wren was appropriately obsequious.

"How may I serve you best? Is the gift for a lady or gentleman, madam?" Wren cooed.

"It is for my husband. Let's move this right along. I haven't got all day." A small frown appeared between the eyes and a quick smile across the lips. "He's quite fastidious about his attire and grooming habits. He travels out of a trunk for months on end, back and forth to Europe. Just took a Roosevelt appointment. A voracious reader. Books might be the ticket. No dear, put that away. He picks out all his own ties. He's mad for his horses and dogs, though. Do you have saddles or leashes? I'm in a bit of a rush." The woman's quick eyes darted from left to right and then she turned her back entirely and was gone. Wren shut her order book and pulled her handkerchief out of her sleeve.

"I'd like to see that." Mrs. Matron returned a minute later and pointed her stubby tan finger to something gold and gleaming in the locked display counter. "It" was an eighteen-karat-gold dressing table set that came in its own crocodile traveling case.

"Oh, it's very grand. Made by Morabito in Rome." Miss Wren unlocked the case, removing the octagonal beveled mirror, the hairbrush, cloth brush, and traveling clock one by one after donning a pair of jeweler's gloves so as not to leave any smudges on the smartly styled toilet set. The tortoiseshell comb set in gold with raised gold beading was sleekly masculine, like all the other pieces shimmering yellow gold in the bright store lighting.

"The only other set like this in the world was sold to Miss Barbara Hutton as an engagement present for her husband, Prince Alexis Mdivani," Miss Wren boasted. Salesladies were expected to know the shopping tastes and marital status of international celebrities. The Woolworth heiress's comings and goings held the attention of every shop girl and society matron in the nation.

"Poor Babs. Hope it lasts." The woman inhaled her words. "This is really quite handsome. May I?" The customer turned the gold toothbrush holder over in her hand, then examined the sophisticated scrollwork on the pillbox. Both carried the names of the craftsman engraved on the back.

"The entire set is solid gold so it will never need polishing," Wren added. "Quite practical."

"It is nearly identical to the one my Mr. Harrison admired so in the Royal Scottish Museum in Edinburgh last summer," she mumbled like a ventriloquist. "Especially made for the third duke of Richmond in the sixteen seventies and given to him by *his* wife after he accepted a royal commission." Mrs. Harrison was smug.

"Well, perhaps it might be just the ticket for your husband and his commission," Miss Wren piped in, chipper as a magpie. "So appropriate."

"Why, how clever of you. I'll have it then. My husband's appointment from the president is like a royal commission, and he's quite the collector, too. This is a work of art. Four thousand five hundred, is that with tax or without?" The woman read the price tag without the benefit of glasses. "May I have it holiday wrapped and boxed? I don't have a shred of Christmas paper in the house."

"Will you take it or shall we have it delivered?" Miss Wren had to keep herself from jumping up and down.

"If it can be in Tuxedo Park by December twenty-fourth, then you can ship it. Otherwise . . . oh, and I'll need a little something for the Roosevelts." As she signed the sales ticket with a flourish, Miss Wren craned her neck to read Ophelia Harrison's finishing-school script.

The woman wasn't nearly as old as she looked, Wren decided. Weatherbeaten, yes; perhaps summers on the rugged coast of Maine, sailing, horse jumping, gardening, carelessly uncared for as if she were above all that kind of middle-class foolishness. Mrs. Harrison gave Wren her East Coast aristocrat's address through a clenched jaw, known as Locust Valley lockjaw among the sales-girls, that peculiar way of speaking that allows velvety mum-blings to escape from a mouth that is moving only at one corner, moving barely, imperceptibly, if at all.

Uppercrust all the way, thought Miss Wren, beaming and tak-ing a proprietary interest in her customer. Probably summered in Newport. Her chest cold had just up and left, flying south for the rest of the winter. Leaping lizards! She had made not only a sale but one of the biggest. Forty-five hundred dollars! Wren was ju-bilant. She had certainly caught her fish. The gifts could be de-livered in three days. She would never forget Mr. and Mrs. William Henry Harrison IV of Charlotte Hall, Winding Way Road, Tuxedo Park, New York. No number necessary.

Claire inhaled the smells of walnut dressing, steaming sliced turkey, and cranberries from her plate. She smacked her lips as the butter pad melted into the hollow scoop of her piping hot pota-toes. Claire couldn't imagine how Christmas in anybody's home could be nicer than Christmas at the Walnut Room. The food was more delicious, the tree was bigger and, of course, far more beau-tiful than any other in the city. This year, Field's tree was a bal-sam fir from the woods of Michigan. Seventy feet tall, it was festooned with fifteen hundred handmade angels, snowballs, icicles, and other ornaments, as well as with thousands of yards of strung cranberries. A beautiful wooden painted angel with wings shot with gold dangled directly over Claire's shoulder. She longed to reach up and touch her, but Claire had been taught by the Aunties that impetuous behavior was a breach of good manners. So instead she craned her neck toward the entrance and then broke into a radiant smile.

"Look, it's Auntie Wren now," Claire said excitedly, waving her arms so Wren could find them in the dining room with its richly patterned carpets and ornately carved walnut walls.

Other guests in the dining room spun around to watch the tiny lady lugging big green Field's shopping bags in each hand and under her arms bustle into the room. An oversized pin in the shape of a holiday wreath was pinned to her ample bosom. The Christmas Eve supper was reserved for certain employees of the store, special friends, and out-of-town guests. The mood in the room was festive. This year Miss Wren was taking Claire to midnight mass at St. Peter's for a Catholic celebration. Last year, because Christmas and Hanukkah happened to coincide, they'd also attended services at Rodfei Zedek Temple, as Wren was determined that Claire's spiritual education be ecumenically correct. Claire and her mother were pretty much Protestants, Wren was a lapsed Catholic, and Slim a devout Pantheist. When they worshiped together, it was at the Unitarian church in Hyde Park. But as Auntie Wren said, "the Lord is everywhere," and Auntie Slim always finished with "especially at Marshall Field's at Christmas," where the devoted ladies celebrated Christ's birthday along with Claire's.

God had certainly been good to them this Christmas, and just in the nick of time. They were in a very gay mood. Claire laughed and clapped her hands together now, and Violet and Auntie Slim laughed along as they waited for Auntie Wren to join them. All this gaiety was due to the largesse of the Tuxedo Park Harrisons,

Mr. and Mrs. William Henry Harrison IV to be exact, who had with one ring of a cash register closed out their debts, paid their rent, and were allowing Auntie Wren to play Mrs. Santa Claus to her loyal friends and their collective child born in the store eleven years ago.

"Wren says Mrs. Harrison looked quite understated—plain almost—but her voice, it just reeked money." Claire loved rehearsing the story of Mrs. Harrison.

"You can always tell by the voice. Money and breeding just tumble out of their mouths." Slim pursed her lips as if she were going to pull out a cherry pit.

"Thank goodness we're having Christmas." Violet sighed happily.

Field's had rewarded Wren by reinstating her permanent position at the store and giving her a bonus and the best table in the house for their Christmas supper. A triumphant Wren had told the others to gussy up and meet her there but to start without her as she had a lot of last-minute shopping to do. When she reached the table, the small-boned lady with the puffed-up chest dropped her heavy load of presents and wiped the perspiration beads from her temples.

"Oh, Auntie Wren. We thought you'd never get here! Hooray for you, darling Auntie Wren." Claire threw her arms around Wren's birdlike neck and kissed her rosy cheeks.

"Sit down, Wren. You deserve it." Violet pulled out her chair, letting her have the one with arms. "You've truly saved the day. You did a smashing job. And just in time."

Wren beamed. It felt so good to be helpful and even better to be necessary.

Tomorrow morning the ladies would open their presents following a lazy breakfast of Wren's special *apfelpfannkuchen*—apple pancakes laced with a touch of calvados to bring out the fruity taste and topped by Violet's homemade plum jam and fresh peach preserves. Wren, however, had insisted on "bending" the ritual this year so that her gifts to the others would be opened in Field's dining room.

She shooed away a white-gloved waiter who appeared with the giant tasseled menu, eager to press directly ahead with her bags of boxes. She plucked a glossy green-and-red-coated box off the top and pushed it across the table. "Violet, you're first." Wren tilted her face, looking girlishly expectant. It was such a thrill for her to be able actually to give something other than a hug and advice.

Violet was thrilled with her gift of a delicate wristwatch. She hadn't had one since Wren had accidentally sat on hers over a year ago. She held it up for the others to admire.

"You were such a game girl when I smashed yours." Wren blushed and blinked her tears away. The difficulties of the past year had stimulated her tear ducts so that her handkerchief was working overtime.

"You're next, Auntie Slim. Go on."

Claire's soft curls fell over her porcelain-fine china skin as nearby diners turned to stare at the three happily chirping ladies and the pretty child taking such pleasure in their Christmas. Their happiness was contagious as it spread around the room.

"Oh, what beautiful leather." Slim looked puzzled as she ran a polished red finger over a long, narrow wallet. She'd never had much cash to carry around with her and wondered about the practicality of a fancy holder for her decidedly loose change.

"It's a passport case," Wren explained.

"Is there a ticket to Paris inside?" asked Claire, leaning over the table for a look.

"Claire!" Violet raised a feathery eyebrow.

"Heavens no, dear!" Wren laughed. "I'm only newly reemployed, not Daddy Warbucks. But there *is* something that goes along with it." Wren smiled puckishly as she handed Slim another box. "It's a sort of theme present. Paris, Paris."

Slim loved her second gift, the French perfume Paris Nights, and lightly touched the stopper behind both of her ears as well as Claire's. The wide childish eyes were fixed on the perfume's packaging of a man and woman in silhouetted embrace. It made her reflect that the only thing missing from the table and their lives was a man with a good steady job.

This long year had in fact taught Claire that good times and good moods came with financial security. The sting of her mother and aunties' anger at her for charging the Amelia Earhart case was still with her; having to return it had crushed her. All these months later, she still wasn't over it. So Claire was gleeful as she pulled back the white and gold tissue paper to reveal an Amelia Earhart traveling case, one that bore Amelia Earhart's autograph and the personal message inscribed especially for Claire. Wren had rescued the luggage tag and put it aside for her until the bad times eased up.

"Oh Auntie Wren! You remembered! I think you are the loveliest person in the world!" She hugged the dear lady and smiled triumphantly at her mother over her aunties' shoulders.

Claire suddenly knew exactly what she was going to do to make sure they'd never have hard times again.

"Here's to Wren for giving us a wonderful Christmas after all." The Aunties raised their sherry glasses in a single three-armed salute.

"Thank you, Lord. Thank you, Jesus and all the powers above, for looking out for us." Wren bowed her head solemnly. They all lowered their eyes in prayer.

"Yeah, and let's hear it for the Harrisons of Tuxedo Park!" Slim lifted her glass high again.

"To the Harrisons!"

Claire was perched on the enormous elk-horned hat rack in the Men's Shop like an owl. Her feet were demurely crossed at the ankles, her lace-scalloped socks turned down in a neat fold as she sat hidden in the branches of the elk horns hung with homburgs, two riding derbies, a trilby, several tweed caps, and a straw boater. The man she had been studying for three-quarters of an hour was directly beneath her. He was perfect, in her estimation. She wondered if she should ambush him or just seduce him. She had seen ambushes in the Hopalong Cassidy films and had heard all about romantic seductions from Auntie Slim. She sighed.

What would Shirley Temple do? Claire pondered. The pint-sized actress who was four years younger than she had been in the store only last week. At seven, America's darling was well on her way to becoming the nation's top box-office star. Even though Shirley Temple had an officious phalanx around her, which included her mother, bodyguard, fan-mail secretary, personal hair curler, and store executives, she and Claire had managed to escape the adults long enough to slip their feet into the fluorescent X-ray machine in the Children's Shoe Shop on Four. There they had giggled and joked as they each took turns sticking their feet into the large wooden machine for determining shoe size and shape, and stared down at their skeletal bones as they wiggled their toes and watched their bones dance. It reminded her, Shirley told Claire, of her staircase number with Bill "Bojangles" Robinson in *The Little Colonel.* The girls wiggled and jiggled their toes until they were discovered by the anxious grown-ups and marched on toward the Doll Department, where even the little star was overwhelmed by the selection of dolls from all over the world.

As Field's child-in-residence, Claire was acting as the store's special hostess to the miniature movie star for the day, a scheme cooked up by the store's publicity department. Later, as both girls gamely posed for photographers, each holding a Shirley Temple doll, a big seller for Field's, and the star's mother urging her to "sparkle, Shirley, sparkle," Claire tried to sparkle, too. She thought how pretty Shirley was with her cheery round face. Was it any wonder that every man in her movies wanted to be her father or adopt her? Why, she could even melt the hearts of gangsters. She was always bringing couples together in her films so that they fell in love, eventually adopting the character Shirley played. She had brought Gary Cooper and Carole Lombard together in *Now and Forever,* and in her latest film, *Curly Top,* she played matchmaker to millionaire John Boles and Rochelle Hudson, Shirley's older sister in the movie. Every Shirley Temple movie had a happy ending.

"How do you get everyone to fall in love with you?" Claire had asked in all sincerity when they were at the marble water fountain together.

"By being nice," the little star had answered. "And by remembering to always dimple after reading my line." She twisted a plump finger into one of the famous circles penetrating either side of her mouth.

Contemplating her present situation, Claire decided she would probably be stuck in that man's hat display forever just by being nice. Dimpling just might work. Or maybe she could try one of Auntie Slim's seductions.

"So do you come here often?" she called down to the man from her owl's lair.

The gentleman was visibly taken aback. He didn't shop by himself very often. He usually left that to his wife and daughters. He looked around before he looked up.

"And who are you, young lady? The Cheshire Cat or a talking hat?"

"Oh, neither," Claire uncrossed and recrossed her ankles on her precarious perch. "I'm one of Field's personal shoppers. And I can help you pick out almost anything in the store. I know where everything is." She fluttered her eyes like Shirley Temple had shown her and wished she could have extended her arm in a languid arc like she'd seen Jeanette MacDonald do in *Naughty Marietta,* but she realized if she wasn't careful she'd fall out of the hat rack and break her neck. And how could she be adorable in a cast?

"Don't you have anyone to shop for you?" she asked pointedly.

"Well, that's the problem. I have too many people shopping and charging it to me. Now it seems I need a few things for myself. Really now, can I help you out of there? You're not a circus performer or something, are you?"

"No, I'm just a working girl." Claire paused as if she were exhaling some of Auntie Slim's cigarette smoke. "And I'd like to help you." Her voice sizzled with what she hoped was sophistication.

The gentleman broke into a warm, friendly, fatherly laugh. He held up a hand to her.

"Allow me," he said, "to assist you."

Claire hung on to his hand, a nice big gruffy hand, and stepped out of the hat rack and onto a column and then down on the counter where shirts were stacked in neat rows by collar size and color.

"I notice you're buying two of everything. Was your luggage lost?"

"No."

"Did you have a fire?"

"No."

"Do you have a wife?"

"I'm in that gentleman's limbo somewhere between marriage and divorce," he announced before he caught himself. There was something disarming about this girl-child.

Bingo, thought Claire. And now he was separating from his wife. Evidently Claire had caught him only on his second day out of the nest. She had no allegiances to the institution of marriage; she had never even known a real family except from storybooks and store catalogs. So now Claire concentrated on sparkling. Somehow she'd pull him into her trap, just like Shirley.

"That shirt you're buying is from last season's stock and that collar is smart but trendy. You look like a man who'd want something more conservative, that would wear from year to year." She pitched him with one of the lines her mother always used on her lady customers.

The gentleman looked impressed.

"But what's wrong with this shirt? It's got a turn-down collar and is plain white so it can go with everything."

"Look over here," she said, taking him by the hand. "You'd be much handsomer in this."

"How are you such an authority? Where are your parents?" His expression turned serious.

"My father is missing and my mother works in the store."

"Well, shouldn't you be running along to her?" He gave a helpless look around the emptying floor. He noticed that he was the last customer. He'd purchased just what he'd needed for a few nights' stay at his club. When he'd moved out of his house, he'd only taken his briefcase.

"Nope. My mother's at home. She's probably worried half sick. I was supposed to meet her but I got stuck in those antlers and was too embarrassed to ask for help."

"You should never be embarrassed to ask for help."

She lowered her lashes and looked at the buckles on her shoes.

"Would you help me get home? If you hadn't come along, why, I could have been stuck in those horns all night!" she fibbed.

"Well, I'm glad that I did. I have a driver outside and we are going to take you home, young lady. Should we telephone your mother so she doesn't worry?"

"Oh yes." Claire looked directly into his eyes. "How gallant you are." She repeated Auntie Slim's mantra like a parrot from the Pet Store on Eight.

"But enough about me." Claire took his arm as they made their way to the Men's Grill with its bank of telephones. "Let's talk about you." Wouldn't Mother and the Aunties be thrilled. She'd tell Mother to put on her prettiest blouse. She was bringing home a man for her. She was bringing home the bacon.

Chapter Four

Give the Lady What She Wants

A woman is like a finely plumed bird. If she is to survive, she takes on the colors of whomever's nest she is inhabiting.

—Old Folk Proverb

Claire's arrival with her catch at the Winderemere had set off a waving of arms and tricky pirouettes worthy of the Ballets Russes. Violet and Aunt Wren reacted with elaborate body language and stunned silence in the shock of the moment. Claire had picked up a man and brought him home to Violet like a box of chocolates.

"Oh, you'll have to forgive Claire. She is only a child." Violet colored to a high pink in embarrassment and tucked her delicate profile into the ruffles of her blouse. Wren fluttered off into the kitchen as if her exit had been choreographed, leaving Violet alone for her big solo.

"I have four daughters of my own," the man said kindly as he introduced himself. "You've done a wonderful job raising her. Really. She's an outright delight."

"Well, you're being very gracious, Mr. Pettibone," Violet murmured, deliberately leaving out any reference to Mrs. Pettibone and the daughters who spent money like water slipping through their I've-simply-got-to-have-that fingers.

Mrs. Pettibone was high on Violet's list of names of ladies who handled their clothing bills like Board of Trade transactions, bartering, exchanging, and begging Violet to hold on to them until they could get their husbands "in the right mood." The Pettibone listing of accounts due was thick in Violet's ledger. What a coincidence that Claire should bring *him* home. Claire. The child could take a cup of sugar and turn it into a three-tiered wedding cake.

Violet smiled at Claire's gentleman. Mr. Pettibone was very attractive in a reliable sort of way. Solid bearing, gentlemanly demeanor, a Patek Philippe watch cupping his wrist, he was well groomed but not handsome; Auntie Slim constantly drummed into Claire's head that the lady should be the pretty one and the man her stable foil.

Violet offered to make him a cup of herbal tea. As he sat down in one of the threadbare slipcovered armchairs, she stole a second look at him. There was a husbandly gentleness about him that came through his burly manner.

For a split second, Violet wondered what she might do if Millicent Pettibone wasn't her valued customer and if she wasn't mother confessor to her and her spoiled daughters.

She needn't have bothered. The living room door flung open and in slinked Slim, her hips moving so that Violet could practically hear the hip sockets grinding in and out. She had slipped into something "comfortable" after Claire and Mr. Cyrus Pettibone's phone call and doused herself with Paris Nights. She smiled at him with her vinyl-slick lips, boring straight into him with her kohl-lined eyes. Eyes that suggested all sorts of things that Mrs. Pettibone had probably never even heard of.

The rest was rumor.

"Hitler who?"

"Adolf Hitler."

"Adolphe, like Adolphe Menjou?"

"Honestly, Cilla, don't you keep up on world events?" Hope Wentworth threw a gardenia at her.

"Cilla's been in a coma for the last two years." Daisy Armstrong was putting curlers in her hair.

"Oh, *that* Hitler." Cilla remembered the maids talking about it. Poland and France were where the household's girls came from, and the maids had been anguished when Germany invaded their homelands.

"All of Europe's at war and Adolf Hitler is the ringleader. Daddy says he's the madman leading Europe straight into a nervous breakdown."

"Holland and Belgium were seized by Hitler too."

Cilla Pettibone looked bereft. "Does that mean I can't get my thousands of tulips from Holland for my party?"

"Not unless you're planning to invite Hitler, kiddo."

"Well, Hitler was just this short little mucky-muck in Munich when I was visiting my sister and Brenda Frazier at school over there. We used to see all the funny SS men in front of the opera house and the monuments. They'd parade up and down the boulevards at night with torches and we'd think, Oh what a fabulous parade!" Lily Dunworth had actually met the Führer. "My sister and Brenda got invitations all the time from him. Brenda Frazier even had lunch with him." She gulped a giant sip of iced tea in a dramatic pause.

All the girls perked up when they heard the name of the girl who turned being a debutante into being as famous as a film star or Eleanor Roosevelt. When she "came out" in New York in 1938, her dark delicate features, powdery white skin, and liver-red mouth had even made the cover of *Life* magazine. The girls fell silent listening to Lily. Even Claire lifted her eyes from her book.

"Hitler used to invite all the English and American schoolgirls in Munich to his little teas." Lily pulled the mint leaf out of her glass and placed it on her tongue.

"Hitler had tea dances?" Snookie Cuthbert made a face.

"No. Just tea. He and his sidekicks."

The girls were snuggled for the night into the recently redecorated glass-roofed solarium of the Pettibone estate on Green Bay Road in Lake Forest with its pearly marble floor, cozy overstuffed couches, and majolica vases crammed with dozens upon dozens of summer roses and peonies. They were planning their participation in the annual Passavant Cotillion Ball held during Christmas break, and Priscilla Pettibone's at-home debut party. The double social whammy would tax their nerves, their parents' bank accounts, and test the girls' physical stamina, but they were preparing to perform their upper-class culture's rite of initiation into the adult world with committed gusto.

Claire was the invited but unwelcome guest at the girls' weekend sleep-over at Cilla's, the youngest of the Pettibone daughters and the last to be launched out of the gilded nest. After a day of tennis, swimming, and poring over row upon row of boys' names from the best families around the country to be invited to her debut party the night before the big cotillion, the sun-kissed girls were pruning and weeding their list like social gardeners. Green books and blue books, regional social registers with summer and winter addresses and private phone numbers, unlisted anywhere else, were scattered around the floral swirled needlepoint rugs.

It was only July, still five months away from Cilla's presentation to society, but preparations were in full swing. Lester Lanin's band had been booked, starvation diets begun, and the caterers hired, along with the invaluable Violet Organ from Field's to coordinate it all. Violet was a recognized authority on Brenda Frazier's coming-out party at New York's Ritz, as all her clients wanted to incorporate at least one "Brenda" detail into their own launches, be it the bridal-like bouquet of orchids she held in the receiving line or the four-strand pearl bracelet she wore at her wrist. To the girls' chagrin, along with that jewel Violet came her sappy daughter. The prettiest dresses and the best balls all had Violet's practiced hands on them. And Claire Organ, perennial wallflower, was part of the "arrangement." Of course the girls didn't understand that their mothers' allegiances to Violet were still held in that "other" social registry, Violet's ledgers of IOUs.

Violet's little experiment in extending credit during the long Depression was paying off in social spades. In her genteel way, Violet, clad in her basic black with the bouffant bunch of long-stemmed silk violets at her shoulder, planned the social gatherings of Chicago's elite. She never raised her voice. She didn't have to; the power of her leather ledger combined with her credo of quid pro quo resonated through even the softest of whispers.

Her services were so valuable that the quiet words "It would make me so happy if my Claire could be included" were enough to propel her reluctant daughter right to the top of a party roster. Easing Claire into a world where she might find a suitable husband had become Violet's raison d'être. Little did she understand that her mission had also become Claire's bête noire.

Claire peered over her book. The slim, wholesome, pale-skinned seventeen-year-old was conspicuously out of place among these girls, some of them looking a good ten years older than they actually were with their sophisticated, tony images. She preferred bridge to boyfriend bingo, and was an avid reader as well as an ardent stamp collector. She was going to try for a college scholarship but she knew the Aunties were pushing her down a more heavily traveled road. So the serious attitude that had begun to cover her face, masking her perfectly arranged features, was rendering her solemn instead of plainly beautiful.

Claire was what the mothers referred to as "a girl with potential," as if she could be coaxed to bloom with a little watering from a gardening can and a ton of face powder. Aloof and alone, she felt more at home among the fine pieces in the quiet Antiques Section of Field's where she worked part time than in her mother's gossip-driven all-female department. "The Bitchs' Boudoir" was what Auntie Slim called the salon. Claire wasn't "coming out," nor was she participating in any of the cotillions like the Passavant, but she was nonetheless Cilla's guest this weekend because both mothers had separately insisted on it. Claire had read enough in the *London Times*, available in Field's Reading Room, to worry more about the turmoil in Europe than her chances of picking up either social credentials or a husband in this fast social company, and she certainly knew that Hitler was more than a crooked politician. Sometimes she wondered just what was it some of these girls learned at their snooty boarding schools anyway. Daisy Armstrong, the one tough-talking and irreverent deb Claire found rather interesting, liked to say they were sent off to learn to "mix a stiff drink, develop a stiff upper lip, and make their potential husbands stiff with desire." Perhaps between her public school education and the lessons she'd learned at Field's, Claire hadn't done so badly after all. She sighed quietly to herself.

Snookie Cuthbert caught her sigh and fixed an analytical stare on her. She thought the out-of-place girl had a quiet, cool way about her that could beat any one of them out of the gate if only Claire had had the wherewithal to race. Luckily for them she didn't. How could anyone see those astonishing eyes if she never raised them? Snookie had seen that kind of nonchalant handsomeness before, and calculated that Claire didn't even know she had a "look." Snookie's father had married three times, and the last two wives had that same kind of unstudied charm. Claire, feeling Snookie's eyes on her, blushed and shivered simultaneously, turning her attention back to Lily's fond memories of Munich before the war sent them home. Snookie's stares were making Claire uncomfortable, so she pulled her book up to her forehead.

"Brenda said Hitler had terrible halitosis." Lily still held the other girls riveted.

"Well, all of Europe is at war with him now and we may soon be too, and then your whole guest list will be in uniform."

"Yes, shooting it out while your daughter is coming out."

"Does that mean I can't invite that Hapsburg boy we met in London?" Cilla put down her half-eaten doughnut and frowned.

"Who even knows if he's still alive?"

"Or a Nazi."

"Well, then take him off the list. I don't want to have to change my seating arrangement at the last minute. I only want live boys. Preferably who know how to dance the rumba." Cill Pettibone waved away that unpleasant business in Europe with a childish chubby hand, polished with dark red nail enamel—just like Brenda Frazier wore.

"Aren't any of you aware how serious this European war is?" It was Claire who spoke. "Even if we're not pulled into it, we're all affected."

All the girls turned to stare at their companion, whose long hair was pulled back off her face in an Alice in Wonderland style. She was spoiling the mood. When Claire furrowed her brow, only Snookie noticed that it was enhanced by a widow's peak that gave shape to her square jaw and broad cheekbones. The chiseled cheeks were the scaffolding of her symmetrically constructed face. Since Claire's thick brows were left unfashionably unplucked and feathered high over her naturally dark lashes, the impact of the explosive violet eyes was diminished. The dazzling color was the only thing about Claire every girl envied, and the fact that her thick lashes were black as indigo without the benefit of Maybelline's cake mascara.

"She's the kind *fathers* find attractive, you know, with that wide-eyed dreamy look. Any modern boy is going to find her drippy," Cilla whispered into Lily Dunworth's ear.

"She's like a spy with the sneaky way she just listens, reads, and never joins in," Lily stage-whispered back.

"My God, she smells just like a vanilla bean." Hadley Tipps sniffed, the tip of her nose practically brushing the white patch of skin between her eyebrows. She was referring to the vanilla-based aroma Claire had had a French perfumer touring Field's mix up for her. Claire preferred this homey brew, a reference to her Candy

Kitchen girlhood, to the expensive perfumes like Quelque Fleurs and Shalimar favored by the deb set.

"I hear her evening dresses are borrowed from the store. They have to be back first thing in the morning. Like curfew."

"But you have to admit she has a certain grace." Daisy Armstrong's family had the largest fortune on the North Shore, so she could afford to be generous. Daisy usually tried to buffer Claire from any real cruelties, more from a sense of noblesse oblige than niceness, but Claire was thankful nonetheless. The girls' sniping, snubbing, and ridicule hurt Claire more than they could guess.

Claire had lost much of her perkiness, Miss Wren's word for her spunky courage, as she grew older. As long as she was a small child, she was the store's pet. In the early years everyone laughed at Claire's precocious charm, admired her golden curls, or pinched her pink cheeks. Then gradually, as she grew taller, and older, her thick hair now dark and merely wavy, Claire had become a problem.

She was too small for one peg and too big for another. The mothers of more awkward debutantes among her mother's clients were jealous of Claire's well-versed talent, and of her even more evident porcelain skin, but consoled themselves with the fact that the penniless girl didn't have a social chance in hell. Suddenly, Claire Organ was out of place no matter where she was.

So she was simply ignored. Mothers and their daughters whom she had known as friendly customers all her life now looked right through her as if she were transparent, talking about things as if she wasn't standing but two feet away from them handing Madame Celine straight pins in Field's fitting rooms while their dresses were altered. It galled her to find herself being treated the same way certain careless people treated taxi drivers, waiters, the household help, or anybody else who they thought didn't matter enough to care about. Only the Pettibones, the Armstrongs, and a handful of her mother's best clients remembered to include

Claire at their daughters' dances or gatherings, even though Claire disliked being there every bit as much as the girls resented having her around—although they all pretended otherwise.

"So non-us," Lily Dunworth had described her.

Claire wished she didn't have to go to these little gatherings where part of the sport was snubbing her. And then there was her discomfort, too, of being a guest in the enemy camp, with her guilty knowledge of the five-and-a-half-year affair between Auntie Slim and Mr. Pettibone—although by now she had learned enough to keep her own secrets. Mr. Pettibone had even brought Claire back a small gift after he'd first whisked Auntie Slim off to Paris—a little French ballerina turning on her music-box stand to the strains of "Clair de Lune." Upon their return, Slim moved out of the Windermere to the North Side, where she currently resided in a sun-filled one-bedroom apartment at the Churchill on State Parkway, decorated with a Coromandel screen and suede upholstery, just like Chanel's private quarters above her salon at 31 Rue de Cambon. A pull-out couch was set aside for Claire's weekly visits, except on the evenings when "Uncle" Cyrus might be stopping by.

Claire wondered what Cilla Pettibone would do if she knew her father had not only been to Paris with her Auntie Slim, but that the same life-sized picture of Cyrus Pettibone that hung in the vast foyer of the Lake Forest house also sat in a small silver Christofle frame on Slim's skirted bed stand.

As the debs-to-be and Brenda Frazier wanna-bes chatted on about dresses and boys and guest lists, Claire self-consciously looked down at her fingernails, as naturally unpolished as Amelia Earhart's. She could hear Auntie Wren in her head telling her that she must be a very hardy girl, the half-moons of her fingernails being so wide and all, taking up almost one-third of her nail, a true sign of health and well-being.

She supposed she had a stronger constitution than most. In fact, the only time Claire remembered being truly sick was in

July 1937, when a viral episode coincided with the first reports that Amelia Earhart's plane had gone down somewhere in the Pacific after having taken off from New Guinea.

It can't be, the devastated girl had thought then, becoming glued from that moment on to the radio, her knees pulled up to her chin as she rested fitfully on the couch listening for news of the flier's whereabouts and fate. Had the Japanese detained her, or had she been captured by savages off New Guinea? Or had the plane, more mundanely, experienced mechanical difficulties? As the world waited and speculated, Claire instinctively knew the answer. Her navigator had let her down with his geography. Just like her father. Eventually, when the search was called off, with nary a piece of wreckage or luggage having been sighted, she put away her girlish dream that one day her life would cross again with the flier's. It was a little blow absorbed and almost forgotten, much like the phantom father.

"Hitler's changing the entire geography of Europe," Claire spoke again, leaving her private thoughts behind. Her eyes were flashing. "Any maps we have will be useless. We should be worried about that and the terrible suffering that is going on there and not about who's coming to your party."

"That reminds me, I almost forgot the McNally boy," Cill piped up, referring to the Chicago family that manufactured all the world's maps, globes, and atlases.

"Oh, Claire," Lily moaned. "You're so tiresome."

"Oh, what a bother." Cill would go to her mother again to complain about Claire having to participate. Why did Claire Organ always have to be included? She was a nobody.

"There must be some kind of butlers' ball with a polka contest Claire could debut at," Daisy tittered into Lily's ear.

"Doesn't she know the reason our grandmothers invented society in the first place was so that everybody could belong to their own class?" Hadley stage-whispered back.

The girls shouted with laughter, stealing sidelong looks at the object of their scorn, who flushed hotly but kept her eyes on her book.

Claire quite agreed with the others about not belonging there. But Claire wouldn't have revealed herself in front of the Priscilla Pettibones of this world for any amount of money, even as tears now stung her eyes and her lips quivered. She couldn't wait to leave the world of women behind her. She had been in a cackling henhouse without a rooster long enough. The hens had gone berserk and were pecking her to death. A real tear slipped down her cheek in spite of her best efforts to detour it.

"So the Armour boys, Marshall Field the Fourth, and Andy Ryerson, who's at Yale. He's so utterly handsome." Cill continued, taking no notice of Claire. "Hanky Clifford from New York, and both—"

"Is there a Rockefeller in our age group?" asked Lily. "Have him."

"Oh, and Phipps from Oyster Bay. He's my brother's roommate at Dartmouth."

"Don't forget Reg Dickerson the Third from Tuxedo Park. I met Dicky at the Everglades Club in Palm Beach last winter. Too divine. Maybe he'll come."

Claire lifted her violet eyes and hastily wiped her cheek dry with her fingertips.

"Tuxedo Park. Yes, ask Harry Harrison too." Lily was busy dabbing her toes with Debutante Pink.

"Oh, he's such a twit. He'll probably just keep his nose in a book the whole time."

"But aren't they awfully rich, the Harrisons?"

"Of Winding Way Road?" Constance read from the blue book.

"And isn't his father an ambassador or something?"

"S'pose. But he can't dance!"

"So don't ask him."

"I'll have to," Cill lamented. "His father went to Princeton with Daddy."

Claire bit her lip and wondered what kind of books Harry Harrison read, and if his father didn't have a fourteen-karat-gold dresser set from Marshall Field's & Co. The Harrisons of Tuxedo Park. Could they be the very same Harrisons who had saved her little Christmas years ago and indirectly "bought" the Amelia Earhart overnight case for her? Claire half smiled to herself and felt a twinge of excitement for the first time in months. Maybe this ball wouldn't be so terrible after all.

Chapter Five

Family Values

There is no doubt that it is around the family and the home that all the greatest virtues, the most dominating virtues of human society, are created, strengthened and maintained.
— *Winston Churchill*

William Henry Harrison IV didn't carry his ancestors around lightly. He ducked his silver gray head to avoid a summer branch as he easily took the jump over the fieldstone fence that intersected the north end of his Tuxedo Park property. As usual, his son Harry was several jumps behind. Both of them cut youthful figures with their trim male bodies gracefully wedded to the horses they rode. Father and son were casually and almost identically dressed in brown leather riding boots, tan jodhpurs, white shirts, and houndstooth jackets. But then there weren't many choices for proper sartorial attire in Tuxedo Park. Only forty-odd miles from roistering Manhattan, Tuxedo Park was a rustic enclave in the Ramapo Mountains restricted to New York's most elite, well-bred WASP families, along with their deer, horses, partridges, pheasants, wild turkeys, and whiskey sours. The horsey patrician residents guarded their privacy aggressively within their slabbed-stone walls, and tried to conduct their well-ordered aristocratic lives quietly and with valor, regardless of the fact that young Griswold Lorillard had given their private park a notoriety of sorts when in 1886 he and a few of his puckish friends had daringly worn tailless dress jackets to the Tuxedo Club's autumn dance, inventing in the process the tuxedo, the gentleman's preferred formal evening attire now worn everywhere by everyone. The Lorillards held the property on the eastern boundary of the Harrison estate looking down over the lake and, like the rest of their neighbors, these pillars of Tuxedo Park society elected to preserve their privacy more than fifty years after "the little notoriety" of the birth of the tux. The Tuxedo people regarded being written up in the New York "café society" columns as akin to having mug shots published in the *Police Gazette*. But there were exceptions, like the time Ophelia's great-aunt had gone mad and shot the butler who was serving her cold tea, winging him on the ear with a pocket pistol. The family was glad to see this nasty little episode reported in "Talk of the Town" instead of on the front page of the *New York Times.*

William Henry Harrison IV, called Harrison by his wife, Ophelia, and his close friend Franklin Delano Roosevelt, expertly dismounted his horse. He was exuberantly greeted by his prized Airedale terriers, Tippecanoe and Tyler, wag-tail references to his direct descent from a signer of the Declaration of Independence, a Virginia governor, and two United States presidents, one of whose campaign motto inspired the call names of his purebred dogs. Harrison affectionately rubbed their short-haired necks with both hands and gamely accepted their wet tongues on his cheek. His son, carrying the heavy mantle of his highly respected father's name with the Roman numeral V affixed to it (he thanked God hardly anybody called him "Cinq" anymore), dismounted with a little less expertise and joined him at the stone mounting post in front of the stables connected to the main house by a worn russet brick path just two hundred yards long.

"Harry." The elder Harrison beckoned. "Let's have a word before we lunch with Mother." Both Ophelia's handsome husband and gawky twenty-two-year-old son called her by the same maternal title even in their most personal moments.

Traditions and obligations had long since replaced mere middle-class emotions at Charlotte Hall, the pastoral piece of real estate where they resided. The estate was more than cobbled gray stones and manicured green hedges where stoic-faced servants served highballs at dusk and weathered stone lions guarded whispered family secrets and lush sprawling lawns. It was a cherished way of life even with all its codified rules of behavior and pecking orders. For the Harrisons, Charlotte Hall was a refuge, a place of order and beauty in which they could shield themselves from the noisy confusions of everyday life. Decorated with inherited furniture and hung with sepia-tinted photographs and oil portraits of Harrison's eminent ancestors, the house stood like an emblem to the best of the past, secure in the notion that it would always be so. The Harrisons were confident that eventually their heirs would sit in their favorite chairs and walk the same walkways, just as their ancestors once had, replacing them physically but keeping their spirits, ideals, and family values alive.

As they approached the great house, Harrison placed his hand on his son's shoulder in a rare show of affection, a gesture that indicated to young Harry that this would be a serious father-son discussion. Evidently his father had already read his letter. As close-knit as their family was, important communications were still laid down formally in writing.

Father and son continued to walk at an unhurried pace like a man and his longer shadow toward the large gray stone Tudor manor, a solemn house, their hands stuffed into the pockets of their jodhpurs, matching one another stride for stride.

"You articulated your position quite nicely in your correspondence, Harry." Harrison usually had this kind of conversation with overzealous ambassadors or warmongering Pentagon generals. "I admire you for your enthusiastic spirit and sense of decency, but I am asking you to wait on this decision for a couple of sound reasons."

"Sir, too much is going on in Europe for me to watch from the sidelines. I don't think I'm cut out for law. I'm a good pilot and ready to fight for the Brits. Now. I want to fly." He squared his shoulders in an earnest display of manly persuasiveness. Harry had already submitted his application to join the British fliers in the RAF and was waiting for his certain acceptance at any moment. It wasn't every Princetonian who had his finesse at the throttle, what his flying instructor called his "aptitude for altitude." So far flying was the only thing in his life that Harry felt he was really any good at, something that no Harrison ancestor had ever attempted before him. He searched his father's face anxiously for any indication of the "yes" he needed to proceed.

Harry had graduated from his father's alma mater this past June and was expected to enter Yale Law School as his father had before him, in just a matter of weeks. Enlisting in the RAF would be the only way to avert this certain fate.

"You'd make a fine flier." Harrison's face was an unreadable blank as he preceded his son through a free-standing stone arch.

"I'm not bad now, you know." He could hear his flight instructor jokingly telling him he was like a goose on the water and a swan in the air. Harry's face momentarily relaxed into a grin that covered the entire width of his face. The same grin—only more confident—was mirrored back at him.

"You'd make a fine lawyer, too." Harrison raised a woolly eyebrow. "That's a decision only you can make and I will certainly respect. But as a senior adviser to the president, I simply cannot have my son fly for a foreign country in a war in which we are not officially involved. It would be an embarrassment to the president and undermine our position."

Sensing his son's disappointment, Harrison breathed deeply and stopped walking.

"Don't you see, son? It's impossible." The frown lines were deep in his forehead. "With Russia in the war now, the opposing political pressures on us to get in or to stay out mount each day. Between the interventionists and the isolationists our adminis-

tration is in an untenable situation. It's just out of the question."
Harrison watched his son's face collapse in dismay.

The elder Harrison lowered his pitch from his speech-making
tone to the *entre-nous* voice he used with the president.

"And when we enter this war, nothing would make me prouder
than to have you flying for *our* country." His hazel eyes were
steady beneath their gray, bushy brows. "And I can tell you, un-
officially, that day is coming."

What he could not tell his son was what had transpired at a
cabinet meeting just a few weeks before, when Franklin had
thundered at Secretary of War Henry Stimson for dragging his
feet about getting promised help to the beleaguered Russians. It
was one of the most complete dressing-downs Harrison had ever
witnessed and totally uncharacteristic of the president.

Later that afternoon, President Roosevelt had summoned his
trusted adviser to the Oval Office.

"Harrison, I want you to take charge of this matter," Franklin
had told his friend. "It's been six weeks since they were invaded
and we've done practically nothing to get the Russians any of the
equipment they've asked for. Please get that list from Stimson
and with my full authority—use a heavy hand—act as a burr
under the saddle. Get this thing done!"

Although America wasn't at war, it was nonetheless supplying
the British with part of their navy fleet and now sending planes
to the Russians. The administration was also trying to decide to
what extent it should build up the nation's own military forces.
Secretary of the Interior Harold Ickes was convinced that "if we
strip ourselves to supply England and Russia we will save im-
measurably in men and money because these two countries between them can defeat Hitler."

Harrison disagreed.

However, he took his instructions from Franklin Roosevelt as
seriously and with no less zeal than a sworn knight of King
Arthur's Round Table. Devoted to his president, or the "gover-

nor," as he sometimes referred to FDR out of habit, Harrison's subdued, thoughtful manner and quiet, patrician bearing belied his crusading passions and fervent belief that it was America's moral duty to stop the black Nazi boot that was stomping through Europe.

The pragmatic side of Harrison's investment-banking background even reasoned that America's going to war might be a boon to the economy. But the moral question hammered at him as much as it did Roosevelt. Did the American people want to fight this war, a war in which the finest of America's young sons might be sacrificed? Including Harrison's own boy. His only son.

These decisions had been weighing heavily on him in the last few months. Today was the first time he had been home in weeks, and he was shocked to find it was suddenly the end of the summer in Tuxedo Park. Harrison spent as much time in this country haven as he could. In Washington he worked with brilliant minds, which were often in disagreement with his views on the business of government. Here he was in the company of his social kindred spirits. While FDR had his Hyde Park, Harrison had Charlotte Hall. The stately manor, named after his wife's Yankee heiress grandmother, had been part of Ophelia's dowry along with her Standard Oil shares, while Harrison had brought the pedigree of his illustrious American ancestry to the table. Harrison, with his tempered financial skills and cool rational mind, had tripled their net worth, even managing to make money during the Depression when his peers, many considered brilliant and ruthless, had lost theirs.

His old college roommate, Cyrus Pettibone, president of Chicago's stock exchange and nearly bankrupt at one point in the crash, had cast his IOU lot in with Harrison. The two of them now quietly owned companies, pieces of or the whole, that they had picked up for a song, bulking up their assets from other people's Depression losses like trolling bottom fishers. Together they owned controlling interests in a burgeoning radio network, rubber companies, bicycle plants, and a mattress manufacturer. They were even silent partners in the razzle-dazzle Ice Capades starring the short-skirted Olympic skater Sonja Henie.

Honesty and integrity were Harrison's main virtues, and if some of his assets were more "blue-collar" than "blue chip," he would never let his snobbery interfere with his financial successes. He knew wealth had its value and so he pursued it ferociously, but, like his politics, he never brought home the baser and muddier sides of either government or business. He protected his wife and son from the more unpleasant elements of acquiring vast wealth. At forty-six years old, William Henry Harrison IV's upper-class habits and values were still deeply ingrained in him.

On this September morning's ride through the idyllic trails of Tuxedo Park, he had detected the first notes of the fall of 1941 in the air. The sailboats and racy wood speedboats were out in force as if for the last flotilla before they were covered up and hauled into their boathouses dotting the shore of the lake. Yes, summer and the season of indecision were over.

There had been no vacations for anyone in the Roosevelt administration this summer. Harrison had had little opportunity to walk through the English-styled gardens patterned after the tall boxwood landscaping and colorful floral formations at Berkeley Plantation in Virginia, the birthplace of his first presidential ancestor, William Henry Harrison. He hadn't spent more than a few undisturbed hours on the lake at the helm of his sleek mahogany boat, the *Silver Fox*. Nor had he had the leisure to study in his book-lined library with its vast collection of volumes of ancient history and comfortably lived-in cracked and faded burgundy leather chairs. There he kept his prize piece of furniture, the desk used by his great-grandfather, the ninth president of the United States, William Henry Harrison, for the few weeks he had inhabited the White House. Old Tippecanoe, as his war hero forebear was called, had caught pneumonia in March 1841 while delivering his lengthy inauguration address—at almost two hours, the longest in history—on the chilly Capitol steps and, unfortunately, had died a month later, setting a record for the shortest presidency in history as well as providing comics with a century of Harrison jokes. Ophelia had even needlepointed pillows for all of Harrison's offices that carried the family's unofficial motto: "Wear an overcoat and keep your speech short!" The embarrassment was somewhat lessened by Harrison's Uncle Benjamin Harrison, who became the nation's twenty-third president and did not die until he was well out of his one term in office.

Harrison was the family's first Democrat, and a New Deal Democrat to boot. Great-Grandfather President Harrison had been a Whig and Uncle President Harrison a Republican. Harrison had been converted to "Democratism"—"his new religion," Ophelia always explained to amused dinner guests—by FDR when he recruited the leading investment banker from his New York firm, Harrison, Stokes and Phipps, the year Roosevelt became governor. They had been bonded together in ideology ever since. Thirteen years FDR's junior, Harrison held the president and his philosophy as a testimony to what greatness even men of inherited financial status and privileges could attain. It was Harrison's belief that if the parents were firm-handed enough, a child needn't be born in a log cabin to have "get up and go." He had hoped his son would show signs of the Harrison individuality, and the drive that would lead him to the accomplishments that Harrison frankly expected from him.

"Helloooo. There you two boys are!" exclaimed Ophelia, her husky voice greeting them from the awninged and ivy-draped back terrace. "My dear boys back at last. Come along," she said, waving them up the grassy knoll to the weathered bluestone promenade that could be entered from their vast house by any one of twenty sets of tall mullioned glass-paned doors.

"Alas, the leaves are getting ready to turn—much too long since I've had the pleasure of my two men together." Ophelia's eyes smiled although her lips appeared to be set in the cement lock so prevalent in her social class. "I'd love to keep you both here with me until the first frost, but we all have our obligations, don't we?" She roughly rubbed Tippecanoe's ears in a display of happiness, the heavy sapphire ring she wore prominently on her freckled hand knocking against the dog's collar.

Harry reached down and hugged Tyler, causing the dog to wag his tail. Many families might have hugged and kissed one another in greeting at a moment like this, but not at Charlotte Hall. The dogs and horses were the surrogate receivers of affection. But while they were by habit and class undemonstrative, the feelings the Harrisons held for one another were genuine and strong. Even though this was one of the only weekends of the summer the three of them were actually physically together at home, their family bonds were firm.

"E.R. and I had a fine time with our little projects while we were all out and about. We saved another boatload of Jews from Portugal and got some Negroes into the navy. I'll tell you all about it at lunch." Ophelia was one of the spokes in Eleanor Roosevelt's circle of friends and helped turn the first lady's wagon every bit as much as Harrison kept FDR's ship on course. But while Ophelia would give up her left arm to save the lives of Jews fleeing the Germans and to push for advancement of the "colored" people's education, it never occurred to her to have one of the "peoples" she worried so much about to lunch. She was one of the first lady's most loyal friends, but nonetheless, unlike E.R., she never crossed the line between whom she helped and with whom she dined. Like many of their neighbors, her activism ended at five o'clock sharp with her iced gin martini, shaken, with a lemon twist. As philanthropic as the Tuxedo people were, most didn't bring their social consciences to the elegant dinner tables in their dignified homes.

"Incidentally, Harry." Ophelia pronounced each syllable as though she were pinging a tuning fork against one of her handcut crystal goblets. "I've got a little surprise for you." Ophelia whooed and trilled at the same time. *"Luncheon guest."* This last was silently mouthed.

"Uh-oh." Harry laughed. "Do I detect another prospective fiancée on the noon menu?" Ophelia's greatest ambition in life was to have her only son well married, preferably to one of the Tuxedo girls, and produce blue-blooded grandchildren to romp and grow under her watchful eye. She already had blueprints secreted away in the vault behind the portrait of her grandmother for the house she was going to build Harry as a wedding present on the four adjoining acres she would give him.

"Are you ready?" Ophelia Harrison's eyes popped even wider than any owl's. "Minnie Mortimer! Toots and Avery's daughter. You haven't seen each other for at least two years now. I know how you like your girls intelligent and all—she's been to Bryn Mawr—and she's a horsewoman too, soooo I've just gone ahead and bit the bridle, so to speak." A tiny laugh sneaked out of her perpetually clenched lips.

Harry shuddered. He remembered Minnie Mortimer.

"Yes, Mother, she's wonderfully horsey." The girl practically neighed. "In fact, I think she is a horse."

If he remembered correctly, she had nearly crippled Harry several seasons ago at the Tuxedo autumn ball by stepping on him with one of her hooflike feet. With her long face, endless row of teeth, chestnut mane, and wide rump, she was about as "horsey" as a girl could get without fulfilling Preakness entry requirements. But, like a fine brood mare, Minnie Alexander Mortimer's bloodlines were impeccable and Harry knew that in his family circles, that was what counted. Since they had known one another all of their lives, naturally their parents hoped they'd one day marry, uniting both their distinguished families and their properties.

"Come now, Harry. Minnie cuts quite a handsome figure."

Suddenly all Harry wanted to do was to escape to the estate's private grass field, climb into his single-engine plane, and take off. Instead, he looked over at his father.

"And your opinion, Father?" he asked imploringly.

"Oh, no." Harrison chuckled as he raised both hands defensively and shook his head. "The last thing I want is to be involved in the selection of your wife."

"I see, sir. It's one thing for you to help decide whether a nation goes to war but when it comes to family duty, looks like Mother's commander in chief and I've just been drafted."

"Oooh buck up, dear, she's a sporting girl. The kind we like." Ophelia stooped down to pick a late-summer garden mum from a stone urn. She pushed it into her son's tweed riding jacket as a boutonniere. Ophelia's outdoorsy life had left her face as weatherbeaten as her husband's, but whereas time and nature had made Harrison's sculpted features even more distinguished looking, the ravages of the elements had left her face as lined as a Chinese sharpei.

"Well then, I'd be delighted to see Minnie, Mother. Lead the way." He sighed in surrender. He fleetingly wondered why women were not considered tough enough for war.

The three of them walked around the main house to the side terrace facing the pool pavilion where a round luncheon table beneath an enormous ancient elm had been set with colorful summer china and picnic crystal. Minnie was already standing at the table, waiting as eagerly as a filly at the starting gate raring to go.

"I had forgotten how you can see our house from this exact spot if you stand on your toes. Well, at least the chimney. Come look, everyone." Minnie spoke out one side of her mouth as if she had had a partial stroke. She was pointing a toned, bare arm off into the distance.

"Oh yes, dear, you're absolutely right. Come look, Harry." Ophelia didn't move her lips at all. The Tuxedo Park ladies communicated with one another like snooty ventriloquists.

"I haven't seen you anywhere for the longest time, Harry. Not at the club or at any of the dinner dances. What have you been doing with yourself all summer for fun?" She dug at a loose brick with the toe of her shoe and lowered her head.

"Flying. Would you like to go up with me?" he asked politely.

"Heavens no. It's too high-danger for me. If I can't get there on Thunder or by the New York Central, I don't want to go at all! Umm, unless maybe it's in the adorable red roadster Daddy just gave me for winning Best in Show. Did you see it in the driveway?" she blurted out excitedly. "Why don't you come for a ride with me?" Her voice boomed out into the fresh air as if she had spent a lifetime entertaining hard-of-hearing relatives. Her hair was pulled back in the equine style she wore when she rode, a thick chestnut-colored French braid to match the mare's. At least she'd had the good sense not to wear her ribbons. The Harrisons and Minnie all took their appointed places at the table, Minnie next to Harry.

Harry closed his eyes for a moment and was caught off balance by the high whinny of Minnie's laughter at one of Ophelia's jokes. He bolted from the table, dropping his napkin to the terrace.

"Mail's just arrived and I'm expecting a letter. 'Scuse me." The reluctant recruit in Ophelia's army wondered if he'd be shot at dawn on the terrace, or just be sent to his room without dessert for going AWOL.

"Well, what do you think, Harry? She's something special, isn't she?" Ophelia and her son were waving Minnie down the quarter-mile-long driveway at dusk as she sped away in her red roadster through the scrolled Tudor archway into the sunset. His rude manners at luncheon had been forgiven.

"Really, dear, I wish you would be serious about your future. All this"—Ophelia indicated the house, horses, acreage, and the four million dollars she held in her own trust fund aside from what her husband was worth—"must have its proper guardian. With inherited wealth, dear, comes inherited responsibility. Best shared by two individuals from the same world."

Harry jammed his hands into his pockets. Ophelia noticed the line of freckles running across the bridge of his nose. He looked so young.

"Aren't you rushing me, Mother? I have all the time in the world."

"Not if you're thinking of becoming a fighter pilot, you don't," she snapped in a way that reminded him of a crocodile clamping its jaws down hard on its unsuspecting prey. Seeing his reaction, she changed her tactics and softened.

"You know, dear, your father and I were 'fixed up' as you call it, and nudged into a marriage when I was only seventeen and he was just out of Princeton, and it's worked out very well indeed. Very well." She nodded grandly.

Harry envisioned his own arranged marriage, in which Minnie would win horse ribbons and he, flying ace and war hero, would eventually settle into the family banking firm and father dozens of grandchildren for his mother. He could imagine Ophelia marching her heirs around and dictating the hour-by-hour structure of their little Harrison lives, just as his had always been planned out on his mother's Adams writing desk in the sun parlor each morning. He thought he had been free at college. Now he realized he had only been following the plan. His mother was leading him to a proper Tuxedo life with Minnie Mortimer or someone just like her. But duty and conscience were what propelled the Harrisons. Who was he to meddle in the unknown fires of passion?

"Of course, dear"—Ophelia was gleeful—"you can lead a horse to water but you can't make him drink."

"Don't you mean make *her* drink?" He hoped she would smile, but she prattled on about duty and family, inheritances and familial responsibility. Even the leonine stone statuary on the grounds seemed to be staring him down.

"Okay, Mother. I'll see her again if it will make you happy. But no promises." He made an intense effort to look intractable, like one of the Harrison portraits in the Great Hall.

"Your father would like you to go to Cyrus Pettibone's daughter's debut in Chicago over the holidays. He's hoping to pull Pettibone into one of his hush-hush transactions in this European war business. But he's got to be with FDR on government affairs that weekend. Take a look around if you like. There'll be plenty of nice girls from good families, but trust me, they won't be like Minnie. I've been your mother for a long time. She'll bring out the best in you." Ophelia's eyes twinkled. "Take your plane," she advised, "and," she said, conjuring up one of their presidential forebears for good measure, "don't forget to take an overcoat and keep your speech short." They both laughed. "And Harry"—she patted him on the back—"lots of grandchildren."

"Father, I'm sorry that I put you to the loyalty test this morning—me against the president. I know he's walking a fine line." Harry entered the library. His still boyish voice held an edge in it. In the soft light cast by the antique American wall sconces and his father's hooded brass reading lamp, the heavily waxed dark wood floors gleamed like embers in the fireplace. As was his custom, Harrison had retired to his favorite room in the house following a quiet family dinner in the smaller of the two dining rooms.

Harrison looked up from his official documents, and, indicating the crystal decanter of brandy beside him on the desk, asked, "Won't you join me?" He seemed less intimidating to his son beneath the vastness of the two-story wood-beamed vaulted ceiling.

"Thank you, sir."

There was a long silence.

Warmth was not Harrison's strong point, but he did put before all else his devotion to duty and God and loyalty to his friends and family. He struggled here to find the right thing to say, and to appease his son in the process.

"You'll get your chance to fly, Harry." He stood up and poured them each a short glass of sherry. "We're moving cautiously into this thing. It's very mature of you to grasp the gravity of the situation. When you're older, you'll understand it's the big picture that needs concern us. I appreciate you trying to see the overview with me. Sit down, son. I think you'll be interested in what FDR and I were up to this August."

"I heard you sailed up to Nantucket on the *Potomac*."

"It wasn't aimless holiday sailing." Harrison's thick brows knitted together into a bushy gray hedge. "We did take the presidential yacht but we made a top-secret rendezvous with some of our American warships. Harry, you've heard about this. The Joint Declaration."

"Churchill?" Harry folded his arms and leaned on the short-lived ninth president's desk, his eyes aglow. "You were there?"

Harrison nodded, a slight smile curling his lip. "The president and I secretly transferred over to the heavy cruiser, the U.S.S. *Augusta*. Fine ship." Harrison sipped at his sherry. "Even Eleanor and your mother weren't told where we were going."

"Father, I had no idea. Tell me what it was like." Harry's awe of his father was real.

"It reminded me of kindred spirits coming together. One of the most emotional moments I've ever witnessed. The world's two great leaders were as nervous to meet each other as a couple of young people on a first date." Harrison's usually cool delivery was awash in warmth. "FDR stood straighter than he's stood in years. He wouldn't use the wheelchair or the crutches. The only assist he'd use was the support of his son Elliott, and as the navy band struck up 'God Save the King,' Churchill boarded. I've never seen such a look of elation cross FDR's face. He was determined to greet the legend and be standing on his own to do it. I wish you could have been there to see it."

"And Churchill?"

"When he moved toward Roosevelt, I could swear the tough old fellow had tears in his eyes. Many of us did."

Harry couldn't tell whether it was from the light reflecting off the glass decanter or the smoke wafting up from the lit pipe or the emotion ignited from the story that caused his father's eyes to glisten.

"Mark my words, Harry, together they will annihilate this darkness stalking the world. Mark my words." For a moment, Harrison's voice resonated exactly like President Roosevelt's.

"Mr. Harrison, sir," the butler interrupted them.

Both father and son spun around.

"Excuse me, sir, but there's a call for you from Hyde Park."

Harry watched as his father crossed the room and picked up the telephone. He thought to himself what a distinguished-looking gentleman his father was. With his thick, sleek gray hair, aloof air, and trim, athletic body, Harrison looked as alert for action as a man of half his years. But his demeanor exuded concern, self-discipline, and a sense of the serious matters crowding his briefcase. Harry almost felt apologetic for bothering him with his modest problems.

Harrison put the receiver to his ear as he purposefully picked up the fountain pen from its inkwell, a plethora of Harrison presidential memorabilia and photographs crowding the desk. A nerve in his left jowl twitched.

"She was a remarkable woman. We will all feel her loss."

Harry stood at attention.

"How is the president taking it? . . . I see. Yes, Mrs. Harrison and I will leave first thing in the morning. Of course. Yes. Thank you for calling." He gently lowered the receiver back into its cradle.

"The president's mother, Sara Delano Roosevelt, has passed away and Franklin's very undone," Harrison announced. In the darkening room, dimly lit, Harrison, deep in thought, cast an unusually large shadow.

Watching his father, Harry reflected how difficult it must have been for him to succeed in the shadow of two presidential forebears and such high expectations. But he had, first on Wall Street and now as senior adviser and intimate confidant to the president of the United States.

Harry wondered if he could ever follow in those exalted footsteps. As a breeze blew in from the terrace, rustling the important papers on his father's desk, Harry suddenly felt he cast no shadow at all.

A wintry blast lifted the heavy hem of Claire's coat, blowing her snow-matted hair across her face as she sidestepped over an icy patch and into the Marshall Field's employees' entrance. She ran up the silent and still escalator two steps at a time. It was shut off for Sunday, the store's day off but not hers—she was late. Mother and the Aunties were probably already there laying out handbags and gloves to go with evening dresses and cocktail suits. The Aunties were dying to get their busy hands on the reluctant party-goer, fix her mouth into a smile, puff up her hair, and deck her out in an evening dress required to be at once "elegant" (Mother), "sweet" (Auntie Wren), and "a head-turner" (Slim). Claire would just as soon be facing the German measles.

Just a few employees were taking inventory today to prepare for the Christmas rush, the burst of year-end revelry that would fill the dressing rooms of the new but already touted "28 Shop" for weeks to come. Field's expensive and deluxe "Store within the Store" was her mother's kingdom, and Violet had poured herself into it just as her clientele poured themselves into the newest pencil-slim fashions from Mainbocher and Claire McCardell. The September opening had been covered by every important magazine and paper in the country and hardworking Violet, finally rewarded for her years of service, had been appointed the new salon director.

The newest jewel in Field's crown was breathtaking. Joseph

Platt, who had created the Hollywood sets for *Gone With the Wind*, had been dispatched to design the shop with the single instruction to "outmatch anything in the world—even the most fashionable establishments of Paris." And so he did.

The twenty-eight dressing rooms were sinfully spacious and each decorated in uncompromised luxury. The "salonettes" were arranged in fourteen opulently designed pairs, with each room facing its twin in a circle around a grand oval foyer. The spacious, regal main salon, with its customer-flattering recessed lighting and hand-rubbed pink oak walls, was furnished with Louis XV gilt tables and Regency chairs covered with gold-studded turquoise velvet and silks. And if gossip ever had a home before, now there were twenty-eight private parlors for high society's greatest pastime, dishing the social dirt. Since each dressing room was decorated in duplicate, any customer could have her favorite room even if it was already in use by a rival, a friend, or the subject of another woman's unflattering remarks. One pair of dressing rooms was a dazzle of cut-glass sconces, beveled mirrors, and tufted rose-satin banquettes; another pair was done up in black marble trim and peach silk; while a third set of private salons, reserved for the viewing of casual hacking-around clothes, was covered with café-au-lait pigskin. English tea was served to the clients from elaborate silver services, and while the salesgirls walked softly and spoke in whispers, the noisy customers had a whale of a good time in the party atmosphere, trying on clothes and trading juicy tidbits.

And there was no tidbit juicier or more vigorously dissected than the long-running affair between Slim and Cyrus Pettibone. It had been six years since the day young Claire had brought the unsuspecting Mr. Pettibone home to tea. For four of them, knowledge of the quiet little romance had stayed within the protective quilted cocoon of Marshall Field's fitting rooms and immediate environs, whispered about and speculated upon by shop girls, society matrons, caterers, hairdressers, hem fitters, and down the fashion food chain. The latest news often circulated with malicious speed, moving along the telephone wires and onto the pastel carpet of the 28 Shop's fancy fitting rooms.

"Slim is taking elocution lessons so she can talk like his hoity-toity socialite wife," a fitter confided to a customer.

"I don't think it's her elocution he's interested in."

"Slim's got a body most models would kill for."

"She could be killed for her body now, by Mrs. P."

"Pettibone won't walk out on a wife and four daughters."

"Not if he wants to continue to be on the board of the Art Institute." Mrs. Armstrong poked her aquiline nose out of her fitting room.

"Not to mention the Chicago Stock Exchange." Mrs. Dunworth inhaled.

"Slim won't be able to close this sale. Even if she bathes in Paris Nights all day long," the Jean Harlow blonde modeling a satin figure-fitting evening gown drawled.

"I hear he's taking her to Paris."

Every saleslady in the custom salon was struck dumb.

Mrs. Winterbotham's jaw dropped to her girdle. Too bad she couldn't run with it, but gossip wasn't "hard news."

Every woman within earshot poked her head out of the dressing room, no matter what stage of undress she was in.

"But nobody's actually seen them together, have they?" she queried.

Miss Violet waltzed in with a gown draped over her arms. "Ladies, ladies, we can't wear rumors. Facts and fabric, that's what we deal with on Six." Violet's singsong denials were Slim's best defense.

"Poor old Cyrus must have been seduced in his sleep," Cora Woodnorth told two friends next door in the beveled-mirrored dressing room. Like a slinky incubus armed with a nightie from Lingerie on Field's fifth floor, they whispered to each other, Slim had aroused his desire, driving him insane for six years.

"And to think"—Hanna Rusk stamped her foot, splitting a stitched seam and sending an arsenal of straight pins flying all around the ultraplush fitting room—"I purchased that silver dinner suit from her only last week." She shook off Slim's taste. She'd never wear that outfit again, out of deference to Millicent.

So the women customers closed ranks in the pinky beige foyer of the 28 Shop with the kind of unity only seen when one of their own was facing childbirth, breast cancer, or divorce, while the salesladies secretly rooted for Slim's success. And amidst the din, Cyrus was forgotten and forgiven, as if he had innocently fallen out of a tree, pants off and ready to go, and landed right in Slim's conniving lap.

Each time Cyrus had to cancel a romantic rendezvous, Slim fell onto the steady shoulder of her loyal friend Violet, who led her to their usual table at Trader Vic's for a good long cry. Slim, her mascara streaking down her cheeks, would ruin martini after mai tai as the colorful paper umbrellas stuck into the exotic drinks couldn't keep her tears from falling into her frosted glass. Gloomily, Slim would return to her apartment alone, slip into a black peignoir, smoke two packs of Gauloises, and retire to her bed, where she reread Fannie Hurst's *Back Street,* the popular tearjerker about a woman in retail who was also in love with a married man. And then Slim would be ready to face the world again.

Yet despite appearances, the years as a married man's mistress had been kind to Slim. He had, in fact, provided for her. Not only was the State Parkway apartment, where she lived with her Persian cat Chat and a canary for company, put into her name, but he also built a small stock portfolio for Slim that included five hundred shares in the Ice Capades. It made Slim feel very proud indeed to take Claire to an evening performance seated in the best box seats on the ice, her full-length mink coat, a Cyrus present, thrown around her shoulders to keep off the stadium chill, knowing she owned a little piece of the show. And Claire took it all in as just another dimension of her after-school education.

Well, here she was, not liking it, to meet her mother and the Aunties to select a dress for Cilla Pettibone's debut dance, just a fortnight away. Claire had been in the background of enough of these black-tie rites of passage to know that they were little more than chic cattle auctions where the sons of the wealthy could choose from among the daughters of the rich. With their imported, out-of-season orchids and papier-mâché stars, these evenings had in fact little to do with love and romance and everything to do with mergers and acquisitions. Claire sighed, squared her shoulders, and resolved not to deny the ladies their pleasure. Yet she worried sometimes over the weight of expectations they placed on her as if she, daughter of the hired help, with one quick spin around the dance floor would find true love, a husband, and financial security (in that order), just because she had on a pretty dress. Claire had no illusions. Having nothing to merge, she was not worth acquiring. The best she could hope for was a passing hors d'oeuvre, a waltz before supper with a nice boy who didn't mind twirling a nobody, and a quick smooch in the bushes. Auntie Slim had unwittingly shown her as much.

"Hi, Mother." Claire smiled and leaned down to kiss Violet's powdered cheek and give her a warm squeeze.

"You work too hard, Mother. It's Sunday. I thought success meant you got to work less."

"Success can only be measured by busy hands," quoted Miss Wren, rushing up to Claire and offering her a Frango mint from a crystal candy dish usually reserved for the customers. "But don't eat too many, dear, we've picked out the loveliest dresses for you and then your mother is taking us all for Sunday supper at the Blackstone." Miss Wren started to return the candy dish to its proper place but kept getting confused, between all the mirrors hanging as big as doorways around the salon.

"Wren, put those bonbons away!" Slim was directing this production. A strong-smelling French cigarette dangled from her fire-engine-red lips. Somehow the last couple of roller-coaster years had only made her more beguiling. "We're redoing Claire for the ball, girls, not fattening her up like an Armour hog for the slaughter!" She turned so quickly that a glimpse of a well-shaped thigh was exposed.

"Oh, that reminds me." Violet was all business. "Where is the white velvet we have on hold for Bitsy Armour?"

Slim reappeared from behind a plaster Corinthian column with an armful of gowns that had been especially ordered for the gala debutante parties. A dozen girls were due in tomorrow for their fittings. As a buyer for the shop, Slim spent as much time in New York as in Chicago. Of course, before Hitler's invasion of France, she had spent a great deal of time in Paris, too, either buying or "copying" designs for her customers. These excursions quietly coincided with Cyrus Pettibone's overseas business trips.

Slim's travels had allowed her to befriend the great European couturiers, her favorite of whom was Coco Chanel. Chanel had closed up her design house when the Germans marched into France the year before, but Slim had her ways. She had coaxed the last two Chanels out of Paris via London. One was currently being steamed free of wrinkles by Madame Celine for Claire in the back room and the other, far more elaborate and costly, was sailing on the USS *Coolidge* for New York in Priscilla Pettibone's precise measurements, or at least the most recent measurements, for the youngest Pettibone had chronic weight fluctuations.

"Bring out the Dress. Our little Orphan Annie is here ready to be done over." Slim called back to Celine, rolling up her sleeves. "Hurry up, Claire. Give me that coat. Your auntie Slim had to use every pull in her pouch to get Coco's seamstresses to whip up this masterpiece. It's straight from her sketches." Slim smiled excitedly.

"Isn't Chanel fraternizing with the Nazis?" Wren worried, following at Slim's heels to the most grand of the fitting rooms.

"*C'est la guerre.* A woman has to do what a woman has to do to keep her head afloat. Besides, I'm sure she doesn't really like them." Slim picked up a lank strand of Claire's hair.

"What is your hair saying, Claire?" She frowned, dropping the strand, which fell in all directions full of static in the dry radiator heat of the store.

"Your hair is making no statement whatsoever. Not saying a thing." She shook her own short, sassy, pitch-black hair.

"And just what, Aunt Slim, would you like it to say?" Claire laughed.

"Who you are, dear, who you're going to be. Men are very responsive to a woman's hair." When her lips stopped moving, her smile was quite pretty.

"No, it's the legs. Everyone knows that." Wren pushed the fitting stool directly beneath the chandelier. Since she was top heavy, her thin legs were her best feature.

"Nonsense, you two," Violet corrected. "It's brains and stability that a man wants in a woman. And that message can be conveyed by what she chooses to wear. Goodness knows I've dressed enough women held in high regard to know a thing or two here."

Slim interrupted. "High regard? Well, all the men *I've* known would rather hold a woman in their arms!" She blew out her cigarette smoke, encasing her words in a puff of parentheses.

Violet soothingly adjusted the light in the fitting room to simulate the low evening light of a debutante party. "Now then, let's all get in the right mood."

"Precision."

"Right mood?" Claire rolled her eyes. She couldn't believe that one fussy old maid, a virgin for sure, one head-over-high-heels-in-love-with-love kept woman, and her mother, who hadn't been touched by a man that way in seventeen years, were now going to advise her on how to be alluring.

"Celine, aren't you done with that Chanel yet?"

"No, Madame Slim."

"Well, in the meantime, let's see this deb dress. This one is simply to die. So chic." Slim shook a Valentina at her niece.

"Valentina dressed Garbo." Wren helped Claire step into the folds of duchess satin.

"What's this dress saying?" Slim put her fist to her chin like Rodin's *The Thinker*.

"It's saying I'm flat chested."

"Yes, dear, we can hear it."

"Take it off me." Claire struggled with the silk-covered buttons.

"To thine own self be true," Wren comforted.

"Yes, but do we have to emphasize my faults? Don't I have enough of them as it is?" Claire groaned. "Poverty, social obscurity, breasts as small as our bank account."

"Oh dear, we can fix that bust nicely with a little stuffing like I do all my ladies," Violet said kindly, while tucking some tissue into the bodice and rebuttoning the back.

"Eleanor Roosevelt says, if you have to compromise, compromise up." Wren pushed her hands up under her own full bosom. She hadn't completed a single day without an Eleanor quote since the day she sold her the knitting needles back in 1932. She read Eleanor's daily column, "My Day," aloud every morning over coffee in the employees' lounge.

The Aunties all took a step back, like fussy fairy godmothers, to assess their work so far.

"Well, the bosom looks fuller now." Slim straightened the padding in the watersilk bateau neckline, adding curves to the poker-straight bodice.

"And the full skirt hides the fact you have no hips."

"Well, you ladies have certainly camouflaged me."

"We're just getting started."

"Sure, but how do I get in the door? Sideways?" Claire turned counterclockwise on her pedestal to view her billowy silhouette.

"At last. The Chanel!" Slim exclaimed as Madame Celine finally appeared. A piece of couture designed by Chanel in her last season, 1939, the dress was embroidered, embellished, and hand-sewn by the couturiere's seamstresses, as a favor to Slim. The pale silk baby rosebuds at the bodice looked as if they had just been plucked from a secret garden.

In unison, the Aunties and Celine gasped in awe.

"A work of art."

"A fairy-tale dress."

"A dress that will shower you in magic."

"And confidence." Violet unfastened the velvet sash and silk buttons of the Valentina, gently pulling off the suddenly very second-rate gown.

"Fit for a princess." Celine stood back, entwining her fingers together into a steeple, before returning to the back room to prepare for the next day's onslaught.

Claire eyed the delicate eggshell-colored masterpiece appreciatively. She just knew its beauty would shield her from snubs and whirl her into an enchanted evening. Even if it was for just *one* enchanted evening.

As the Aunties slipped the party dress over her head, piled up her hair, and hung a string of costume pearls around her neck, Claire slipped into the mood. She only hoped she could live up to the exquisite dress's expectations.

"Ah Paris, Paris. Just a rustle of satin and I am transported back to the Avenue George the Fifth. Paris, the city of romance." Slim heaved a sudden sob, arching her small shoulders so high they brushed her golden dangle earrings, sending them twirling and spinning crazily like little Ferris wheels.

Wren handed Slim her handkerchief in anticipation of the tears that would be flowing from the woman still in the throes of backstreet love and the fall of Paris.

"Take it." Wren pushed the wadded-up hanky into Slim's hands.

"No, no." Slim waved the hanky away. "Let these tears flow. These are tears of joy. Pure joy. You see, Cyrus has proposed. He is finally going to marry me."

Wren spilled all the straight pins from Celine's box onto the floor.

"Oh, no, here we go again," she wailed, wringing her hands as she knelt down to pick up the pins.

"*C'est vrai.* It's true." Real tears flowed down Slim's white, powdery cheeks. "He's leaving that old dragon right after Cilla's debut. We'll be man and wife by Valentine's Day."

Wren looked at her woefully, shaking her head in doubt.

"No, really. Why would I lie?" Slim's eyes shone in all sincerity beneath her straight bangs.

Suddenly, three pairs of widened pupils were riveted on Slim, who was draped elegantly across the satin chaise and dabbing theatrically at her moist eyes. She looked vulnerable and fragile in the pink dressing-room light, real tears streaking mascara down her heart-shaped face.

"It's true." An astonished Wren sank to her knees. They rushed to Slim's side.

Wren took Slim's hand as much in comfort as feeling around for a diamond ring.

"Oh girls, *mes soeurs,* come close." She motioned them toward her. "I've been dying to tell you but I wanted to wait until we were all together." She exhaled weeks of secrecy and gazed victoriously at their dumbfounded faces, stopping to pull Claire's palm softly to her cheek.

"And it's so right that it should be here at Field's, in this place"—her eyes rolled up to where the Tiffany dome would be—"where we first became a family."

"But how did it happen? Why is this happening now?" Claire hoped she was being delicate.

"Cyrus has always told me that it was his intention to stay with Millicent only until his last daughter was launched." She swung her arm as if she were launching a cruise ship with a champagne bottle. "Cyrus is a man of his word. I never reminded him of his promise nor expected him to keep it. You know, it's not in my nature to be demanding. I was resigned to live for a moment here, an evening there. Just a little romance. But two weeks ago he asked me if I would still have him. If I would be his wife." The width of her grin could have landed her in *Ripley's Believe It or Not.*

There was a moment of silence as they all sniffed into their perfumed handkerchiefs. No one spoke until Violet cleared her throat.

"Oh, we're thrilled for you, dear. It's just that it comes as such a surprise."

"Oh, Auntie Slim. I'm so happy for you." Claire extended her long arms around Slim's petite shoulders. "And here I am hogging the limelight and standing in what is definitely a wedding dress. Cream lace, satin, pearls, and all." She planted a kiss on both of Slim's cheeks, in the French way, just as she had been taught. "You should have this gown."

"No, dear." Slim brightened, her eyes sparkling. "I have a little Mainbocher evening suit tucked away in the back."

"Just like the duchess of Windsor." Miss Wren clapped her happy hands together. "That *other* American girl who married up. Well, everything's starting to look up around here for our little clan, isn't it?"

Violet, her composure returned, suddenly moved into action. "Here, let's have some music to celebrate Slim's good fortune." She reached behind her to snap on the radio. "And Wren, run up to Gourmet and bring back some bubbly."

Added to the reassuring music of infectious laughter came the strains of Artie Shaw's band in an upbeat melody.

"Oh, it's Artie Shaw himself. Lana Turner's new husband."

The swing music wafted across the satin-tufted dressing room, and Claire, still dressed in the elegantly understated Chanel, gleefully danced Auntie Slim around the floor as Auntie Wren passed a silver tray of fluted champagne glasses from the eighth floor filled to the brim with Moët & Chandon. Even Violet got into the festive mode, removing her silken violet corsage and placing it in Slim's hands like a bridal bouquet.

Suddenly the middle-aged women appeared as young and full of hope as they had that very day seventeen years ago when Claire entered the world on Five.

"Just think, finally, a wedding in the family."

"Our first."

"But not our last." Slim raised her glass, glowing.

"To Slim." They raised their glasses.

"To love." Slim crooned as the band played. *"Toujours l'amour."* The music was suddenly interrupted as the urgent voice of an announcer broke in.

"Japanese bombers have just attacked the U.S. naval forces at Pearl Harbor in Hawaii. Heavy casualties have been sustained. The attack planes may be on their way to the mainland. We will stay tuned for a message from President Roosevelt. A declaration of war is expected. Repeat: The U.S. has been attacked. We are at war, Mr. and Mrs. America."

One by one the shocked ladies solemnly set their celebration glasses back onto the silver tray. Each of them tried to make sense of what she had just heard.

Slim worried that she might be a war widow again. Surely Cyrus would be asked to lead a battalion.

Wren said a heartfelt prayer for Mrs. Roosevelt and her four sons, all of military age.

Violet moved immediately to embrace her daughter and hold her next to her heart.

For Claire, the world was at war and all its social snobberies and rules were suddenly shelved, crumbling topsy-turvy, opening up unheard-of opportunities for the shop girls' daughter. Claire was about to be thrust into circles inaccessible even to the daughters of social privilege who snubbed her. The world would never be the same. Nor would Claire.

Chapter Six

The War Bride

Last year, time was no object . . . to Dine, to Dance, to Meet, to Marry. This year, time is of the essence. A soldier's Leave is reckoned in Days, Hours, Minutes. Dates are timed to the split second and girls no longer keep boys waiting. Are you free next Wednesday from 4:30 to 8 P.M.? I've special Leave. Can you lunch today? I'm being shipped overseas. Can you marry me tomorrow?

—Vogue, *1941*

There were two stupendous news flashes that filtered through the Pettibone manse on Lake Forest's Green Bay Road, setting off a flurry of telexes, cables, telephone calls, and a good measure of tears and hand-wringing. One was the December 8, 1941, radio address to Congress by President Franklin Roosevelt condemning the "unprovoked and dastardly attack by Japan" that had now plunged the American nation into war. Cyrus spent the frenetic morning cloistered in his walnut-paneled study talking to his business associates, Board of Trade economists, and after a lengthy private but revelatory conversation with his friend William Harrison IV, he put his personal plans, sex life, and Slim on the back burner in a vigorous surge of patriotism.

The other bitter piece of news coursing through the sacheted upstairs parlors and bedrooms and sending the maids and daughters into a swoon was the sinking of Cilla's party dress. The USS *Coolidge* had been torpedoed one hundred and twenty-five nautical miles off the coast of Newfoundland, sending the seed-pearled and lace-embroidered gown slowly sinking past the surprised sole, salmon, and roughy to settle at the bottom of the icy North Atlantic. The sinking of the Chanel by a German torpedo caused as much havoc in the floral carpeted corridors and upstairs boudoirs of the household as the sinking of the Pacific Fleet was stirring up at the Pentagon.

"Those selfish Nazis," Cilla wailed. "What am I going to wear now? It's my coming-out party and I can't wear just anything."

"Oh, good gracious, first Pearl Harbor and now this!" Millicent was beside herself. "Why, *Town and Country* is covering my baby's ball. What to do? What to do?" Frownies hung from Millicent's face in disarray, making her look like a heavily bandaged war casualty. The antiwrinkling sleeping adhesives had come unstuck and were swinging precariously as she frowned herself into a frenzy. All the movie stars used these press-on overnight patches to stave off crow's-feet and facial lines, or so the Field's salesgirl had promised her. In Millicent's case, she was also trying to stave off an aggressive mistress. If only Field's sold something for that.

"Oh, where is Violet? She'll know what to do." She clasped her hands to her bosom. "Somebody find Violet. I'm having a nervous collapse." She pushed her pink satin eyeshades over her head like a headache band with both bright-pink manicured fists. "I can actually feel myself aging, I'm so upset. And where is your father at a terrible time like this? Jean Marie, take these Frownies off my face!"

Jean Marie, her ladies' maid, flew out of the room sobbing. She also had received bad news, a letter informing her that her father and uncles in France had been rounded up by the Germans in a random act of retaliation after partisans in their hometown had attempted to assassinate one of the occupying Germans. It was presumed in the letter that they and the other town leaders were being shipped off to a camp somewhere in Poland. Jean Marie's cries were heard all the way down the hall and echoed ominously from the back stairs to the kitchen.

"Oh, somebody stop that wailing! You'd think we beat the help around here." Millicent put her hands to her forehead and rubbed distractedly. "Oh, why does everything always have to happen to me? Why did they have to torpedo Cilla's dress? Couldn't they have waited until after the party?" She was waving her hat pin dangerously like a sword in her hand, putting everyone in the room on her best field-hockey guard. "Even if we'd had torpedo insurance, the Chanel is irreplaceable. Where are we going to find a suitable dress now?"

Sally Pettibone Lambrecht, lounging on the edge of her mother's rumpled bed, took a sip from her brandy-laced morning tea and dramatically pointed to the drapes.

"That is *so* mean," said Cilla, recognizing the reference to Scarlett O'Hara's postwar wardrobe.

"Sally, have some sympathy for your sister. She's trying to come out." With one last shove and a heave, she was in her dress without the help of Jean Marie. "You've already had your big debut, and two husbands, too. Look, you've made Cilla cry." She turned to her youngest daughter, who was sobbing and nervously popping buttered breakfast muffins into her mouth.

"Don't worry, my pet." She brushed the crumbs from Cilla's chin. "We won't let a war get in the way of your future. Violet will know what to do. She always does."

Six-eighty Green Bay Road was ablaze with twinkling lights and glitter. The house shone like a beacon of faerie light for miles around in the clear, wintry night. Six months of intense preparation had paid off. Chicago in winter had been transformed into Venice in summer, and Cyrus Pettibone's pseudo-Normandy castle had been extravagantly made over into a doge's palace.

An army of stylists from Field's display department had fashioned and tented the five main salons with heavy Scalamandré silk and covered the walls with tapestries and hand-painted murals depicting Tintoretto-inspired vistas of a starlit Venice. A real Canaletto had been purchased through Field's Art Department and hung in the main library. They had even erected a ten-foot plaster-of-Paris *Santa Maria della Salute* outside on the terrace, the dome dramatically illuminated by floodlights borrowed from Wrigley Field. The lightbulbs' hue had been changed to pink, just for the Pettibones' pleasure. And with Mrs. Wrigley's full consent. The chewing-gum heiress was coming to dinner, of course. All the place cards had been penned in Field's Calligraphic Department and were even, at this last second, being rearranged to satisfy the somebodies over the nobodies.

The sunporch had festively been turned into the Lido Beach, complete with striped awnings and lounges, while a miniature Grand Canal ran around the house in a refurbished, heated drain-pipe. An authentic Venetian gondola stood rocking in the watery enclosure should any hearty fur-clad guests or those too drunk on champagne to feel the chill choose to take a canal ride. Millicent had spared none of Cyrus's money.

Dozens of chandeliers festooned in pale orchids and orange blossoms languidly dripped their petals onto the floors buffed for dancing Viennese waltzes and the "Conga Chain" as well as Glenn Miller's swing tunes. In keeping with the theme, a string quartet from the Chicago Symphony Orchestra, their heads topped in tri-cornes, played Vivaldi under the torchlit, tented entryway to welcome the guests and set the mood, even as the young people were singing along with the skinny crooner belting out "Chattanooga Choo-Choo" around the Venetian-bannered bandstand in the Winter Garden Pavilion where Lester Lanin was playing, a concession to Cilla's crowd.

The only thing missing were the flocks of pigeons from St. Mark's Square. Millicent had declared pigeons too "filthy and or-dinary" for her daughter's ball and so the exhausted party plan-ners substituted a last-minute dule of doves. But the birds were

presently stashed away in the greenhouse since no one could figure out what to do with their guano, as her Peruvian gardener
called the doves' unpredictably aimed droppings.

All in all, Venice had been faithfully re-created in satins,
Fortuny silks, painted backdrops, gold papier-mâché, and great
expense, thanks to Millicent's careless extravagance, and paid for
by Cyrus's guilty conscience. In an odd way, Slim told Claire as
she dressed her for the gala, her auntie's invisible hand could be
felt in all this. Had there been no Slim, there most certainly
would have been no four-hundred-thousand-dollar ball celebrating the watery Italian city, now a trophy in the Führer's Axis
showcase. Cyrus would have put his foot down.

Slim, her kittenish eyes big as saucers, was as excited about the
ball as if she were going herself. This was not just Cilla's coming
out gala, she reckoned, but Millicent's going-away party. Hang
the cost.

Claire walked through the doorway of the house her aunt was
dying to claim for her own. She glanced toward her right, and
caught a glimpse of Mrs. Pettibone draped in peach chiffon and
brown velvet in deep discussion with the mayor and her husband,
Cyrus (Auntie Slim's fiancé), who was standing smiling at her
side. Peeking back at them over her shoulder, Claire thought
Millicent certainly didn't look like a woman whose Vuitton luggage was all packed and ready to leave for Reno in two days. A
high-pitched laugh trilled through Mrs. P.'s lungs as Mr. P., the
mayor, the chairman of the Continental Bank, and Sally
Pettibone Lambrecht all chimed in like a merry peal of church
bells. No, it certainly didn't look like a fallen family on the verge
of collapse.

"Sally dear, find your little sister. We must form our receiving
line again." Millicent gave a startled look at Claire's costume, re-
garding her up and down and up until she stopped and left her
nose in the air.

"Gracious, she's certainly putting on a brave front," Claire marveled, gathering up the folds of her stiff gown as she climbed the polished marble entry steps. A chill shuddered down Claire's surprised spine, when at the very same second Cyrus Pettibone winked at her, he gave his wife a kiss on the cheek.

"Come Pett, let's greet our guests." She looked like Caesar's wife entering Rome as she strode arm-in-arm with her husband into their former living room, now a brilliantly candlelit ballroom fit for an emperor.

Claire gazed after them, a slightly puzzled look crossing her brow. Suddenly, she was swept up in a surge of Donnelleys, Smiths, McCormicks, and Fields gaily entering the ball.

Turning to the left of the main vestibule with all the other invited girls to check her cloak and freshen up, Claire squared her nervous shoulders and took a deep breath before she entered the ladies' powder room, four times the size of the Windermere apartment and jam-packed with strapping girls in big dresses and elbow-length gloves noisily primping in front of the gilded Chippendale mirror.

"Did you see him? Gawd! A man in uniform. Isn't he spiffy!"

"Tall, dark, and solvent."

"Oh, you should marry him." Daisy Armstrong looked fetching, stuffed into a white strapless number with yards of tulle stitched into consecutive tiers widening like a Christmas tree. It was said she had the finest pair of shoulder blades on the North Shore.

"Yes, marry him. He's going off to flight officers' school in a week."

"Not until I sleep with him." Snookie Cuthbert swigged a glass of champagne. "I don't want to wake up some morning to a limp regret." She giggled and everyone giggled with her. Snookie had already been through the receiving line twice and the champagne-soggy dance card dangling from her wrist was already full of names followed by a Jr. or a Roman numeral. Her evening, like her future, was already laid out.

"Well if you don't snatch up Edward McCormick, somebody else will. All of them are getting engaged or married before they ship out."

"If there was ever a time for a girl to act like a woman, it's now." Daisy puckered her lips, brushing some Red Madness across them.

"Oh, hello, Claire," she said into the mirror, not bothering to turn around. "I hardly recognized you." Daisy tossed her lipstick back into her evening bag and returned to her conversation.

"*Vogue* says time's awasting."

"I'll say."

"Claire, when did you grow a bosom?" Snookie studied Claire's new glamour-puss silhouette.

Ignoring Claire, Lily Dunworth returned to the matter at hand. "Shouldn't you get engaged first, the old-fashioned proper way?" she asked.

"Not in these times."

"Marry them before they go to war, my aunt Susan says, or you'll be too old when they get back." Weezie Rusk blew two perfect smoke rings over her shoulder.

"*If* they get back."

"Oh shut up, Lily. That's not very patriotic."

"Yeah, and then you'll be left behind like those spinsters from the last war."

"Or a salesgirl." Snookie flashed a look at Claire.

"You're such a slut, Snooks. You've already slept with Tony and now you're plotting to marry his big brother."

"All's fair in love, war, and haute couture."

Claire quietly slipped off her cloak, handed it to the ladies' maid, and hesitantly joined the chatty lineup at the gilded mirror.

Suddenly all she could see was the Dress. The delicate Chanel masterpiece had the air of privilege and propriety as if the wearer were about to sit for a Winterhalter portrait. The seed pearls gave the dress a subtle shimmer, as if its glamour was just whispered. The peach and pink rosettes at the collarbone gave the gown its fresh quality, so that it had an understated innocence. It was perfection. The Chanel made all of the other dresses appear far too sophisticated to ostensibly herald a young woman's entry into polite society.

Claire stared at it in the six-foot-wide dressing-table mirror and then slowly lowered her eyes. Somehow the Dress made even Cilla Pettibone look lovely.

Yes, what should have been Claire's was now Pettibone property. On that day after Pearl Harbor when the hysterical Pettibone women had marched onto the 28 Shop floor to avenge the sinking of Cilla's dress, the quiet salon had been thrown into turmoil. Miss Slim was shoved by Miss Wren into the private elevator, and, with one stab of the Down button, was sent into lower-floor oblivion where she would be safely out of firing range. Wren then frantically tried to locate Violet, tracking her down at last in the window-design warehouse, where she was on her hands and knees scouting for last-minute party props for the ball. In the twenty minutes it took them to travel up the escalator full of holiday shoppers, Millicent Pettibone had muscled her own way into the 28 Shop's off-limits back room and after aggressively pulling out dress after dress, had found the "other Chanel." Covered by a Field's garment bag, the gown had simply been marked, *Reserved for Violet's Customer.*

By the time a breathless Violet sprinted on her flat-heeled working girl's shoes to the scene, it was too late. The Dress, painstakingly and lovingly fitted to Claire so that it hugged her tall body, rendering her a princess for one night, was already being pulled apart, let out, and patched together by a tearful Celine for the hefty debutante who was determined to fit into the Dress as if it held all the power of Cinderella's glass slipper.

Violet was crestfallen. Her daughter's dress was in tatters and now belonged to her best customer. The length of the masterpiece had been hacked off for rebuilding into the width. Only after Millicent and her daughters had cleared the store two and a half hours later and a weeping Celine sat sewing together patches and pearls was Slim summoned back in the private elevator on which they had posted an Out of Order sign, just in case.

There had been no time for tears.

Slim sprang into action like an uncoiled jack-in-the-box, calling up old debts and promising new favors until at last she had located a Charles James runway sample that was en route from New York to Elizabeth Arden's Chicago salon for a Women's Service League fashion show. The dress, she was told, had impact. It was every shade of nature's soft greens, changing hues with each billowing fold of the faille and slipper satin skirt, which hung like fresh petals from a tightly cinched waist. The dramatically elongated folds that crossed over the torso were artfully arranged to create cleavage where there was none, and to emphasize the gentle slope of a strong shoulder. This dress was what haute couture was all about. Fashion arbiters would point to it for years to come as a masterfully cut construction. More important, the Siren, as the sophisticated dress was called, was Claire's size and available for the night—just as long as it could be returned in mint condition the following morning.

Claire stared pensively into the mirror as the flock of girls suddenly rose up and took off like geese going south for the winter. Their nests were already feathered and secured, as were their positions as future social matrons or society gypsies. They already knew what charitable boards they would sit on, which schools their children would attend, to which clubs they would pay dues, and where they would spend their holidays. They could afford to be frisky and wild because they were only soaring free for a year or two before they landed feet first, smack into the respectable lives mapped out for them in the Rand McNally. Oh, there was the occasional eccentric, the brother who wore kilts or the sister who ran off with the tennis pro, but this was all just part of their familiar landscape. Only Claire's future was in question. Where would she land?

As Claire studied her reflection, she suddenly thought she looked ridiculous, done up like a magazine page photographed by Salvador Dali. Her Max Factor makeup had been so heavily applied that it was hard to see her features. Her eyebrows had been plucked, making her violet eyes jump out with star drama. Her small, pale lips were drawn into a wide red mouth big enough for Joan Crawford. She was unrecognizable even to herself. Her dress was exquisite, "certainly the most high-priced one there," Aunt Slim had gloated earlier as she had gotten Claire ready, only the gown was much too sophisticated for a girl of seventeen.

Claire felt like a fraud and a phony. Worst of all, she felt like she was trying to be like one of them.

Just then the bathroom door opened. Two dowagers breezed in and Claire busied herself with her dress, trying to make herself invisible.

"One of those El Morocco types," one whispered to the other, gesturing toward the avant-garde gown's sexiness. "Nightclub people." Her raised eyebrow said it all.

"Such a commotion." The turquoise dress fanned herself with her monogrammed handkerchief, a wide cabochon circlet of rubies concealing her bony wrist.

"A bit overdone." It was unclear whether they were discussing the party or the dress. Or both.

"But then, Millie has reason to celebrate. Cyrus is home for good and there's to be no divorce."

"Thank heavens." The dignified heiress sighed. "A family needs to stay together during these dire times."

A feeling of outrage imploded in Claire. She seethed as she thought of poor Auntie Slim in her silk lounging pajamas waiting expectantly by the telephone to hear all of the ball gossip.

Then Claire flashed back to the wink Cyrus had given her earlier while his lips simultaneously bussed his wife's ample cheeks. That phony. He'd done it again.

"When will these social-climbing shop girls realize our crowd comes together to hold our families intact?" The older woman pushed a hairpin into her nest.

"We may be polite but we use our claws when we have to."

"And our charge cards."

"Yes, but it was Bill Harrison who took him to the woodshed, lovey."

"Harrison has pulled strings to have Cyrus appointed to the War Production Board."

"What a distraction it would be from his important war work if he were to be involved in a scandalous divorce." The silver-haired dowager adjusted her snood with hands gnarled from years of golf, bridge, and meddling.

"Good thing Millie got Ophelia to intervene. I'm sure it's the last we've heard of the slutty Miss Slim." She brushed the Slim/Pettibone affair away with her hands like yesterday's lint.

"Well, ducks, there are so many *important* things to occupy us now. Millie is hosting a Red Cross tea next week and we're putting together travel kits—Field's is donating them, oh that Saint Violet—for our boys going overseas. They'll need pocket knives, wallets, and dobb kits. And stationery sets." Both of the women nodded in agreement.

"Well, back to Millicent's Piccolo Venice."

"Yes. Funiculi funicula." The silver chignon laughed.

Claire's face suddenly turned white, her mouth went dry, and she wished she could disappear into the antique Chinese wallpaper with silver birds flying over the mirror. She stood by the sink trembling as the two society queens rustled out of the room, oblivious to the damage their gossipy buzz bomb had ravaged.

Standing in the debris of insults, Claire started to shake violently and the tears at the back of her eyes streaked their way down her cheeks. Violet and Slim, one all common sense and the other all sensuality, had had their chances, and were locked out, as if in some perverse game of Red Rover. They'd call you over but never let you break through their daisy chain of closely linked arms. Claire would certainly not be content to sit on the fringes of a closed little circle. She had a suitcase. She'd find a place to go.

"I'm not going to turn out like Saint Violet, sucking up to society shoppers and dragging around their dirty dry cleaning," she swore to herself. "Not me! And I won't be whispered about and pointed to like Slim just for being honestly in love."

Her lower lip quivered as she thought about her aunt, whose only mistake was leading with her heart. Claire hoped that she'd never have one.

"No heart for you, glamour-puss." She pointed to her fancy image in the mirror. And with that, she pulled out tissue after tissue and a pyramid of cotton balls from their crystal decanters and began wiping every ounce of artifice and makeup from her face. She picked up an expensive French linen towelette and rubbed vigorously with that, too, as if with a handful of vanishing cream she could rub out all of her little family's misfortunes. She reached for the swan-shaped faucets and twisted them on, splashing cold water over her face with both hands. The astonished maid handed her a towel and Claire rubbed her face dry. Her skin was natural again, her perfect complexion enlivened by cold water and anger.

"I am not one of them!" she told the mirror, referring to the girls who taunted her. "I am destined for better things!" she vowed as she unclipped the jeweled barrette from her updo and let her shiny tangle of hair tumble free over her bare shoulders. She hiked the bodice fabric up to her collarbone, flung her falsies on the dressing table, and stood back to survey her new reflection.

Face clean, falsies tossed, and modesty restored, Claire gathered up her now quite lovely party dress and with her chin up hurried out of the powder room and into the small, dark, private library across the hall, shutting the door behind her. She looked around for the phone. She'd call a taxi. She was going home.

Her head was spinning and all she could see was black, white, and black. She leaned against the doorjamb a moment to collect her thoughts and gain some composure.

"Ohhhh! I will *not* go to their stupid ball. I am going to get out of here. If only I had wings!" She shouted to a wall of books.

Harry Harrison turned around in a leather wing chair where he had been browsing through an oversized atlas, and echoed her sentiment.

"I'd rather be flying myself. It's a spectacularly clear night." He stood and poked his head out the bay window.

Claire's jaw dropped.

"Oh, excuse me. I didn't know there was anybody else in here."

"Well it's not exactly the public library," he said. The young man in dress blues galumphed across the room, extending his hand.

"I'm Harry." His grin was sincere and stretched from ear to ear. He shook her hand like he was pumping water.

"I'm Claire."

"Nice name. Nice dress." His goofy grin was immediately disarming.

"Really?" Her shoulders relaxed. She lifted her violet eyes and cocked her head. He was taller than she.

"Oh, it's grand."

Claire couldn't help smiling. He looked awfully handsome in his naval lieutenant's dress uniform. Something about the uniform made her feel safe.

"So are you really a flier?" He certainly looks the part, Claire thought to herself.

"You bet. And a good one. Just call me the Winged Mercury." He pointed to a bronze statue of Mercury, the kind you could find in the library of anyone with an annual adjusted income of over two hundred thousand. Only this one was wearing a Venetian party hat.

"I met Amelia Earhart once. I even have a letter from her."
Claire's eyes grew more violet in her animation. She began to forget just why she had come into the library in the first place.
"Imagine, a flier in the library." She smiled shyly, closing her eyes.
"'The drone of the plane, the steady sun, the long horizon all combined to make me forget for a while that time moved swifter than I.'" She opened her eyes wide to Harry. "Beryl Markham, *West with the Night*. I'm reading it now. Do you know it?" A log popped in the quietly burning fireplace.

"Afraid not, but she's that gal who flies in Africa, isn't she?"

Claire nodded. "Tell me where you've flown." She moved closer to look at the atlas map with him. He smelled like fresh air, soap, and airplane hangars. "Where will you be going? Please show me. I'm good at geography." Claire was starting to dimple like Shirley Temple.

"Only if you'll let me escort you into the ballroom. I still have to march myself through that dull receiving line, but it would be much nicer with the prettiest girl here on my arm." He said it with all the sincerity of an Eagle Scout—and she believed him. He had none of that yawning diffidence about him—done that, been there—that boys who usually went to these affairs demonstrated. He was holding his arm out to her.

"On your arm? Why, I'd love to." Claire's voice was like softly blowing heather.

"I don't suppose you have any dances open on your dance card?" He tried to sneak a peak.

"Well it's awfully late and most of my dances are gone, but you being in the war and a flier . . ." She shook her empty dance card off her wrist and tucked it in her bosom like she imagined Daisy Armstrong would do.

Together they walked lightly into the bombardment of champagne, cigar smoke, orchestras, combos, butlers, and smells of candle wax, youthful perspiration, fresh salmon, and the expensive apricot and jasmine odor of Quelque Fleurs, the evening's most prevalent perfume.

Claire's light mix of vanilla, musk, and cocoa knocked all the other smells from Harry's olfactory memory. He leaned down to her slender neck to catch the delicious aroma that was like an oasis in the midst of society's many heavy smells. In the candle-light her lavender eyes were so bright, and her questions about his flying expertise so earnest, that he suddenly erased from his memory all the other girls' dance cards, upon a dozen of which his name was neatly written. Stepping out, they joined the others in the flickering ballroom.

He put his arm around her waist. Without knowing it, he was following her very subtle lead, just as she had learned all those years back at Field's dancing school. She had the knack; he felt like Fred Astaire. Funny, he was usually so awkward. Minnie always said he danced with the gawkiness of a giraffe. But now he had a sudden impulse to whirl this pretty girl around in a fancy step.

She beamed a radiant look back at him. The band struck up Cole Porter's "Night and Day." He pulled her closer as she hummed the melody into his ear.

He wondered what it would be like to kiss her fresh lips and put his hands on her pale shoulders. He liked the way her pretty pallor was natural, no cosmetic colors painted on her face that stained a soldier's dress shirt when he took his girl into his arms.

"I suppose you must be exhausted from all this ball business. Crammed into just a few days. Are you coming out at the cotil-lion tomorrow night?" It was too much to hope that she might be free and just have a quiet dinner where she would be all his.

She blushed and nodded, looking away at another dancing cou-ple. No need to tell him yet that I'm an impostor, she thought. Not just yet—it would spoil the moment. This wonderful bor-rowed moment. Besides, she rationalized, Auntie Slim would be disappointed if she caved in and fled now. She'd want Claire to make an effort and hold her head high. She'd expect her to act like her girl with guts. More importantly, she was starting to have fun. What was the harm in staying?

"Oh, finally, we've found the roving receiving line." Harry nudged Claire forward. He was feeling proprietary and they hadn't even exchanged last names yet. Now the Pettibones formed a semiformal queue in front of the main salon's brightly burning fireplace, festooned with garlands of holly and greenery dotted with white gardenias and red roses.

Cilla, standing with her parents and two of her recently un-married sisters, carried a bouquet of pale Alice roses in her pudgy hands. She smiled eagerly at Harry. He may be boring, as the other girls repeatedly groaned, but both her mother and much-married sisters pronounced him quite a catch. But what on earth was he doing with Claire? Somebody ought to fill him in, and that somebody would be she. He would be grateful and that would start the ball rolling. She jumped out of line to greet him.

"You know, Claire is *help*," she whispered into Harry's ear as he leaned down to congratulate her.

"Oh, she's a great help. She actually made me, the clumsiest man alive, look like Fred Astaire out there on the dance floor."

"I mean, she's not one of us." Cilla was cupping her hand to his ear and standing on tiptoe. "She's my mother's saleslady's daugh-ter. Oh, don't get me wrong, we love her mother to pieces. It's just that she's poor as a church mouse." There, she'd saved him. "I didn't want to put you in an awkward position." She flirted with him with her squinty brown eyes.

"As poor as all that," Harry echoed politely.

This Claire was someone who appeared both independent and able to look up to him, Harry Harrison, on whom no one had ever relied. His mother and Minnie were always telling him what to do. From the moment he had laid eyes on Claire he had somehow felt important. Like the perennial groundhog who pops out of his burrow looking to end a long winter, for the first time in his life, Harry saw his own shadow.

"Well, thank you, Priscilla," he said. He didn't bother to tell her of the dinner talk at Charlotte Hall during the heart of the Depression when Cyrus Pettibone, bowler in hand, had come begging to Harrison for a handout and hand up. But he'd been poorer than a church mouse. He *owed* millions. If Harry's father hadn't rescued Cyrus, putting his old friend on his feet again and bringing him into his fold where they had made even bigger fortunes, Priscilla Pettibone, now scurrying back to her place in the receiving line, would not be in a position to snub Claire tonight.

He wondered how this lovely creature beside him was able to be so dignified with so many malicious girls out to hurt her. It brought out his protective male instincts. Why, this girl might actually need him. Back home, Minnie Mortimer, his forced fiancée, had never even allowed him to select a restaurant or to pull out her chair at dinner. She never even let him win a game of backgammon. She was totally self-sufficient. Hell, Minnie gave lie to the adage that it takes two to tango. The few times they'd made love, he got the impression that she'd just as soon be in bed with Thunder. Yes, he thought, standing up straighter, Claire needed someone to protect her.

Millicent Pettibone spotted Harry down the line, and waved. "Well hellooo, Cinq!" she sang, calling him by his least favorite pet name. Millie adored people with ancestors.

Claire looked from Millicent to Harry. Was this some new Lake Forest society custom she hadn't heard about? Did all the guests get numbers in French? What would hers be, Zéro? She gulped. She was next in line to shake hands with Mrs. Pettibone. The old feeling of unease came over her. Mrs. P.'s chin was jutting out at her like a rock in a storm. Suppose she publicly chastised Claire for her aunt's behavior in front of Harry? Then Auntie Wren's words rang through her ears: "Remember Claire, there's no defense like elaborate courtesy."

"Good evening, Mrs. Pettibone. It was so nice of you to include me. Everything is so perfect." Millicent regarded Claire with a superior smile coming from a cold and condescending height. Claire ignored the slight.

"Cilla." Claire put her gloved hand in the deb's kid-gloved hand, leather to cloth, skin never touching skin. "You have the most beautiful gown here. Chanel, isn't it?" Her voice was like silk. "You put all the other girls to shame." And quickly moved along to Cyrus. She had always thought of him as a benevolent benefactor, but tonight she thought he looked like a two-timing lout. He gave her hand an extra squeeze as she passed down the line. One of the sisters snapped open her enamel cigarette case with a diamond *P* on the top and pulled out a Chesterfield instead of shaking Claire's hand.

Claire mustered up all the false courtesy she could and smiled kindly. She could shrug them all off. If she didn't care, they wouldn't matter. Plus she had the security of being escorted by Lieutenant Harry. But Harry who? Harry whoever. She whirled around. Harry the Fifth in French seemed to be Millicent Pettibone's most favorite guest.

"There you are, dear. Cyrus said you were probably hiding that aristocratic nose of yours in a book in one of our libraries. *We* are a literary family, too. Aren't we, girls?" She hugged Harry to her bosom. "My, but aren't you handsome in your uniform. Your parents must be soooo proud. Do you have any medals yet? And engaged to the Mortimer girl. What a respectable coming together of fine families. My goodness, but what with this war I suppose you'll be married in one of those jiffy ceremonies. Why, these days a girl comes out on Friday and marries on Sunday. Isn't that right, Sally?"

"Guess it saves on flowers." Sally shook his hand. "Nice to see you, Harry. Been a long time."

Claire looked over her shoulder at her "engaged" escort. Well, what could Auntie Slim's niece expect? They had probably singled her out and told him, "Engaged and on your own? Well, hit on her. She's a nobody. She'd be perfect."

She felt deeply wounded. The same feelings that she had felt earlier in the powder room washed over her. Her mouth went dry again. Her knees felt weak.

"Claire. Are you all right? Can I get you something to drink?" Harry picked up a glass of champagne off a passing silver tray.

Get out of my sight, you louse of a man, she thought. He wasn't even married yet and he was already cheating on his wife.

"Yes, thank you," she said. "Perhaps we should toast your engagement." She gave him her sweetest smile.

"Hold on. Wait a minute," he spilled some Dom Pérignon on his sleeve as he guided her back into the little library, steering her through the party people as the orchestra played "Embraceable You."

"There," he said finally. He shut the door and shut out the party. She continued walking straight to the telephone.

"Let's see, I was about to call for a cab before you startled me from your hiding place."

He put two fingers to his lips and studied her, cradling his elbow in his other hand. Was this young woman, whom he had just met, whirled twice around the dance floor, and whom he was dying to kiss, jealous? Was it possible that this high-strung, beautifully mannered peach of a girl liked him enough after a few spins around the room to feel some kind, the same kind, of chemistry he was feeling? But, he thought, moving toward the telephone, boring Harry Harrison never inspired any feelings in women except their bossy side.

"Hello, I'm calling from the Pettibone House. I was wondering if you could send a taxi over right away. What? Organ. Claire Organ. Yes. Chicago."

"How do you do, Claire Organ?" Harry took her hand, pumping it again and grinning. "Harrison. William Henry Harrison the Fifth. Tuxedo Park. Friends call me Harry."

She dropped the phone.

They were married four days later.

Chapter Seven

The Two Mrs. Harrisons

The day after that wedding night I found that a distance of a thousand miles, abyss, discovery and . . . metamorphosis separated me from the day before.

—Colette

Claire tucked her tweed traveling skirt under her knees, Wren-like, and lowered herself straight back onto the eighteenth-century Salem side chair, her posture in strict alignment with the chair's fluted splat. Charlotte Hall was still reverberating from the news of Harry's elopement. Claire imagined that even the faces in the classical figures carved into the pediments were frowning down upon her in disdain. Ophelia, exhausted from a night over the telephone long distance with a stunned Millicent Pettibone, sat in silence in her own mother's high-backed Queen Anne chair. The inquisition of the new Mrs. Harrison by Ophelia was about to begin.

Claire was apprehensive and unnerved but as prepared as possible for the verbal assault on her humble birth, peculiar upbringing, and store-learned virtues. She looked to her husband for support. He seemed subdued in his mother's presence. Harry cowered uncomfortably in the shadows of the eighteen-foot-high mantel beneath the family coat of arms as a roaring fire bellowed from the great hearth. Surely the enormous fireplace was big enough for a human sacrifice. Claire bit her lower lip and wondered if this grand room wasn't a replica of the waiting room to purgatory.

She looked around at the proper opulence of the room. Every antique was authentic, the arrangement of the pieces precise and correct. The vastness of the house with everything in its place reminded her of the expensive dollhouses on the fourth floor at Marshall Field's.

The new bride steeled herself by looking straight into the formal library's fire, remembering how she and Harry had spent the rest of that first evening quietly closeted in the Pettibones' small library, the rest of the party shelved. It gave her confidence and brought a comforting smile to her lips.

The low fire had crackled and Harry gallantly added the occasional log as need be, each of them tossing in their gold-embossed seating assignments and place cards. They sat across from one another, knee to knee, soul to soul, and talked in the soft, breathless voices of mutual discovery as a light snowfall began to flurry outside the library window, encasing them in their own private bell jar.

They were moving into that secret soundless world of first love, dropping the ins and outs of their own lives into the conversation.

"Oh, it's a rather odd family, you see. I have three mothers." She turned the faintest shade of crimson.

"Hmmm," Harry said knowingly. "Dad's a bit of a ladies' man, is he? We have plenty of those where I come from."

"No." Claire laughed, holding out her hands in protest. Harry took them both, holding them tightly for safekeeping.

"It's two aunties and one mother. I never knew my father." She lowered her lashes. She wasn't embarrassed. It was just a fact.

"Dead?" he asked compassionately, inching out of his chair. There was so much kindness in his voice. Just the way he asked was enough to endear him to Claire.

"It was all a long time ago." When she turned her profile to the fire, he could see the exquisite contours of her face.

"I've had the happiest of childhoods, really. You can't imagine how much fun it was to be raised running loose in a department store." She laughed.

He couldn't imagine. He envied her. He was desperate to know everything about her. He listened, enraptured, as she created lovely story pictures of how it was. In her exuberance she slid off her chair onto the floor, her hands still in his, a rustle of slipper satin and a whiff of vanilla, a pale green confection kneeling at his feet.

Suddenly, he wanted to hold her in his arms very much. His long fingers reached for her tentatively, gently tracing the slope of her cheek in slow circles. Claire warmed to the touch of his rough, sporting fingers on her own soft skin. She felt herself leaning toward him. She gasped as he brushed his lips against her slightly parted mouth. The corners of the room were rounding into a whirling circle as she let herself fall into its spin.

Looking up at him, she observed how solid he appeared, a soldier come to save her, just as his family had saved hers, so many Christmases ago, with a single purchase of a gentleman's gold traveling set. She wondered whether the elegant fingers stroking her now had ever touched those luxurious combs and brushes, pushing back that stubborn lock of brown hair off his forehead.

"Tell me," she protested. He had to lean forward to hear, her voice was so soft. "I want to know everything about you! Where you'll be flying. When do you leave?" He watched, beguiled, as she pulled her hands back and lightly ran them across the bare skin at her throat. "Will you be fighting?" She drew her brows together in concern, a foreign line crossing her smooth brow. The room was coming back into focus.

Harry did his best impersonation of his father, stern-faced and aristocratically nonchalant.

"I'm teaching navy pilots right now—and I'll . . ." He paused; it was against his nature to lie. "I'll be flying combat missions, probably in the Pacific, as soon as I've fulfilled some family obligations." His voice descended into a baritone, just as his father's would have.

"Family obligations." Her own high spirits were dashed. Claire couldn't see his face as he retreated back into the brass-studded leather chair out of the light of the fire.

The fiancée, Claire thought, is this where she comes in? She waited.

Harry cleared his throat and clasped his hands under his chin. How could this girl be expected to understand that in families like his, marriages were deals? How many times had he been cautioned that matrimony was the glue that bound together good families and good genes, and that the heart had no place in this anatomy? Harry turned toward the window. He couldn't meet her eyes.

As if by intuition Claire could read his thoughts: She was losing him.

Out of her gilded female past, she summoned up her teachers. She needed their guidance to hold his attention. What would her practical mother have done? Claire puckered her lips as if she had just bitten into a sour apple. Probably have handed him over to the Pettibone girls, like her dress, as if Claire weren't worthy of him.

What about Auntie Slim? Claire frowned. Auntie Slim would be no help. She wasn't interested in becoming a rich man's mistress or the target of powder-room slurs.

And Amelia Earhart? What would her heroine have done? Claire wondered. Amelia wouldn't let him just fly away, that's for sure. Not the adventuress. But how would Daisy Armstrong have stopped him?

And then she knew.

Claire blushed. She laid her arm on Harry's jacket sleeve. Her angel-light touch brought Harry back, away from his Tuxedo Park promises.

Two powerful urges were at work. Their passion was pulling them within a hair's breadth of one another. And the practicality of their respective escapes was pushing them even closer.

Harry could, with one full bend of the knee, acquire a wife and fulfill his obligation to the Harrison ancestors so that he could fly in this war instead of only train other air jockeys. And he could release himself from his unofficial engagement to Minnie. Harry grinned mischievously. He could return to Tuxedo with this pretty girl on his arm, striking out in independence with a single defiant act even while fulfilling his duty to ensure there would be a Roman numeral VI to follow his own V. Yes, he thought, putting a protective arm around Claire, by tangling his fingers in her silken hair, by making her a Harrison, he'd get his freedom to fly without the ball and chain of Minnie. Looking now at Claire's face in the firelight, he could barely remember what Minnie looked like.

"I think you've bewitched me, Claire Organ."

Claire studied him as she would study one of her stamps under a magnifying glass. Harry's rangy good looks were appealing, as was his bookish curiosity; she found his sincerity and fine manners attractive, his honesty truly wonderful. In fact, in a vague whirl of fleeting images, he reminded her of someone. Someone important to her. She also couldn't quiet the recurring thought that he might be her ticket out of a dead-end job at the store.

The firelight danced on her face as she widened her violet eyes, inviting him in. It suddenly dawned on her. He resembled an awkward version of the man she had danced with in a thousand dreams. If he were only gray at the temples and a little more aloof, he would look just like the man she had been in love with since she was five: the man from the Marshall Field's catalog.

And so, motivated by a surge of youthful passion coupled with earthly practicality, their mouths moved nearer to one another and, closing their eyes, lips touching, they soared into the future with a kiss.

His mouth closed on Claire's with such intensity that her lips opened in surprise, allowing his breath to sweep into her. She lifted her hands up to Harry's face to hold him there in the most natural untutored impulse. Her hands rested on his ears, blocking out all other sounds and sensations other than the pull of their continuous kiss. He managed to take in some air without removing his mouth from hers and she sucked the breath gently out of him as if they were sharing oxygen. He was stirred to every part of his body.

Harry had been taught the relevancy of God, Duty, Country, Family, but never the pleasure of guiltless love or the fine-tuned maneuvers of a naturally gifted lover.

They were perfectly suited to one another. He drew her up to him and her lithe body molded to his like molten lava so there was no space between them. The lights and the fire caught him standing over her so that his darkened shadow covered the wood-paneled wall behind them. Opening her eyes as she kissed him, she suddenly turned her lips away and pointed.

"Look, Harry Harrison. You're larger than life," she exclaimed. "Look at your giant shadow."

Harry was gone, lost in a waterfall he had never fallen over before. He buried his head in her breast, inhaling her, his fingers tangled in her loose hair, enveloping her body, messing up her dress. If it weren't for the cumbersome dress, he might have been inside of her, their contours were so indistinguishable, his shadow swallowing hers.

Finally, Claire shook loose and pushed him away. Her laugh was clear and silvery and her high color genuine as she deftly smoothed the folds of her bodice that his hands had rearranged. Her eyes were coy as she lowered her lashes and glanced quickly to see if her small, high breasts were covered.

"Excuse me, fly-boy." She was breathless. "I was wishing that you'd take me flying, but I was kinda hoping you'd use a plane." She dimpled at him.

"What are you doing tomorrow?" He studiously examined his Cartier tank watch like a flight plan, his lips on her ear. Tomorrow was only an hour away.

"It's my eighteenth birthday," she whispered, a private smile on her lips. "I'll be a woman, legally."

There was a moment of stillness as he looked at her. "You already are."

Harry wrinkled his forehead, the brows becoming a single furrow. "Well then, I better take you home so I can pick you up." He pressed his mouth against her cheek. He couldn't seem to stop touching her.

A date. He was making a date with her! But he still hadn't explained away the sort-of fiancée.

"Your birthday!" Now his grin was wide. Claire recognized his teeth as rich people's teeth—big and white and well tended to. "How would you like it if I took you flying? Really flying."

She clapped her hands together, dismissing once and for all the invisible fiancée. As she well knew, if the merchandise wasn't out on the counter, the customer stopped wanting it.

"I'll be by for you at ten," he said. "I'd suggest you lose the dress for some trousers. Unless you think you're going to need a parachute." The dress. She looked down horrified at the pricey, voluminous borrowed Charles James that now looked as if it had been rolling around the hayloft.

A grave look suddenly fell over Harry's features. Minnie had come trotting back into his thoughts. "How do you feel about horses?" he asked.

"Horses?" she asked. Claire had no idea how much her answer mattered.

She put his hand on her cheek. "The only horse I care about is Pegasus. He has wings."

Delighted, Harry kissed her full on the lips and sped off to prepare for the Claire-filled day ahead.

Back in her closet-sized bedroom, Claire slung her dress over a straight chair, ignoring the padded hanger and tissue paper, and dived into bed. She had only a few hours to dream until Harry would be back to pick her up. She snuggled naked under the covers, for the first time leaving her flannel nightgown in the drawer, kicking Raggedy Ann and Pooh Bear off the bed. It had been an hour's drive from Lake Forest to Hyde Park and it would be another hour back. And then back again. Claire had tested his interest in her and he had passed the long-distance marathon. In the morning, she absentmindedly pushed past her mother with a breezy kiss and told the Aunties to put her birthday on hold. She was going to meet some friends.

"I love you, dears," she called over her shoulder to the astonished ladies.

"I didn't know she had friends." Miss Wren clucked in surprise.

Claire was already out of earshot and far down the hall, bypassing the slow elevator to skip down the stairs instead.

In the driveway, Harry, grinning and daylight handsome in the cool morning air, was holding open a leather flying jacket for her. She slipped her arms into the sleeves as he enfolded his arms around her.

They were aloft. Flying high over the planetarium, Marshall Field's, and city hall, Harry turned left and buzzed the Windermere Hotel. Claire gave him the thumbs-up from her backseat bird's-eye perspective as he swung out over the copper-domed Museum of Science and Industry and headed east out to the lake, until there was nothing but a brilliant morning sky, ice-blue water, and Harry and Claire in the Lockheed Electra.

There was snow. From the air, the frozen ground was a precise quilt laid out in blocked squares of white lace and linen. It felt as if the world below them, nestled under its winter blanket, mattered so much less than the closed space they inhabited together within the silver hull.

Claire inched closer to her handsome pilot. The engine noisily reverberated through the plane. Peering out the window, Claire was lost in a trance. The trees were trimmed in ice ornaments, sparkling like white diamonds in the morning sun. It was magic. She had never felt like this. Freely flying, time lost to space, soaring like Amelia.

She looked at Harry's large hands pulling back on the throttle. She liked the look of his strong neck as he turned from the task to her and back. She liked the way his leather aviator's jacket cracked as he expertly swung the plane around, in complete control. The ride was smooth. He was so good-looking squinting into a sun brightened by the snow's reflection. His eyes crinkled at the corners and he pushed on a pair of aviator glasses. And then he turned to her.

Either he was the handsomest fellow she had ever encountered or she was falling in love.

So Claire was merely shy but not offended when Harry drove directly from the airfield, where small planes hastily commandeered for Illinois Civil Defense were being painted camouflage colors, to the Palmer House. Packed with young men in uniform in the cocktail-hour commotion, the hotel's revolving door spilled out equal numbers of navy, marine, and army recruits with colorful precision in a parade of white, blue, and khaki. Laughter floated out from Trader Vic's like some tropical port of call. It was an eerie last hurrah for these untested military men, many of whom would soon ship out and likely die trying to recapture the very South Seas islands this hot spot gaudily imitated with its tiki torches and Polynesian totems.

The irony of the moment was lost neither on the well-read Claire nor on Harry, who was already savvy to War Department secrets. The Japanese had attacked the Philippines, Malaya, Wake Island, and Guam the day after Pearl Harbor. Harry knew of the reclamation plans and that even he could lose his young life for a piece of dirt on one of these palm-tree pockets of paradise in the South Pacific. Upstairs in the main lobby, music from the Empire

Room rumba-boom-boomed with an urgent hilarity. There was more swaying than dancing going on as Claire and Harry poked their wind-blown heads inside to watch the clenched couples for a moment before he guided her to the brass floral-engraved elevator doors.

On the ride up, Claire nervously studied her boots as Harry awkwardly searched for the room key in the side pocket of his jacket.

What was she doing? she asked herself. She fought down the grown-up feelings he had aroused in her. Had she lost her mind? Was she going to give her virginity to a total stranger? Well, she assured herself, not really a stranger after a dozen dances, seven hours of conversation, and a ride in the sky. In the days before Pearl Harbor, the intensity of their night and a half together would have stretched out for months and been considered a long courtship. War hormones simply speeded up the process. Why, then, was she feeling like a village virgin about to be sacrificed to the lord of the manor, who was off to fight the Crusades?

She folded her slender arms across her chest. "I think we should shut down the engines right here. Slow down a bit. I mean, I'm not that kind of girl." She realized too late that she'd just let a schoolgirl cliché tumble out of her mouth.

"I mean, Lieutenant Harrison, aren't you being just a bit presumptuous?" She wished the rush of erotic feelings inside her would be still.

"Geez, Claire," he ventured cautiously. "I thought you'd like a little supper and some private time . . . like last night."

"In your suite?" she queried sharply in her mother's voice.

"Well actually, it belongs to my dad. He owns an interest in this hotel with Cyrus."

The Pettibones again. Was she actually going to lose her virginity in one of their business holdings? She flashed Harry an angry look.

"I . . . certainly didn't mean to give the impression . . ."

Harry's words were pleading forgiveness but his eyes were full of desire. "You see, there isn't a decent restaurant in town that hasn't been invaded by some branch of the military. I figured the only way we could have a quiet dinner was in a private suite." A shock of hair fell into his hazel eyes. As Harry brushed it aside, an irresistible grin spread across his face. "Besides, we had to fall out of the sky sometime, didn't we?"

"But that doesn't mean we have to fall straight onto a mattress."

"Look, if you'd rather, we could eat downstairs at Trader Vic's or at the nightclub with all the other soldiers and their girls. I simply thought you'd prefer someplace quiet where we could talk. I thought you might enjoy it. Claire," he said softly, "it's only dinner."

He waited earnestly for her answer.

With all the other soldiers and their girls. Yes, Claire thought, *their* girls. She stole a glance at Harry's patrician profile. Beguiled by his boarding-school manners and Ivy League look, tonight, even if it only lasted until the clock struck twelve, she would be like one of those swaying couples downstairs, closely held and possibly even cherished.

The elevator stopped at the penthouse. Claire took a deep breath then reached for Harry's arm and stepped out. "Which way to private dining? I'm famished." She twinkled at him. So what if she might end up being dessert? She laughed, giddy with the prospect of the evening before them.

"What's so funny?" Harry ushered her into the marble entry of the suite, flipping on an enormous crystal chandelier with the stem of his aviator's glasses.

"I was just thinking about dessert."

"The lady is already contemplating dessert?" Claire found the slow grin spreading across his face very appetizing. "I thought you were the one who wanted dinner." He studied the menu on the desk. "How about a bottle of wine? Shall we start with a little game hen? A hock of ham? And maybe I can scare up a cannoli or two from the Pettibones' *troppo* Italian table?"

"Can you imagine? Mussolini is the bad guy and the Pettibones have the audacity to throw a goombah *carnevale*!"

"Well, what do you expect?" Harry smirked. "All the women in that family have linguine and clams for brains."

They both started to laugh.

She moved over to the couch and sank down into its plush burgundy velvet while he picked up the telephone to order.

"It'll be a while. Catering says there are three wedding parties going on downstairs and a bunch of soldiers' farewell bashes. Do you mind? Can I get something for you? Canned goods? Some army rations?" His grin was lopsided.

"You could light the fire." Claire crossed her trim ankles and leaned back lazily on her arms.

She watched as he tossed his leather jacket over a satin chair, loosened his Princeton tie, and unbuttoned the first button of his white shirt. Perspiration stains made half-moons under his arms. The firelight sparkled across his handsome face as he stoked the flame. She rose and walked over to him. It seemed only natural that he should take her in his arms and bring their lips together. After all, both of them had been thinking about it all afternoon. They took their time, taking each other's breath away, dropping their inhibitions as they listened to one another's heartbeats instead of following the Boy Scouts' handbook. He was pulling off her cashmere cardigan and laying it over his jacket. She was turning her slender figure toward him, now emphasized by the matching gray pullover and slim trousers she wore.

"Your hair is beautiful in this light," he said, gently pulling the side barrettes out so that the length of her hair tumbled over her shoulders.

"Yours, too," she brushed the errant shock of hair out of his eyes.

"You just want me to see better so I can tell you how lovely you are."

She lightly placed her fingers on his crocodile belt and then lifted her eyes to his. He took her fingers from his belt and brought them to his lips, swallowing hard.

"Is it the war or is it me?" His question was sincere.

"I'm not sure." She bit her lower lip.

"An honest woman." He smiled, regaining his composure.

"Then be an honest man . . . Is it me, or is it because she's not here?" Claire took a step back, the reflection of the fire dancing on her hair and slender neck.

"She's nobody I want."

"But somebody you'll marry?"

A look of annoyance crossed his face, a fleeting moment of indecision, then a look of resolve.

"I'd marry you, Claire." Harry's voice was trembling as he pulled her face to his, and then he suddenly lifted her in his arms in a single movement and carried her into the bedroom with its vast bed draped in silk and fringe.

He hesitated for a moment, watching the changing expression of her face, until the pouty mouth opened and the eyes fluttered shut signaling her readiness, then he laid her across the width of the bed and covered her in kisses. Gently, he pulled off her sweater, her boots and knee-high socks. She responded by unbuckling his belt, then tentatively pulling it through its loops, watching, fascinated, as he removed the rest of their clothing. He pulled his hands from her firm small breasts and told her how beautiful she was, running his fingers down the smooth slope of her legs and across her flat stomach. Naked, she was at once girlish and womanly. She gently traced the hair on his chest with her fingers and then lightly rested her hands on his thighs, pausing uncertainly, slow-dancing, both of them watching, inhaling each other's scents, not wanting to miss a single discovery. They were like two grown children, exploring, desiring, wanting, tasting slowly, with the most natural instincts in their purest desire to please one another.

He tenderly took her and she felt that a year had passed between last night and this moment.

"You hungry?" He burst into the room like he had just taken San Juan Hill. He was holding a bottle of Chateau Margaux 1934 like a saber. Harry was covered from his athlete's waist to his knees with a plush bath towel, hastily pulled around him in order to receive the room-service cart.

"No," she whispered. She was still naked on the rumpled spread, her knees shyly pulled to her chest, as if playing peek-a-boo with her lower body, her hair cascading over her breasts, covering them. An uncertain little girl had left the ball with the handsomest boy there. And he had wanted her enough to make tender love to her, to guide her over the threshold into womanhood. A private smile was on her lips. She'd been proud of the way her body had responded. And if she hadn't quite lost herself in the depths of blinding passion and heard the trumpets described by Slim, she had taken to it instinctively. She exhaled. She had never felt so cherished.

"I'm not hungry at all. In fact, I'm feeling quite satisfied." She threw back her head and stretched her arms and neck behind her, catlike, exposing her bare bosom.

He watched her greedily. He had made love to her and he desperately wanted to make love to her again. Her body had responded to every move he had made. Suddenly he didn't feel like awkward Harry anymore. He had pleased this pretty creature with the warm laugh who shared his passion for flying. His sexual experiences until now had been scattered and unsatisfactory. Minnie straddled him like Thunder and called out instructions like an animal trainer. Before her, there had been just a handful of girls, boldly sophisticated, who'd feigned virginity and blamed their ardor on the alcohol. Claire was the real thing, and she had just made beautiful love to him with no apologies.

He grabbed two glasses from the bar, holding both of them in one hand as he expertly poured the wine like a naked sommelier.

"For mam'selle." He placed a glass in her hand. Noticing goose bumps on her flesh, Harry covered her with his leather flying jacket, gently pulling up the zipper. He had never felt so masculine before.

"Harry?"

"Ummm." He plucked a leg from the well-garnished cornish hen sitting on the room-service table.

"I'm happy it was you. For the first time." Claire blushed the exact color of the rose tufted headboard behind her. "In fact, it's always been you. You keep rescuing me, you see. And you don't even know it." Tears welled up in her eyes. He put the wineglass down and stared at her.

"Come on in," she said, patting the bed. "Next to me. I want to tell you a story. A bedtime story." He pulled back the spread and sheets and shot into bed.

"Are you settled in?"

He kissed her neck. "Yes."

She brushed her heavy mane of hair off her face with the back of her hand.

"Once upon a time," she began in a soft voice, "there was a little girl who lived in an enchanted department store with her three fairy godmothers. They loved her very very much, and she loved them in return. The fairy godmothers and their little girl didn't have much in the way of possessions, but they worked hard and were happy. There weren't any men in their little cottage so they learned to chop the wood, cook potluck meals, and play the wind instruments, bringing music into their lives." Claire glanced up to see if he was with her.

"Go on." Harry rested his head on his elbow.

"Then one day a great plague came over the land, called the Depression. Suddenly, the three fairy godmothers lost their powers. They couldn't grow food, their cupboards were bare, and one of the godmothers lost her wands and her job. It was bleak. The snows came. And the wolf howled outside their door. Then one day, an important lady came into their store and said, 'I need a very special gift for my husband, for he is prince of the Tuxedos and ambassador to the court of King Franklin.'"

Harry looked at her, puzzled.

"One of the fairy godmothers showed the great lady an ermine coat since it was Christmas and very very cold. The heat had even been turned off in the godmothers' cottage and their little girl had to sleep with one of them every night just to keep warm. But the fancy lady said the ermine coat was too grand, for while her husband was a great man, he was not a showoff. The next fairy godmother showed her silk scarves to tie around his neck, but the princess shook her head no saying, 'The prince of Tuxedo is fastidious about his clothes and picks out all his own ties.'

" 'Oh,' said the third fairy godmother. 'Then I have the perfect present. It is a set of golden combs and brushes and bottles and boxes for the prince to take with him when he travels to other courts in the land. And it comes with a special magic that will protect him from harm.' The fairy godmother didn't tell the princess that she had cast a secret spell on the gold treasures so that the prince's son, when he grew up, would one day return to rescue their little girl from all the mean witches who lived in the big castle.

" 'Yes,' said the great lady. 'Wrap it in crocodile skins and I'll have it.' She handed over a bag full of coins.

"How the godmothers rejoiced! There was food on the table again, coal for the furnace, and presents under the Christmas tree. The little girl was safe from harm and her little family was saved. The godmothers were so grateful for their good fortune that every Christmas thereafter they said a special prayer for the princess, prince, and their young son to safeguard their castle, Charlotte Hall, Winding Way Road, Tuxedo Park, New York. No number necessary."

Claire beamed up at Harry after her tale. He looked down at her with a feeling so strong he could only imagine it was love.

Suddenly, he kneeled before her and, wrapping the plush towel tightly around him so he would be decent for his proposal, asked: "Claire Organ, will you marry me and be my princess?" The answer was in her kiss.

Slim sat slumped at her breakfast table, a puffy-eyed forty-something waif in a creamy satin robe, marabou cuffs wiping away mascara-tainted tears.

Cyrus had sacrificed her for his country. After all, this was war, no time to desert his nation and his family. Romantic notions of them joining the French Resistance together flew out the terrace window, along with the crumbled croissant she had flung at him when he had put his hat on his head and walked out the door, leaving a consolation prize from Cartier lying on the table. So this was appeasement.

Aside from how she had made little jokes to him about how she would do the patriotic thing and be his private lieutenant for the war's duration, or how she would go on as his mistress with a stiff upper lip, the fact remained, to paraphrase Churchill, that this was her darkest hour.

Glumly dejected, she didn't hear her front door open or Claire bounding over to greet her with all the elation of a child bursting in from school with a perfect report card.

"Auntie Slim!" Claire took her hands and pulled her from the table to whirl her around the room. Her face was radiant. Her eyes shone like amethysts.

"Oh gosh, I'm so happy! I know I didn't call you after Cilla's party like I promised. I'm a whole day late. But what a day!"

"*C'est ne pas rien.*" Slim sighed. "Cyrus has been here. He's explained it all." Her eyes wandered languidly around the room until they landed on the butter knife. "I know what I am. A woman tossed out on the seas. Another one of the war's casualties." She lifted her arms and struck a pose worthy of Isadora Duncan.

"Oh, how could I be so selfish to burst into your sorrow with my happiness?" Claire's eyes moistened.

"Happiness? What happiness?" Slim was immediately alert, her arms dropping to her side.

"There's someone outside I want you to meet," Claire said shyly, indicating the foyer.

"Someone?"

"Yes. William Henry Harrison the Fifth. My fiancé!"

Within the hour, pleasantries had been exchanged and the preparations drafted. Slim, her sorrow gone, wondered to herself just how the boy's mother, father, and the rest of the fine people of Tuxedo Park were going to react, but the young couple was eager to marry at once. Harry believed it was much better to bring home a wife than a fiancée. For practical reasons, he said. Slim heartily endorsed the plan, knowing it was much harder to return the goods after the merchandise had been sampled. "Besides"— she lifted Claire's chin with a slender finger so that their eyes met—"delay is no friend of love." If they were going to land Claire on the beaches of Tuxedo Park without proper social credentials, they could at least arm her with a marriage certificate. But it had to be done fast. Tomorrow was too soon, but the day after would be perfect.

Back at the 28 Shop, Violet wrinkled her brow, dropping her engagement calendar and cool composure. Why such haste, she worried, gathering up the date pages. Couldn't they at least wait until after the holidays? Violet sighed. Of course she wanted the best for Claire. Indeed, her very existence had been a means to this end. But now that it was here it was happening too fast, like a tornado whirling by before you had gotten everyone safely into the cellar.

"Don't be a dark cloud!" Slim scoffed. "They don't have tornadoes in Tuxedo Park." She dropped her voice. "Violet! Think. Winding Way Road." She pronounced each syllable as if she were speaking to Helen Keller. Her lovely Claire had hit the jackpot; she wasn't about to allow the girl's mother to stand in the way.

Wren, swept along by Slim's fervor, begged to be a bridesmaid. After all, she was still single. She hurried off to purchase the hunter-green dinner suit that had just gone on sale in Matronwear.

By another happy coincidence, Slim just happened to have a wedding suit in her closet, a blue Mainbocher. Celine could alter it for Claire in a jiff. Something borrowed; something blue. What else was required?

"I've got it!" Slim laughed, pulling a sleek Chanel with white collar and cuffs from her closet. "Something old." The sparkle was back in her eyes, and the kick in her walk—she was the chicest maid of honor while Violet, in dove gray, pushed aside her better judgment and let the winds of love sway her. She gave her daughter away marching down the aisle of Reverend Caldwell's study; all the As and Bs in Violet's officiator's Rolodex being already booked.

Lieutenant Ogden Hammond, a Princeton classmate of Harry's, was commandeered from his bar stool at Trader Vic's to be his practically sober best man. Field's Services provided the narrow diamond-baguette wedding band; the lilies and gladioli; the wedding brunch of scrambled eggs with chutney, creamed chicken in noodle baskets, orange and grapefruit walnut salads, vanilla ice cream topped with fresh coconut; and the wedding cake—a ravishing four-tiered confection with chocolate frosting created overnight especially for Claire by Field's pastry chef. The champagne toast was full of good wishes: "Bless you both," Wren said. "Live so that you keep the precious thing you now have. Keep patience in the daily rubs of life. Enjoy life together and with those you love."

A smart set of matched leather traveling cases had been sent down, compliments of Field's president, who still looked on Claire as the store mascot. No bride had ever had a more quickly assembled trousseau representing the best in quality and splendidly tailored good taste, each garment selected by the doting Aunties. They had arranged for their surprise to be waiting for Claire on the train that would carry the newlyweds east to New York, to Claire's new relations, and to her new life. Slim had personally picked out the peignoirs. The ladies fervently hoped that they'd remembered to snip all the price tags off the new clothes.

The merry little band arrived laughing and twittering at Union Station, Claire clutching her groom's hand and her battered Earhart overnight case. Strings had been pulled to get the young couple a private compartment, and it was only as the train chugged slowly out of the station, Claire's white-gloved palm pressed against the rice-splayed window (Mother and the Aunties hadn't missed a trick), the women wiping tears and locomotive steam out of their eyes and waving, that Claire realized she was leaving the store, Chicago, and her family for the first time in her protected life.

When the porter brought in the ice bucket of champagne and pulled down only one of the beds, as he had been instructed, she wondered if it wasn't too late to jump off the train in Indiana and go back to her old life. It was only when Harry reached over Claire's shoulder to lower the window shade, shutting out the telephone poles and billowing furnaces of the steel mills rushing by, when he took her in his young muscled arms, that she relaxed and gave in to the movement of the train.

For the remainder of the journey, they never left their compartment, and the shade was never raised.

                              *   *   *

Harry placed the tree trunk–sized log on the Harrisons' fire, now churned up like a homey hell. A spark popped out, landing near Claire's cheek and breaking her reverie. A stray cinder brushed her jawline. Was this to be an inquisition by torture?

"Claire, darling. Are you all right?" Harry was by her side in a flash.

"Oh, I'm fine. Really. How kind."

"You're doing great. I think Mother really likes you," he whispered into his bride's ear, as if being gorgonized by Ophelia Harrison were a social privilege.

"Perhaps Claire's chair is too close to the fire, Mother."

"Nonsense," Ophelia mumbled through her tightly controlled lips. She bore the pinched look of a peevish woman. "It hasn't been moved in twenty-five years."

Harry gently brushed an imaginary ash from Claire's cheek, letting his fingers linger on her skin.

Ophelia pushed on her glasses to examine her besotted son. It was clear to her that Harry was under the young beauty's spell.

"But do go on, Miss Organ. Just how were you raised?"

"Very nicely, I can assure you." Claire's voice was soft and apologetic. Had she really married Harry? It was as if she were back in the Pettibones' sunroom with Cilla's snooty friends.

"No. No," Ophelia bellowed impatiently, picking up her crewel from her lap. "I meant religion. Your religious instruction. In case of children." Her unplucked brows dominated her face even with the wire-rimmed glasses.

"Well," Claire stated, choosing her words carefully, "ecumenically. I was exposed to every organized religion. The Aunties and Mother felt God was everywhere."

"Pantheists. Oh dear. That's quite a broad view. But what was your mother?"

"She's a Protestant. We both are." The words moved invisibly out of Claire's mouth even as she maintained a courteous smile.

"And the other mothers?" Here Ophelia's brows arched into a circumflex.

Claire fought an impulse to rise out of her chair in anger but she heard the Aunties' cheerful voices in her head: "Remember Claire, the best defense for insult is extreme courtesy."

"All God-fearing women, I can assure you."

"Oh. I thought your people, being in the retail profession, might be of the Jewish persuasion. So many are these days. More India tea, dear?"

"No thank you, ma'am." Claire was so warm from the fire she was dying to unfasten the first velvet button on her suit, but didn't dare. She shifted uncomfortably in the heirloom chair, causing it to squeak. She blushed, turning her cheek crimson. Claire's pretty neck was still in line for the annulment guillotine and her lock-jawed mother-in-law was jabbing at her handiwork like a Locust Valley Madame Defarge as she fired off question after question at her new daughter-in-law, who apparently had no bloodlines whatsoever.

"And who are your people—on your father's side? You couldn't just have been born in a hatbox!"

Claire was exhausted. In the reckless course of the last seven days, she'd turned eighteen, lost her virginity, become a war bride, and made love for two whole days on the *Twentieth Century Limited*. She had also moved a thousand miles away from everything familiar. At this moment she was missing her mother and aunties with an ache in her heart. Nothing her new mother-in-law could say would tear Claire's loyalties away from her little family, even if they weren't cut in the conventional mode or up to society snuff.

"Minnie Mortimer's coming to dinner. With her father and mother. One of each. It'll be nice for you to have some friends your own age in Tuxedo." Ophelia stabbed her long needle into the cloth and laid down her handiwork, darting a quick look in Harry's direction.

Harry's eyes were on his bride.

"Well, Miss Organ. What a perfectly ugly name. No wonder you were in such a big hurry to change it. I know you must be fatigued. After that long train ride and all. I'm sure your rooms should be ready by now. You've got a private sitting room and bedroom on the third floor. Harry can show you. Dinner's at eight. Please be on time. Mr. Harrison will be home."

"Mother!" Harry flushed, suddenly full of confidence again. "This is my wife, Mrs. Harrison, and if you don't mind we'll be staying together." He stood behind Claire's chair like the husband in an old-fashioned tintype.

My goodness, thought Ophelia. The girl must be a sexual sorceress.

"Really, Harry. Your father and I have never shared a bedroom."

Claire stifled a gasp and didn't have to wonder why Ophelia Harrison and Millicent Pettibone were such good friends. She wondered if Mr. Harrison had an Auntie Slim too.

Freshly bathed and rested, Claire slipped down the stairs early. Her new dinner pumps were soundless on the deep pile carpet running down the mahogany stairs, garnished at each riser by a brass rail. The house was strangely silent. She had met six of Charlotte Hall's staff: the butler, the chauffeur who had picked them up at Penn Station that morning, the two upstairs maids who had unpacked Claire's new wardrobe, and the gardener and the groomsman who lived in the gatehouse at the entrance to the estate. She wondered where any of them might be. Perhaps she should find scissors or a letter opener to scratch up the soles of her new shoes so she wouldn't slide across the high-buffed floors. Where was everyone?

Did the Tuxedo people all take a siesta before their evening highballs? Or perhaps she had flunked the entrance exam into the Harrison clan and they had left her alone in this gray stone Tudor house to wander around like a character in a Charlotte Brontë novel.

Struggling to get her bearings, she looked back over her shoulder up to the top of the stairs and had to laugh. Harry was still asleep, exhausted from his Olympic lovemaking. She had suspected that he was athletic, but his attentiveness was going to leave her with little time out of bed. Claire wondered how her mother, having tasted love, could have lived without a man all these years.

She carefully turned a gold door latch almost as high as her shoulder and walked into what appeared to be a gentleman's study. The entire west wall of the room consisted of six French doors looking over a flagstone terrace, the doors each containing a dozen panes of beveled glass. She spied a letter opener on the desk and walked over to it.

Suddenly, something pulled Claire to the windows. She was startled to see Harry. He was coming up the snowy hill, two dogs jumping and running around him, obviously their master. How had he managed to be in two places at once? Did the man need no sleep? She instinctively opened a door, allowing an icy blast to enter the room, and called out a warm hello. The dogs lifted their heads. She held her arm in the air and stopped, frozen, when she realized she had the wrong man.

He came up the path with purpose, his tweed jacket softly nipped in at his waist. Authority was in his stride like a man who moved comfortably through the corridors of power, each step taking him someplace. The hounds bounded in a second before him, his vanguard.

"The bride, I presume." His brown eyes were flecked with hazel, his thick hair groomed back like his son's, although prematurely gray and raked with silver.

"Yes." She extended her hand, her mouth widening. "I'm the new Mrs. Harrison."

"And I am the other *Mr.* Harrison."

They shook hands and studied one another.

His handshake was firm and his physique as trim as his son's, but self-confidence granted him the bearing of the dignified statesman he was. She was visibly stunned. If this was how Harry was going to age, Claire thought, she had everything to look forward to. Her father-in-law was the flesh-and-blood image of the Marshall Field's man.

"Have you been introduced to Tippecanoe and Tyler?" His voice was surprisingly friendly.

"May I pet them?" She knelt down, her open expression eager for an answer.

"They seem to have taken to you."

Claire rubbed their necks and they nuzzled their wet noses on her velvet dinner dress. She didn't seem to mind. She kept her eyes averted on the dogs.

"Hello, boys. I bet your pedigrees are better than mine. I'm glad you like me." She laughed, and Harry's father liked her instantly.

"And so with eighty-three poor Jewish refugees aboard and the *Quanza* about to sail back to Europe, E.R. and I simply had to intervene." Ophelia rang the silent dinner buzzer under her foot, signaling for the fish course to be removed and the meat course served.

"We had enlisted Negroes in the navy the week before, so we were chock full of missionary fervor. Thank you, Charles," she mumbled discreetly.

"Go on, Mother."

"Yes, do," Mrs. Mortimer chimed in. "It's riveting." Ophelia had assured her that Harry's marriage wouldn't last. She and her daughter watched squinty-eyed as Claire correctly placed her fish fork on the right side of her plate.

"Well, as Harrison knows, Franklin wasn't lifting a finger." Ophelia tilted her bushy eyebrows first in Mr. Mortimer's direction and then at her husband. "It falls to us women to bring compassion into the world. Remember that, girls. Men may be the brains of this nation, but we are its heart and helping hands."

She helped herself to a heaping platter of cauliflower, carrots, russet potatoes, and well-done roast.

"There are some people in the War Department who would consider it meddling." Harrison speared a potato.

"Rest assured that Eleanor Roosevelt doesn't meddle. She deserves a medal of honor for her work. And if we hadn't 'meddled,' if you insist, my dear, those Jewish refugees would be in one of the German camps we keep hearing about but that the State Department refuses to believe exist."

"Please tell us what happened, Mrs. Harrison." Claire leaned in closer. Mr. Korach in Better Shoes had a brother still in Germany and worried about these rumored camps.

"Eleanor and I were at Hyde Park when she received word. You and Franklin were out sailing the *Augusta* with Churchill, as I recall."

Harrison nodded, unable to hold back a smile. That was more or less accurate, he thought, secretly glad that Ophelia would never be his biographer.

"So here comes the *Quanza*, steaming into New York Harbor, with its passengers packed in like sardines. No *Queen Mary*, this ship, children." Ophelia loved holding the room's attention. "Everyone with an American visa disembarked except the Jews from occupied France, who were pleading to come ashore, but no. Our ridiculous bald-headed bureaucrats said, 'Not without your papers.' I ask you, where is the compassion in our government?" She examined the red wine in her glass as if it held the answer.

Claire looked startled. Harry's mother was evidently capable of great social good as well as drawing room mischief.

"Well, these people should have had their passports with them. I mean I always have mine, even at the horse shows." Minnie felt she should participate in the conversation since Harry loved politics.

"So the boat sailed off to Mexico just like one of those Caribbean holiday cruises"—Ophelia's knife sailed through an imaginary sea—"except that those poor souls weren't allowed ashore *there*, either. Lickety split, they were turned around to return to Europe and an almost certain death. Whole families, can you imagine? Luckily, the boat had to load up with coal in Virginia and that's when the Eleanor forces quickly sprang into action. We had everyone onboard certified a political prisoner so the entire ship could disembark. So clever. Those tedious immigration people at State said we were in violation of the law and tried to stop us. But it was too late: Our Jews had landed! Like Pilgrims!" Shoulders lifted in her moment of triumph, she swung her arm out over the tablecloth, accidentally pinging the china with the large sapphire on her finger, like a clash of cymbals ending a symphony.

"But that's wonderful, Mrs. Harrison! You are a saint." Minnie applauded.

"Yes, we're thinking of having Mother canonized. Aren't we, Father?"

"If that would make her happy, I am sure it can be arranged." Harrison raised his crystal goblet to his wife. He had the look of a man who had long ago drummed out his wife's speeches.

"Nonsense," shot back Ophelia, looking pleased.

"We took hell in the White House over that one." Harrison waved his white napkin like a flag of truce. He was proud of his wife, but his first duty was to protect his president. "Franklin had been trying to keep us out of the war and now that we're in it, we can't handle every European political situation that arises."

"And what's more, if we take all these refugees in, where are we going to put them?" Mr. Mortimer pounded a weak fist on the table. He shared the prominent Mortimer chin and nose with his daughter.

"Oh, can't we talk about something more fun," Minnie whined. "Claire, do you ride?"

"No, I'm afraid not."

"That's too bad," Minnie's mother said tragically, as though Claire were a social quadriplegic. "Almost everyone rides in Tuxedo. How about tennis?"

"No, I never learned." She pushed her peas into her potatoes. A big silence dropped over the table. Claire could see that Harrison dinners were a constant game of "keep up."

"Could it be golf?" Minnie asked like it was a game of charades.

Harry gave Claire an eager look of "Come on and join in."

But she couldn't.

"Mummy and I went to the Winter Antique Show and, Mrs. Harrison, you won't believe it, there was a dining room set just like yours." Minnie indicated the grand piece of furniture they were dining at, the seven chairs on which they were seated and the seventeen more spaciously parked around the magnificent Chinese-wallpapered room. "Good thing you inherited yours, because Hepplewhite costs a fortune."

Claire, having added nothing to the conversation, was now relegated to being a piece of furniture herself. She looked over her shoulder and studied the row of mahogany chairs.

"Chippendale."

All the eyes in the room turned toward her. The ball was in her court.

"Hepplewhite," Minnie thundered.

"Chippendale, decidedly. It's a fine example of Philadelphia Chippendale," she said to no one in particular, like she was back in Field's antique section. "Mid-eighteenth-century, pre-Revolutionary. A fine example, too." She smiled.

"And just how would you know that?" Minnie was losing her home-court advantage.

"By the cabriole legs. See? The overall air of delicacy. And the clawed feet on the pedestal balls. Eagles' claws." She imitated a clutched claw with her hand and arched it in Minnie's direction.

"Claire, how clever. Is antique collecting a hobby?" Harrison asked.

"Oh, no sir. The only thing I collect is stamps."

"I'd suspect you'd collect something small." Minnie glanced over at Harry.

"Probably an authority on Chippendale beds, too." Minnie's mother whispered into Ophelia's ear.

"What a wonderful coincidence, Claire. I'll have to show you my stamps." Harrison was truly delighted that his new daughter-in-law shared his solitary hobby.

"Isn't she wonderful, Father?" Harry beamed.

"Tell us, what are all the young people doing for New Year's Eve?" Ophelia interrupted, changing the course of the conversation.

"Well, everyone's going to the club, just like every other year. Except now most of the boys are in uniform or"—Minnie looked at the man who had been her New Year's date up until a few days ago—"married."

"We were thinking about taking Minnie away to Palm Beach for the holidays," Mrs. Mortimer added quickly. She knew it was time to surrender. "It's sure to be very gay and far removed from the war."

"Hardly. The Breakers Hotel is probably going to be turned into a military hospital."

"Heavens, Ophelia." Minnie's mother's wheels began to turn. "The Japanese wouldn't invade Palm Beach, would they?" She struggled for breath. "Think of the Everglades Club. Men with sabers and women in kimonos on the croquet court! What is the world coming to?"

"Don't worry." Harrison laughed at her silliness. "The membership committee would never let them in."

"Cigars and brandy for the gentlemen." Ophelia stood. "Enough of this nonsense." Claire had earned her seat at the table—for now. "We ladies shall adjourn to the drawing room— but only for fifteen minutes while the men have their smoke. Perhaps I can interest you in some of the war relief work E.R. and I are cooking up."

"Yes, Yes!" Minnie was up like one of her jumpers, swiftly taking Ophelia's arm. "Did you hear about Marjorie Merriweather Post Davies? She's giving her yacht the *Sea Cloud* to the navy. She's such a trooper!"

When Harry joined Claire some minutes later, his too-big Havana still smoking in his mouth, Claire didn't respond the first time he called her Mrs. Harrison. Nor did she respond when it was echoed in an even lower, more resonate timbre. It was only when he tapped her on the shoulder and Claire spun around, her velvet skirt following her by seconds, that she realized that both father and son were addressing her by her new name.

"Mrs. Harrison."

"Mrs. Harrison. Mrs. Harrison, would it interest you to see some of my stamps now?"

Claire lifted her head, nodding happily while Ophelia lowered her gaze.

Now there were two Mrs. Harrisons in the house.

"She has her charms. And she's got spunk. I'll give her that. But she has absolutely no pedigree! Perhaps if her great-grandfather had *invented* the organ. Why, we checked on Tippecanoe and Tyler's bloodlines for the preceding five generations before we brought them into our home!" Ophelia was helping pack her husband's Vuitton hardcase. He was returning to Washington early the next morning, at the president's urgent request. "And if we hadn't spent Christmas at the White House with Churchill, Harry wouldn't have gone to the Pettibones' alone and unprotected, and none of this would have happened."

"The dogs seemed to like her well enough."

"Pleasing an Airedale is one thing. Placating our neighbors is quite another." Ophelia snap-latched the double locks on his well-worn crocodile travel case with the gold-plated grooming implements.

"I find her unspoiled and refreshing. She'll be good for Harry."

"Harrison, what exactly do you suggest I give to the society pages in the way of an announcement? Ordinarily, the *New York Times* wants to print the relevant details about the bride's family as well. You know, their professions, clubs, summer houses, in addition to the bride's finishing school, what season she debuted in, all the milestones. Frankly, I'm at my wits' end about something Harry picked out at Marshall Field's."

Ophelia needn't have worried about embellishing Claire's abysmal social history. Walter Winchell did the honors. From his regular Table 50, Winchell spied the newlyweds dancing at the Stork Club on New Year's Eve. They had decided to escape the Tuxedo Club's certain stares for New York and an overnight getaway before Harry reported to officers' training school and an assignment overseas.

The wide-eyed Claire, in cream satin and a pair of sapphire clips borrowed from Ophelia, was caught in a newspaper photo seated in a booth between two men in uniform, her husband and Elliott Roosevelt, the president's handsome son who was on his way back to England as an army air corpsman. The black-and-white picture showed her shaking hands with Brenda Frazier and her new husband, Shipwreck Kelly. This popular photograph ran in *Life* magazine, all the New York dailies, and the *Chicago Tribune*, establishing Claire on her very first visit to a nightclub as a former deb from the Midwest, a well-married young woman, and a society party girl. Claire's makeup-free face, highlighted only by a dash of Maybelline, stood out in fresh contrast to Brenda Frazier's sickly pale powdered skin and liver-red lips. And while the photo was crunched up and discarded in certain Lake

Forest living rooms, in the Aunties' modest apartment it was prominently displayed in a silver Field's frame.

An investigation of the fine print revealed that Claire was no longer the other Mrs. Harrison, but in Winchell's freshly minted phrase, "Claire Harrison of *the* Harrisons."

Chapter Eight

The Second Front

Dearest Leona,

The knowledge that your letters are flowing to me in a never-ending stream is enough to tide me over as many CENSORED *as the APO cares to inflict on me. Have I ever told you what a comforting feeling that is, honey? We are at the point now when some of the flimsy alliances contracted in the States are starting to crack under the strain of separation, and I thank God a million times a day for blessing me with such a true and devoted wife. We have enough jilted boys on this island to open a branch of the Brush Off Club. The only consolation I can offer those boys is that it is just as well to have the truth show up now as later.*

—*Sgt. Robert Barry*
14th Bomb Squadron
12 November, 1943

Their young, feverish love never had a chance to dwindle from the honeymoon stage, since by March Harry was gone to fight and fly. Indeed, Claire's pregnancy had been the ink on the deal.

"Couldn't you stay a week or two more? You could learn one more safety parachute maneuver," she pleaded.

"I can open a parachute now in my sleep. It's sleeping alone I'm worried about." Harry ran his fingers down her cheek, memorizing it.

Claire buried her head in his uniform and inhaled the smells of him. It might have to last her weeks or months or, heaven forbid, longer. He wasn't just leaving her, he was leaving her behind.

"Take me in your pocket. I'll fly with you. Like before," she whispered.

Ophelia and Harrison stood back at a discreet distance near the canteen where hot coffee was being served to the hundreds of soldiers boarding their trains who were still bidding farewell to their loved ones.

"I'm afraid you wouldn't fit in my pocket for long. Not with that small bundle coming alive down there." Harry pulled his officer's coat around them, hiding his hands as he touched Claire tenderly, his palms gliding over her hips and across her belly. She fervently pressed her lips to his and the familiar tastes of their mouths mingled, tainted by her light, salty tears.

"Harry, I'll write to you every . . ."

Claire's soft voice was drowned out as the conductor called out the last "All aboard" and Ophelia stepped between them.

"You mustn't be late, dear." Ophelia bussed Harry on the cheek and chided him as if he were just going off to Miss Chase's Dance School with the other privileged youngsters. "Try and get an upper berth," she trilled, always aware of their lofty social position.

"Be brave, my boy." Harrison firmly shook his only son's hand and clasped him on the shoulder with his gray leather glove.

"Be safe." Claire mouthed, pushed aside in the same moment her young husband leaped aboard the train, already pulling out of Grand Central Station. The combined steam from a half-dozen locomotives sent up a fog so thick that even people wrapped up in their final good-byes lost sight of each other.

So Claire waved to a dozen lieutenants, any one of whom could have been Harry leaning out of the Pullman's open windows, all the boys waving back, whether or not they even had someone seeing them off in this human sea of worrying wool coats, raised trilbys, and waving white handkerchiefs. In this world turned upside down, the image of a pretty All-American girl with a look of I'll-wait-for-you-until-you-get-back was a picture they all needed to carry overseas as much as they needed their dog tags. And so they waved to the tall, shiny-haired girl standing on tiptoe on round-toed high heels, the indigo blue of her coat skimming her slim ankles.

Harry watched Claire for as long as he could, her small waist cinched by the coat belt, her nose tucked into the fur of her beaver collar until the smoke erased her. He waved happily even if she couldn't see him anymore. Thanks to her, he was free. Free to fly and soar.

"Don't forget to wear an overcoat, Harry," Ophelia called out last as if wrapping him up in the family motto was as good as a hug and a kiss.

"Well, I'm off. To the war effort, you know." Ophelia turned abruptly on her sensibly low heels to board her own train, which was leaving momentarily for Washington, as if the real work at hand was going to be done by her at DuPont Circle from her volunteer's desk at the Office of Civil Defense. She brushed her cheek quickly against her husband's and nodded to Claire's belly.

"Take care," she said crisply, more to the growing embryo who most emphatically would not be born in a department store than to her daughter-in-law of twelve weeks. In Ophelia's mind, Claire's baby was a gift that would belong to her, never mind the unsuitability of the maternal packaging it arrived in. Claire was just the delivery girl.

"Remember, stay off step ladders and drink your milk," she barked.

"Yes." Claire was too stunned to assemble any more words. The steam, the noise, the heat, and the Harrison inside her all conspired to make her swoon. She'd had morning sickness all day.

A steadying arm caught her elbow and turned her away from the tracks and back into the crisp air away from the station.

Harrison strolled with her down Forty-fourth Street, allowing her fawn deerskin-covered hand to rest on his coat sleeve, generously adjusting to her shaky rhythm when he would have characteristically led the way. They paused at the curb in front of the Commodore, Claire's head falling against his square shoulder, the hem of her coat hitting his houndstooth trousers. She bobbed in and out of reality, and drew in deep breaths of air in a brave effort to compose herself.

His voice was as elegantly smoky as rich rolled tobacco.

"Would you like a cup of tea? We're not far from my club, if you're feeling well enough." He checked the monogrammed pocket watch he kept tucked in his vest. "I've time before I'm due at La Guardia."

La Guardia? Was the whole family shipping out tonight? she wondered. Perhaps they had booked her on the *Titanic II* sailing at midnight.

"I'd like to drive you back to Tuxedo, but I have yet to pick up my diplomatic pouch. Averell Harriman and I are flying the Pan Am Clipper to London, in just a few hours."

The cold air and all the Harrisons' traveling plans were quickly clearing her mind. There were nightly bombing raids in London and death among the rubble. No wonder the family had all been so blasé about Harry's departure. They were all going to the "front" in some way or another.

"So you'll be going to war as well." She brushed her hair from her forehead, tidying up, and looked into her father-in-law's distinguished face.

"Just as a citizen soldier. Armed with pouches of paper ready for negotiations." His eyes twinkled as the corners of his mouth, Harry's mouth, lifted in a wide, disarming grin. No wonder Harrison was so good at diplomacy. That ingrained response of modesty had left permanent creases around his eyes and jaw, adding character to his handsomeness.

"I feel so useless."

"Nonsense, Claire. You have the most important job of all of us. You're carrying the next Harrison. My grandson . . . we hope." He stopped smiling. It was suddenly apparent that he wasn't offering idle words of comfort.

There was so much more to this send-off than was outwardly acknowledged, she could see that now. If the Harrisons' only son were killed without a male heir, the illustrious family line would end right here. To Harrison and Ophelia, having this child was much more compelling than whether Claire or Harry was in love, or if she was a good wife, or if indeed his parents even liked her. A surge of elation invigorated her with the realization that they were all counting on her, depending on Claire to do the one thing this proud family could not do for themselves.

When Harrison took her hand it was to shake it formally as if they had just reached an understanding. They were allies now, each off to perform their separate but equal duties. He to deal with Churchill and Roosevelt, and she to bear a son. No one had to tell her that her future rested on her ability to deliver.

So Claire returned to Tuxedo with her one assignment. Like a good soldier she would fly their flag and hold the fort. But with her husband in the South Pacific, Harrison shuttling between Washington and London, and Ophelia at Eleanor's elbow, Charlotte Hall seemed more of a musty museum than ever, especially to a young girl aglow with new life inside her. She rattled around the enormous house, wondering if she would go the whole nine yards without ever seeing another soul. Her loneliness was all the more acute when she considered that Harry might still be gone when their child was born. A sudden chilling thought snaked its way into her mind. Just like her own birth. Her father had been thousands of miles away and was never heard from again. Claire shuddered and shook off the comparison. Harry would be back.

In the meantime, she tried to enliven the long, empty days before her. Up early, breakfasting by herself in the sun parlor, poring over the *New York Times,* Claire listened intently to the Philco radio for news of her husband's carrier group or her in-laws' whereabouts between commercials for Carter's Little Liver Pills and Old Gold cigarettes.

Claire hungered to have a real conversation, even if it was only to sell someone a pair of knitting needles or a Chippendale chair. Trying to engage the stiff household staff in friendly chitchat was out of the question. They were like Field's nose-in-the-air floorwalkers, only making themselves visible to tell her what not to touch or to scold her with an icy "Mrs. Harrison wouldn't like that." So among the sixty-odd rooms at Charlotte Hall the only ones she stuck to were the bedroom she had shared with Harry and her father-in-law's book-lined study. He had even earmarked some books on foreign policy for her and she devoured them, committing whole passages to memory.

It irked her that the regiment of servants who ignored her took hours tending to chores she and her aunties could have whizzed through; and it worried her that as soon as her child was born, a delegation of nurses and nannies reporting to Ophelia would take charge. She had overheard as much.

As the afternoon light lengthened and the dogs napped in the still house, she indulged herself in one of the few activities that truly gave her pleasure. She explored Charlotte Hall like a social archaeologist for clues to Harry's childhood. A porcelain music box painted with his initials yielded a lock of his baby blond hair, along with a picture of Ophelia holding her small son. A double passport issued to him and Ophelia when he was six showed that they had visited Venice and Paris many times and Claire concluded that mother and son had rarely been separated. By taking his silver trophies off recessed shelves, tracing her fingertip along the inscriptions and touching his blue ribbons, she learned that he'd jumped horses until he was twelve and shot skeet at the Greenbriar on holidays, winning prizes for his marksmanship with clay pigeons. She particularly liked the photo of an eighteen-year-old Harry with his fly club, their matching emblem *P*s worn as jauntily on the sleeves of their leather jackets as their cocky grins.

She couldn't quite decipher, though, which fellow the college-age Harry was in the picture of the Princeton water polo team hanging on the wall in his closet. All the boys were tall, thin, and wiry, and with their wet hair flattened on top of their identical WASP features any one of the eight could have been her husband. After some time with a magnifying lens she thought she found him in the middle row, third from the left.

After several weeks of these "excavations," Claire uncovered the single most interesting fact. She realized that she didn't know her Harry very well at all. By carefully going through the albums and seeing him grow over the years with the same circle of relatives and friends, and by reading the Rudyard Kipling stories he kept by his bed, she was beginning to get a picture of someone she hadn't met yet.

She had known only the passionate young flier in a uniform and in a hurry. She'd fallen in love to the strains of Benny Goodman, her dashing young lieutenant's hands holding her tightly. She'd dined with the polite heir who told her he didn't care about *her* ancestors, but whose own house proudly displayed crowds of them on all four floors, each in carefully tended-to frames.

Their time together so far had been recklessly romantic, full of sweet tenderness and forever promises, their excitement enhanced by the drama of separations and anticipated returns. Their wedded life had been a patchwork of hurried golden moments on sporadic evenings, where touching took the place of words, and of intense weekends sandwiched between flight school and family, until, too soon for her, Harry's final orders came through. And then he was gone.

Her isolation and Tuxedo's frosty treatment of her, the discoveries of her daily "excavations," the hormonal changes—all of it caused her to question whether the peacetime Claire would be up to Harry's Hudson Valley standards. Her instincts told her she would have to find a way to blend in, to learn whatever she would need to know to make him happy.

In the meantime, the long letters she and Harry wrote back and forth filled her evenings and sustained her. Nestled in Harrison's study, a cherry plaid blanket thrown over her elevated legs, the dogs snoozing on either side of the buttery leather lounge and ottoman, she read:

> *April 24, 1942*
> *USS* Hornet

My darling,

I am wistful tonight, my dear, and a picture I crave is of you and me sitting on a soft couch somewhere in the complete quiet, where we might watch a smoldering fire and just be together. Or perhaps out in the pine woods somewhere beyond C.H., lit by the stars and moon, stretched out on a blanket of needles, just feeling the touch of you and staring up at the limitless sweep above, where no one cares where you come from, just that you are the sweetest girl in the world and you are mine. I know we Harrisons do not show emotion easily or express our feelings well, but I can only tell you, my dearest, I am yours alone.

I have put the picture of you and me and old Elliott at the Stork Club over my bunk onboard and even though there's not a single fellow here I prepped with or who attended Princeton or Yale Law, I have bonded more closely with this squadron than any group of fellows I have known before. They are all quite smitten with you and your beautiful face, although one of the guys, a good pilot and a grocer's son, might have been just a smidge more impressed that old FDR's son was squeezed in next to you. Well, at least they can see this is a Democratic war. No favoritism in this man's army. What with the commander in chief's boys in the thick of things. Elliott is already flying over CENSORED *reconnaissance missions in unarmed photographic planes.*

Yours truly will be flying to an island off the Philippine mainland called CENSORED. *Sounds like one of those Trader Vic drinks we indulged in, doesn't it? I wish I had you in my arms now, my dearest, and the wonderful fresh vanilla smell of you in my nostrils, and your silky hair lying across my chest. I cherish you and our little bundle that you are carrying within you. I wish I could be there, too. Write to me, Clairest. I long for your voice.*

Yours,
Harry

"Why aren't your lips moving? Are you all right, dear?"

"Of course, Mother." Claire had her face twisted up like her mother-in-law's in a poor rendition of an Eastern Shore aristocratic accent.

"What, dear? I can barely understand you. Whose mother is queer?"

Claire relaxed her lips and spoke in her regular clear midwestern voice. She had been practicing her diction as part of her campaign to conquer Locust Valley.

"No, no, Mother. I'm so glad you're *here.*" Obviously Claire's newly affected diction needed work.

"Come and hug me then. We're all just a bunch of sad sacks without you."

"Me too."

"Claire, you're as thin as a sparrow. Are you eating enough for the baby?"

Violet was spending a rare but much anticipated weekend with her daughter. Civilian travel was expensive and discouraged, not to mention that Violet's impeccable good manners wouldn't allow her to stay longer than was proper in a house in which she didn't feel entirely welcome. She hadn't seen the Harrisons since that disastrous January weekend when she and the Aunties had been invited to Charlotte Hall for what they assumed would be a round of black-tie postnuptial parties. Instead, the visit had gone like a Noel Coward comedy that they could laugh about only now.

Upon arrival, they were ushered into the lead-paned solarium for tea sandwiches with Harry and Claire, their bags whisked upstairs. Instructed to dress for dinner, Wren caused a small commotion before she realized the upstairs maids had only unpacked for her and were steaming, not stealing, her two outfits. By the time Slim descended the spiraling oak staircase holding her long enamel cigarette holder aloft while blowing smoke rings directly into the faces of the ancestors lining the wall, a slack-jawed Ophelia had made up her mind to cancel Saturday night's dinner at the club and Sunday's brunch with her Tuxedo neighbors. She told Harrison she simply wouldn't mix fruitcakes with caviar. Even Claire was aghast. She wondered what had happened to her proper aunties. Since they had arrived in Tuxedo they were behaving like the Marx Brothers.

So the lady houseguests were secluded like social lepers in the great house, a band hastily hired to provide dinner music Saturday night so that Claire and Harry could dance while the "mothers-in-law" tapped their toes like out-of-luck wallflowers.

Throughout it all, in contrast, Violet had behaved so properly that by the time the ladies departed for the Sunday night train back to the Midwest, she had probably intimidated her hosts as much as she had impressed the servants. She had left the help exactly the right amount of tip money for their weekend stay and discreetly left a dozen silk hangers and scented drawer liners for Ophelia to open after their departure as well as a beautiful fountain pen in a stand for their host.

Still, for all the pleasantries and promises exchanged, Violet felt like she was meant to be just an occasional houseguest and resolved not to intrude on the Harrisons' hospitality any more often than was necessary. Besides, she was needed at the store. So it was just a quick visit and a little maternal aid—both emotional and financial. Just because her daughter was well married didn't mean the largesse spilled over into Claire's pocketbook. Like most of the very rich who budget for the cook's groceries and the chauffeur's car polish and the gardener's manure, Violet observed, no one had thought to give the new Mrs. Harrison a dime. So Violet slipped a twenty-dollar bill into Claire's palm as her daughter hugged and waved her off in the Harrisons' chauffeur-driven town car.

After Violet's departure, the silences in the house became overbearing. Claire sometimes thought that unless she could find something useful to keep her occupied she'd go crazy herself. She'd read every baby book printed in English. But there was a war on and she had to find a way to participate.

It came together in the oddest way. Minnie Mortimer telephoned to invite Claire to a horse show at which they would be selling war bonds. Would Claire be interested in manning one of the tables? No one would need to see Claire from the waist down; some of the Old Guard of Tuxedo didn't fancy seeing a pregnant woman out and about, especially at a blue ribbon event. Minnie's offer was a prickly olive branch. Claire didn't bother to tell her that she still wasn't showing yet, just that she'd be there.

Sitting at her makeshift desk a good nervous hour before the bond drive began, Claire conscientiously pored over the literature neatly arranged on the table.

"A woman is a substitute," one War Department brochure began, "like plastic instead of metal. Women are needed to do the work of men now that they are away." "An idle typewriter," a pamphlet from the Office of War Information trumpeted in bold type, "is just another weapon for Hitler." Fascinated, Claire read on, pulling her cashmere cardigan closer. All of the literature was designed to encourage women to take secretarial jobs in Washington, where the mountain of paperwork necessary to move a nation through war was triple anything the capital had ever seen before. She itched to get close to the action. Later that

afternoon, when the bond drive was over, Claire, an event calendar in her hand, motioned Minnie into the corner with an excited
"Eleanor Roosevelt's coming!"

"Whose house?" Minnie yawned as though she couldn't have
been more unimpressed.

"How far are we from Poughkeepsie?"

"Thinking of entering Vassar?" Minnie looked at Claire sideways.

"No, Eleanor Roosevelt is going to be speaking at a plant near
there. I think we should go."

Minnie pursed her lips and wondered if her old fiancé's new
bride had been kicked in the head by a horse. "If you want to go
that's fine, but why me?"

"Because I haven't learned to drive yet." Then Claire flashed
her a smile every bit as charming as the diplomatic Harrison
Senior's. She was learning.

The dogwood and forsythia along the roadway to upstate New
York were in robust bloom, as were bright-hued tulips prying
their way up from the moist earth, but all of them paled in comparison with the yellow silk daisies bunched on the first lady's
hat. The two well-dressed girls arrived at the factory just as Mrs.
Roosevelt was mounting a platform to speak with several women
welders by literally walking the plank, the only means of ascending the makeshift platform erected four feet above the ground so
that everyone in the crowd would be able to see her.

Mrs. Roosevelt's voice was mellifluous and pleasant, lifting up
to the rafters of the former Waring factory, which now made
small airplane parts instead of eggbeaters and blenders.

"If you've sewn on buttons, or made buttonholes on the machine, you can learn to do spot welding on airplane parts." E.R.'s
voice sang out like a high-pitched contralto. "If you've done fine
embroidery, or made jewelry, you can learn to do assembly on

time fuses and radio tubes. And if you've ever poured batter for a bundt cake, you can pour the lead for our bullets. Are you ready?"

A cheer went up and Claire's heart leaped.

"I am here today to commend you, and you are here to tell me what needs to be done. Once in a while down in Washington they listen to me when I have something to say." She smiled. "I say, if our country needs its married women to work so that we can win this war, then the government needs to step in with day nurseries and play schools adjacent to our plants!"

Clapping, Claire turned to Minnie and said, "Isn't she wonderful?"

Minnie looked back at Claire and shrugged. "She sounds like a socialist to me. Besides, that's what we have nannies for."

Claire turned away from her and inched closer to the applauding factory worker on her right.

"As I have traveled the country I am invigorated to see college girls and career women, shop girls and stenographers, housewives and widows, girls whose fathers are army men or girls whose husbands are flying planes and driving tanks, picking up the slack to do the work the men have left behind." Claire applauded vigorously and thought of Harry. Surely she could think of some way to help her own flyboy.

Back at Charlotte Hall after the speech, Claire's step was lighter and her mind on her immediate goals as she raced up the elaborate floral carved staircase two steps at a time and whizzed past her father-in-law's bedroom. Something caught her eye. She backtracked and poked her head into the normally unoccupied suite. She was surprised to see Alice and Katy, the upstairs maids, involved in an elaborate bed-making ritual. As they shook the thousand-thread-count second sheet, one girl on either side of the four-poster bed, the Egyptian cotton and silk blend fabric was billowing up into a huge balloon over the bed like a perfectly shaped cloud. As the luxurious square of custom cotton fell flat, each of the gray-uniformed girls with a starched pinafore hurried to pull the top sheet taut and tuck it into hospital corners before any wrinkles could form in the fabric.

"Could you do that again?" Claire spoke with all the authority of Mrs. Roosevelt, whose no-nonsense voice still rang in her ears. "Please."

"What, ma'am?"

"Have we left any wrinkles, Miss Organ?"

Claire cringed at the sound of her maiden name, but to the maids in this house, there would always be only one Mrs. Harrison.

"Um, yes. And you know how Mrs. Harrison dislikes sloppy work." There was such an unexpected authority in her voice that the startled maids undid their handiwork and began again.

"Oh, and billow it out, yes, high now . . . and hold it, just like that . . . to shake the wrinkles out." Claire directed. Charmed at the lovely sight, she leaned against the door well and watched as the sheet floated so softly to touch the mattress below it could have landed an angel. And then it came to her. Like quicksilver Claire was out of the room, bounding down the stairs again and into Harrison's office. She closed the door and began to type, her fingers flying over the lettered keys, leaving Alice and Katy, who overheard everything at Charlotte Hall, to wonder whether Miss Claire wasn't as batty as those Aunties.

The small private elevator, paneled in wood, was crammed full of crocodile suitcases forming a pyramid up to its vaulted cathedral ceiling. The Harrisons were returning to Charlotte Hall, though one of them—no one bothered to tell Claire which—was a day ahead of the other.

But Claire was busy concentrating in Harry's old nursery. She stood atop a step ladder, her pastel smocked shirt puckered at what used to be her waist, painting cumulus clouds on the walls and ceiling. The puffy clouds were bright white, their linings tinged with pinks, and they sailed through a clear bright sky dotted with shiny silver airplanes wearing big smiles on their fuse-lages. And in the recessed space where the crib would stand was her masterpiece, a striped hot-air balloon flanked by two creamy white parachutes gently sailing a pair of happy clowns to earth. No soldiers or guns in her child's nursery. No horses either.

"Claire. Come down off that ladder!" She was so startled to hear his voice that she tumbled off faster than her feet. Harrison caught her before she crashed to the floor.

"Safe. No harm done." She stood up, recovering quickly. She was seized with a momentary panic as she remembered Ophelia's admonition to stay off ladders. Claire hoped Harrison wouldn't tell his wife. Who knew what punishment Ophelia might try to impose?

"How goes the work of the ambassador of war?"

"Better, thanks to the busy work you've been up to."

So he knew. Claire could tell by his smile.

"I have to admit that when they first told me that Mrs. William Henry Harrison had secured an enormous contract for manufacturing war matériel, turning the leading producer of bed linens and hosiery into our biggest supplier of parachutes, I was astonished that Ophelia could carry off such a coup. But when I congratulated her over dinner, she didn't know what I was talking about. The following day when I looked into the matter and learned that the supplier was Marshall Field and Company, I knew that our Mrs. Harrison was you." Harrison was wearing his genuine grin now, not his diplomatic one.

Indeed, Claire had written a series of impassioned letters lobbying her old acquaintances in the executive office to give up manufacturing Field's primary products, Fieldcrest sheets and pillowcases, and to sacrifice Zionets lace curtains and Fieldbilt lingerie for the war's duration to serve a bigger need. She suggested that by turning over their North Carolina mills and Indiana plants to the production of war goods—silk bags for gunpowder, and parachute cloth, camouflage, and mosquito netting—Field's could make good on the store's motto to "give the lady what she wants," namely a speedy end to the war and her husband's and son's safe return. Little did Claire realize at the time that out of her instinct to help her Harry, she had helped a thousand Harrys.

"I think the war effort could use your persuasive skills more than your paintbrushes," Harrison continued. "Come down from your ladder, Claire, and come to Washington with me."

July 9, 1942
USS Hornet

Clairest,

Fancy that! Father tells me if I have to bail out of my bomber I probably have you to thank for the smooth ride down. Aren't you the resourceful one, turning sheets into parachutes, but then I did get the prettiest girl at the party and shouldn't be too surprised at any of your accomplishments.

Darling, I can't tell you what comfort it gives me to know that you will be safe now with my parents at the Willard where Mother can look after you properly. I am truly delighted she was able to track down and persuade old Bridget to come out of retirement and be our baby's nurse. She was my nurse until I was nine and I seem to have turned out none the worse for it.

Forgive me, Claire, for not wanting to share my war news but rather to hear all about your domestic adventures, whether or not the baby has kicked you in the side yet or if you like the plans for our house to be built on the north parcel of C.H. We will be just a stone's throw from the big house. Do you like Mother's plan for a connecting underground passageway?

I have had my first brushes with the darker side of the war and my greatest salvation is to envision the three, no three and three-quarters, of you, minding the hearth and giving so generously with your own volunteer efforts. But do remember to rest and listen to Mother—at least until our little one is born.

Clairest, write often and oftener. Even seeing your slanted script with your little drawings lifts my mood. When I come back from a mission it is like being handed a bag of coins to receive a parcel of your letters. It was especially important after we dropped the bombs on CENSORED *and on the fly-by where we got to see the mangled damage we had wreaked. All that, and to lose so many boys and then the island itself. I* CENSORED *but* CENSORED. *Our boys' spirits are dampened but the tide in the South Pacific will turn soon, I am sure.*

You are so perceptive, darling. You are right to see this is not the same as shooting clay pigeons. I don't know how it is you always know my mind. In the meantime, I kiss you on the lips and thank God you are waiting for me.

Your Harry

P.S. Please thank your auntie Slim for the monogrammed stationery and portable writing table. Unfortunately the paper is not the right issue but the writing table is a terrific hit in the ship's hospital, where I loaned it to some of the fellows on the mend.

P.P.S. Did I remember to tell you it makes me have wonderful thoughts to hear that you sometimes sleep in my leather flying jacket?

Chapter Nine

Eleanor and Lucy

Mature women should enter politics in order to guard against the emptiness and loneliness that enters some women's lives after their children are grown. Today's women need to have lives, interests and personalities of their own apart from their own households.

—*Eleanor Roosevelt*
"*What I Want Most Out of Life,*"
Success Magazine

In 1942 five thousand new people poured into Washington each month, and early that summer Claire was one of them. Like Claire, nearly one-third of the newcomers were women, mostly young. They came from every corner of the country, these fresh faces in their one pair of nylons and pencil-thin skirts, all in search of jobs, excitement, and, with any luck, husbands. But Claire already had each of these in spades. As the newest staff assistant to the president's senior adviser, her father-in-law, she was dropped smack dab into a heady world of generals, cabinet members, and twenty-four-hour workdays in a city that never shut down. After the sleepy days in Tuxedo, she welcomed the frenetic activity of the capital boomtown.

Where two years earlier the prewar armies had trained with cardboard weapons and flour for gunpowder, now there was a war department so vast it was preparing to move into the largest building in the world, the Pentagon.

Daylight savings—"war time"—was instituted throughout

the country, and in Washington working hours were staggered to ease congestion in the streets and offices. Stuck in a bottleneck of Nashes, Fords, and DeSotos, Claire craned her neck around to better take her first look at the capital's picture-postcard sights— as if Imperial Rome had sent over its leftover marble columns, obelisks, and temples, it seemed to her—from the back of Harrison's polished black Lincoln. His aide and sometime driver Tom Brewster explained to Claire, driving her down Pennsylvania Avenue at a snail's pace, how trees were being up-rooted and streets widened to accommodate the automobile traf-fic that choked the city in spite of the staggered hours and rationed gas. "This town is getting so crowded that Hitler and his tank could be stuck in traffic for hours before anyone noticed," Tom joked. He laughed with a friendliness that reminded her of Harry's straightforward warmth. Tom couldn't have been more than a year or two older than her husband. The appealing impact of his sandy hair, big white teeth, and skin tanned the color of toast was mollified by a pair of thick tortoiseshell glasses. In Washington, with its scarcity of young men, even Harvard-educated noncombatants like Tom, thanks to poor vision and rich fathers, double-dutied as drivers and couriers. "Housing is at such a premium," Tom told Claire, watching her closely in his rearview mirror, "that secretaries working the late shift 'time share' a bed with someone working the early shift. One sleeps on the still-warm sheets while the other works."

Claire listened to Tom's stories, her wide-eyed gaze locked on the Washington Monument, which loomed ahead, as a peachy gray dusk fell over the city. Eventually, they pulled up to the very proper Willard Hotel.

Because of the housing shortage, it had been decided that Claire would live at the hotel with her in-laws. Since the Harrisons didn't share a bedroom, Claire would take the sitting-room couch or the extra bedroom when either was out of town. Not so different from the Windermere, Auntie Wren had pointed

out in a letter. Claire didn't care. Adapting quickly to the impro-
vised arrangement, she was so relieved to be out of her gilded
birdcage at Charlotte Hall and in the center of power and activity that no inconvenience could deter her.

In just her very first week on the job, as part of Harrison's War
Materials Oversight Team, Claire had been called upon to collect
projections from the chairman of Chrysler on how many and how
fast its assembly plants could turn out tanks for the hush-hush
North Africa operation coming that fall. She'd also made dinner
reservations for Cyrus Pettibone and his out-of-town guests, own-
ers of a Chicago scrap metal company, in town for urgent discussions about the quickest way to melt down rusty old tankers and
salvage the sheet metal for airplanes. In Claire's newly opened
eyes, even though the floodlights that had always bathed the
city's monuments in a soft, democratic glow were switched off for
the war's duration, living in the capital was like being in the center of a thousand watts of energy.

"Turkey and yams. That's what you get when Eleanor's in residence. Dry as a bone, too." Harrison said slyly to his daughter-in-
law. He shook the summer rain off his umbrella and handed it
over to the usher as they followed Ophelia up the stairs to the first
family's private quarters. The humidity was high, and Claire
could feel the dark fabric of her summer frock sticking to the
back of her knees. She was nervously excited to meet the great
man himself. She could hardly believe that she was calmly making her way upstairs to the president's parlor.

"E.R.'s stomping all over the country on Franklin's behalf to
learn what the American people are thinking and you're expecting her to prepare a beef Wellington?" Ophelia scolded her husband. She fidgeted with a bow-shaped diamond brooch the size of
a well-fed mouse that dangled from her ample bosom.

Harrison diplomatically took both of the ladies by the arm as
the trio ascended the remaining stairs to the private residence.

There in the Oval Room was the president seated at a table, mixing cocktails. A pince-nez on his nose, he peered over at Claire, his broad grin and cigarette holder dominating his jovial face. His cocktail hour was the only time of the day when he let all the worries of war briefly fall from his shoulders, Harrison informed her.

"Harry's bride! And just in time. Jump down, Fala, and give the lady your chair," he bellowed to his black Scotch terrier, who instantly handed over his seat even as he left his four-pawed imprint on the cushion.

"Eleanor's having a lot of do-gooders for dinner so we have to get the fun in before the first course. Isn't that right, Ophelia?" Ophelia waved hello and skirted out to find the first lady, still at work in her office down the hall. "What can I fix you with, my dear?"

Claire was frozen. Here was the most important man on the face of the earth asking her what she'd like to drink.

He put her at ease. "Most people ask for something with ice on an evening like this."

"Ginger ale," Claire gulped.

"And how about you, Harrison? The usual?" His thin lips curled into a contagious smile when he greeted his friend. Claire observed that the affection between the two men was genuine. Harrison found a leather chair that had acquired a rich glow from years of use and slowly lowered his tall frame. Harry Hopkins handed Claire her beverage from his moist hand. If Harrison was FDR's right hand, Harry Hopkins was his left.

"Thank you," Claire said softly to everyone.

Her eyes swept the room, taking it all in. The president's study was in fact a large oval room lined with mahogany bookcases spilling over with leather volumes and a tumbleweed decor of family pictures, Harvard ashtrays filled with dog treats, and Audubon prints. The ships in glass bottles and slightly askew oil paintings of sailing vessels were a tribute to FDR's love of the sea.

Upstairs at the White House had the cozy look of a well-born family's lifetime of clutter, gathered together for a rummage sale. Claire had no idea that this untidy room—the lived-in version of the formal Oval Office directly below—was in reality the heartbeat of the White House where FDR conducted most of his business until the wee hours of the morning and that his bedroom was only a closed door away. Claire sipped at her cold drink and demurely shook hands with the Morgenthaus, the Sherwoods, Harry Hopkins, and the president's only daughter, Anna. Even though Anna was fifteen years older than Claire, she was still the second-youngest person in the room, and had the warmest smile. As a mother whose husband was also soldiering overseas, Claire felt an unspoken bond with her and so she shyly settled herself into a nearby chair. She was satisfied that at least she looked presentable, with her thick hair softly waved to her shoulders, the crisp white collar and cuffs accenting her silk maternity smock.

"The hardest job in Washington is being Harrison and the second hardest is working for him. How are you holding up?" Roosevelt asked. His broad grin criss-crossed his entire face.

"Well, it's only been ten days." Claire blushed.

"Ten days! Why, usually they ask to be transferred after forty-eight hours to something easy, like active duty!"

The president peered curiously over his pince-nez at the wholesome-looking girl with the violet eyes whose posture was show-horse perfect.

"So, my dear, from where do you hail, originally?"

"Chicago." Claire's timbre was soft and musical, running up and down the octave in some sort of vaguely aristocratic scale. She was finding her own voice at last.

"Ah, Chicago. Come closer. Harrison, you don't know this story either."

They all circled in.

"The day after Pearl Harbor, the fellows at Secret Service suggested I'd be needing a bulletproof armored car. Guess they figured the Japs would try to sink me next. So Mike Reilly"—he turned in his chair to Claire by way of explanation—"he's chief of the White House Secret Service detail. Well, Mike runs into a federal regulation against buying me any car costing more than seven hundred and fifty dollars."

Like any great actor, Roosevelt waited for the shock effect to sink in: a president left unprotected because of a fiscal budgetary rule! "Now"—he pointed down with his cigarette holder, spilling ashes on the Oriental rug—"Reilly's a clever boy. Found out the U.S. Treasury owned a huge armored limousine it had seized in an income-tax evasion case." A chuckle started to escape the side of his mouth. "Reilly had it washed, gassed up, and driven over here. Naturally I asked to whom it had belonged. Thought a thank-you note was in order." He winked at Claire. "Turned out it was a Chicagoan."

"Who did it belong to?" she asked, aware that it was expected of her.

"Al Capone. I'm driving around in his getaway car!"

The room laughed, like it was supposed to.

Anna leaned over to whisper into Claire's ear, "It's *his* getaway car, too. He likes to take it out for long afternoon drives into the Virginia hills. It soothes him."

Claire was beginning to get the drift of the "cocktail hour." It was a scheduled recess for a beleaguered president and his trusted inner circle away from the gloomy dispatches and war operations of the day. All that would begin again after dinner. This was a time reserved for clearing their heads and swapping the day's best laughs.

"Claire, put that glass of spirits down! It's not good for our baby." Ophelia burst in, announcing Eleanor's imminent arrival. Rattled, Claire anxiously looked for a coaster on which to put her glass of ginger ale. It was easier than explaining.

Suddenly, the door opened, allowing a tall Eleanor Roosevelt with a stack of papers in her long, suntanned arms to stride into the room, instantly making it her own. A cadre of shorter, solemn-faced women, marching at her side like social reform storm troopers, flanked her. Claire sensed an instantaneous shift in gears. Where the conversation had been driving along at a pleasant idle, in a no-particular-hurry first gear, it was now thrown into full throttle and everyone sat straight up in their chairs for the ride.

"At last. My dear, I thought that you might have abandoned me for your millions of readers." FDR shifted his cigarette holder from the right side of his mouth to the left with just a slight movement of the jaw.

"But yours is the only high opinion I look for." The corners of E.R.'s mouth lifted as six chins fell behind her, as though the first lady's friends were disappointed that their thoughts mattered less to her than her husband's.

"And what's the good word for our fellow Americans tomorrow?" Claire, too, was an avid reader of Mrs. Roosevelt's column, "My Day," appearing without fail six days a week in hundreds of newspapers across the country.

"Nothing that Hitler or Hirohito will be losing any sleep over, I'm afraid."

"We always have to be sure Eleanor's not giving away state secrets in her articles," Harry Hopkins explained to Claire. Franklin's side of the room laughed in affectionate indulgence while Eleanor's sorority of camp followers snarled and glared rabidly.

"Well, I've called it 'Food for Thought,'" Eleanor responded as the president poured her a short glass of beer. She didn't approve of alcohol but there was reason to celebrate. By gently badgering her husband, she had just gotten him to approve the first government-sponsored day-care center. She had framed her appeal pragmatically, convincing him that doing so was the only way to ensure a stable workforce.

"Tomorrow's piece is a plea to grocers to extend their hours so that women involved in war work can shop for their families on their way home." She gulped down her drink. Eleanor hated wasting time as much as she disliked idle chatter.

"Franklin, we must do more for our female war workers." She reached for her glasses and began to read from her next day's column. " 'I am sure that if the people of our great nation could see the difficulty women have carrying a full-time factory job and also keeping up a family, doing the shopping, housework, and helping with homework, we would do what must be done to ease their burden.' " She folded up her glasses. "I'm asking the butchers to hold back some of their meat supplies until six p.m. and for grocers to extend their hours for women who go to work. Our fighting force behind our fighting force!"

"Good for you, Babs!" Franklin applauded his wife.

Claire smoothed her hands over her pregnant belly and marveled at how the first lady understood what women like her beleaguered aunties had wanted all their lives, only this woman had the power to make it all happen. Power. Power and persuasion skills were her accessories, and she wore them well. Slim had always taught her that a silk scarf and a whiff of perfume were the female's only tools of persuasion. But Eleanor used facts and pragmatism. And, of course, her access. Claire admired Eleanor's kind of accessories.

"Shall we?" Eleanor signaled the group into the family dining room. "I'm off at dawn to fly to Alabama. They've asked me to speak at the FEPC hearings in Birmingham."

The Fair Employment Practices Commission was a hot potato, Anna Roosevelt told a mesmerized Claire as they went into dinner, and the first lady put herself in jeopardy whenever she went down to fight with recalcitrant unions and war-plant employers to hire more blacks for defense jobs.

"Because of Eleanor's efforts, Negroes are working in firms like the aircraft industry that formerly banned them, and in the nation's shipyards black employment has quadrupled," Mrs. Morgenthau whispered to Claire in a pass-the-salt kind of way.

"And not everyone loves me for it." Eleanor had the ears of a bloodhound. As she took her place at the head of the table, she seemed to be speaking directly to Claire but was just as likely putting the words together for her next day's column.

"This wartime struggle will not be worth winning if the old order of things prevails. Unless democracy has real meaning here at home—and by that I mean democracy for everyone, with civil rights and social reform—there's no point in fighting for democracy abroad." The table fell silent in acquiescence.

"Yes. And I'm going along too, Harrison." Ophelia chimed in. "The baby isn't due for another eight weeks so I'll be just fine."

Claire blinked in amazement and nearly rose to her feet. Just who was having this baby anyway?

After the dry turkey and yams came dessert, a soggy vanilla ice cream that had melted down in the summer heat. Ophelia stared Claire down over the rim of her coffee cup until she dutifully drank her glass of milk in one long tilt. Eleanor put down her spoon, which was the sign for her own signal corps to follow suit. Her companions rose like synchronized swimmers from the water in one movement and waited for Eleanor to affectionately hug her husband good-bye so the women could prepare for their early morning journey.

"The South will never be the same again, my dear. Don't make them chew more than they can swallow." He worried that she expected more from people than they were able to concede. With a shoulder shrug, he let Hopkins and his butler guide his tall frame into a waiting wheelchair. Comfortably settled in, he patted Eleanor's hand in a husbandly gesture before she retired to her separate bedroom. "And Babs, fly safely."

"Claire, I've been called to the White House for a cabinet meeting. I don't know how long I'll be. Could you sit in for me at War Supplies and take notes?"

"Yes, Harrison, of course." In the half year since she had acquired a set of in-laws, she had not settled upon a comfortable way of addressing them. She could hardly bring herself to call the cool and distant Ophelia "Mother"; that warm word evoked the trio of dear ladies back home. It was true, Claire had spent most of her childhood searching for a father from her elk's-horn lair, the hat rack in Field's Men's Shop. But now that she had found one who matched her paste-and-clip dream book right down to his graying temples and Scotch plaid suit, the exact "father" she had invented for herself out of men's magazines and catalogs, the word just wouldn't roll over her tongue. Besides, she reasoned, she didn't call Harry "Husband." Thankfully, in the informal atmosphere of the Roosevelt White House, where friends and family intermingled easily, she could fall in with what Tom and the others called him. So Harrison it was.

"And don't forget this afternoon we've got the Armed Services chiefs and War Production czars coming in—rubber, oil, food, and solid fuel. They're combustible."

"Yeah, and we'd better make them check their weapons at the door." Tom nervously waved a memo in his hand. "General Patton is plenty mad because the nuts and bolts he ordered for his tanks got shipped to General Bradley instead. It's going to take us months to sort that out."

"Oh, that got fixed this morning. We just bypassed regular channels." Claire's smile went from enigmatic to Olympic. "The general bought them from Sears."

Harrison lifted his head with an unconcealed look of amusement.

"And to whom were these items charged?"

"Why, to Mrs. Bradley, of course. General Patton insisted!"

The three of them threw their heads back in hearty laughter before Harrison hurriedly escaped out the door, tipping his hat to Claire. The girl just kept surprising him.

But Claire was unperturbed by the generals and businessmen who barked orders to her as they paraded through the office. She had waited on people like that all her life. And if she could help get a few screws overnight that might have taken months from proper military sources through her own initiative and salesgirl know-how, then that was just one more thing she brought to her job.

Harrison had made it clear that time was his greatest enemy. She rationalized that working for her father-in-law was a lot like working inventory week at Field's, only "taking inventory" at War Production never ended. With her organizational skills inherited from her mother and her own easygoing way with people, she was perfectly suited for the position of gopher, soother of ruffled feathers, information gatherer, and emergency substitute for her famous father-in-law at power breakfasts. She even employed some of her resourceful mother's bartering techniques, using her precious nylon coupons and meat rations to sway a secretary to ensure that her overscheduled boss got to Harrison's meeting and not to someone else's. Claire could always be counted on to find a car and good theater seats for the assistant to the secretary of anything, remembering to record the chits in her own IOU ledger. If Harrison asked, she could deliver. It was all part of her cheerful effort to get what was supposed to be finished yesterday done tomorrow. The more Claire learned, the more she was able to expedite Harrison's workload.

And, to her delight, Claire found that she was able to please the demanding Harrison.

"You're as efficient as my last two assistants put together," he told her one morning as he passed her desk. And she basked in his praise.

"We couldn't do without her," a grinning Tom joined in. "Of course both those other guys are at Guadalcanal. We might as well show you all the ropes, as it's unlikely they'll ship *you* out." He eyed the loose jumper she wore with a protruding bump the size of a lunch bucket.

"Nor you," Claire shot back half in jest. She hadn't sorted out her feelings for the bright, good-looking boy she had befriended who wasn't fighting for his country in combat. Unlike her Harry flying in harm's way, Tom with his nearsightedness and law degree was sitting out the danger in this cushy 4-F desk job.

As Claire watched Tom busy himself in paperwork, she fought off a twinge of resentment for him, flying high on the Hill in his pin-striped safety net.

On the social front lines, a truce had been called for Claire. This new Washington was a city that recognized an individual's accomplishments and not his or her place in the genetic lottery. Here she was a no-questions-asked Mrs. Harrison, and so Claire was just pleasantly surprised when she was quickly voted into the members-only Sulgrave Club not only on the basis of her illustrious last name but also on the recommendation of one Hope Ridings Miller, nominating chairwoman and keeper of the blue book. The women had become friends over dinner one evening when Harrison kept Mrs. Miller's husband at a WPB meeting until well past midnight. An apologetic Claire was able to deliver to Mrs. Ridings Miller, for her next sit-down dinner, an exiled archduke of Austria, Colonel and Mrs. Robert Guggenheim, Mrs. Nelson Rockefeller, and Crown Princess Marthe of Norway, all of whom used Harrison's office on a regular basis for important favors. Mrs. Ridings Miller was of the Washington hostess opinion that if you couldn't be a celebrity the next best thing was to feed one. Claire was happy to oblige her, and the appreciative "Hopie" became a social ally.

So Claire joined the white-gloved blue-blooded ladies for lunches and teas in the high-ceilinged rooms of the Sulgrave Club, which reverberated with gossip about the latest power alliances and women who were pushing their own war wagons and social reform. In a town where the right connections were more crucial than plasma, every door was suddenly flung open to the bright, well-married young lady with the socially and politically connected in-laws. And because of her day job, Claire also found herself one of the few women on the guest list for the dinners held at Gwendolyn Cafritz's sprawling glass house on Foxhall Road, where Washington's political elite gathered weekly, their comings and goings recorded by Cissy Patterson in meticulous detail for the *Washington Times-Herald.* Taking to the center of power like syrup to waffles, Claire Harrison was home.

The buzz of the plane's engine cut off abruptly, pulling it into a stall. The small plane hung there in midair, motionless as if trying to make up its mind whether to glide somewhere calmly to safety or to fall straight into the sea. After one tricky spiral, it leveled off and sailed through the air in a soundless descent. The churning water loomed below them, dark and fathomless. As Claire struggled to keep consciousness she turned her head to the left in slow motion to watch the pilot at work. Amelia Earhart pressed buttons and pulled knobs with deft precision and speed, although the perspiration that fell off her forehead betrayed her anxiety.

The radio was long since gone, so there was no way to let anyone know what was happening to them. Despite Amelia's gallant attempts, they were going down. The butterflies in Claire's belly bumped around and then she felt a drop as if half of her body weight was shifting, putting unbearable pressure on her groin and thighs. A heavy ache pulsed through her body as if an airplane part had landed on her lap. She looked at Amelia, who had stopped working the controls and, running her fingers through her tousled hair, turned to grin at Claire, mouthing the words, "You'll be okay."

And then they were in the water. Claire had no idea the Pacific Ocean would be so warm, like foot-soaking water heated in a teakettle rushing and whirling around her and pouring down her legs, which were numbed. The water was everywhere and Claire was sinking deeper into its pull until she heard Amelia's voice somewhere above her and struggled to lift herself up.

When she awoke, Claire was covered in sticky perspiration and was startled to see that the warm water that had drenched the sheets under her was coming from between her legs. Her water had broken and the first heavy pains of labor had pushed her out of a deep, dreamy slumber, the kind only a pregnant woman falls into near the end of her term and from which it is almost impossible to rouse her, even with doorbells, phones, and fire alarms.

Instead of feeling panicky, Claire felt surprisingly calm despite the soaked sheets and the flooded couch. When she stood, a waterfall of warmth poured down her legs, soaking her nightgown and drowning her feet.

Feeling light-headed and loopy, she saw no need to hurry as she brushed her hair back, pressed a cold washcloth to her temples, and threw off her drenched nightclothes, substituting them for a sleeveless dress and a matching ribbon for her hair. After all, Amelia had said everything would be all right. She winced as a sharp pain jabbed her in the lower back, and she could hardly believe her own presence of mind as she picked up the phone to call her doctor, vaguely making out his home number lying alongside the alarm clock. Four A.M. She apologized for disturbing him but she explained about the sheets and her water. He laughed kindly in his sleepy voice and told her to meet him at the hospital.

She packed her battered Amelia Earhart overnight bag, put a trench coat over the back of her dress, which was already nearly soaked clear through, and on very unsteady legs went to Harrison's door. She tried to knock but her fists felt so heavy she turned away and stumbled to Ophelia's door, where she turned the knob and stood over her mother-in-law until she awakened with a start. From then on it was Ophelia's show.

It infuriated Claire that Ophelia had seen the baby before she had. In fact, Ophelia had seen the baby even before the doctors, delivery nurses, and all-seeing God Himself. Seated at the foot of the delivery table with her gloved hands folded, wearing a silk dress and a straw hat, she had observed Claire's labor like a stony-faced theater critic, glued to her chair, an imperial witness to her grandbaby's birth. Later, Claire would swear that just before they put the ether mask over her face, sending her into twilight sleep, she had caught a crazy glimpse of her mother-in-law donning a coal miner's hat, the kind with a light on top, so that Ophelia could better peer into the birth cavity from her best seat in the house, front row center.

When she awoke in the dry, starched sheets of the hospital bed, she was thirsty. Moreover, she was curious. She quenched her thirst first with a few sips of ice water through a glass straw and then lurched up with a panicky start to find herself with a flattened belly. She ran her hands over her stomach again to convince herself it was not a dream. The baby inside was gone.

"Where is my baby?" Claire asked the nurse, still looking around the room as if they had hidden something from her. "Can I have my baby?"

The gray-haired pediatrician, who was a social friend of Ophelia's, broke the news.

"It's a healthy baby girl for the Harrisons!"

What was with this "Harrisons" stuff? Claire wondered with a trace of irritation. This was *her* baby's birth, not a relay tag team's. And then it registered.

A healthy *girl.*

"May I see her?" she asked quietly, suddenly crestfallen that she had let down the team. A girl.

"As soon as Ophelia's done fussing down at the nursery. Are you planning to breast-feed?" She hadn't, but perhaps she should. Surely Ophelia couldn't do that.

"Why yes."

"So many of you modern girls prefer not to these days. The formulas are excellent nourishment. As good as mother's milk."

"Is everything all right with . . ." Claire stumbled as her question remained awkwardly suspended and incomplete. What was she going to call the baby? They had all assumed it would be William Henry Harrison VI. She slipped her arms into her bed jacket, a gift from Slim, and swung her hair over the lace collar.

"You have a beautiful baby girl, Claire, and she's perfectly healthy. Perfect, in fact, in every way. He beamed a reassuring look in her direction and flipped a page on her chart as he started out the door. Then he turned on a dime, his stethoscope knocking against his chest. "Are there many redheads in your family?"

Claire shook her head. "Why, Dr. Hastings?"

"Because your daughter looks so much like her grandmother, feature for feature. I thought that maybe the red hair came from your folks."

Claire responded with such a spontaneous look of alarm on her face that he lingered for a moment longer.

"Of course, many towheads are born with reddish hair and after a few months' time the first hair falls out and we get the real color. Congratulations on your daughter, my dear."

Claire nodded, her hormones and hurt feelings welling tears into her eyes. She was supposed to have delivered a boy and instead she had presented the Harrisons with a redheaded girl who would be bald in a matter of weeks. She hoped Harrison wouldn't be disappointed. Or Harry.

Ophelia was jubilant. Her pink-cheeked grandbaby had actually stretched out for her with her tiny arms. Even Dr. Hastings had witnessed it. Sara Woolsey Harrison, with a fine set of lungs and a bright-red corona crowning her head, was whisked from the hospital and ensconced in Tuxedo to be attended to by a chorus of nurses, nannies, and society pediatricians. Ophelia had insisted upon "Woolsey," it being her own mother's maiden name, and "Sara" was a grand gesture honoring President Roosevelt's mother, deceased nearly a year to the day of her namesake's birth. How could Claire argue with that? Ophelia promised her she could name the next one as she sat busily opening up baby gifts.

Claire watched her as Ophelia scissored her way through the pretty ribbons, wondering if she would ever be able to cut through the Harrison traditions that were rolling right over her. Claire agreed to everything in order to keep the peace. For now, Sara's apple cheeks and her milky baby smells eased any friction at Charlotte Hall.

Even the recessive red hair was assimilated into Harrison family lore as portraits of two distant ancestors, formerly relegated to the quiet basement, were dusted off and relocated to the grand foyer's walls because of their like-colored hair. There they were hung on either side of the Titian with its own russet-haired beauties. Claire and Sara's names were added to the traditional Harrison family greeting card to be sent that December. This year the Christmas message featured the priceless foyer masterpiece on its front, designed by Tiffany & Co. especially to Ophelia's specifications.

Peace in the New Year read the gold-letter engraved sentiment inside. Determined to preserve it, Claire chose not to share with Mrs. Harrison, Sr., the resolution to the mystery surrounding baby Sara's red hair. Her father's mother had red hair, Violet had whispered, careful not to let the Aunties overhear; and some of the Organ cousins had purportedly been carrot tops, too. Her mother's news had made Claire feel infinitely better. She had had a hand in creating Sara after all.

The family routine they fell into was ultimately to everyone's liking. Ophelia, Harrison, Harry (by letter), and finally Claire had all agreed it was the best choice. Even little Sara had had a voice.

After a few weeks back at Charlotte Hall, Claire was finally made to realize that what it took to raise a Harrison was a team. Whereas Claire had originally thought she and the baby would move into the Willard so she could continue her war work and wait for her husband, her romantic balloon was burst by a hundred pin-sharp reasons. The air in Tuxedo was fresher—there was no smog, no pollution, and no heavy humidity hanging in the air to pollute Sara's little lungs. Charlotte Hall's gardeners would grow the vegetables and fruits fresh in the garden, or the winter greenhouse, straight from the stalk to the plate, just as Harry had been nourished, and hadn't *he* turned out a healthy specimen.

Then there was the surprise-attack issue. If the Japanese or Germans ever made it over again—Remember Pearl Harbor!—wouldn't they shell Washington before they bombed the peaceful idyll of Tuxedo Park? As all his inner circle knew, even the president kept a gas mask hanging from the side of his wheelchair, just in case. And why would Claire want to give up the work she was so good at, especially now that Harrison had requested that she assist him in highly sensitive dealings conducted from his White House office?

Claire had agreed to think about it and even sought Anna Roosevelt's thoughts on the matter when, over a cheese soufflé lunch at the Sulgrave, she had suddenly asked the president's daughter to be little Sara's godmother, realizing that since moving to Washington she had been living in a man's world and hadn't made any other good female friends. The two women, following their first meeting, had bonded instantly. Like Claire, Anna had felt frustrated and impatient being the only member of her family excluded from the great events of the war. And like Claire, she had been determined to find relevant work and to help the war effort in a meaningful way. For the last few months she had been working in her father's White House office.

"But you must come to work in the White House!" Anna said, her eyes shining like a schoolgirl's. "Don't you know it's lonely being the lowest man—I mean lady—on the totem pole. Since you're younger than I . . . I'll finally have someone to boss around." She flashed the famous Roosevelt grin. "It's almost like a promotion! Oh, please do!" Anna reached across the table. "We'll have such fun!"

Claire's decision was temporarily pushed aside when that fall she welcomed President and Mrs. Roosevelt to Sara's christening. Claire's face was radiant as she watched Anna hold the child in front of the golden baptismal bowl, Sara resplendent in Harry's antique lace christening gown. And it was with a lump of pride in her chest that she was able to introduce an overjoyed Auntie Wren to her heroine Eleanor Roosevelt, as she recorded the moment and all the day's highlights on her Kodak box camera so Claire could send the snaps to Harry. Violet, elegantly dressed in her eponymous color from head to toe, and Slim, glamorous and sophisticated in her chic black suit with ropes of costume pearls wound around her neck and wrists, were enlisted right on the steps of Tuxedo's Presbyterian church by Ophelia, all business once the ceremony was over, to support her wartime plan for bringing up Sara. Claire would work Mondays through Thursdays at the Capitol, for as long as the war continued, arriving back in Tuxedo by noon Friday to spend uninterrupted time with her daughter until Monday morning.

"After all," trilled Ophelia, glancing at the other two Aunties, "you yourselves were working mothers, and look how well your Claire has done." Ophelia made her case with a sharpshooter's precision. Bull's-eye, thought Claire as she watched the flattered ladies vigorously and noisily signal their approval. Even E.R. had agreed, in a short handwritten note. While extolling the joys of motherhood, she reminded Claire that in times like these, everyone had to make sacrifices. Claire just wasn't sure who would be giving up more, her or the baby.

Nevertheless, it was a plan. Full of promise, mothering, excitement, and productivity. And in Claire's mind the arrangements were sealed when after four weeks Sara had simply refused her mother's milking breast, pushing the primed nipple away with her tiny fist and making a sour face and pursing her lips like a finicky gourmet. Looking up at Claire fitfully with those dark, arrogant Ophelia-like eyes, her moon-faced daughter had gone on an ear-piercing crying jag until nurse number two had calmed her baby with a prewarmed bottle of formula that just happened to be in her apron pocket. Claire watched in surprise as Sara hungrily sucked from it as though it was her beverage of choice. And so a schedule was arranged and they all followed it like the civilized people they were.

Deep down in her heart, Claire knew that a conspiracy of Ophelia's nurses had secretly wooed and weaned the infant away with their vanilla-scented formula. The nurses were white-uniformed tricksters in Ophelia's army—an army the Aunties had unwittingly joined as outlying troops in support of Ophelia's common sense and against which Claire felt she had no defense. In almost an act of revenge Claire's breasts had burst into bloom, voluptuous forever, full of milk as a regular reminder of just who the real mother was.

Secretly, Claire was glad her new full, creamy bosoms seemed to have no intention of returning to their natural prematernity rosebud size. It brought a private smile to her lips as she assessed her altered shape in the mirror naked, admiring her transfiguration. With her long, slim legs, thin-boned body, high aquiline nose, and recently found composure, the new high bosom and motherhood had turned Claire into what she had only stood on the precipice of before: a full-blown beauty.

It was with new confidence then, head up, posture perfect that she walked up the marble stairs of the old Executive Building to the headquarters of War Production on a glorious October morning her first week back. Ambivalent as she may have been about leaving Sara, she had to admit it felt good to be in Washington again with its high-pitched energy and sorry shortage of qualified workers.

Tom wolf-whistled as Claire strode into the door in her new custom-cut suit and hand-stitched high heels.

"Is this a Hollywood goddess come to sell us war bonds? No, wait," he said, "it's Gene Tierney, isn't it? Gosh, Miss Tierney, you're looking good."

"Oh Tom, you're such a child." Claire pushed him away with a nonchalant wave of her hand and then with the other hand brushed a lustrous Lauren Bacall wave out of her eyes. The suit did flatter her new figure, and she'd sensibly bought three of them, identical, so she'd always look fresh and smart but not like she owned an extravagantly huge wardrobe.

His grin was unstoppable. "Let me guess. There's two of you now, the motherly one back in Tuxedo and the fancy glamor-puss here."

For someone who'd never really had a platonic friend, though, Tom had become the closest thing to it. Secretly, Claire was glad he noticed the effort she had put into her appearance.

"Is Harrison in yet?" She pulled off her brand-new kid gloves that matched her suit.

"Nope. Left for London with Averell Harriman this morning. I'd say, ten days."

Claire suddenly felt let down. Harrison could have told her, she thought. She was supposed to have attended a dinner meeting with him this evening. The frown on her face echoed the down-stitched darts on her jacket. She'd assumed that with her new higher-security clearance she could share everything with Harrison. Claire was thinking so hard she didn't even hear Tom.

"I said, there's a new batch of Harry letters here. Came with the morning drop."

Claire brightened a little and took the packet. One of the perks of being politically connected was that things came to you quickly that others had to wait for. But Harry's letters had become so much the same of late; she held the stack unopened in her hand for a moment, as if weighing them for the postage. She didn't want to be pulled into Harry's war, with its injuries and bloody backdrops, just yet. Not when they were in Washington fighting so hard on their own front. Not when she needed him here at home to fight for her and her baby.

Because of delays with military mail, his letters were full of news she'd already known about for weeks. On the other hand, he somehow always had Ophelia's nursery news even before Claire could cheerfully put it down on paper herself. She sighed. She also didn't want to feel the pressure of his poemlike dreams neatly scribbled across the pages in his Ivy League penmanship. Dreams that featured Harry, Sara, and Claire, unrealistically perfect in their red brick house connected by a passageway to Ophelia's. She hadn't realized how attached Harry was to his mother.

Harry was still writing to Claire like she was the little girl back home when in only fifteen months' time she had developed into a woman. Now she was a mother and a trusted intelligence aide with White House security clearance, as well as possessing a permanent place card at the best dinners in town.

"What, no tearing through your husband's sweet nothings?"

"Look, any more wisecracks and I'm going to turn you in to your friendly draft board and tell them there's nothing wrong with your eyesight. In fact, I shall recommend that they send you straight to the front so you don't have to strain your baby blues looking for the enemy." She batted her own eyes at him as she put the letters into her pocketbook, snapping the clasp shut. She'd read them later. There was real work to do now.

"Where's the Chrysler folder? Isn't Knudson scheduled for today?" she snapped at him. Chrysler and the rest of America's automotive giants were high on Harrison's patriots list. King Bees was how she and Harrison referred to them. The industry that had once built four million cars a year was now building three-fourths of the nation's aircraft engines, one-half of all its tanks, and one-third of all machine guns.

"Yep. And a dinner with the three big grand pooh-bahs from Detroit. Guess with Harrison and Harriman dodging dinner bombs with Churchill that makes you tonight's host . . er, hostess." He ran a long look up and down her new figure. Tom's grin was unbearably toothy, his banter reminding her how much she had missed their verbal sparring. Nanny talk and arguments with Ophelia over puréed peaches had left her intellectually parched. With a pang of disappointment she realized just how much she had been looking forward to hosting this dinner with Harrison tonight.

She peeked into his empty office, hoping he hadn't really left. Ten days without Harrison would be ten long days. She tapped her red polished fingernails against his stapler with a rat-a-tat sound. Impatiently she decided to open the first of Harry's letters. It was addressed to Sara Woolsey Harrison and was a month late in arriving.

> *My darling Sara,*
>
> *I know your dear Mother and Grandmother will have to read this for you, but I feel I must spell out my joy at knowing you exist. Because of the love that your Mother and I share, you, little Sara, the miracle of new life, have come to be. Although we have not yet met, I can assure you that as your Father, I will be more attentive and gallant than any knight in the fairy tales your Mother and Grandmother read to you in your nursery. A nursery, my sweet daughter, in which I slept and dreamed when I was small and your Grandmother . . .*

There was more but Claire didn't want to be late for her Chrysler meeting, and then she was off to the Cafritzes' for a reception in honor of the Luces. She couldn't wait to meet Clare Boothe Luce.

That night after dinner, with tank talk and proposed landing dates reeling through her brain, Claire lay in her hotel bed unable to sleep. A batch of Harry's letters was strewn around her like amulets evoked in a magic spell to conjure up a distant lover. It worried her that some days she was unable to imagine his face or even remember the sound of his voice. But it bothered her even more that an exact phrase from his letters would be used by Ophelia to criticize her.

Strange, it was as if the war that had brought them together was now conspiring to drive them apart. Privy to top-secret information with her new security clearance, she couldn't share with him the work that was so important to her, so she stuck to her idle, chatty reports about the child she adored but who preferred Ophelia's nanny squad to her hand these days. Keeping secrets became part of her job even if it put up another wall between her and Harry. She feared that the distance between Harry and herself was growing far greater than the distance between the Potomac and the Pacific.

She wished she could tell him about her work. She wished he could see her now. How accomplished and capable she had become. How much she had learned. Indeed, how very different she was from the unsure, unworldly girl he had fallen in love with in a forty-eight-hour courtship. Deep in her heart she knew the truth: If they had met today, they probably would never have married. Under normal circumstances Ophelia would never have allowed it. It all seemed a thousand storybook pages ago. Had they really been so much in love? Or had Harry married her just to get into the war? Was this child born out of their passion? Or had a baby been a son's present for his mother, part of some cold family bargain? The only real thing to her these days was her war work, and it consumed her.

Harry. She needed to see him. Know he was real. Touch him and talk to him. If only the two of them could be together with their daughter. Then everything would fall into place again. She puffed up two pillows and sat up higher in bed, wondering if his sleeping quarters were comfortable, and why it was that she had never dreamed about him.

Claire felt tremendous loyalty toward Harry; because of him, all this had happened to her. She tried to find a word for what she really felt for him. Tenderness . . . and gratitude. But she was somebody else now and you didn't dream about people to whom you merely felt grateful.

She switched on the light. She wasn't being fair. Just because she had grown up, the spell shouldn't be broken. She read a second letter.

But Harry's letters had all the forced humor of a flat gin fizz. He was flying, bonding, and bombing. He was bonding, all right. His "gang" was all there when in a third letter Harry was calling her "Little Claire" and his buddies Buzzy and Flip had both signed it as well, asking her to send some stationery from the White House so they could requisition more beer from headquarters. It was clear "the bombers" were bombed. She shook her head, laughing. She could be a good sport and read between the lines. They were obviously drunk on beer and celebrating a tough mission completed. But the cerebral side of her couldn't help wondering which one she was married to. Larry, Curly, or Mo. Flip, Buzzy, or Harry. They were kids.

Harrison was concerned. Twice in the last fortnight Claire had casually wandered into his dreams in the short sleeps he allowed himself. That graceful form so familiar to him had stood on a hill behind Charlotte Hall waving a soft, billowy scarf. And he had been glad to see her there.

This troubled him. And so he did what any high-principled man schooled in serving God and Country would do.

He fled.

"Tom, can you pack up for me? London again, I'm afraid." On the other hand, Harrison reasoned, once his flying boat was safely halfway across the Atlantic, it seemed totally logical that Claire should be part of his fitful slumber during these days when his mind was doubled over with the numbers of supplies that hadn't

been delivered in time. And Claire was just part of his overcir-
cuited workday. Hadn't he dreamed about Eleanor Roosevelt a
few nights before? And he hadn't given that nocturnal visit a moment's pause. He was sure he was uncharacteristically overdrama-
tizing. That was all. The Stateside version of battle fatigue must
be what he was suffering from. Like the flu. There was nothing
even remotely pertinent about an overworked middle-aged man's
dreams. He dismissed the whole business as he and Harriman
smoked their Cuban cigars and read the latest telexes in the thin,
pointed light of the airplane. A few more hours, God willing, and
they'd be in London.

England was a distraction. Harrison had friends here and the
highest regard for even the ordinary Londoners who had stoically
suffered years of blackouts, the terrible drone of the buzz bombs,
and the more horrible silences that came just before a hit. There
was a bravado bred into the Brits that Harrison admired. One
night after a particularly wearying working dinner at Churchill's
country house, Chequers, with Harriman and an assortment of
Allied generals and military strategists, Churchill's wife,
Clementine, and their daughter-in-law Pamela joined them. It
was eight-thirty and Churchill looked exhausted, but the perky
Pamela announced that they had a feature film for the evening's
entertainment and everyone should grab their overcoats, because
it was cold in the cinema room.

Harrison sat down with a whiskey and soda and a small bowl
of popcorn. The movie was a British film, long, dull, and very
badly acted. So Harrison watched Churchill's daughter-in-law instead as she played hostess in the darkened room—shy
Clementine having chosen to turn in early—lighting cigars,
making everyone feel comfortable, and lifting the mood.

Watching Pamela hover over her father-in-law as she pulled a
blanket over his shoulders with such daughterly concern made
Harrison forget his own overblown worries. Sometimes it took

putting an ocean between you and a problem to see it clearly, he
assured himself, and filed it along with the other solved problems
in his briefcase.

Claire arrived early. She took the six A.M. train from Washington
to Grand Central and then the commuter to Tuxedo. The spring
weather was fine, and she longed to hold her child in her arms. A
walk around the grounds, the dogs on either side of Sara's high-
wheeled Silver Cross carriage, and a picnic for all of them were
uppermost in her mind. She paid the taxi driver who had brought
her up from the station to the front of Charlotte Hall's iron gates
and generously overtipped him. Unannounced, in her eagerness,
she had taken the quickest way instead of calling the house for a
lift.

She carried no luggage, just a huggable teddy bear under her
arm, and as the morning was so peaceful, she thought she'd walk
the three-quarter-mile driveway to the house. The front gates
were locked, she discovered as she jostled them. Standing on her
tiptoes, Claire tried to peer into the gatehouse, but the heavy
drapes were drawn. It was a little after eleven and she had told
Ophelia she'd arrive around suppertime. Obviously the Harrison
security force was in operation.

Claire turned and walked back down Winding Way Road a bit
until she got to the place where the sculpted boxwood substituted
for the property fence, and slipped in through a break in the
corduroy-thick hedges, careful not to snag Teddy on the poker-
sharp branches. She wished she hadn't. A demon dog, all black
sleekness and a gnash of white teeth, flew barreling down the
road, stirring up gravel dust as she stood there in the open like a
carnival-duck target. She let out a scream and, covering her face
with the bear, tried to roll herself back into the bushes.

Something sharp bit into Claire's leg and she cried out in pain
before a series of men's names were shouted and then the dog
called off her with a hysterical "Down, Hecker."

When she regained consciousness, she was lying in her room, Ophelia coolly appraising her condition.

"It's for Sara's protection. And security for the rest of us," she explained, less than sympathetically. "There have been incidents. Harrison is in the paper so much and everyone knows he has top-secret access and of course there was the Lindbergh kidnapping way back and one of the . . ." Ophelia blathered on.

"I'm the mother. Not a kidnapper."

"You arrived on your own schedule without any regard for how it might upset ours and we cannot run a smooth household with people popping in under the bushes. With your name splashed all over the society pages it's a wonder we haven't been burglarized." Ophelia sneered. "And with Churchill due on Monday with half the Cabinet, we had to put in security measures."

"Please bring Sara in." Claire was feeling groggy. The shots the doctor had given her were making it difficult to stay awake.

Nanny Bridget brought a skittish Sara to the door, but the two-year-old clung stubbornly to the doorjamb, shaking her red curls and refusing to go in; the smell of alcohol swabs and her mother's leg sewn up frightening her. Claire fell off to sleep and when she awakened, it was already dark outside. She thought she was alone until Nanny Bridget rose from the shadows.

"Mr. Harrison called from overseas." She switched on the lamp.

"Harry?"

"*Mr.* Harrison. He's had the dog removed because of you. You have a visitor."

As Tom entered the room he was wearing a comforting grin. "These are from the boss." He laid the long bouquet of cut flowers across her bed.

"Oh, they're lovely." Claire reached down to pick them up.

"Well, I know Pam Churchill keeps her son, young Winston, out in the country while she works in London, but I don't think they turn the dogs on her when she drives out to visit."

"Hush, Tom. It was an accident, not an incident. I just want to forget about it, okay? And not a word to the papers. It would embarrass Harrison."

"Oh, right. Sure. Why didn't I think of that? So, which foot did they amputate, the left or the right?"

"You goof. It's just a scratch. Fourteen stitches isn't much. Could you ask the nurse to come in? I want to get up and see Sara. Go have your tea with Ophelia."

Claire maneuvered herself clumsily onto her crutches and into the nursery. The pain she felt when she saw the room was sharper than the one the damned dog had inflicted on her. Her expression was one of disbelief. All of her pretty handiwork, balloons, planes, and drawings had been wiped out and painted over since last week's visit. She felt as though she had been erased.

Instead the nursery had become a pastel carousel of pink and green unicorns and horses framed by scalloped borders like an outdoor awning at the Tuxedo country club.

"Lovely, isn't it, Miss Claire?" Nanny number two appeared in the doorway with an armful of freshly laundered diapers. "Sara loves her horsies, and now everything's spruced up for the big company coming."

Claire burst into tears. But that was to be expected, Ophelia told the staff. The Doberman had frightened her out of her wits, but she'd be just fine after a few days' rest.

After ten days in Tuxedo with Sara, Ophelia, the nurses, and picnic parties that included the visiting dignitaries, Claire's leg was as good as new. She practically ran back to Washington.

The learning curve in wartime Washington was by necessity driven by speed. Over the next turbulent year, Claire learned by running alongside Harrison's heels. And one of the things she learned was that underneath his proper, tweed facade, Harrison had the guts of a truck driver.

Throughout the past several months he had been called upon

to make countless important war decisions and now, in January 1945, he was needed more than ever. With supplies running low, FDR had made it Harrison's job to oversee and coordinate what the military needed with what private industry could manufacture. The pressure upon Harrison was enormous, and he was being badgered from every direction. To Claire, it seemed like the whole future of the free world rested solely on her father-in-law's already burdened shoulders. As Harrison sped up his work and his metabolism, Claire made herself even more available to him; she was more devoted to him than if she'd been his own flesh and blood. Shared secrets and mutual respect bonded them. The war was depending on Harrison, and Claire protected him like a doting hawk. Some days they would be at the office until well past midnight, and when his schedule couldn't be stretched an iota more, she would step in after conveying Harrison's apologies, pass out his agenda for the meeting, and just usher him in for the closing. She protected him and his time and, as she grew to understand him better, revered him all the more.

Sometimes the things she did were of a more personal nature. She would happily make sure his cigar pouch was replenished, pushing the Havanas into place one by one, or simply add lighter fluid to the silver ribbed lighter that carried his monogram, a gift from Ophelia.

Today, sitting rod-straight on the edge of her chair, wearing one of her custom signature suits, Claire had only to wave a folder and lift an eyebrow to get his attention. They had their own silent language by now. Once she knew she had his attention, a fact no one else could detect, she slowly raised a manila folder with a blue sticker to her shoulder, indicating that the text of his prepared remarks was now obsolete.

A flurry of new telexes had turned their latest figures upside down, and if Harrison was to keep the public confidence alive on the president's behalf, he couldn't be a day late in the updates delivered at this news briefing.

Harrison understood her movements immediately. What others saw was the aristocratic war materials czar, one of the president's chief advisers, quietly acknowledging the elegant young woman in a superbly cut suit and a string of pearls worn short. What they didn't see was him ad-lib his speech until the folder would be handed to him by Tom or a page, as she never stepped on the podium herself; until he had the proper corrections about the latest supplies and delivered the war news in his serious, undramatic way. She would stay in her seat and listen, feeling his sincerity and solemnity quiet the room as he spoke. He would single out a particular face in the audience, and by explaining his case to that single individual, hold the rest of the room.

She marveled at how in his quiet way he was imposing and commanded not only silence among the unruly press corps, but also respect. Sitting straight-backed on the edge of her chair, her legs crossed at the ankles, her hair softly arranged around her heart-shaped face, Claire was as in awe of Harrison's talents as if he had been Frank Sinatra crooning at the mike to the bobby soxer she could have been. As Tom hurriedly entered the room, head down, with mimeographed sheets of the immediate changes to hand out to the newspaperpeople, he looked from his boss to Claire and stifled a frown. Was he the only one of them who could see what was happening?

"You did wonderfully well. I expect we'll have national coverage of the war materials czar's encouraging remarks." Claire spoke with quiet adulation. "And then the war materials czar can push Ford and Chrysler to full capacity."

Harrison leaned his head in her direction as she whispered the names of the three newly appointed heads of the latest alphabet agencies, who were walking directly toward them in the congressional hallway. Then Harrison held out his hand in greeting, calling each new face by name as they approached him.

Claire spoke softly into his ear, a private reminder even Tom couldn't hear as he closely flanked Harrison's other side, but

Harrison was nodding and almost cracked a smile. In a normal voice Claire continued, "The president's secretary called and asked if you might join him for a quiet supper tonight. E.R.'s away. The Red Cross trip. She's in uniform this time and the soldiers are loving it. Shall I see if Ophelia wants to join you?" Her eyes were pooled in sincerity.

"Ophelia's with Eleanor. Boarded the train at the last minute. She's in a Red Cross uniform too." It was impossible to detect either sarcasm or disappointment in his flat tone. "But tell them yes and that I'm bringing the other Mrs. Harrison."

"Oh, how very nice of you to include me. Thank you. Perhaps Anna can come as well."

Claire had cultivated her new voice to perfection, a soft voice that reeked of culture, refinement, and while not exactly Vassar or Franklin's Hyde Park, it was a lovely patois of all the best places but did not tether her to any particular geography. Her newsy chatter that she stored up to amuse Harrison was now delivered in a musical medley of twangy midwestern clarity with certain phrases elongated in Tuxedo's high-tea tony vowels. She had observed that in Washington a quality voice could cover a mountain of misinformation.

Claire and Tom had to hurry to keep up with the agile Harrison as they climbed a steep well of white marble stairs and followed after his trim figure until he darted into the offices of the senator from Michigan. They walked on, just the two of them, to the parking area, Claire turning a head or two as they hurried down the Capitol steps. One step from the bottom she turned to Tom and asked, "Who's Lucy Mercer?"

"Why?"

"She's lunching with the president today."

Tom looked around the white-stuccoed driveway and the park beyond to see if any temporary recruiting booths hadn't sprung up nearby. He suddenly felt an urge to join the army, just to be somewhere safe. He could see clearly now. He jammed his hands into his trouser pockets as he walked in long strides with his head down, just like he was looking for land mines ahead. And then he told a startled Claire the story of President Roosevelt and his great love affair with Lucy Mercer.

It was an oysters-and-bourbon kind of evening. There were candles on the table, which was set with the floral presidential china, and a second course of roasted beef and wine. But it wasn't the food or the flowers that mattered. It was the gay, romantic mood that pervaded the room.

"Watch *me*. It's better to use your fingers and let the little suckers just slide down your throat." The president demonstrated his oyster technique with flair.

"Franklin, show us again." Lucy Mercer spoke in a soft, husky voice underscored with mirth. "It takes a former secretary of the navy to know the best way to swallow a fish."

"Yes, that's me. Poseidon of the sea!" FDR flashed his famous grin.

The president seemed to have lost twenty years in as many hours. Where two nights before Claire and Harrison had sat up with Eleanor and the president as he fought a fever, tonight FDR had the look of a young man refreshed. Lucy Mercer Rutherfurd was seated to his right. Eleanor's chair was left empty, but it was obvious to everyone there that the president's old flame was the reason for the color in his cheeks. Lucy's grace and beauty belied her years, and her easy laugh and comfortable silences made the room feel like all the windows had been thrown open to let the springtime tumble in. *She* was the perfume that was scenting the room.

The president himself had picked Lucy up at the station. Anna had made the arrangements, betraying her mother unthinkably, and Claire, observing the look of puppy love on the president's face, wondered at it all. So the man who was the moral beacon for a nation, Eleanor's husband and the father of five, whose fireside wisdom inspired millions and who just days before had begun his unprecedented fourth term in office, was a man just like any other, with the same back-street desires of a Cyrus Pettibone.

"If Franklin hadn't been so politically ambitious, he probably would have divorced Eleanor for Lucy." Tom's gossipy words rang in Claire's ears. "His mother threatened to disinherit him if he did. That would have cost him not only all the money, but his beloved Hyde Park and his career as well. It cost him plenty anyhow. Even though he promised Eleanor he would never see Lucy again, they say the marriage has never been the same."

Claire looked over at the elegant, well-bred Mrs. Rutherfurd, with her exquisite manners and skin the color of freshly fallen snow. Her fair complexion was accentuated by the black lace cowl circling her long neck, a subtle reminder of her recent widowhood. Speculation aside, Anna assured her that Lucy Mercer Rutherfurd had genuinely grieved for the much older, wealthy man she had married on the rebound.

"Lucy, do you mind if I tell that story about the time we motored up to Allegheny?"

She shook her head, never taking her eyes off him.

Reserved in a soft, feminine way and wearing a lovely smile, Lucy seemed to relax the president with her very presence. Claire hadn't heard that jovial bellow in a long time. Lucy Mercer was tonic. Above all, she was a good listener, even when it was apparent that she was hearing a story for the umpteenth time. It almost made it easier for her to laugh in just the right places. Claire noticed how opposite she was from the vital Eleanor. Lucy Mercer sat listening raptly to FDR, never once interrupting him whether he was talking about vermouth or Vermont, on which both subjects Eleanor held dissenting opinions. And when the man who had lost his waning appetite called out for seconds, Claire was sold. She realized that in her gentle way, Lucy was more alluring than any woman she had ever encountered. For some men, a great listener was as enticing as a great pair of legs.

She also realized that there were two kinds of women in the world: the Eleanors and the Lucys. Violet was an Eleanor and Slim a Lucy, but which one in this time and in this place was Claire? She blushed. Was it possible to be a little bit of both? Franklin was now telling the story about a weekend drive they had taken together, years ago, before she was even born. It kindled a hint of fire in Lucy's warm blue eyes, but it was a flame that sparked only for Franklin. And while she politely engaged her other dinner companions in conversation from time to time, her attention was on FDR and undivided.

Claire leaned over to Harrison to see if he too had fallen under Lucy's spell.

She had developed a sensitivity for reading his moods. But all she picked up tonight was the pleasure he was taking in seeing his great friend buoyant again and almost carefree. It made her smile.

Relieved, Claire picked up the coffeepot to refill Harrison's cup just as he reached over to fill it himself. Their fingers touched and one or the other let them linger lightly for a moment, although they didn't look at one another.

Their closeness to each other had become casual and familiar. But somehow the accidental contact seemed different in this candlelit setting. Tonight when Harrison had leaned over to speak quietly into her ear, a simple act he had done a thousand times before, she could feel his warm breath on the back of her neck and it disquieted her.

Their wineglasses refilled, an unusual occurrence at the White House, Franklin toasted his guest. Anna hesitated but for a moment before lifting her glass. Her eyes met Claire's in a look that said "I'll do whatever I have to do to keep my father well. Whatever it takes," apparently even if it meant arranging lighthearted evenings with a woman her mother despised.

Claire felt ashamed that she had even questioned her friend's judgment. She appreciated the tremendous risk Anna took when she conspired to bring Lucy into her mother's house, and how crushed Eleanor would be if she knew.

"To bombs and liaisons!" said the president, and they all raised their glasses.

And anyway, Claire thought, sipping her wine, who was she to criticize? How many times had she run interference for Slim and Cyrus? Had she forgotten that it was Slim who had taught her to "take love where you find it"?

When Claire said good night to the president, he hugged even her in a rare embrace, his strong upper body enfolding her from his armless wheelchair, so great was his exuberance.

"It was lovely to meet you, my dear." Lucy's handshake was wraithlike and fleeting, as if she were a merry ghost they had all dreamed up.

Franklin's gay mood was affecting them all like a third glass of champagne. The festive high accompanied Harrison and Claire out the door and down Roosevelt's private elevator. But when Harrison reached for her elbow to help her into the car, he took it with such force that she thought about making a wisecrack that escorting a lady home was not a contact sport. She didn't because that was a joking-Eleanor thing to say and she was still in the Lucy Mercer moment.

As they sat in the front seat together, Harrison at the wheel, it occurred to Claire that going back to the hotel alone, just the two of them, something they had done hundreds of times before, suddenly felt awkward. Ophelia seldom spent the night at the Willard anymore. She traveled a lot with Eleanor now. Tonight they were in New York for a meeting of the European Children's Refugee Fund along with Mr. Marshall Field IV, who was president of the organization. The two women would be staying over at the apartment Eleanor kept for herself in Greenwich Village.

Harrison seemed to be deep in thought. He drove almost too fast down Pennsylvania Avenue; for once the traffic was unusually light.

Claire broke the silence. "Anna told me tonight that it looks like Stalin will be bringing his daughter to Yalta, too." The Yalta conference was in February, in less than a fortnight, and the allied leaders were meeting in Russia for crucial talks. Harrison had planned to take Ophelia, but with Churchill, Roosevelt, Stalin, and Averell Harriman all bringing their daughters, it was turning into a girls' international slumber party. Ophelia complained that she wanted no part of it, and so Claire was substituted.

"I'm going to call State again tomorrow and see if I can get that itinerary out of them. As I understand it, the Russians keep changing the schedule. February in Russia. Whose idea was that? Do you suppose we'll be dressing for dinner or just dressing to stay warm?" Claire turned to Harrison and whimsically fought off an imaginary chill.

As the car pulled under the canopy of the hotel, the light illuminated Claire's face in the darkness. Harrison was staring at her as if he were seeing her for the first time.

Claire shifted in her seat self-consciously and then moved to her side of the door.

He stiffly handed the keys to the doorman, letting Claire fend for herself, and as they walked to the elevator, he stopped at the desk to check his messages. There were half a dozen. Harrison flipped through them as they rode up in silence. Turning the key in the door to their room, he switched on the ceiling lights as she crossed the living room to relight the fire. Having stirred the flame, she stood warming her back, ready to fix him a nightcap, or take dictation, or whatever would drive away the problem that was obviously distracting him. He hadn't said a word to her since they'd left the White House.

"Shall I put up some coffee for us?" She let her overcoat fall to the couch as she knelt down to pick up the new message that had been slipped under the door. She was unprepared for what happened next. Harrison stepped between her and the door and lifted her by her shoulders. For a crazy minute she couldn't tell if he was drawing her closer or pushing her away.

"I'm going back to the White House. Now." She wondered what he could have left behind that was making him so upset. "And I'll be working late so I'll just sleep over in the Lincoln Bedroom. Do you understand?"

No, she didn't.

"Anna's sleeping in the Lincoln Bedroom." Her mouth was inches away from his. She was nodding her head and simultaneously starting to tremble.

"Then I'll take the Rose Room!" His mouth was so close to hers that Claire could almost taste the oysters and bourbon on his lips.

"Good idea. You can keep Mrs. Rutherford company," her voice was as soft as the quiet draft at the whining window. Perhaps if she made light of his unexpected flash of temper, she could put things back together again.

"Are you ill, Harrison? Or is there some danger?"

"Claire." He released her only to take her face in his hands. The feel of his elegant fingers against her skin made her instinctively want to close her eyes, to relinquish her face to his fingers. She fought an overwhelming urge to let him cradle her face in those hands. She could feel his need like a jolt to her body. She had always thought of him as a patrician tower of strength, something noble and marble. Why was he suddenly acting so human?

And worse, why did she yearn to respond?

She opened her eyes wider to make the room stop spinning.

"I'm not taking you to Yalta!" Harrison had never raised his voice to her. She opened her mouth to speak, bewildered. What was it about tonight that had unleashed this surge of feelings? Claire pedaled back over the entire evening but shook her head blankly.

"Do you understand? I can't." He released her abruptly.

She tried to read his face for an explanation, but the terrain of his handsome features was as unrevealing as the outside of his diplomatic pouch. He started toward her again, composed himself resolutely, turned, and left. Stunned, she waited until the door closed behind him before she exhaled.

She stood there feeling like a stranded soldier on a battlefield after everyone else had gone home. What had just happened? Numb, Claire walked from the living room into Harrison's bedroom. The gold brushes and combs from his travel set were neatly lined up on top of the highboy, winking at her from the shadows like the old friends they were. She gently fondled the gold handle and boar's bristle. In his haste to leave, he had left them behind.

Claire's head was beginning to pound. She suddenly acknowledged to herself that she longed to reach out for him, smooth away the tight lines in his face and soothe him in his obvious distress. After all, this was the man she worshiped. While she had been with Harry for only three months, she had been by Harrison's side for nearly three years.

Having been through everything together, they had developed their own private telepathy, a shorthand with which they read each other's mind. Why couldn't she read his now? Claire sat down on Harrison's bed, hugging herself with her hands. She was feeling so cold and alone. When the first blue lights of a winter dawn peeked into the room, she was still sitting on the bedspread, puzzling. What was she supposed to do? Maybe she should take Sara back to Chicago and wait for Harry there.

Harry was her far-away husband, Sara the child she had borne for them all, but Harrison, what was he to her? It finally dawned on her in the glare of clear morning as the alarm-clock buzzer sounded.

He had become her life.

Claire had thought her feelings for him were admiration for one of the world's great leaders. When had it changed? Somewhere after a late-night planning session when she had shed tears on his shoulder over boys lost in battle or another time when they had shared a victory of their own together, a line had been crossed. A forbidden border. If she even thought about what was happening, she had tried to hide it. Even from herself. Evidently he had thought about it too. That would explain tonight. Fuzzily, she rose and walked over to Harrison's mirror, to see herself as he saw her. The statuesque young beauty staring back at her was someone she hardly recognized. In this light, in this mirror, she wasn't Harrison's daughter-in-law, nor was she merely the "other" Mrs. Harrison; she was a sensuous woman in love. Just how long could they both go on pretending?

She heard the key unlock the latch and turned toward the door, half hoping it was the hotel maid, half hoping it wasn't. When a haggard Harrison stood in the door, need and despair etched on his face, her first impulse was to go to him. She stopped herself at the foot of the bed. She had to think. Whatever she did now would change the rest of their lives. All of their lives. The pounding in her head was unrelenting. It was in the middle of the room that they met, each taking a few hesitant steps in order to comfort the other. The love they felt for one another was so intense, it wavered there like a third person in the room. And when she stumbled, exhausted, he did what any gentleman would do. He took her in his arms.

Chapter Ten

Bombs and Liaisons

"To hell with public opinion."

—*Clare Boothe Luce*

Their world turned upside down overnight. Roosevelt was dead. The nation fell into such a deep mourning for the man who had led them through three presidential terms and was its Sunday fatherly voice of hope that a communal wail began to rise from one end of the country to the other. The president died in Warm Springs, Georgia, with Lucy Mercer by his side. Eleanor had been elsewhere and unaware.

But as Claire well knew, secrets could be kept even about the most visible men on earth. Lucy's presence would be eliminated in the lore that would surround his legend as soon as Eleanor rushed to the cottage in Warm Springs to learn the truth. By the time the draped funeral train rolled slowly back to the capital, a new version of his death would be invented.

Claire had been sent by Ophelia to pick up Harrison at the airport. Harrison looked bereft as he climbed down the metal steps of the *Sacred Cow*, the president's private plane, until he saw her standing alone and off to one side of the tarmac. He caught a whiff of her light fragrance even before he was close enough to touch her. His pace picked up as he rushed to her side and they embraced like the hundreds of other couples hearing the news that the president was gone.

They hugged, her windblown hair brushing against the black

armband he wore out of respect for his friend. It was the first time they'd seen each other since that dangerous night when passion had separated them from all their good instincts, three months earlier.

"I didn't want you to come home to strangers."

She held out a handkerchief in case, a lace extravagance from Slim; even a leader could cry.

"The embassy called us a few minutes after it happened and flew us back." There was a tremor in his voice.

Claire looked closely at him and thought: ashes. His face is the color of cold ashes. With heartfelt worry she lifted a hand to touch his forehead. He gently removed it and placed it in his own, folding his fingers over hers.

"I've missed you." His whispered words made her use the handkerchief herself. The husband and wife a few feet away wept openly. A quiet darkness enveloped them all. Even the cherry blossoms and dogwood coming into their April bloom seemed to hush and fold.

"How is Eleanor?" The statesman's usual voice returned to its owner. For Claire, it was like the temperature had dropped ten degrees.

"Distraught. She's on her way to . . ." she hesitated for the correct words, "bring the president home." The next question she answered before it was asked, as she hadn't lost her knack for reading his mind. Not even after their long absence from each other, a self-imposed interval in which she'd dreamed about him every night.

"Eleanor was at the Sulgrave Club when he died. She was speaking to a women's group." Claire's eyes flickered over Harrison's tall frame. She had never seen him look so haggard. Or so handsome. The gray at his temples had spread like silver moon rays through his thick hair in the time they'd been apart.

He pulled a leather cigar tube out of his inside suit pocket.

"We all knew he wasn't well. Eleanor should have been with him." Harrison's voice splayed indignation as he flipped up the lid and removed the hand-rolled Havana. He pointed the cigar holder outward as if looking for someone to blame. "I don't like to think of Franklin dying alone."

"Mrs. Rutherfurd was there." Claire's voice was barely audible.

"And so Lucy made a back-door exit." It was impossible to tell whether the frog that rolled with his words from the back of his throat was tragic or sarcastic.

Harrison chomped off the top of his cigar. "A rather shabby thank-you to a woman pinch-hitting for the wife."

"Oh, Harrison. It's no one's fault. Eleanor had her job to do, too." She pulled at the jacket of her neat tailored suit while they stared at one another awkwardly. She knew he kept his lighter in his left coat pocket so she reached in to retrieve the silver accessory. He took a few short puffs on his cigar as she held an unsteady flame.

What she had to say next was difficult.

"I've taken a room at the Fairfax. It seemed best . . . after everything that's happened." They both knew she wasn't referring to the president's death, but to the eight hours of forbidden love at the Willard that had marked their last fateful evening together.

Afterwards she had bolted.

Claire had taken Sara and returned to the homing nest. There, the Aunties had hovered over her like warm breasted birds, feeding her and soothing her confusion, for it was evident that something had gone very wrong in Washington. But since Claire wasn't volunteering any information, the doting mothers wisely left her alone. The pattern had been set long ago. She protected them as much as they nurtured her.

Sara, bratty and demanding at first, had taken to the fourth floor of Field's like the mischievous toddler she was, grabbing at dolls and life-sized carousel horses the hugeness of which she'd never seen even at Charlotte Hall. Auntie Slim had opened her hat boxes and chock-full jewelry cases to her "girls" as play toys, and Violet had just opened her arms wide to love them both.

Finally after two months of unconditional love and warm reunions with old friends at Field's, Claire was feeling like she'd been given a healthy dose of homemade chicken soup. Some of the store folk made her feel self-conscious, treating her with the same adulation they gave Dorothy Lamour after she'd quit running her Field's elevator to star in the Road pictures with Bob Hope and Bing Crosby.

In her own mind Claire had done nothing right but marry well, and for this she was being given a hero's welcome. Swept up in the ticker-tape mood, she had even allowed her old nemesis, Cilla Pettibone, to throw a cocktail reception in her honor at the Casino Club, the almost secretly private club downtown, co-hosted by Snookie Cuthbert, who now latched on to Claire like a long-lost best friend. The post-deb set had read about her with envy in the Washington columns and *Town and Country* and were woozy with curiosity. Cilla was deep into psychoanalysis and Snookie newly on the wagon after her latest "drying cure." Daisy Armstrong Fitch, who still had the finest set of shoulder blades on the North Shore, now had the widest hips too, having given birth to a fine set of twins three years earlier. Pretty Lily Dunworth, divorced but gung-ho on remarriage, inquired earnestly about the man market back East.

"Claire, you got so *lucky*." She threw her voice like a ventriloquist into the V-shaped glass of her Bombay gin martini, and it echoed throughout the marble-floored room as the other girls joined the chorus of "To Lucky Claire!" It reminded her that for all their noisy friendship, they still thought of her as the poor girl from behind the ribbon counter who'd cleverly tied one humdinger of a matrimonial knot.

Although she was the picture of refinement in a navy crepe de chine cocktail suit with a white rose in a tiny crystal vase pinned to her lapel, Claire was suddenly pulled down to her former station. It was painfully evident to her, 28 Shop graduate, that she'd need more than a new suit if she and Sara moved back to Chicago. Apparently it wasn't an option. She thought everyone here could see how much she'd changed. Weren't the pearls worn short at her neck real? Hadn't she gotten Field's to make parachutes out of pillowcases? Hadn't she earned their respect yet? For close to three years Claire had engaged in top-secret war work, been invited to join old-guard eastern clubs, and charmed bad-tempered generals, becoming a welcome fixture at the upstairs White House. Claire had taken pride in the way she had adapted to her new life, and the fact that this bunch could see only the old Claire was a bitter disappointment. They were applauding her all right, but only because they thought she'd slept with the right man.

Recovering her poise, Claire brushed a stray hair off her embarrassed cheek and graciously promised to fix Lily up with Tom as soon as she got back. Back? After what had happened was she ever going back?

While she delayed a decision, Claire arranged her social calendar like she was still in Washington with important appointments to keep. Today, Slim was taking her out to the Cape Cod Room for gossip and lunch. That morning she'd had a preview of the coming conversation: It was to be about Slim's travails simultaneously going through menopause while being a married man's trinket. Hot flashes and hot sex were evidently a tough combo. Claire laughed lightly while weighing how much about her own life to confide in her romantically free-thinking aunt. There could be quite a lot to talk about. She arrived punctually, a discipline picked up from Harrison.

"Remember, Claire, the real world runs on time. If you want to be a player you have to show up on the stroke." She half smiled to herself, remembering his words. Slim never took time seriously and somehow, even though she took the extra time to look terrific, she was always left at the post. Shaking her head in daughterly indulgence, Claire settled herself on a red leather wing chair in the lobby of the Drake to wait and read her husband's latest bulletin from the war zone.

So the summons calling her back to Tuxedo, when it came, was in the form of a letter. Harry was merely the process server carrying Ophelia's subpoena.

Iwo Jima Island
March, 1945

Claire,

Good news from the South Pacific. The temperature is a balmy 77 and the seas turquoise, perfect weather for capturing an island with coconuts in the palm trees and grass huts camouflaging the Nips' big guns. In our new B-29 we were able to shoot out most of the Japs' firepower from the air so that our landing forces could capture the island just by cruising up to the shore in their PT boats, after Buzzy, Flip and I cleaned up the beaches for them, of course. I have to admit capturing Iwo got a bit messy. These guys never give up. After the battle only 200 soldiers out of 21,000 were still alive and rather than surrender like good sports, they committed harakiri by jumping feetfirst into the flaming Suribachi volcano. Talk about sore losers.

But never mind, my darling, this island with its funny name makes me think of one of those drinks from Trader Vic's. Toast me from Chicago with a Mai-Tai, will you? You can celebrate the fact I have just made Lieutenant Commander.

And then the newly promoted officer issued his first command.

Clairest, Mother is deeply concerned that you not keep Sara away from her routine and real home for too long. I certainly can understand your homesickness—I feel it so often—but Mother is right about this. She's afraid the Aunties will spoil her and undermine Mother's efforts in bringing Sara up the Harrison way. So be my good girl. Treat yourself to a shopping spree and head back to

Tuxedo. On the next train. That's an order. Don't go AWOL, otherwise Mother and I will send out the marines! Let's keep it in the navy.

Love from Lt. Commander,
Harry (Tux) Harrison

A stunned Claire didn't know whether she should feel like a prisoner of war or a double agent. She rose, wadded up his letter, and threw it in the lobby fountain where other people made their wishes.

While Claire had gone home to her mother, Harrison had exiled himself to London. But there he was forced to take stock of his personal feelings, something he had never been required to do before in his self-assured, on-track life. Ever since that night when he had broken the rules and succumbed to a wilder call, he had wandered aimlessly, sleepwalking through his work.

As rich as he was, he had endured an impoverished emotional life for years. Now tasting true passionate love, he was seized by the need to be with her again. Only guilt had kept him away; as much as he wanted Claire, he had to remember that she belonged to his son. But in spite of being a father, he was also a man, and all the elements of her unavailability made her that much more enticing.

He had been in shock when he boarded the special plane back to Washington within an hour of Roosevelt's death. But once in the air he used his first unscheduled hours in ages to think. High above the real world, his mind floated back to the one lovely thing in his life, Claire. This tall and willowy slip of a girl had taken possession of his heart with an iron grasp. Claire had an uncanny ability to follow his intellect and comprehend his every thought, and an eagerness to please him. All of it thrilled him. Most of the world considered him an important man, but only Claire had seemed able to make him really *feel* important. He anguished over whether or when to see her and what he would say. And then Ophelia sent her like a test of mind over heart to greet him.

His spirits lifted instantly when he saw her standing off to the side hatless, her hair blowing in the spring wind as she hesitantly lifted her arm for him to find her. The invisible grip she held on him immediately tightened. The fact that she would stay at a different hotel was the practical decision, one he would have made. She had, as always, anticipated his thinking. Stealing shy glances, barely lifting their eyes from the sidewalk, they began to make their way toward the car.

"You're looking well," he said, searching for ground at sea level. He had to get out of the clouds. If he were another kind of man, he would have said "beautiful," but Claire, who understood the subtle shadings of his vocabulary—as well as his intent— merely smiled. She instinctively laid her arm across his as they walked, their heads bowed toward each other, talking softly. Finally, she slipped her arm through his in the most natural way.

There would be a lot of busy hours ahead. The business side of Harrison took over as he outlined the assistance Eleanor would certainly be needing, preparing for the state funeral in Washington and the private burial at Hyde Park, as well as packing up twelve years of personal possessions from the White House—daunting tasks. Harry Truman, the new president—the name tripped over his lips—would undoubtedly be relying on Harrison's experience and would want them all to stay on. With the end of the war in Europe in sight, this was no time to desert his country. The business side of Claire nodded her agreement. If he stayed, so would she. They would be colleagues again. It was a safe zone, familiar and tested; and who better to help him? She fit his mold so well because he had poured it himself.

But as he lifted Claire's elbow to help her into the car, both of their memories returned to the last time they had ridden together and to the hours that followed their dawn encounter at the Willard.

She had moved into his arms with a push and pull that betrayed her guilt and anxiety, the luminous morning making it all so much more forbidden. But after the touches, caresses, and kisses, they both felt that nothing so good could be wrong. Then she ceased thinking as he touched her again, this time running his fingers through her hair, which was unruly after her restless night. He piled a mass of it on her head, taking his time to examine the planes of her delicately chiseled face, letting the heavy hair fall slowly, strand by strand, to her shoulders. She watched him, mesmerized, as he lifted her chin with a finger and then brought both hands down to trace the outline of her body from her shoulders to her hips through last night's pale ivory silk dress, his touch setting off an involuntary shiver. There was something erotic about the sight of evening clothes first thing in the morning. He felt unrelenting arousal in wanting what he wasn't supposed to desire.

For a man who had regularly breakfasted on oatmeal and a slice of white toast at the same time every day for thirty years, standing there with her in last night's rumpled clothes, still tasting like last night's smoky oysters and brandy was foreign and intoxicating. The light of the beginning day seemed only to illuminate his desire. It was like exploring dark, silent mysteries in the brightness of noon. The curves and softness he might only have felt in the propriety of darkness were blatantly defined for him. He not only wanted to touch her, but needed to see her, not only for the beauty of her body but to see if there was desire in her own eyes.

She had heard his thoughts that morning and helped him as he unbuttoned the back of her dress. He had dug his fingers into her shoulders and brought his mouth to her clavicle and the soft valley of flesh below. His elegant hands made their way to her perfect breasts, risen since motherhood like white-and-pink-petaled roses that had blossomed overnight.

She arched her back to lift them closer to his mouth. He pulled the rest of her lace slip away and buried his head in the mounds as smooth as pressed satin. He had watched them for months take their new shape beneath his furtive glances in the rooms they shared, trying to deny his growing desire. Now he reached out for her, excited by her faint smells of vanilla and talc mixing with the brandy on his breath, a heady recipe for a man accustomed to dry toast.

His long fingers traveled down her torso, igniting her hesitant passion. Her eyes fluttered shut as he set about touching places on her body he had dreamed about with such inexorable frequency it had almost driven him mad. Slowly he caressed the scar on her leg. Harrison found the jagged dog bite sexy. It emphasized her vulnerability, and it excited him more than anything in his marital memory.

They were friends first, admirers of one another of the highest order, and nonsexual lovers already. Theirs was the love of lingering looks and sighs. After all, the logical man inside him reasoned after they had consummated the physical act, they were relatives only by marriage. And as the electricity of one ignited the other, even that distinction faded. When they were spent, lying in one another's arms, softly breathing each other's breath, lightning bolts didn't strike them, nor had they gone blind. They had just fallen hopelessly in love.

After all these months they were alone again. This time in the cocoon of the gray-felt interior of the Lincoln. There was no mention of that night. And in Claire's mind there never would be, though every night before she went to sleep she listed all the reasons they could never be together, like a mantra.

He leaned toward her, apprehensively. His smooth hand resting on her sleeve, her hands at the wheel. He peeled back the white gloves from her light skin like a delicately operating surgeon and tried to turn her toward him by taking her two hands in his own.

As their fingers touched, an involuntary heat ran through her body.

"Why did you run away from me?" His voice gripped her.

"Because one of us had to."

"I'm supposed to be the gentleman. I should have been the one to leave."

"I've made arrangements to be with Anna tonight." She pulled her cheek away, taking stock. "She needs me." While her demeanor and words were impersonal, Claire's soft eyes betrayed her feelings as she turned to face him.

Harrison abandoned his patrician aloofness.

"*I'll* need you."

"But, I thought we decided—"

Harrison finished her sentence by closing her mouth with his. It was such an uncharacteristic public display of affection that it startled even him. Perhaps he was going to hell in a handbasket, but the world had gone mad and Franklin was dead. Harrison pulled back, reflecting silently on his friend's life. At least Franklin had been with Lucy at the end. Perhaps Harrison should take a cue from his friend's example and grab what little happiness he could in this life.

"Mother keeps avoiding me. She acts as if I'm responsible—I don't know how to talk to her." Anna kept her chin down as she hoisted a stack of watercolors of Campobello, then a model sailboat FDR had built himself and forlornly laid them into a cardboard packing box with some of her father's papers. There were tears in her eyes and on her moist cheeks.

Claire knew better than to try to respond, so she silently continued helping Anna pack her famous father's lifetime into crates. There would be enough to fill twenty army trucks before they were done. Eleanor had promised the Trumans she would be out of the White House in a week, and her promise would be kept. Anna was busily helping out with guilt-edged fervor even as mourners were gathering downstairs.

"Oh, Anna dear, she'll come around." Claire squeezed her friend's hand. Both of them were dressed entirely in black.

"I only did as he asked. Which one was I supposed to please? Mother or Father?" She put her head in her hands for a moment and then pushed the tears away with her palms so as not to stain FDR's letters.

"Grace told me how terrible it was. She was there when Mother found out," Anna confided, referring to Franklin's private secretary.

Claire nodded her head slowly. The newspapers had reported that a grieving Eleanor had arrived in Warm Springs at midnight. She waited for Anna to continue.

"You know how Mother is, always the emotional rock. She comforted everyone gathered around her and then sent them all off to bed like children who were having a bad dream. Now that she was there she would make everything better." Claire understood. She had seen that Eleanor a thousand times.

"Finally alone with her cousins Daisy and Laura Delano, Mother sank into a couch and asked them to tell her exactly and precisely how it happened."

"According to Grace, they all just looked at one another. No one knew what not to say. And then Laura—you know how gossipy she is—blurted it out, claiming that Mother was bound to find out sooner or later. 'Franklin was sitting for a portrait right over there,' she said, and actually got up and pointed to the specific spot. 'And he was looking better than he had in weeks in his double-breasted gray suit and crimson tie. Lucy Mercer Rutherfurd picked out the tie herself. The portrait was going to be his gift to her.'

"Claire, can you imagine Mother hearing this!" Anna ran her fingers through her soft, waved hair and went on reliving the moment.

"Mother clenched her hands and struggled for her next breath. But Laura wasn't letting her up for air just yet. Oh no. She told her, 'Well, we can be grateful for the fact that the last thing he was looking at was the smiling face of a beautiful woman.'

"With that, Mother rose and walked into the bedroom where Dad's body was laid out on the bed. You know, we kids used to know whenever Mother was feeling really troubled because she would walk unusually erect with her head held high. She's been walking very erect since."

Claire looked compassionately into the face of her friend who bore her mother's mouth and her father's lustrous eyes. The devoted daughter had just lost one parent and perhaps the respect of the other. What could Claire possibly offer in words? She knew better than to tread on other people's betrayals. All she could do was be a good listener and help Anna through these next hard days.

"Let me get you a cup of tea," Claire said. "You'll need your strength for this afternoon. I'll be right back." She shot a look at her wristwatch. The State funeral was at four.

She rushed toward the family kitchen but skidded to a halt when she spotted a rigid Eleanor walking purposefully, her head bent forward several inches ahead of her black stockings and shoes, toward the East Room, where the president's body lay in a closed coffin. Claire backed into the curtained alcove so as not to disturb her. Too late, she realized she was in the red-velveted cubbyhole where the grandchildren spied on State receptions without being seen.

The honor guards at the door started to speak to the first lady but she waved them away, saying "I would like to have a few moments alone with my husband," and asked them to open the casket. Claire hid herself in the shadows, a reluctant witness. She watched as Eleanor stood over the president, gazing lovingly down into her husband's face, her head hanging so that she looked like a bereaved blackbird. She spoke softly to Franklin, a last farewell before she slowly lifted a handkerchief to her eyes. Then she slipped a gold ring from her finger and touched it to her lips before tenderly placing it on her husband's hand.

When she finally turned to leave the room, she was dry-eyed and her face displayed the composure of the public Eleanor. Claire watched her stop and ask the honor guard that the casket not be reopened. Her good-bye would be the last. At least she'd had that.

Claire had never been to a funeral, and she knew this was a day she would never forget. She stood beside Tom a few yards behind Anna, Eleanor, and Elliott. Harrison and Ophelia were on the other side just behind President Truman, with the cabinet members, Supreme Court justices, and Russian ambassador Gromyko. Claire looked over at Anna and studied her grieving friend. Having never known her father, she couldn't fathom losing one.

She looked across at Harrison. The corners of his mouth twitched; his lips were hidden as if he had pulled them in so as not to let the anguish he felt escape.

The crowd's silent mourning was broken by Fala barking at the booming military salute. Claire lifted her head during the singing of the final hymn to watch Eleanor in her grief. She searched Eleanor's stoic face for signs of the hurt she was concealing. This was a noble wife indeed. And she couldn't help noticing that there was no place for a Lucy here. It was unbelievable to Claire that Eleanor had actually known about Lucy, but Anna had implied it was the Lucy Mercer affair that inspired her mother to reinvent herself like a chameleon, wresting her out of the world of tangled emotions and into the world of deed.

For survival she had entered into the male-driven world of activity and accomplishments and made her mark there. Pushing into uncharted territory with the passions other women reserved for their lovers, she had created her own daisy chain of women workers and transformed herself into a magnificent leader. Clearly, Eleanor had reinvented herself. At that moment Claire Harrison wanted nothing more than to walk behind Eleanor forever.

All through dinner they had eaten in silence. Harrison's sudden announcement startled Ophelia out of her self-absorbed thoughts on legumes, Chinese wallpaper for Harry's bedroom, and the rest of her son's house going up a few hundred yards and a duck pond away from Charlotte Hall.

"I've decided to take the president's offer to oversee the Allied economic rebuilding of Europe."

Ophelia looked appalled. "You mean that haberdasher in the White House?" She held her heavy silver spoon in midair and then spilled some rich vanilla cream over her pie.

"He was sworn in as president weeks ago, my dear."

"Not in front of me." Her voice was as cold as a North Atlantic iceberg.

"Ophelia, I'd like you to come with me. It will be an interesting time to share. Europe is coming alive again."

"I don't want to go to Europe. It's dirty and quite overrun with refugees. There are no fresh vegetables. One can't get a decent meal. They're out of everything over there. Europe's suddenly become our poor cousin."

"But we can change that. My commission will funnel civilian supplies and services, medicine, food, and building materials into the liberated areas, all under the aegis of State. Once we've identified who needs what, this project will supply Western Europe with everything it needs to return to life. It will be a humanitarian gesture we can make together." It was a plea by Harrison as much as an invitation. If she did accompany him, at least he'd be fettered by familiar restraints. Then his fantasies would continue to remain in his head, and he could convince himself that that one night with Claire had been an accidental collision, merely their version of battle fatigue.

"No."

"Please."

"My loyalties were with our Roosevelts, not to some poker-playing hatmaker from Kansas."

"Missouri."

"Don't correct me, Harrison. I'm still prostrate with grief. Our vegetables will be coming up in the garden soon. Stay home and enjoy our life here."

"I don't want to go alone. I need my wife." The intensity of his words escaped a tightened mouth. Ophelia looked as startled as if mighty Jupiter had just said he couldn't make one more thunderbolt without his wife Juno beside him lighting up the furnace.

"Oh, come now, Harrison." Her voice was the verbal equivalent of a shoulder pat—well-meaning yet affectionless. "Someone's going to have to take a broom to Europe before I return. Anyway you've got Tom and Claire going already and a whole delegation from State if you feel you need company." She was content to sit in her living room at Charlotte Hall with her crewel work in her lap and her granddaughter learning at her feet.

Harrison looked down the long table at the two sets of salt and pepper shakers at the head of their respective place settings. Apparently they didn't even share condiments anymore. He sighed.

"Very well, my dear." Harrison's mind wandered off to Belgium, Italy, London, and Claire. She had agreed to join the group and assist in writing up the commission's study on the assurance that Ophelia would be part of the team. In fact, she had even made reservations for weekend side trips for Mr. and Mrs. Harrison. Would she change her mind now without the bulldog presence of Ophelia? he wondered. Since that last kiss in the car, their good-bye kiss, they had behaved toward one another like etiquette-school cum laudes—polite but not excessively so, correct but not intimate. If her "good morning" was too effusive, he shied away. If they accidentally brushed against each other in the office hallway, she stiffened but went about her business. After work hours, as near as he could tell, when she wasn't in Tuxedo with Sara, she'd have the odd night out with Tom and other young people. Evidently, they both had come to their senses.

"Go on to Europe, Harrison. Save the starving masses. Perhaps I'll join you later."

During the long flight, Claire fell into a heavy hemlockian sleepiness, so her first impressions of Rome were the slow-motion visions of someone waking into a Technicolor dream. It was as if colors she'd only seen on Renaissance canvases existed for real just in Italy. Terra-cotta earth, a Titian orange sun, a Bellini blue sky whirled around her even as the sun-darkened olive-skinned people outside in the street bustled by, speaking a language she couldn't comprehend but whose word endings seemed to vibrate with fortissimo.

Claire turned the dials on her Timex so that her watch would be readjusted to European time.

"Claire, for Christ's sake—what kind of clothes have you got packed in this suitcase?" Tom dropped her suitcase with a thud. The members of the mission had been allowed to take only two valises each on their flight over.

"There aren't exactly clothes in that one," she fudged.

"But exactly what?"

"Sugar and soap."

Even Harrison looked up from the task of collecting his luggage.

"Sugar and soap?" Tom echoed.

"There's an orphanage in the Trastevere, near Santa Cecilia, that my auntie Wren has always supported through her church.

It's what they asked for." Claire's voice was as soft as the breezes blowing through the cypress trees.

"Sugar and soap. Well, guard that bag with your life. Everyone in Europe is desperate for these commodities. It's like taking six sacks of gold for a walk on Wall Street."

"We'll put it in my car. You can take it there after we've checked into the Excelsior." Harrison's smile was generous.

Harrison had been in a gloomy frame of mind ever since Franklin's death. In the last few months he had wondered if he'd ever shake off the dark specter of his loss. It had begun to happen on the plane.

Claire's aura had loomed larger as the plane had climbed higher, and the air he breathed became lighter. Seated next to her and across from Tom in a club-car configuration, Harrison occasionally looked up from his European Relief Program folders to watch her craning her long neck across both of them, her upper teeth biting her lower lip as she concentrated to peer out the round window of the four-motored silver C-54. She shifted in her seat, wrestling with a fold-out Rand McNally map of Europe, marking all the places where they would attend conferences on their junket and waving the smoke from Harrison's Havana and Tom's Chesterfield away from her line of inhalation.

"Let's just send her up to the cockpit and let her drive the pilots batty," Tom finally suggested in good humor.

"She's fine where she is," Harrison countered above the drone of the plane's engines.

Tom was about to tell his boss he was joking but thought better of it and went back to his report on the feasibility framework for rebuilding the Italian economy.

Harrison redirected the overhead light to shine only on his reading as Claire's tired head finally came to rest on her shoulder.

After a yawn-filled dinner with the delegation that was over by ten-thirty, Claire suddenly felt alert again. Whether it was travel lag or the difference in time change, she was fully revived. The bellman showed her to her room on the fifth floor of the Excelsior, the shabby, once-grand deluxe hotel recently vacated by the Fascists. Claire walked into the black-and-white-marbled bathroom, which was twice the size of her old Windermere bedroom but offered only a slim bar of rewrapped soap and a single oversized bath towel with most of the fluff washed out of it. She turned on the white porcelain handles that controlled the broken faucet, from which only a trickle of water flowed. It would take forever to fill this tub with its grandiose marble lion's feet. She sighed as she pulled her hair into a ponytail. She'd worried whether she'd brought enough toiletries and clothes to wear in the one bag she had allowed herself, but then dismissed the notion. Her small sacrifice had been worth the grateful looks on the faces of the nuns and bone-thin children. They'd have sweet dolci and biscotti for a month.

The plan for the rest of the night was simple. Her energy up— she quickly calculated it was eight hours earlier in Washington— she'd take a long soak, whenever that bear of a tub filled. In the meantime, she'd draft a letter to Auntie Wren to tell her what a success the sack of sugar and soap had been. She'd craft a clever postcard for Sara and dash off a "safely arrived" note to Harry, who, oddly enough, had wholeheartedly endorsed this particular trip right on the heels of his mother's urging her to go, especially after Ophelia herself decided to bow out. So that was how it was now. Because his mother approved, so did Harry. Claire sucked in her cheeks as she turned each side of her face to the mirror.

After her lukewarm bath, she brushed her hair one hundred strokes but was still wide awake, so she slipped on a sleeveless sheath and a pair of sandals and took the stairs, not the elevator— "*L'electricity signóra,*" the majordomo had told her, was "*come si dice,* iffy-offy"—and scampered down the wide staircase to post her letters.

While the electricity annoyingly flickered on and off in the dim lobby, the downstairs bar was softly candlelit. She approached slowly, drawn to the silk-lined room where the blinking chandeliers and the tall ottocènto chairs cast shimmering shadows on the fabric-sheeted walls.

"Do you know anything about Italian antiques?"

Before she could attach the voice to a name, Harrison leaned out of the Baroque shadows, a smile lifting his lip.

"Ohmigosh!" Claire's hands flew to her heart and her laugh jumped a scale. "For a moment there I thought I'd flown all this way just to run into an old Field's customer!"

A stealthy waiter dropped out of nowhere to inquire whether signóre would like to buy signóra a drink.

After Claire's lighthearted interpretation of the finer points of Roman antiquities, for the most part made up, came Harrison's inquiry.

"Are you sleepy?"

"No." A short shake of the head.

"Me either. Shall we take a walk?"

"Mmmm."

He led the way through the palatial lobby that looked less rundown in its spotty darkness.

Outside, the round moon was astonishing, glaring like a circle of wired electricity that hadn't been dimmed by war, broken cables, and bombed-out power plants. Suddenly they could see each other clearly. Her face, fresh and earnest, was a perfect unlined stage for the moonbeams to dance across. His was already chiseled from the summers in Maine, autumnal fox hunts, outrunning the Depression, and inhaling secondhand presidential tobacco. Each line had a reason and told a story she yearned to hear. In this light their silhouettes were the focus. They were almost identical. They were tall, lean, willowy, had long-muscled limbs; she averted her eyes in embarrassment as she suddenly remembered the rocklike thigh muscles she had touched when they had made love. They walked down boulevards and turned onto narrow, crooked streets that eventually emptied into a piazza four-squared by ancient villas, coming to stop at a high wrought-iron gate with a mossy green coat of arms, its gold patina long ago dulled. He pulled his shoulders back and stepped away from her.

"I know this house."

"It's very grand. Is it an embassy?"

"It belonged to friends of mine."

"Do you think they still live here?" A picture of them dining al fresco in this beautiful villa's lemon garden plied its way into Claire's romantic imagination.

His gaze ran up and down the three-story stone structure, its portal urns untended, its awnings in tatters.

"Probably gone, I'm afraid. They were Jewish." He turned to her slowly. Sympathetically, she took his arm and lightly laid her fingers across his sleeve as they continued to stroll.

"It's so strange. I don't know who of my old friends is alive and who isn't." Her fingers tightened their grip on his sleeve. "We've all been so busy in this damn war we've forgotten the people."

Claire followed his pace in silence.

"Do you mind walking a little longer?"

"As long as you keep talking."

He stopped and took her by the shoulders. She knew what was coming and could have prevented it with a word or a gesture. But she didn't. He drew her lips closer to his, her mouth was already open. When he pulled her closer her hands instinctively circled his neck as she leaned into him, their thighs and hips pressed together with no ancillary space. It was a long, hungry kiss.

When she opened her eyes their lips lingered. Well after midnight on the Via Collina in a city resting from war, there was no one to fault or judge their behavior. In America one kiss might have been their limit, but here in the heart of the Roman night with the smells of their clean perspiration mixed with the scents of almonds and orange blossoms filling their nostrils, the kiss only whetted their appetites.

Claire heaved a long sigh, and pushed her arm through his and then cradled it with her other hand. Everything seemed different. In this place filled with crowds of ancient ghosts and ringed with hundreds of centuries of monuments and ruins, built by a pantheon of gods who took mistresses, and deities masquerading as swans to seduce virgins, their passion for each other seemed tame; their kiss so small on the moral compass of everything that had happened around them. A warm wind rustled down from the hills, lifting the balmy, moist air. Beads of perspiration glistened on her hopeful face as they approached the hotel.

"*Buon giórno, Signóre and Signóra Harrison!*" Alberto the concierge in his gold-braided uniform greeted them as if they were a couple and, in that pink and golden moment before dawn, that is what they became. It had just struck four o'clock in the morning, and in the eternal city they were now "the Harrisons."

"Shall I bring up to you the coffees?"

"No, *grazie.*"

"Ah." Alberto nodded. He had often put Mussolini's mistress to bed and consoled homesick Germans. "*Buona notte.*"

The sound of their shoes crossing the foyer clicked across the marble floor. The red runners had been taken out to dry-clean away all the Fascists' footprints. Harrison gently took Claire's hand as they ascended the staircase to his suite. Dawn was blatantly sweeping into his rooms. They met it in one another's arms.

It was as if a stiff mask had dropped from Harrison's face, revealing a warm man given to easy laughter.

"Even foreigners begin to feel different after being in Italy for a short time," the enterprising Alberto remarked, winking, a few mornings later as he palmed the gratuity Harrison had just given him. He glided the handful of coins fluidly into his pocket as he saw the distinguished American guest into the sedan taking him to the Quirinal Palace for the day's first session.

Claire routinely followed a punctual hour later, after having shampooed the night's ardor out of her hair and scrubbed the look of a radiant lover off her face. While patting the lightest layer of Pond's cold cream onto her face, she saw to the "little details," as Slim called them: arranging for Harrison's shirts to be properly laundered and hung and stocking the humidor—salvaged by Alberto "from a guest who left in a big hurry in 'forty-four"— with Harrison's favorite cigars, procured by the resourceful concierge from black-market contacts with whom he had an excellent working relationship.

Occasionally Claire was able to gather up a short stack of day-old English newspapers and week-late *Time* magazines to add to the homey mood she tried to create in the suite. Having lived with Harrison the last few years in their odd arrangement at the Willard Hotel, she knew all his habits. And having grown up at the Windermere Hotel with the Aunties, she knew exactly what was needed to turn these impersonal rooms into their private haven. A saffron-silk scarf from the Via Veneto was draped over the table lamp to cast a warmer glow; an idle ice bucket was commandeered to hold ivory-colored Banks roses, and a silver bowl was kept filled with fragrant olives on the bar table that she had set up to mix Harrison's after-work martini. Claire even persuaded the chambermaid to give them fresh bed linens daily, a luxury not available to the other guests. The knowledge that the fastidious Harrison would sleep more comfortably was well worth the special treatment.

At the Quirinal meetings, briefcase in hand, Claire joined Harrison, taking his notes and telexing his messages, but all at a much more relaxed pace than they had kept up in Washington. The days were filled with presentations by members of the nine European delegations attending, and Claire could feel the excitement build as she began to appreciate just how ambitious the recovery program would be.

But the moment that touched her most deeply came on the

first night of the twelve-day conference when she watched the delegates, most of whom hadn't seen each other since the onset of war, embrace and weep with joy to find their friends still alive. She listened as they shared their stories, describing how they and their family members had survived blitzkriegs, buzz bombs, concentration camps, and other, unimaginable hardships. Dinner that night was a true banquet, and afterwards they made Chianti toasts—to one another's survival, to the great Victory, and, poignantly, to those missing friends who had not lived to see it. Then these paler, thinner versions of their old selves raised their filled glasses to the future. Claire watched, not surprised but spellbound as one dignitary after another greeted Harrison—respected, as she already knew, but obviously beloved as well—grabbing his hand, pumping it up and down, hugging his straight-postured shoulders like eager children, thanking him for his exhaustive wartime efforts on their behalf and for keeping the American focus on coming to Europe's rescue. Claire watched Harrison use his handkerchief to wipe away tears from the corners of his eyes. It made her love him even more.

For the first time since she had known him, Harrison was overcome with a surge of feelings; and when she came to him that night, slipping off her robe to press her bare skin next to his, he reached out for her and pulled her close, a man drowning in deep emotions and clinging to a buoyant life raft.

He lifted her hair up off the nape of her slender neck, kissing the little place he had earmarked for his own. She let her head gently lean to one side and then raised her bare arms over her head in a stretch. He brought his hands down the front of her nakedness, coming to rest at the tuft of soft brown velvet below her waist. Feeling him without seeing him, her back to his chest, was an odd sensation, but she liked it and let him know. His elegant hands traveled down her body like a cellist in an unhurried overture to their lovemaking. In response to his caresses she instinctively flowered open, giving him as much awareness of herself as possible.

She could hear her body start to sing as he ran an imaginary bow across the belly of her curved torso. To bring the rhythm of their lovemaking to a different pitch, he paused to stroke other parts of her body that men of less nuance might forget to linger over.

Her very being was by now as tightly strung as a Stradivarius, a responsive instrument so sensitive that even the lightest feathering of his touches caused her to tremble in exquisite pleasure. He turned her over to face him and she showered him with butterfly kisses from her soft, moist lips, parting them as she continued to open herself up to receive his well-orchestrated thrusts.

His brain led his body like a maestro conducting a symphony, holding himself back as he gave her the gift of extra pleasure and she shuddered in a crazed atonal finale with flutes and crashing cymbals over and over again until she fell off a jagged edge, her breath gone, her heartbeat racing. He caught her.

Quietly he cradled her face in his hands to calm her rapid breathing, until she cooled. Coming down, she kissed him back a dozen times and, gathering up her strength, she used every muscle she had newly discovered to please him. The next movement was in her hands, and she took the baton. She stroked him lyrically with her fingers until she grasped him and then unhesitantly brought him to her parted lips.

She could tell by the way his body tensed and swelled within the pink moistness of her mouth that her boldness had rekindled his insatiable desires. She felt the pressure of his arms on her naked body and knew they had crossed all the borders of good taste, leaving Italy, lapping each other up, drunk in one another's juices until, finally exhausted, supper long forgotten, they fell asleep.

Their days moved along like airy cloud puffs speeding across a flawless summer sky. For the first time since the war, an opera was performed at the opera house. Tom joined them as a patched velvet curtain rose over Verdi's *Il Trovatore*. Although they didn't mean to, later, at their after-theater supper of cannelloni and red wine, they somehow shut out Tom's chatter about commission gossip and news from home. Claire teased him that his face was beginning to look as glum as the stone gargoyle spitting a steady stream of water into the fountain of the walled garden restaurant.

The next day Tom was grumpier than ever during the private tour for commission members of the Barberini Gallery, the guide directing his comments to the American delegation in a pitch to solicit funds to restore Italy's art treasures. When he extolled the virtues of Raphael's *Fornarina*, a portrait of the very young, bare-breasted baker's daughter generally believed to be the artist's mistress, Tom turned abruptly on his heel and stormed into another gallery hung with vivid crucifixions. Later that day, Tom announced he was going on ahead to prepare for the round of mini-conferences at Interlaken, Brussels, and London, where more data would be collected for the American fact-finding study. He would catch up with "the Harrisons" in London, he said. As far as Tom was concerned, he had uncovered one fact too many.

With their chaperone having called his own curfew, Claire and Harrison were free to roam the city alone after five, when the meetings and relief requests ended for the day. They liked blending invisibly into the crowd. Claire, a scarf over her head, and Harrison, in a linen suit, joined an anonymous line of pilgrims following the Appian Way, one of the routes of St. Paul, walking with flickering candles down into the catacombs where the early Christians had hidden and held their religious services.

Later they attended a moving hilltop ceremony where the remains of American soldiers who had fallen at Anzio were being transferred for interment in the English cemetery outside Florence. Harrison and Claire walked quietly hand in hand, both of them silently mourning the hundreds of young men they had never met but for whom they had worked so hard to arm back in

Washington. By the time the open-air car driving them back to Rome finally delivered them to the hotel, Claire and Harrison were smothered with rust-colored dust.

Entering the lobby, Harrison brushed some ancient dirt from his lapel, turned to his companion, who looked as if she had been crop-dusted, and asked, "Did you ever cancel those reservations for the weekend at Lake Como?"

"Oh dear, I forgot. The one I made for you and—"

Neither one of them wanted to say her name. For one crazy, dark second Claire had a vision of Ophelia riding a broomstick over the Colosseum trying to chase Cupid out of the sky. She instinctively took two small steps back to avoid the imagined calamity.

With a touch to the small of her back, Harrison steadied her. "Why don't the two of us go?"

"You mean—?"

"Of course. Weren't the reservations made for Mr. and Mrs. Harrison?"

Claire looked at him as if he had just announced he was going to fight the Christians *and* the lions.

"And if I'm not mistaken, that is the name on your passport."

"But Harrison, it's . . . a resort," she stammered. "I don't even have a swimsuit."

"Then don't wear one." Her eyes grew as wide as his grin.

Harrison turned to Alberto, who was never far away from a potential tipper. "Be a good man and have the desk prepare my bill. We're checking out."

"Certainly, signóre. I also ask the kitchen to pack *del pane e formaggio*. Right away. And I will see to the cigars. Como is very very beautiful place but has a no good black market." In his eagerness, Rome's best concierge clicked his heels together and shot out his right arm in a reflexive Nazi salute; catching himself just in time, he slammed his hand against his forehead like a good American GI.

"I'll have to shower first."

"Good. We'll save time and water and shower together."

Alberto bowed away backwards, pleased as punch. He knew a big reward was coming. Sometimes guests paid more to be forgotten than remembered.

Her long, wet hair lay against the salt-and-pepper short hairs on his chest. His lean torso, conveniently hollow in places, made way for her soft curves. Claire lay languidly in Harrison's arms, the muscled limbs of a man who had held the reins of thoroughbreds.

Thrown wide open, the fourteen-foot floor-to-ceiling windows let in the pleasing sounds of Lake Como lapping against its medieval stone walls, the humming motor of a single Riva cutting its sleek way through the cold water, a dark mahogany sports machine with blue and white leather seats carrying groceries to a villa across the way. A mountain breeze blew in the white sheers, shrouding silk-sleeved armchairs in gauzy cover before billowing out again. It reminded her of parachutes.

Claire lifted her head like an alert sentry. She was determined not to let Harry and his arsenal of obligations land on the beach and storm their Italian idyll. The last thing Claire and Harrison needed was reality shrapnel splintering their glass palace and the loveliness of what they had together. So she reinvented her mood, playfully shaking water from her wet head, bringing buoyancy back into the bedroom.

Harrison pushed her away, laughing. "Are you trying to drown me?"

"Only with love." She leaned over his pillow and kissed the creases around his eyes to coax a twinkle. What had been lines of worry in the not-so-far-away Washington years now fanned out like pinwheels on a child's toy.

These lazy afternoons at Lake Como had taken on the dream quality of a wall fresco, soft colors ombred into earth tones, tugging on their imaginations and taking them out of real time. If the beautiful still water outside their second-floor suite was their lake, then the bed—a four-poster antique hung with bronze brocade drapery puddling onto the pale-green-and-salmon terrazzo floor—was their island.

Their days fell into an idle pattern, beginning ambitiously enough with a swim before breakfast. Claire would speedily breaststroke her way across the bottom of the pool, emerging out of the slapping cold water a few inches from Harrison, who'd be doing some sort of steady WASP crawl. Invigorated, their laps completed, they made plans for the day over breakfast. A tour of the Isola Bella's gardens, a hilltop climb above Cernobbio—it didn't matter where. Plans always fell away when, coming out of the shower tying his robe, he would step into her embrace. The smells of unwashed salty perspiration and sun oil on her skin refired his urges and pulled them back into the eddy of their lovemaking. As they spun and twirled around one another like bedridden dancers, lunch was missed, dinner delayed. Room-service trays went untouched and telephone bells unanswered as they took their nourishment from each other and from naps in the rumpled sheets and the softness of each other's arms.

Claire knew the difference between holding a lanky man in her arms with his youthful self-doubts and dreams and another with seasoned ambitions. She had stroked the stubborn lock of a young man's hair back into place and known zesty lust with him, but it paled with the feelings that had been newly aroused in her by the man who had stroked her heart with his intellect, and although his body was less firm, his embrace was stronger.

It made her feel special to know that this accomplished man who could have spent his time with anyone on earth had selected to be with her. Finally she had found the very man she had searched for as a girl on the men's floor at Marshall Field's, in every catalog, and around every corner. She felt loved, secure, and, for the first time in her young life, chosen.

*   *   *

All too soon, it was time to return to business. London couldn't be delayed. They had skipped Switzerland, Harrison sending a substitute and his regrets, but now commission efforts reasserted their claim on their time. Bidding *ciao* to Lake Como and Isola Bella they boarded the train for Calais, and from there, ferried their way to England.

London was all meetings and deadlines. The devastation seemed far worse to Claire than she had heard. From the height of St. Paul's Cathedral, she could easily see where houses and shops had once stood and could take in at a glance the destruction of an entire block. Her room at the Savoy near Tom's faced the Strand, while Harrison's suite overlooked the Thames, his windows framing a broad view of the heavily trafficked river. She realized how much she missed the water when they all attended a Wednesday morning staff meeting in his parlor.

Before they broke for lunch, as a parade of room-service carts rumbled in, Harrison pulled Claire aside to tell her they'd been invited to Markenfield Park, Lord Dashwood's country house in Buckinghamshire, for the weekend and he hoped she'd want to go. The pleading in his eyes made her jump for joy, although in a roomful of people she wisely kept her eyes averted to the foxes leaping across the burgundy silk of his tie.

"Who's sitting next to Pamela Churchill?"

Emerald Cunard stood behind the heavy dining room chair, a scotch in her hand, and peered over her lorgnette at the crested place card held aloft by two silver hoofs of a jumping horse. There were twenty-four of these polished equine place-card holders arranged on her long mahogany table.

"An extra man." Lady Dashwood exclaimed proudly.

"What luck!"

"Quite a remarkable feat in these times."

"And what does the extra man do?"

"Binky says he's some sort of pirate."

"How glam. Does he have a peg leg and eye patch?"

"No, some sort of financial privateer. Made a bundle in rubber during the war." Wissie Wolfington whistled through her teeth.

"Oh, rubber. As in tank tires and those plasma tubes. Just like a pirate to profit from our war."

"Now he's going for gold. Been sucking up to Will Harrison for the big construction jobs. Shipping, too. Duccio's so vulgar you can practically smell his olive-and-vinegar breath before he enters."

"Oh, *that* Duccio! I think he's rather cute. A little short, perhaps, too dark with too much hair on his arms."

"If he was a horse, I wouldn't have him in my stable." Wissie sniffed.

"Well, I've heard he's hung like a stud." Emerald Cunard flashed her famous witty eyes. "But is he Pam's type? Poor Pami. Edward R. Murrow's gone back to his wife and America, and Averell Harriman gone to mother Russia and eventually back to his Marie."

"Don't pity Pam Churchill."

"So does the pirate have a wife?"

"Single."

"Oh my." Emerald lightly dusted the single pirate's chair with the hem of her chiffon evening dress.

Claire cleared her throat in the doorway so as not to appear to be eavesdropping.

"Ah, the lovely Miss Harrison. Join us, dear."

"Is your room all right? I put you right next to your father-in-law. Lord Dashwood says Harrison's the one to know but that you're the one with his appointment book."

"Sort of like the gatekeeper. Frightfully good to keep it in the family."

"Yes. Would you care for a drink, dear?"

"No, thank you. And the rooms are so lovely. Will I have time for a tour of the gardens before dinner?"

"Hardly. You'll be in quite a haste to slip into your dinner clothes as it is." Both Lady Dashwood, longtime wife of Britain's press lord and hostess of one of England's great country estates, and Emerald were dressed in slim gowns that skirted their ankles.

Claire looked down at her well-cut suit. Here her reliable war uniform didn't seem quite up to snuff.

"Oh, I'm truly sorry, Lady Dashwood." Claire's cheeks turned the prettiest shade of pink, like peonies. "I'm afraid I didn't think to bring black-tie clothes along." Or jewelry, she thought, stealing a look at the enormous sapphires and diamonds encircling the neck wattles of the two older ladies. "I'm not sure Harrison has a tuxedo with him, either."

"Oh, he's always kept a suit of dinner clothes here. Even during the worst of the bombings, we dressed for dinner. One can't let the Nazis spoil a good dinner party, Binky's always said. Bad for morale." Her hair was crimped in a stiff tidal wave of curls.

"Come with me, dear." Emerald Cunard, whose family had launched a thousand ships and who loved a good makeover almost as much as she enjoyed a juicy society scandal, took Claire under her chiffon wing. "We'll find something for you. You have such a lovely figure. So slim." She raised her lorgnette to inspect the young girl's well-rounded bosom. "See you at half past, Wissie." Emerald's mind was on her wardrobe in the Vuitton steamer trunk she had packed for the weekend.

"Please do. One hour of highballs and then dinner is promptly at half past eight." A frown crossed the hostess's high brow. Why couldn't the Americans, with their casual ways, understand the importance of keeping up a good show?

Standing in her slip in front of the Victorian mirror, Claire was reminded of Aunties Slim and Wren and, of course, of her mother's antics in gussying her up for the Pettibone debut. There she had allowed the overzealous ladies to deck her out like a Cecil Beaton Christmas tree. Now, more sure of herself and her own style, she would not be misled.

"That one's the ticket."

"What, that old thing? It's what I wear when I have to dress up after somebody's died."

"It's simple and if it's a little large I can easily belt it. See." Claire held up the black crepe to her bare shoulders.

"Fine then. Well, at least it's got good cleavage. On you the front will be scandalously slit to the waist. Perhaps we'll seat you next to the pirate and stir up the dinner talk." Her mischievous eyes brightened at the prospect. "But you'll be needing a piece of jewelry."

"But . . ."

"I insist. Dressed all in black and no jewelry, someone will ask you to draw a bath. Ha-ha!"

Claire beamed back at her as Emerald fluttered out of the room like a lady butterfly.

She spun around as Emerald Cunard's apricot poodle darted into the room to hide a precious hambone. Food. That was the crack in this incomparable British courtesy. Food was so short that the government issued free cartridges to anyone wanting to shoot gray squirrels. The minister of food even hawked tasty recipes for squirrel pies. And while the table downstairs in the great dining hall would be elaborately set with Meissen platters, George II silver gravy bowls, Minton china soup tureens, and tortoiseshell candy boxes, the sugar bowls, butter tubs, eggcups, and sweetmeat dishes would be bare.

Claire looked away from the mirror to the window and out to the perfectly manicured turf behind the house, which was set up for croquet and lawn tennis. Beyond that the ground was stepped, descending to the grand parterre's vast expanse of lawns and hedges arranged in the Italianate manner. However, the grove of ilex trees was now home to a dozen or so sheep, and Claire knew that part of Lady Dashwood's prize rose garden had been sacrificed for beds of cauliflower and turnips. She also knew from Wissie's fingernails that the lady of the house tended the precious vegetable garden herself.

Claire examined herself critically in front of the mirror. The dress was too large and cut too low. She shook her head. Harrison wouldn't approve, she was sure, and this was the perfect opportunity to make herself desirable for him. So Claire used her shopgirl ingenuity to do like the Brits and make do with what was.

As the clock bells chimed seven-thirty she moved as quickly as if she had been inspired by the Aunties' fashion wand. The lustrous hair was swept up into a French roll so that the special place on the back of her neck could be visible to him from any angle. She pinched a crocodile belt from his drawer to make the size ten fit her size six and, still wondering how to conceal her full breasts, suddenly spun the sheath around, fiddling with the opening so that from the front she was demurely covered from her collarbone to her wrists but her strong back and tapered waist were entirely naked from behind. Quite satisfied with herself, she heard a soft rapping on the door.

"Come in," she called out.

Emerald Cunard's personal maid made a short curtsy as she handed over the red box.

"These are for you, ma'am."

"Oh, how lovely." Claire held the luminous, perfectly matched string of round South Sea pearls up to the fringed lamp shade just for a second before she fastened them around her neck. The diamond baguette clasp rested at *that* spot on her neck.

"Oh, thank Mrs. Cunard for me. Please tell her I'll be sure to return them first thing in the morning." Claire's skin glowed with the same luster as the pearls at her throat.

"Oh, no, ma'am." The maid curtsied again as she hurried away. "These are from the gentleman."

Claire smiled with her gleaming American teeth and, glancing over her shoulder at her reflection, wondered if she could just *back* into the drawing room.

As Claire swept down the inlaid satinwood staircase, her coltish legs supporting her regal posture, she had only one ongoing hope. If, if, and if Harrison would return to Lake Como with her forever. Could he be content surrounded by books and his papers, writing political histories and his memoirs of the war? Who better to assist him than she, the woman who truly loved her great man? Wouldn't it be wonderful if the impossible could happen? If it could happen anywhere, it would be on their idyllic lake. Mornings spent in quiet research, he writing, she preparing the next day's text; then lunch on the veranda; and after the afternoon's work was done, a walk in the garden, a cappuccino, and long evenings entangled in one another's arms, their passion free to soar in the bed they'd share without the charade of separate rooms. If only he could lose his senses, as she had lost hers, they could return to Italy. She wouldn't even have to change the initials on her luggage—or her last name.

"Dance with me, darling," Harrison daringly whispered into her ear in the moonlit darkness. Claire and Harrison rose to join the other couples fox-trotting on the flagstone terrace overlooking the vast acreage of pleasure grounds and forests and ultimately the Thames, which snaked its way around Lord Dashwood's private park.

Harrison slipped his fingers into the deep V of Claire's dress, his hand on her bare back. She closed her eyes and hummed along with the melody. They were locked like that in a private trance until the smell of Italy penetrated Claire's nostrils. But this was not the smell of their Lake Como, she thought, as the pungent odors of sandalwood cologne and garlic shook her out of her English primrose garden. Her eyes blinked open to the little man with the slicked-back hair and unctuous smile.

"May I borrow this dance, Miss Harrison?"

"Thank you, but . . ."

Pamela Churchill was looking desperately anxious to switch partners too.

"Oh please, Claire, do. Dance with Duccio. It'll give me a chance to ask Harrison a dozen questions."

Reluctantly Claire changed partners. Fulco Duccio boldly introduced himself as Claire lowered her arms to dance with him. He was a whole foot shorter than Harrison. She looked longingly over her shoulder at Harrison, always the gentleman, stiffly squiring a very gay Pam.

Beneath a brow that concealed a wind tunnel of dark thoughts, Duccio studied her.

"I have never met a girl with purple eyes before." His words rolled out as smoothly as if they had been soaked in olive oil.

Claire turned to this man holding a thick hand against the bare small of her back and shivered. He watched her intently through eyes the color of a pitched sea.

"I am in the debt of your—how do you call it in English—father-in-law." He smiled. "He is making it possible for us to steady our feet again. We are busy making business together."

"Of course. My . . . father-in-law is one of the most brilliant minds in the States."

"It is why I pursue him like a suitor." His friendly laugh was genuine.

Fulco Duccio ignored the music, staying in the square diagram of polite dancing he appeared to have learned in a manual. When he accidentally pulled Claire the wrong way, his apologies were effusive.

"Forgive me. I am very good at making money and very bad at social graces." This time his laughter was boyish. "I hope I have your sympathy. One two three. One two three." He smiled as he counted out the steps. "They didn't teach us proper English dancing where I come from."

"And where is that, Mr. Duccio?"

"Calabria."

His hair sat immobile on his skull as if it were anointed with salad dressing. But, Claire thought as she relaxed into his clumsy lead, there was something undeniably dynamic about his brutishness, as though he were the only bull in a pasture full of cows.

"Claire, may I escort you upstairs? We have that early morning ride with the Dashwoods." Harrison was at her elbow. Claire happily took his arm.

Duccio bowed like a headwaiter and assured Harrison the deal they had struck that afternoon would be mutually beneficial.

"Good night, then." Harrison was already leading Claire away.

"Good night," Duccio called out after the Harrisons.

"What do they call him again?" Claire whispered.

"The Pirate."

Claire heard a soft click as the door connecting her room to Harrison's unlatched. She felt him slip into the ironed sheets of her bed, where she was naked except for the circle of pearls. After they made love, more tenderly than ever before, he wound his fingers around the necklace.

"And who is your wealthy suitor?"

"Why you, of course." She laughed.

"These are really very beautiful, but they're not from me."

"Then they're on loan from Emerald."

Harrison cupped her face in his hands. In the dark, his eyes flickered with protectiveness. "You shouldn't have to share anything with anyone."

And Claire nodded, agreeing with all of her heart. If, if, and if.

Not only was William Henry Harrison IV, statesman and American envoy, in hot demand by the new leaders of postwar Europe, but after two months in Europe the Harrisons were coveted dinner guests in all the best homes. Some offers they declined, others they dutifully accepted, but when the engraved card inviting them to dine on the Boulevard Suchet as the guests of the duke and duchess of Windsor arrived, Claire became as excited as the twenty-one-year-old girl she was.

"Oh, *please*, Harrison. How could I ever tell Auntie Slim I turned *down* an invitation from the duchess of Windsor?"

"As far as I can tell, she's just a silly woman who gets her hair done twice a day."

"But you can't imagine how important she is to the Aunties! We lived vicariously through her since I was a little girl." Claire pulled her long legs out from under her and excitedly hopped onto his bed. "Why, she's practically the Patron Saint of Shop Girls!" Her raised hands were inches away from the crystal chandelier.

"Well, if it will keep you from jumping on the furniture as if it were a trampoline." He smiled indulgently. "I suppose, provided it's not in conflict with one of my more important duties, we can go."

She excitedly wrapped her arms around his neck, delaying him from some of his other pressing appointments.

The two days before the Windsor dinner, the Slim part of Claire's personality dominated all the other aspects. The black crepe evening dress, a present from the adoring Emerald Cunard, was tried on with the V neck in the front, at both sides, and, finally, the back. The circle of pearls (as it turned out, an inappropriate thank-you from a grateful Fulco Duccio, who had received the American contract for carrying scrap metal in his newly acquired tankers) was twisted every which way around her neck.

Harrison had allowed her to keep them "for now," but as they had been appraised as priceless and Harrison didn't want to be beholden to the little Pirate, he had warned Claire that they should be considered a collateral loan.

Claire, like liberated Paris, was filled with a wild, unfamiliar happiness. As she dawdled down the Avenue Foch in search of the appropriate house gift for the Windsors, she walked in her own dazzling private light, and other women on the street turned to smile at the lovely girl obviously in the throes of Paris's charms. Looking into a window, she found the perfect present, royal blue suede collars and leads for the Windsors' pet dogs, whom, she had heard, the duke and duchess talked to like "substitute children."

Using her Field's skills, she directed a surprised shop girl how to wrap the gifts specially, even tying the flat ribbon into an entwined *W* and *E,* the romantic way Wallis and Edward, the duke and duchess, engraved all their personal possessions. She left the shop with a light step, her exquisitely wrapped package in her arms, just in time to see a flock of little girls in white tulle veils climb up the cracked steps of the Sacre Coeur for their first communion. She followed them into the church, feeling she had much to be thankful for.

The minute Claire walked through the doors of the Windsors' temporary home on the Boulevard Suchet with Harrison, she knew they had entered a charmed circle. Her eyes grew wide as she took in the duchess's details: the water in the flower vases was as clear as the ice in their drinks, the tablecloths embroidered to match the priceless Lowestoft china, and George IV's (the duke's relative) silver candlesticks arranged so that the duke could gaze unobstructed across the table at the duchess.

It was clear that Wallis took her hostessing duties more seriously than her husband had taken his coronation vows.

The duchess's order of the day was evidently to cheer up and charm the pampered guests of her table, and while the invitees (a dress designer, a prima ballerina, various counts and countesses, as well as the British and American ambassadors) didn't carry the power of some of the other Europeans Claire and Harrison had dined with, they were treated as if the world's continued spinning on its axis depended on them. There were individual Sévres butter pots with porcelain-handled knives at every place setting, and a waiter at the ready behind each chair. But the one detail Claire memorized to take away as her own was the duchess's habit of writing down with a small gold pen on a little jeweled pad the observed preferences of her guests and little things she might do next time to please them.

Claire was quite taken back when she read the duchess's calligraphic menu cards standing at each individual place setting. How had the duchess managed to find food when all of Europe was on rations?

WE

Dîner
Mousse de homard froid
Concombres à la crème

Perdreau rôti sur canapé
Bread sauce

Riz sauvage aux petits pois
Céléris branches au beurre

Salade mâches et betteraves
Bombe glacée aux fraises

Petits gâteaux
Crème chocolat

As the other guests read the cards, eyes wide and mouths watering with the thought of delicacies they hadn't tasted in years, the duchess laughed. In reality, there wasn't a lobster to be found in France, not even for Paris's most famous hostess, and fresh peas were as scarce as truffles.

But what the duchess couldn't deliver in food she made up for with her contagious wit, and her guests soon let themselves be carried along by the duchess's delicious food fantasy. While hot dogs from the U.S. were served instead of the inscribed cold lobster, salad russe made from tinned vegetables and canned ham from the American officers' club—garnished with black-market eggs—stood in for the roast partridge, the evening was four-star.

The duchess apologized only once. "Why, I *never* serve soup at dinner anyway. After all those cocktails, it's just another drink." And suddenly the food seemed as rich as the conversation. When, during the Spam course, she spied France's ranking British officer raising an eyebrow at the porcelain monkeys that crowded her amusingly decorated table, each chimp sporting a gold coronet on his head, the duchess laughed merrily. "*Some*body has to wear a crown in this house."

Just as the waiters began serving melted Hershey bars instead of crème chocolat and raisins instead of the imaginary *bombe glacée aux fraises,* a far more serious bomb was dropped. Their maître d'hôtel handed the duchess a yellow envelope on a silver tray. Her pointed face blanched beneath her white powder as she directed the missive to "His Royal Highness."

With great solemnity, the deposed king stood and clanged his spoon against his wineglass.

"As the former king of England, I feel I should inform you that the Americans have dropped an atomic weapon in Japan on a place called Hiroshima. There are at least one hundred seventy-five thousand confirmed dead. Gentlemen, I assume many of you need to return to your embassies." And from the tone of his voice, Claire could tell that the man who had given up his throne for the woman he loved only wished he had someplace important to go.

As the stunned guests rose to leave, Claire and Harrison gripped each other's hand. They both knew that the war, and their own private party, was over.

Chapter Eleven

Domestic Damage

Him that I love
I wish to be free—
even from me.

— *Anne Morrow Lindbergh*

Hands across the sea?" Harrison made a feeble attempt to cheer Claire up as the *Queen Mary* sailed into New York Harbor. Far enough away so that they could only just make out the art deco tip of the Chrysler Building and the green needle-top of the Empire State Building, Harrison and Claire entwined their gloved fingers.

"What shall we say? How shall I behave?" There were tears in the violet eyes beneath the brim of her fedora, her elegant waves blowing softly in the open-air breezes.

"Like a Harrison." His response was distant and faraway, but his fingers tightened around hers.

She didn't want to behave like a Harrison. She wanted to hurl herself into his arms like the girl on the cover of *Modern Romance*. "I won't be able to sleep without you." She couldn't imagine a night without hearing his breathing or inhaling his smells.

"You're too young to have circles under your eyes," Harrison said as he tilted Claire's head toward him.

"And you. Will you be able to sleep without my head on your chest?"

"I'm nearly forty-eight years old." He frowned. The age distance between them seemed to widen as Wall Street came into focus. "People expect me to look tired. They don't expect me to be giddily in love with my daughter-in-law. After all, I'm a man of 'high ideals.'"

How far removed it all suddenly seemed from just a few hours earlier, when they had desperately fought with all their sexual powers to keep the morning fog from rolling in. Last night as they made love on the gently pitching seas, Harrison would have cut any kind of deal with Poseidon to give them a week, another day, or one more hour adrift on the Atlantic, and now here he was, almost cavalierly throwing out a wreath to bury their love at sea.

Damn all the Harrisons and their high ideals, Claire fumed, damning herself in the process. If carnal sins had been committed, she had been a willing sinner. She watched in hopeless silence as efficient deckhands scurried to dock the huge ship.

"Who-hooo! Harrrrison! Clairrre!" Ophelia trilled like a mockingbird. "We're over heeere!" The little trio, waving three sets of arms, was immediately visible among the throng of mostly female humanity waiting on the dock. Nineteen forty-five was a year of homecoming. All over the world governments had released some sixty million men, and to Claire it seemed as if all their mothers and sweethearts were waiting excitedly on Pier 54 in New York Harbor. Claire's hand retreated from Harrison's and rose in the air to wave back. Suddenly she was confronted with her past pledges: a young husband and their little girl. For there was Harry, tall, tanned, and rangy, standing in the front row on the pier with a decked-out Sara on his shoulder. And she was as happy to see him as if he were Aunties Slim and Wren wrapped up in one. Like a sister, she ran her appraising eyes up and down the returned lieutenant's commander's proud physique. No bullet wounds, no limp, healthy, home, safe.

She turned to Harrison, stiff, tight-mouthed, hands jammed into his pockets, and caught the look of fatherly love in his eyes.

What were they going to do? The question was moot. Ophelia, already pulling strings and making decisions, had arranged for the famous diplomat and her son's wife to be escorted down the gangplank in VIP style before the masses of uniformed men hit the boardwalk.

Claire kissed her daughter happily before she hugged her husband hello. She pulled back awkwardly from Harry, this charming stranger, her pen pal, as Ophelia issued orders, commandeered their luggage, and ushered them into their awaiting town car. From the two leather jump seats, Sara and Harry chattered nonstop while Claire, relegated to the backseat bump, sat tightly squeezed between Ophelia and Harrison. Her confused heart beat erratically as Harry swiveled around and squeezed her ungloved hand at the same moment her knee was jostled against Harrison's leg.

Only the pedigreed manners and ingrained social behavior handed down through two centuries of Harrisons could have allowed the present company to converse politely in a moving car where a little girl was just learning to know the father she had never met and seeing her mother after a three-month absence; where a former devil-may-care flier was now ready to settle down with his bride and child and a stable job trading securities at the family firm; where the patriarch was wildly in love with his son's wife; where the matriarch had everyone's future neatly mapped out at home on her morning desk; and where an achingly torn young woman's thoughts ping-ponged between wanting with all her soul to be a good mother and wondering if the family would be better off if the car just crashed and they all developed amnesia.

"How was the weather in the South Pacific? You've got terrific color."

"Fine, Father. A lot like Nassau, only the humidity and heat were much more intense, since it's closer to the equator."

Claire was stupefied. With all the entanglements swirling around them, and an absence of years, father and son chose to discuss the weather. Lifting herself up, Claire rose to the moment.

"England was beautiful. You could see crocuses blooming in the cracks the bombs made. The world is going to return to normal." And for a moment she thought it just might.

"Oh, Claire, it's *such* a shame. Sara's had *two* visits from the tooth fairy since you've been abroad, and you've missed them both."

"Look, Daddy! The tooth fairy left me two silver dollars!" Sara waved a little Cartier coin purse in the air.

Claire sat forward, throwing a sideways glance at Ophelia. "My goodness, that's a generous trade. Where I've just come from, little girls are so hungry they could live off one silver dollar for a whole month."

"Oh, Claire, don't scare Sara with your little ragamuffin stories. This is a *happy* time, and tonight at dinner everyone can tell their what-I'm-thankful-for story. Save it for then." Ophelia could still deliver an insult without moving her lips. "Oh, Harry, did I tell you the Mortimers are coming?"

Harry, home for just three days now, was relieved that everything was just as it used to be. Every soldier wanted to come home to the exact same picture he'd carried around in his pocket since the day he left. The war was really over, and now they could all pick up where they had left off.

When Harry grinned at Claire, anticipating the night ahead, she was surprised that she had forgotten about his dimples.

It wasn't until she had missed her first period and suffered two weeks of morning queasiness that Claire decided she had better finally reconsummate her marriage. She stood sweating in the bathroom of their new house, flushing the toilet for the third time.

Claire was pregnant, and she didn't need to kill a warren of rabbits to know. As she pulled a brush through her hair, she counted not to one hundred but back to that last night on the ship. Harrison had wanted her with such fervor and her desires had dulled her brain so entirely that neither one of them had taken precautions. When she'd left for Europe she had no intentions of sleeping with Harrison and therefore no need for her diaphragm. And once they had begun to make love, it was he who had taken care to protect them. Somehow that arrangement let her feel less culpable, as if unplanned sex was nobody's fault.

The porthole had been open. The misty salt air had swept into the stateroom and they inhaled it like divers drawing in their last breath of oxygen before plunging into the sea. Harrison had held on to that spot on her neck and her breasts with such ferocity that he'd unintentionally bruised her. She in turn, wanting to cling to him forever, had dug her fingernails into his back. If the sounds that escaped her throat had not been drowned out by the high winds and waves hitting the ship, some unsuspecting steward might have come to their rescue. When Harrison entered her, he thrust deeper than he had ever gone before; Claire felt as if he had entered her very womb.

Now it appeared he had.

Holding a damp washcloth to her temples, she forced herself to consider her options. How could she be so selfish? She wouldn't be. She reached for her pink peignoir and pinched her cheeks to match. Claire was suddenly going to recover from the "episode of shyness" she had felt "about being intimate with a man again after such a long time," her proffered excuse for not performing her marital duties. If she didn't put her finger in the dam now, the domestic flood that would follow would destroy them all.

Squaring her shoulders, she resolutely entered their bedroom, decorated with Ophelia-ordered separate beds, one of the few of her mother-in-law's interfering favors Claire had been grateful for. Harry, long since accustomed to reading himself to sleep, was propped up on his pillows, his knees supporting Gibbon's *The Decline and Fall of the Roman Empire*. She cleared her throat. "Why don't I go downstairs and bring us a bottle of champagne? You know, we've never properly celebrated our reunion."

Harry let Gibbon and the Romans fall from his fingers. "You mean you're feeling better?" His voice was boyish.

"I think it's about time we start building our own empire."

Claire left to fetch the champagne as Harry ran to the bathroom to gargle with mouthwash and slap Aqua Velva on his beardless face, uncertain that he could rise to the occasion. There wasn't a doubt in Claire's mind. Every motion and caress that had been instinctive and natural with Harrison she now mechanically applied to satisfying her real husband. Harry was hers again, no questions asked. When she demurely announced her pregnancy a few weeks later, practically all of the Harrisons were pleased as could be.

Like a true chameleon, Claire reinvented herself. She laid aside her Lucy Mercer lessons along with her backless dresses and pearls and concentrated, in her tweed skirts and Belgian loafers, on Sara's lessons and running the house Ophelia had built—like clockwork. Even if the house wasn't to her taste, it was at least their own, and the duck pond and fifty yards of alléed grape arbor provided some degree of separation from Ophelia. After the birth of William Henry Harrison VI—nicknamed "Six," to her displeasure—Claire evolved yet again into something she had never been before: the good mother. This time there was no discussion that nannies would be kept at bay, and when Ophelia tried her formerly successful chicaneries at weaning Six from his mother's breast, Claire simply laid down the law. Her mother-in-law would hold no more domain over her baby or her breasts.

She competently—if not exactly cheerfully—presided over her husband's business dinners, keeping a pad, like the duchess of Windsor, at her table place to record the likes and dislikes of her guests. And like the duchess, the water in her vases was clear as crystal and the conversation lively. The young Harry Harrisons always served an interesting variety of both guests and vegetables. Although Claire would never leave home before Six had been tucked in and she'd told Sara her favorite bedtime story, she somehow managed to accompany Harry to at least half of the events he begged her to attend. Uninterested in his friends and wishing to be back home, she nonetheless engaged in after-dinner games of charades with the same group of cronies her husband had known since childhood and who practically had their own private sign language. She disliked going with him to dances where the couples changed partners with each song, the same songs she'd hummed sexily into Harrison's ear. The only Stork that interested her these days was not the swanky club in Manhattan but the one who had brought Claire her beautiful baby boy with his father's smile. To shield herself from Ophelia's interference, she kept a revolving schedule of her own house-guests, making sure Mother or one of the Aunties was always present and available for baby-sitting duties. And although Harry might gripe at his office on 51 Wall or on the back nine of the country club about his wife's frosty disinterest in the bedroom, he couldn't complain about the meticulous way his home was run or Claire's bottomless love for his children.

It was Sunday night and between Aunties. Harry, Claire, Sara, and baby Six were having an early dinner with Grand-mère and Grandfather Harrison. Just before blueberry pie, Six cried for his supper. Claire quietly picked him up and strode into the morning room, shutting the door behind her. It was quiet in here, and private. Her back to the terrace window, she opened her blouse and brought Six's plum-red mouth to her nipple. She sang a melody in his ear and softly rocked him as he sucked milk from her breast. Claire didn't hear the glass doors open behind her and didn't know how long Harrison had stood behind them watching before she felt his presence.

"Forgive me, Claire. I didn't mean to intrude."

Claire turned around, inviting him into their space with her warm smile. They hadn't been alone for months, but he was never out of her daydreams.

"Look how he eats, Harrison. Look how strong he's getting!" He was standing directly in front of mother and child.

"Claire, I'm deeply indebted to you for giving us this grandson to carry on the name."

Suddenly the prewar promise she had made to him and then all the other promises they'd whispered to each other rose like a dream before her.

"Oh, Harrison." She smiled gently. "Haven't you figured it out? He's not your grandson."

And while she patted Six's sweet mouth with a diaper, Harrison fell to his knees and sobbed.

"How *could* you?" Harry was furious as he stormed into her room. "I've just found out. Why have you deceived me?"

Claire tried to swallow, but her reflexes were frozen. A dozen domestic dramas flashed before her, the kind that ended with emergency rooms and police reports. Although Harry had always been even-tempered by nature, alcohol and low self-esteem were a frightening combination that if in the hands of a pharmacist would carry a warning label: *Do not mix.*

Harry's hazel eyes were a whirlpool of anger, his head and neck beet-red. In his fist was a crumpled piece of paper. How could he have found out? While she and Harrison had erred in Europe, they'd been nothing but correct in Charlotte Hall. She would never allow the secrets she and Harrison had shared to hurt another member of this family.

"Would you care to explain what you are doing? You're supposed to be my wife, not some coed." He threw Claire's second-semester grade card across the room at her.

Her heart settled back into her chest. "I'm only attending college." Her voice quivered. His violence, directed at her over this little deception, was way out of proportion. It was only deserving if he'd uncovered her real betrayal.

"Claire, I'm truly disappointed in you. Your me-first attitude is unforgivable. I can't understand you. And taking Commie courses to boot. Majoring in social reform! Aren't the Harrisons generous enough for your new liberal ideals?"

Claire bit her lip as Harry went on.

"You have no warmth, no passion anymore. You've become a . . . a . . ."

"A Harrison?"

"That's uncalled for. I was thinking more of a trouser-wearing do-gooder—like Eleanor. The Tuxedo Park Eleanor, that's what you've become. You've made me a laughingstock." The worst of the storm was over. His voice settled into a whine. "You're beautiful and sexy, Claire. Not that you ever let me near you."

Claire could smell the expensive gin on his breath as he drew nearer.

"I guess I'm just not clever enough to know which Claire you are on any given day. Are you going to be Mrs. Benjamin Spock in the nursery or Eleanor Roosevelt with your social reforms?" He took a big gulp from his martini. "What happened to the sweet, giving girl I married?"

"I thought you'd be proud. This family has raised my social conscience. And why shouldn't I be educated? It's only fitting for someone in my position to—"

"You mean in *my* position." It was evident the Tanqueray was feeding Harry's mean side. "Mother *told* me you wouldn't be up to the position. Too bad I didn't get a receipt when I picked you out at Marshall Field's. I understand they have an excellent merchandise exchange policy."

Cruel and angry when drunk, the warning should read, Claire thought. As she turned back to her social studies book, shaking quietly, she was struck by how much Harry resembled his mother. They shared the same shallow eyes.

She wasn't surprised by his outburst, only saddened: She already knew she had married the wrong Harrison.

*   *   *

By painstaking months and inches, Claire was able to pull Sara a little bit closer, but not entirely, to her. In contrast, though, little Sara found her younger brother irresistible. Like everyone else, she was drawn to the blue-eyed, towheaded child whose cherub's face could warm even one of Ophelia's rooms and take the chill off Harry's black moods. Six's cheeks, lit from within, were blushed like summer peaches, and his lips limned so perfectly it was as if Raphael had painted them himself. Claire could only imagine that since she and Harrison had gazed upon so many *Rinascimento* Madonnas with child during their Italian sojourn that the spirit of one of the tender boy beauties had jumped off the wood panel to be reincarnated in Tuxedo Park. Anyone meeting Six for the first time invariably remarked that this child must be a child born of love. With his Bermuda blue eyes and plump, pinchable thighs, he was a born charmer. Even the cold-hearted denizens of New York society, who spent their lives indulging their taste for beauty, melted before this child possessed of a calm, quiet knowing and clear, lucid eyes.

While other children went through awkward stages, when Six got his first two staggered teeth everyone delighted in his jack-o'-lantern grin. True, when he sat for his first haircut, the curls falling away to the floor, he no longer resembled a golden-haloed angel; however, he grew overnight into a more special version of the Harrison Man. Sara gaily retrieved one of the silky wheat-colored clippings from the barber's chair and playfully held it over her mouth like a mustache as Six laughed. When the fun was over she tucked her treasure away into her locket.

And so Six became the touchstone for the beleaguered Harrison family. No longer were they reduced to talking about the weather. Now the inebriated husband, his sour mother, the sorrowful grandfather, and the good mother and her moody daughter found something in common besides nor'easters and hot spells.

Sunday suppers at Ophelia's became bearable. Before Six, there were embarrassed silences between sounds of soup being slurped and the clink of forks and knives being correctly placed on the right side of bone china. Now there were the sounds of laughter and proprietary claims as to from whom Six had inherited which stellar characteristic.

"I don't know *when* I've seen a child who resembles me more." Ophelia was convinced that Six took after the Fisks and Vanderbilts, to whom she was related.

Harrison indulged his wife, but was sustained by the knowledge that this child carried the best of all the Harrisons. The belief he held that his secret son could be the third family president alleviated his suffering. After all, Harrisons were about serving and sacrificing.

Even Harry puffed up with a young father's pride when Six was able to throw the ball the farthest on the playground and ride his pony at a full gallop by age five.

Everyone tended to talk at once, mostly to brag about another of Six's accomplishments. And since Claire had allowed Sara to be the only one besides herself to rock him on her knee and later teach him his ABCs, the big sister felt more protective love than all of them combined. Somewhere in Six's half-dimpled smile and behind the luminous eyes was the knowledge that he was the tender tether that held this family together.

"Six, you've got to stop showing up the other boys. Let somebody else win at soccer. Part of being a good leader is to let the other fellow make a goal once in a while. It's how you inspire team loyalty that matters." Harrison rolled his Brussels sprout over to Six in demonstration, to Ophelia's mild irritation.

"You handled Joe like a true equestrian, darling," Minnie blathered. For years now the Mortimers had been Sunday evening regulars.

"Grand-mère, when will Six and I be old enough to do the Tuxedo Steeple Chase?" Sara had a soft-eyed chestnut gelding named Prancer, and Six's barrel-chested pony, a gift from Minnie, was registered as GI Joe. The two children spent as much time as possible down at the stables, grooming their horses and holding one another's reins as they took turns exercising their ponies in the ring, the only place they were allowed to go unsupervised. Claire thought it was too dangerous for them to venture out onto the estate's trails alone.

"When Grandfather says you can. That's when." Claire shifted the authority to the man she respected.

"Aw, geez, Claire, don't be such a good mother. Minnie and I were riding at their ages." Harry's eyes were bloodshot.

"And look how well they turned out!" It was remarkable how Minnie's mother had grayed without an ounce of wisdom to compensate.

"Please, please, *please,* we want to jump the north field fences this weekend. Can we, Grandpa?"

"If you let the groom go along and it's all right with your mother, you have my permission." He always let Claire have the final say.

Claire frowned, worried about her children's safety. "All right, but wear your helmets." Claire knew that, as delicately beautiful as Six was, he had a reckless brave streak. Already he had broken one arm going for a goal and endured a bloody nose defending a playmate. On his long walks with his mother and the dogs he was forever playing champion to every frog and bunny on their trail.

"You needn't ever be afraid, Mother," he told her one afternoon after a big summer storm. "Sir Six will always come to your rescue."

"Oh thank you, my brave protector." Claire smiled and knighted him gently with a tap of her umbrella on each shoulder.

Claire's love for her own children deepened her concern for the rest of the world's offspring. Although she'd conceded to Harry and quit her social-work courses at Bard, she started her own children's refugee center in Tuxedo, naming it Eleanor House, and found homes for Eastern European children still adrift after the war or the babies newly orphaned by the Communist strikes through South Korea.

Harry seriously wondered if she *had* become a card-carrying Commie or just a daisy-chain lesbian. Maybe those rumors about Eleanor were true. In his increasingly intolerant point of view, Claire was probably both and certainly suspect. Why else wasn't she making love to him? In their unfriendly atmosphere the two were constantly grating on each other's nerves. Just last night they'd had a blowout over which movie to go to: Harry had wanted to see Jimmy Stewart in *It's a Wonderful Life* again, but Claire was set on *Notorious*, starring Ingrid Bergman. Perhaps he should be taking his own Lucy, he thought to himself one morning as he rode the commuter into Manhattan, the *Wall Street Journal* neatly creased at the article he was reading. After all, he *was* entitled, even more so now that their European investments were booming. Every time Fulco Duccio built another shipyard, the Harrisons got richer. As silent partners, they could accrue the increasing riches without sullying the family name. Harry was repulsed by the little Italian—Duccio was such a scumbag. The article on the left-hand side of the *Journal* outlined his rapid progress from dockloader to one of Italy's most successful financiers, leaving out what they couldn't know: who his well-connected backers were. Good thing his father had cut the deal so that one was equally beholden to the other. After all, how could the Harrison tradition continue if they faded away into the hand-carved woodwork like the other mainline WASPs, only doing business with their own kind? Without money these old *Mayflower* families became blue-chip has-beens who consoled themselves with the notion that anything handed down and properly threadbare was better than new money with its gaudy accessories, houses full of Monets with price tags hanging proudly from the frames. Fellows like that could never get memberships in his club; Harry himself had blackballed a dozen of them, with names like O'Reilly and Levitt, men who had gotten rich too quickly after the war building homes for the returning boys and bottling their ketchup. And if the Harrison fortune grew vaster because they did a few deals with thugs like Duccio, it allowed them to live their life of privilege and occasional noblesse oblige. Harry's eyes had been pried wide open when he had been taken into the inner sanctum of his father's firm.

Why couldn't Claire fall into line? Ophelia had volunteered her time and done her good deeds, but she never brought one of the recipients of her largesse home to dinner. Which is exactly where Claire fed her malnourished children, with names like Tatjana and Wang Kon. If she wanted more children, why didn't she just let him do the honors some Saturday night? He should have done like his war buddies, using a pretty girl to satisfy his libido but saving marriage for the girl next door. He chortled to himself. "Next door" in his case meant the million-dollar estate adjoining his, and the girl was an heiress who could hunt and fish with her man but also knew her proper place in the house, which was to laugh at his boyish jokes in the breakfast nook and pour his martinis every day at 5:45. What he needed was a bloody good companion. And as Ophelia had tried to tell him, Minnie knew how to stay put in the saddle. She had this way of eagerly laying aside whatever she was doing when Harry came into the room, and if she smelled too much like harness leather or wet fly-casting boots, these aromas were strong reminders of their happy childhood days together. Reason enough to take her to dinner at the Metropolitan Club before her horse show tonight.

Ophelia cackled out loud when she heard Claire announce at a Sunday supper that she was bringing over two four-year-old or-phans from Seoul. "I thought slavery went out with Lincoln. Pass the cream."

"No, Grand-mère." Six's smile was so disarming that Ophelia missed the flash of temper that had momentarily widened his pupils. He flew his mother's flag. "If bad soldiers took their parents away, I don't mind sharing my toys with them."

"Ophelia, you misunderstand my intentions. I'm not planning to adopt these children. I'm just placing them in nice homes," Claire said, wondering how the wicked witch of Charlotte Hall could possibly imagine that her house was a more suitable atmosphere for two frightened children than a mortgaged Cape Cod decorated with love in a suburb of Long Island. She thought back to her own first meeting and inquisition by Ophelia and shuddered. You didn't save a child from North Korean bombings only to throw him into the society wars of the North Shore.

Sara spoke up, sensing that Six had said the right thing. "I'd love to have a Korean of my own." The Aunties had sent her a Korean doll couple from Marshall Field's fifth-floor Toys, and she kept the pair, with their green silk pajamas and black stovepipe hats, on her Most Favorite Ten Things shelf.

"Well, as long as they're out of here by Christmas." Ophelia swallowed her coffee.

"That's the spirit." Mrs. Mortimer looked around the table pleasantly.

And so with the arrival of the little refugees, the "apocalypse in a thimble," as Slim later referred to it, began.

"Who's been peeing in my Pillsbury?" Cook, flour coating her thick arms, was in a tizzy. She stormed into Ophelia's study to complain about the "slant-eyed savages invading my house." With her aluminum bowl filled with a discolored recipe as evidence, not only the tiny Koreans but also Claire were put on trial. It was the final instance of breaking the rules Ophelia had been waiting for to bring her case to court. In her relentless campaign to purge this misfit from her otherwise perfect universe, the attack on the dinner rolls by Claire's non-toilet-trained orphans was tangible evidence for the prosecution.

"Heaven knows what else they've contaminated. We could be catching Korean cholera just by eating muffins at our own table for all we know. I *insist* you put a stop to this, Harry, and I hope it opens your eyes to the fact that this woman who doesn't love you is only using us. Divorce her."

And if Harry had any misgivings about his mission, the lieutenant commander was constantly flanked by his mother and Minnie to be sure he stuck to his guns.

"Son, if this intruder loved you she wouldn't need to find time away from you with these little yellow creatures," Ophelia preached to him at breakfast.

And during their secret suppers in New York, it was Minnie who manned the guns. "Darling, you needn't uncork your thrills." Minnie shook her finger and pulled the after-dinner bottle of Tanqueray away from Harry. She twisted around, exposing her boyish breasts as she placed the bottle on the bedside table. And there, beneath the Union Club's wainscoted ceiling, in a room reserved for its top-drawer members to freshen up before the theater or unexpectedly stay the night, she wet her finger and used it to satisfy Harry in the way he preferred.

Afterwards, as Harry rested back against the headboard with his jug ears pushed forward, Minnie propped herself up with a bony elbow and massaged his temples.

"Claire's been a fine brood mare and given you two wonderful children. We should be *grateful* to her for that." Minnie didn't bother telling Harry that all the best doctors in New York and Boston had pronounced her infertile. "Let's just give her a big thank-you, a nice send-off, and the freedom she needs to save her lower classes. I have no qualms about doing it our way and writing a great big check to CARE and the Red Cross at Christmas."

"Oh, Minnie, my little pudding. What would I do without you?" Truth be known, Harry had felt more in the shadow of his father than ever, and Minnie was the perfect wall sconce to shine a little light on his secondhand quarter of the universe.

*   *   *

Tom Brewster, whom Harry had sent as his messenger boy, came to Claire with the divorce papers. The two old friends met for lunch at "21," and over corned-beef hash and with miniature Texaco trucks, oil derricks, and New York Yankee pennants hanging over their heads, he outlined to a surprised Claire which assets would be available to her. She had known their marriage was a sham, but she had assumed that to the Harrisons' appearances were too important for something as seedy as a divorce. Tom's papers probably laid out a civilized arrangement, Claire thought, with her and the children ensconced in one of the guest cottages, still under Ophelia's watchful authority.

Her eyes scanned the masculine, childish decor—big boys' trophy toys representing the businesses owned by the tycoons who ate there—and desperately searched for something familiar, like a Marshall Field's truck or an ice-skating Sonja Henie. She leaned the sleeves of her Lord & Taylor suit on the red-and-white-checked tablecloth and pushed the creamed spinach around on her plate.

Her reaction was less emotional than she might have thought. She had been leeched by Ophelia so many times she was almost too anemic to respond to this publicly delivered cut. Tom rattled on in dull lawyerly tones, and Claire noticed a blue-haired friend of Ophelia's whispering into Walter Winchell's ear, both of them trying too hard not to look in her direction but obviously there for the show. She was determined not to give them one.

"Take your time here, Claire, and by all means get your own counsel if it'll make you comfortable. But the Harrisons feel, since it's a friendly divorce, I can represent both parties."

"It's not a party, Tom." A good buddy to her during the war years, when life returned to normal and he'd become the Harrison firm's in-house legal counsel, he'd put some distance between them. Claire was disappointed but understood. After all, what was six years of friendship compared to a six-figure income and a powerful position? "I see no reason to drag this out. The Harrisons are nothing if not honorable. I'm sure they'll be fair." She thought she caught a glimpse of a silly-hatted Minnie giggling in the corner with another girl. The hat, pulled down low, could disguise her horsey face but not that whinnying laugh. Finally Minnie lifted the brim and openly smirked at Claire, as if challenging her to a contest.

Claire restrained herself. She didn't want to behave like the ill-bred shop girl they wanted her to be. "Why don't you have the papers drawn up and send them to me in Chicago? I think I'll take the children to see the Aunties for a few days."

"We can do it now or wait till you come back. That'll be about a week, right? Nobody's forcing you to sign." There was a twitching in his hand as he held his butter knife. She sensed there was another piece of news he was almost sorry he had to be part of. "But it would be the Harrison preference to sign off on this unpleasantness here and now. I'm sure you wouldn't want to a create a drama."

"Has Harrison approved this . . . document?"

"They've been drawn up to protect *all* the Harrisons. Of which you are one." Tom's tone was that of both a friend and a lawyer.

"Oh, why delay the inevitable?" And she signed in triplicate the places he had marked.

"Claire." Tom started to lay his hand over hers as he took back the document. "If there's anything I can ever—"

She pulled her hand away as if he had touched a raw nerve and, clutching at her gray gloves, felt a hint of color returning to her cheeks. She was sure she had handled herself like a lady, and she was glad she had given Minnie and Winchell nothing in her behavior to crow about. Hadn't there been enough domestic damage already?

Auntie Wren's hand-painted banner and colorful welcome-home balloons festooned the arch between the dining room and double living room of their Windermere apartment. The longtime friends had purchased a two-bedroom suite on the top floor of the residential hotel that provided them a peachy view of a tree-filled Jackson Park and four whole windows overlooking Lake Michigan. Violet's financial wizardry and plain old-fashioned thrift had finally made her a woman of property. It wasn't a palace—it wasn't even a house—and while it wasn't in Slim's swanky neighborhood, it was paid for, pleasantly furnished, and home. Violet and Wren had happily gone to the extra effort to greet the tired travelers with the fresh smells of just-baked chocolate chip cookies. The minute Claire and the children entered the sun-filled apartment, decorated with framed finger-painted originals by Sara and Six, the tension of the last few days flew away like the pigeons that took their breakfast on the Aunties' windowsill.

Claire had tried to protect her children from the angry words and accusations hurled at their departure from Charlotte Hall. As usual, the Aunties had the old-fashioned remedy: busy days and lots of laughter. Six preferred the Museum of Science and Industry half a block away, with its giant beating heart you could walk through, and Sara liked the sailboat pond off the drive at Fifty-seventh Street almost as much as she enjoyed doing something she had never done before: grocery shop. She insisted on wearing her best Florence Eisman to tap the grocer's melons, pinch the grapes, and instruct the butcher *exactly* what size and shape to cut their lamb chops before he wrapped them in the shiny white paper. The butcher always called her "young lady" and gave her a sample of something she had never tasted before, like salami or tongue. In the restful evenings—the Aunties took their dinner promptly at seven—the tuckered-out children were content to listen to the Aunties' store stories, the radio playing in the background, and pore over their mother's pretty stamps.

Wren wrung her hands and cried.

"It's the one thing we didn't teach you. What to—you know—how to keep them—that *hormonal* part of a man happy."

"Wren, please! Stop this!" Slim choreographed her entrance like Ruby Keeler.

"It's not the most terrible thing in the world. The duchess of Windsor was divorced *twice* before she married her king, and so was Rita Hayworth. As the French say, sometimes you have to kiss a lot of frogs before you get your prince."

"Well, if that's the game plan, you should be an empress by now," Violet observed sharply.

Ignoring her, Slim continued. "We've always been a special pride of lions, an all-female family." She sighed. "And now God has blessed us with two beautiful grandchildren to cherish, and even"—she hid her deep emotion—"the most special little boy on the planet."

William Henry Harrison VI, "Six" to his East Coast family but called "Sweet William" by the Aunties or just plain William by Grandlady Violet, was a head turner. No matter where he went in Marshall Field's, somebody stopped shopping just to stare at this beautiful child who moved in a part-the-seas way.

Wren was aghast at how anyone could name this angel dropped to earth after a number. "How could they? Like Sweet William was something you could buy at the pastry shop after you've waited your turn."

"No imagination, that's how." Slim explained it away. "Sure, *I'm* named after an adjective, but at least it's descriptive." She ran her hands down her sleek hips. "Six is just something that comes after five and before seven. Isn't it, darling?" She pinched his cheeks with hands circled with clanging charm bracelets, smothering him in a mist of Chanel No. 5 and My Sin.

"I love the way you smell, Auntie Slim." He adored her. For all the special attention lavished upon Six, no one could say he was spoiled. The cherished child, who received so much love, only had more love to give back.

At his request, Six celebrated his sixth birthday in the store's Walnut Room, the same room, they all remembered, where Ophelia Harrison's purchase had bought Christmas in the depth of the Depression and a ticket out of debt when Claire had been just about the same age. While his sister wasn't looking, Six rolled up his sleeve and grabbed a slippery orange goldfish out of the fountain and mischievously dropped it down the back of her party dress. After a few seconds of hysterics, all was forgiven. Nobody, especially Sara, could stay angry at Sweet William.

I've never felt so relaxed, Claire thought as she tucked her nose into the crook of her elbow and swung easily on the fringed silk hammock hanging across Slim's salon. God knows what her aunt and Cyrus Pettibone had done in this contraption, but who was she to judge? No matter where, it felt good to be alone for a lazy half hour. Mother was at the store, Wren was with the children at the zoo, and she was waiting in no particular hurry for Slim to return from "lunch" with Uncle Cyrus. She laughed to herself. Sometimes out of great complications came serenity. At this moment she was seriously considering writing a social studies chapter on how women could come together and raise very fine children.

"You shouldn't have signed the papers." The serious expression on Slim's face as she entered the room was as set as a dead-bolt lock.

"We've been over this before." Claire was still in the lull of the swaying hammock. "It's done."

"Undone, according to Cyrus. Ophelia's filing a custody suit. She's determined to steal both of your children away. Full custody. Evidently those divorce papers you so graciously signed didn't give you as much as you thought. Harder to do battle with the Harrisons without their kind of bucks."

Claire sat upright and brought her feet down to the floor. "But they don't take children away just because one parent's richer."

"No, dear. But they do if the rich parent's family dines with judges and"—the unblushable Slim was embarrassed—"accuse the mother of anti-American acts."

"What on earth can you be talking about?" Claire stood and tried to steady herself, letting the silly hammock swing away. "I've been playing Betty Crocker for five years!"

"Evidently there was a fly in the batter. My dear Claire, I'll testify for you in court. We all will."

Suddenly Claire was truly terrified. A vision of the colorfully hatted Aunties, single ladies all, taking the stand across the room from the gray-garbed Harrisons, long-married pillars of the world's best communities, rattled her so that she fell backwards into the silk swing and hung there dumbfounded.

It was several hours before Claire could fully mobilize herself into reaction. After she and Slim taxied to Hyde Park and the children were given a quick supper and tucked into bed, the four ladies assessed the situation. Slim outlined the story for them all as Claire nervously paced the floor. Evidently private detectives had been following her for months, and since no lover could be found or phantom invented, they had to search deeper. Claire had been a true incarnation of the good mother. She didn't drink, didn't smoke, didn't swear, and never missed so much as a bubble bath she had promised her children. So the only thing left to assassinate was her political character. With Senator Joseph McCarthy finding Reds under every rock, it was becoming fashionable to be frightened by Communists. What with the Soviet Union expanding its party lines left and left, if a very good lawyer could connect the dots between Claire harboring deserted Czechoslovakian children and Korean orphans, importing them into America—literally taking in the teeming masses struggling to be free—and some "all are equal" Communist manifesto she might be in for a very ugly trial.

"We've always taught you to help everyone in need, but it's not

like you're Emma Goldman." Secretly Wren was an admirer of
the socialist firebrand.

"Nor are we your average family." Slim was the reality check.

"Exactly what *do* you know, Slim? The facts will do." Violet
was the calm in the hurricane.

"Well, ever since Cyrus's prostate trouble we do more pillow
talk than anything else in the—"

"The fact, not the finding, will do nicely." Violet arched a
feathery eyebrow. In the afternoon light off the lake there suddenly appeared a fresh touch of gray at her temples.

"Cyrus says . . ." Slim had spoken those words so many hundreds of times over the years that the others had invented their
own eponymous secret parlor game. Violet had always vowed that
she was going to turn "Cyrus says" into a board game one day, sell
it at Field's, and make her fortune.

"Cyrus says there's cause for concern."

Wren envisioned the yellow game pieces moving two squares
back on the board.

"Concern?"

"Yes, Ophelia's confided in Millicent Pettibone, who's confided
in Cyrus." Slim rolled one fingernail over the other as if to explain.

"Thank goodness for pillow talk." Wren put her palms together.

"Quiet. Go on, Slim."

"Tom What's-his-name, the Harrisons' private hatchet man,
has already filed in court in Ramapo County, where all their poor
cousins are judges, to bring the children—let me get this right—
home. Yes, 'home to the only place they've ever lived in.' They
have money, connections, and evidently Ophelia is breathing fire
over this. Cyrus says"—she took a breath—"Claire doesn't have a
mouse's chance in a cat house."

"What am I going to do? How can I save my children?" Claire almost screamed. "They're so much happier here with all of you. Away from *them*." Her voice was a lament.

The phone rang half a dozen times before any of them had the composure to allow an invisible stranger into their crisis. Slim listened for a moment or two and then put down the receiver. She turned to Claire.

"Cyrus says you're to call Mr. Harrison at this number right away."

"Harry?" parroted Wren. "Is there a chance you two children might patch things up?"

"*Merde!*" Slim was furious. "Not Harry—Cyrus says he's going to marry Minnie Mortimer and Ophelia's going to give them Claire's children as a wedding present."

Claire started to swoon.

"Steady, now. Here's the number you're supposed to call for the elder Mr. Harrison."

The concerned ladies moved into the kitchen but not completely out of earshot. They strained to pick up bits and pieces of Claire's conversation with her father-in-law.

Claire, shaking with rage, nonetheless spoke into the phone with the voice of a gentle sparrow.

"How could you? Why would you? Why not just take a knife and cut out my heart?"

And then there was a very long silence. Auntie Wren peeked through the crack of the swinging doors, hushing the others behind her. Claire's mouth was a perfectly straight line—not a natural shape for a mouth.

"I don't understand . . .

"It sounds cold-hearted.

"Arrangements like that can't be ordered. Isn't something like that an affair of the heart?

"Why would he possibly want to help? What's in it for him?"

Everyone in the kitchen held her breath as the next minutes passed without Claire uttering a single word.

"Oh, I see.

"Yes, of course. It would put an ocean between us. And the lawyers couldn't touch us there?"

"I see. Of course. Speed. I understand."

And then the Aunties heard a quivering contralto in Claire's voice they had never heard before.

"And will you make it over?"

And then an icy response. "Of course. I'll be sufficiently grateful. I won't give him cause to be sorry.

"I've never quite understood your negotiating skills before. You really are the master. Don't worry." Her voice dropped away like fallen rose petals. "I'm in. The deal is sealed in rubber and cement."

She stood there, cradling the phone in her hands, listening to the dead signal. Finally she put the receiver to rest and turned stony-faced to the expectant Aunties.

"I need to get passports for the children. I'm taking them on holiday to Italy."

Never had there been so much hysteria over scrambled eggs and bacon at staid Charlotte Hall. The family that handled every crisis with icy calm was now wiping spilled milk and orange juice off the morning pages of the *New York Herald* and the *Times*. There, not on the society pages but in the international news section of both papers, was the announcement, accompanied by separate pictures of the principals, of the surprise nuptials of society matron Mrs. William Henry Harrison V to Fulco Duccio, Italy's playboy businessman whose fortune was estimated in the hundreds of millions. Both Cholly Knickerbocker and Walter Winchell reminded their readers that the dashing Duccio was a regular figure in Europe's fast night life. The *Post* reported that he had recently caused a ruckus at Maxim's in Paris, breaking glasses and chairs when the French ballerina he was dating danced with another man. Mr. Duccio had reimbursed the French restaurant for its expenses and was still a regular at its best table. Mrs. Harrison, attended only by Anna Roosevelt and the bride's children from her first marriage, wore a blue Balenciaga and carried violets. She is best known here for her generous charity work and in particular for founding Eleanor House, a children's refugee center.

Harry read aloud to the rest of the family, a long-faced Minnie at his elbow, while Ophelia noisily rearranged her Lowestoft china with the back of her hand, and Harrison reached into his pocket to light an early morning cigar.

Across the sea, Claire Harrison Duccio was learning Italian and busily reinventing herself.

Chapter Twelve

~

Social Climbing

Out of all the social climbers in Europe, Pamela Harriman was the most athletic.

—The London Times

Near the alpine peak of their summer climb in Gstaad, Claire heaved a sigh of relief.

"Oh, Claire. Claiirre," Pamela Churchill yodeled to Fulco Duccio's glamorous wife. They were all a little breathless. But climbing the switchbacks at a leisurely pace had been more social exercise than sport, as they still had enough oxygen at eight thousand feet to carry on a conversation.

Everyone in the climbing party was in prime physical shape: No one got to the heights this merry band had attained without stamina and a good set of lungs. Not to mention a fierce competitive drive.

"Are we going to picnic here, or go on to the summit?" The pink-cheeked divorcée and European party girl wanted to eat.

"I say let's go to the top and plant our flag." Léonide Massine, famed choreographer and dancer of the Ballets Russes, assumed the classical second position, planting his feet near the narrow foot trail at a level where snow patches circled clusters of alpine roses and tall spruces.

"Which flag, darling? I don't think there's three people in our group from the same country."

"How colorful. Let us plant a new flag. Ve could use my coat of arms." Gunilla Von Hapsburg wore lederhosen, a smart cap over her blond braids, and very red lips over her wide smile.

"I want to hear Pam yodel again. My money says that the chamois antelope ignore her and some Italian playboy comes out from under his rock," Léonide said.

"Look. A skylark." Claire pulled the field glasses to her eyes and pointed out the bird to the others.

"Claire. Ma Clare di luna is finding birds, inedible birds for us to admire." Duccio's shadow fell over his wife. The financial titan didn't find any animal in nature attractive unless he could devour it or deal it.

He leaned his short, sturdy frame against a walking stick that was very expensive but completely unnecessary. As a boy in Calabria he had been nicknamed *Il Capro,* the goat, for his agility. *Duro* was how even his own mother, a fishmonger, had described him. Tough twice over. Every day he had scrambled over the mirthless rocks of his boyhood home and leaned fearlessly over their sheer drops, better able to scout which big freighters on the ink-blue sea would soon be pulling into port. Then he'd scurry down the cliffs, beating out the merchants in both speed and price, in his highly successful campaigns to sell sea-weary sailors meat, goat cheese, fresh pasta, and eggs. By the age of eleven, Irpino Duccio, still unschooled and illiterate, had saved enough to make his way to Naples. There he became an apprentice to a gambling card sharp, and then to a thief who worked the rich villas on Capri. Later he sailed off on a German freighter as the captain's second cabin boy, where he studied languages and kept the supply books—as well as some supplies for himself, to sell later. By the time he arrived in Rome at the age of fifteen, his pockets jiggling with lira, he had assumed the name Fulco (after a noted Roman jeweler he had once robbed), abandoning the unsavory-sounding "Irpino" forever. He became an owner of a few rundown fishing boats, then a salvaged freighter, and then another purchased with borrowed Mafia money. Because he was small, he learned to use his hands as weapons, perfecting a single devastating chop to the clavicle that could knock out a larger man. His temper was so hot and his arms so strong that lesser men simply capitulated to avoid confronting him.

But it was during the first years of the war that he had become rich. He bought Swiss citizenship for the duration of the war, and while his right hand did legal business with the Americans, his left conducted black-market deals with the Germans. Everyone needed sugar and rubber, reasoned Duccio—who was he to judge? And when he had been able to restore some stolen treasures taken from St. Peter's by Nazi vandals, he earned Holy Communion and lifelong gratitude from the fine cardinal in charge of the papal treasury. As a result, his growing fleet flew the neutral Vatican flag and his boats could dock safely at every port. Duccio was very good at keeping important men in his debt.

Duccio's fortunes were truly bolstered, however, when he acquired a Harrison. For the favor of marrying the American beauty, William Henry Harrison IV rewarded him with a continuing column of shipping freight and construction contracts. Once he had those, the business of other rich Americans fell in his lap. While a good French public-relations firm had wiped away any Mafia taint, it was only the addition of a pale American society wife that allowed Duccio to rise to the highest levels of wealth and social acceptance.

At the high meadow just shy of the summit, Claire Harrison Duccio unwrapped the snack that she carried for her husband in her knapsack: quartered apples, olives, soft cheese, and finally his folding saddle seat so that he could bend his short-legged form into a generalissimo position.

Claire saw to his needs like the attentive wife she had taught herself to be. It was in these public gestures that she made up for their lack of private intimacy and the fact that husband and wife slept in separate bedrooms.

"Come closer, my dear. *Vicino a me. S'accomodi.*" He patted the ankle-high patch of grass by his stool.

"Of course, dear."

"*Che meglio.*"

"*Si caro.* I was staying up front with our more athletic guests."

"Always the perfect American hostess. You help me in so many ways." He took her pale hand in his. His hand was the same shade as the bald alpine rock but with a thick pate of black hair clumped across the back.

"I try to be." She lowered her eyes.

"You are the most hostess without even trying."

When she laughed, she displayed perfect teeth. The sight made Duccio cover his own bad gums and brownish teeth with one of his paws. Early malnutrition and untended tooth decay had left his mouth a dental disaster zone.

"Oh, come now, Duccio." She gently pulled his hirsute hand away from his lips. "If it embarrasses you so much, let me take you to a good dentist in London."

"There are no good dentists there. Even the English aristocracy have rotten teeth. Only in America. Let my good aristocratic American wife take me *there.*"

She frowned. Ophelia's lawyers were in America, ready to take her children away. Claire hadn't been back since that night she'd packed up their belongings almost a year ago and arrived on Duccio's doorstep like a mail-order bride.

Tutti, the gun-toting manservant, had opened the door, an impatient Duccio at his elbow.

"Welcome to Villa Duccio." Duccio bowed.

"*Grazie.*" If she was astonished to realize she was reintroducing herself to the man she would marry just as soon as she had showered and changed, she was bowled over by the lavish rococo villa that would be her weekend home. Her violet eyes crossed as they swept over a panoply of arches, niches, medallions, balustrades, and statues of dwarves and maidens unlike any she had seen in a museum. Her host took her wonder for admiration. He was obviously hoping she'd be impressed with both his taste and his undeniable wealth.

" 'You can't depend on your eyes when your imagination is out of focus.' I read that in your American Mark Twain." He stood back with an awkward arm gesture, pulling an imaginary curtain aside so that the twenty-seven-year-old beauty would focus on the rooms instead of his less than statuesque fifty-year-old physique. His gesture had just the opposite effect, however. Pretending to study the enormous Vincenzo Dandini paintings behind him, each rococo fresco taller than its owner, Claire instead appraised her mysterious husband-to-be. He stood as erect as a cypress. His Mediterranean-blue eyes were set deep in his head, the hooded lids impenetrable. Nonetheless the cold, dark eyes radiated a strange intimacy, inviting like the waters they brought to mind. Blue, gray, green, the irises changed as the light fluctuated in the vast room. His feet seemed to grow out of the floor of varnished red bricks from Impruneta, and from above, an eighteenth-century Murano glass chandelier rained colored crystal upon his slicked-back hair. He was certainly dramatic looking, but hardly a man she'd even consider having an affair with, let alone choose for a husband. For a moment she wavered. Duccio caught her with a look. Even though he was shorter than she, he had positioned himself so that he could look down upon her. His tie was too long, his collar too wide, his gestures too effusive, but somehow he made her feel as if he would throw all his considerable power into keeping her and her children away from harm. A very frightened Claire realized that if anyone could beat Ophelia and her hired guns, it was Duccio, who had both the weapons and the ruthlessness to use them.

He motioned her over to a red-and-white-striped silk sofa that seemed long enough for a dozen Claires but seated himself on a thronelike gilded chair backed with cut green velvet. He pushed a vase of roses in her direction so that she would understand that they were for her. Rough and refined artifacts comingled in this drawing room; the surroundings were not unlike their owner. She noticed how soft, almost feminine, his mouth was, contradicting his other features, which were as rocky as the Calabrian coast.

He was solicitous to an extreme. Would she like a mineral water? With gas or *sine* gas? Or perhaps a fresh-squeezed orange juice? The glass of juice was already sitting on the sideboard, the same bright color as the rare Persian rug at his feet. What she had mistaken at first for a sneer was really his crooked smile.

If she were here on a guided tour of Tuscany, this might be a perfectly pleasant idle afternoon. Duccio was obviously a charming host, although neither the decor nor the man were to Claire's taste. What was unreal was that she was sitting on a fourteen-foot sofa with a total stranger whom the man she loved had decided she should marry. All to keep her and her children out of the way of Ophelia's expensive lawyers and the malicious allegations. Claire was no longer foolish enough to think she could beat her foe. If Harrison couldn't stand up to Ophelia's machinations, how could she? Ophelia was too clever an enemy; the accusations they were hurling at Claire were too numerous to be counted. She was accused of everything from Communist activities to lesbianism, anything that would portray her as a woman unworthy to raise her own children. Which was precisely the point. Ophelia was prepared to do whatever it took to send the war-wife away so that her grandchildren could be raised in the house she had built for Harry and grow up according to the agenda she had planned. She would stop at nothing; Claire was an incidental enemy to be rolled over by Ophelia's battalion of legal tanks. So if Claire had to sleep alongside a pirate with more power and fewer scruples than Ophelia, she would adjust. She had to. But for now, she was still so stunned by the frightening turn of events, her throat so constricted with terror, that she wasn't even able to swallow the cool drink Duccio had placed in her perspiring hand. He noticed her hesitation and awkwardly tried to put her at ease.

"So you are wanting to start a new chapter in your life, my little pale one?"

"Circumstances dictate that I must."

"You have such a nice soft voice." He pulled his throne closer. As he drew nearer, she could see his eyes more clearly. They were mesmerizing. Behind commanding eyes like these loomed either a madman or a genius. When she looked only at his eyes, she could almost feel the pull of his attraction.

"Unless you are very tired, I would like to walk you through my garden. It is one of the most beautiful in Tuscany. I have a question there to ask you."

Claire knew what the question was. She was almost touched that this gruff man was trying to make their business arrangement romantic. She stood, clutching her handbag in front of her with both hands. She had steeled to the parameters of the deal that Harrison had set, but found she was nervous nonetheless.

"To the garden, then."

A path crossed a little bridge then led directly to Villa Duccio's voluptuous garden. They ambled down the wide allée bordered with high hedges of bay trees before they entered the main parterre, every bit as green and big as Chicago's Lincoln Park. Claire caught her breath. It was as if nature had developed a sense of humor. Everywhere she looked there were evergreen animals, griffins, doves, a Noah's Ark of manicured topiary protected by battlemented walls of box hedges. Some of the tension started to fall from her shoulders. Following Duccio, she stepped carefully around two lily-filled basins that spurted water twenty feet into the air, splashing her along with the giant stone hooves of satyrs that permanently leered at marble female statues. Red, green, purple, yellow, and orange flowers surrounded the imaginative centerpiece of this garden, a floral coat of arms with *Duccio* scripted in geraniums. Surely this was the place where he would pop his question. She was mistaken.

"There is a lovers' grotto at the end of this path. For three centuries men nobler than I have asked for the hand of their lady there."

Claire blushed and a bead of sweat formed at that spot on the back of her neck. Surely Harrison had told him this was a business deal for which he would be well compensated. Financially.

"Excuse me, Mr. Duccio."

"Fulco, *per favore,* please." He touched her shoulder.

"Fulco . . ."

He put his hand up to stop her. "Right here in the grotto it is said you can see the ghost of a beautiful young woman who sold her soul to the devil to preserve her youth. She thought it would please her lover. A tragedy, don't you think?"

"Yes, but—"

"What foolish women won't do for love. It is the wise woman who realizes marriage is just another contract, one that benefits both parties. It's quite the better way, don't you think? Only practical expectations. Then nobody has to sell their soul to the devil."

Suddenly Claire felt that Duccio, obviously so much smarter than the barbarian she had assumed he was, might turn out to be a bearable companion.

Between the backdrop of undulating rocaille arches and a figure of the goddess Diana surprised in her bath, Fulco Duccio promised to protect Claire and her children if she would preside over his table and entertain his associates. So beneath Villa Duccio's eighteenth-century clock tower and under the shade of ripe espaliered fruit trees, in full sight of an ivy-covered Cupid and a stone goddess of love, where so many young couples had pledged their eternal vows, Claire Harrison and Fulco Duccio agreed to share a public facade.

"We will fly one another's flag, my dear."

Suddenly out of the grotto Tutti appeared, his holster partially visible, to present her with an obscenely large ring from Buccellati. The naked diamond sitting on a black velvet jeweler's pillow looked like a piece of the moon. The rock was cut in the shape of an ice cube, the flawless diamond glowing from hot white to cold blue in the cavern's light. Claire tossed her head back to laugh for the first time in sixty hours. At the same moment, she slipped Harry's wedding ring off her finger, hearing it drop into the lily-laden pond.

"Do you realize it's almost our anniversary?" Duccio asked. "I feel like singing. Do you have my accordion in your knapsack?"

Claire good-naturedly pretended to search. "It must have been lost in the avalanche, dear."

"Da avalanche?" Léonide danced over like Nijinsky as the faun. "This is what we will see when we return to the Riviera and Pam discovers she has converted to Catholicism for nothing. Agnelli has a new woman, one with a long neck who his family will allow him to marry. *Pffttttt!* I can see the landslide now!" He trailed his fingers up his neck as if he were elongating it. "You know Pammie answers the phone '*Pronto!*' now. Imagine a good English girl, married to a Churchill, speaking with an Italian accent. Oy!"

Pamela, wearing pearls over her cable-knit sweater and corduroy trousers, trudged up the hill with a Muslim playboy. "Oh, Claire! There you are! Shouldn't we be getting back soon? Aren't your children coming back from their summer vacation tomorrow?" She dropped to rest on a rock. "We are so—how do you say in English?—exhausted." Her phony Italian accent caused the rest of the party to dissolve into titters. The laughter continued unmitigated until the sound of a bullet zinged through the air. Then the thud of lead hitting something warm with blood shook them.

"What on earth?" Pam Churchill's accent was once again very British.

"Duccio shot a lark!" Massimo, the count of Ruspoli, exclaimed as if the man he worked for had just bagged a lion on safari.

Only Léonide noticed the shadow that crossed Claire's otherwise composed face. He knew better than to bring up in Duccio's presence the only two people Claire really loved. The hot-blooded Russian recognized what nobody else could see: that Duccio had fallen in love with his elegant wife and was insanely jealous because she didn't love him back.

"Over here, my darlings!" Claire beamed so brightly that light radiated from her like a beacon.

Sweet William rushed into his mother's arms, darting ahead of his sister and Auntie Slim, who guarded a mound of luggage against the crowded confusion of the train station.

Claire wrapped her arms around Six and hugged him to her breast.

"You look brown as bears. And you've grown. Both of you. In only one month's time."

"Yes, but everyone knows August is the month for growing." Six patted his mother's cheek.

"And muscles, too. Sara, how you have changed." Sara stiffened in her mother's embrace and wiggled away, extending her hand in greeting.

Almost overnight, Sara had turned into a little Ophelia. From the way she half-opened her mouth to speak and shuddered away from physical contact, it was clear that a month in Newport with the Harrisons had turned her daughter into what Duccio called one of the "garden furniture people"—iron arms and wooden trunks. Her aloofness was all the more evident at Rome's train station, where crowds of effusive Italians hugged and kissed with exuberant arm gestures.

Claire sighed and pulled her lips into an indulgent smile. It would take her months of patient love to undo Ophelia's damage.

"Come, children. Let's help Auntie Slim. I have a surprise for you."

All the way home to Palazzo Duccio, their house in Rome, Six tried to coax the surprise out of his mother while Sara complained about the heat and intense Roman sunlight, at one point yanking down the backseat's window shade with a snap.

"It's *so* much cooler in Newport. And no pesky mosquitoes."

Ten-year-old Sara impatiently batted one away with her copy of *Anne of Green Gables.*

"Oh, Sara. If those were Newport mosquitoes you'd think they were swell." Her brother flashed her an all-American grin.

Laughing, Claire hugged her son and teased Auntie Slim about having to travel for eight days straight onboard ship with two such strongly independent children.

Auntie Slim tried to look annoyed but in fact was besotted with her two charges. "Let's see. Sara stayed in the cabin the first two days with mal de mer and kept iced tea bags over her eyes."

"You should have seen the waves, Mommy. They came up to here." Six demonstrated excitedly.

"He's not exaggerating a bit. We just *blew* over from the States."

Sara felt like fencing. "You can blow me right back. I have friends there now, you know, and Grand-mère says—"

"How is Grand-mère Ophelia?" Claire's voice was as calm as the Tevere River, which they were crossing.

"Quite well," Sara mumbled stiffly.

"I'm so glad." Claire looked genuinely pleased. "Now tell me everything about the crossing."

"Your son took up skeet shooting and banged away quite a bunch of pucks."

"They're called clay pigeons, Auntie Slim. I've got really good aim, too."

"Guns! Aren't you a little young for that?" The first wrinkle of the day crossed Claire's brow.

"All the Harrisons hunt and shoot, Mother. Grandfather taught me." He mistook the faraway look in her mother's eyes for disapproval.

"Oh well, as long as you keep it confined to the wide-open spaces. Didn't you children have a great-aunt who shot off the butler's ear for putting in two lumps of sugar instead of three?" They all giggled as the dark purple and black car pulled into the narrow colonnaded driveway of Palazzo Duccio's time-worn Roman facade.

"I *hate* this place." Sara pulled her straw hat with streamers down over her auburn eyebrows. "Our cottage in Newport was so much nicer. And I detest my room here. It's just like being kept in the attic." She pointed with her *Green Gables* to the third-floor rooms she shared with her brother in the square-shaped palace. What was begun in 1547 by Cardinal Ricci in grand baroque style was now being topped off in the swanky fashion favored by the children's free-spending stepfather.

"So you've said, dear."

Six stepped into the vast marble foyer, cool as an ice palace with its echoing floors, and hung his cap on the bronzed rump of an eternally aroused Centaur.

Slim's head turned to the statue for a second inspection. The half-man, half-horse that dominated the entryway reminded her of something she hadn't seen for a long time. It also reminded her of something Sara had said onboard ship. Evidently Ophelia Harrison was having some sort of legal document drafted about her grandchildren growing up amidst erotic art. She patted the rump in question as she followed Claire and the children up the grand, curving staircase. Sneaking a look on the way up at other statues planted in the arches, Slim saw where a few fig leaves might indeed be welcome additions.

"Why are we going to *your* room, Mommy?"

"You'll see." Claire knew her children disliked the overwhelming grandeur of her bedroom, with its cathedral ceilings frescoed with allegorical scenes of Olympian love and nanny goats in hot pursuit of naked nymphets. Claire had to admit she could never get used to them or the gold-leafed putti holding sheaths of satin over the elaborate cornice above her bed. "I've done a little decorating of my own this summer. What do you two think?" She opened the door.

"Wow, Mom. It looks like home in here!"

Slim poked her head in. "Too much like home. What did you use for inspiration, Early Windermere?"

With some of Italy's best carpenters, artisans, and fabric makers at her disposal, Claire had turned her enormous bedchamber into a compact, four-room apartment. The recessed turret windows had been replaced by prefab American paned units that let the sunlight stream into a cozy family room set with inviting sofas, overstuffed ottomans, and a few child-sized chairs. Three other doors led from the parlor, one to Sara's bedroom, one to Six's, and, in the center, Claire's.

"Welcome home, my darlings."

Toys, books, and globes were neatly stacked around the cheery sitting room. Even the offending frescoes had been covered by pretty tapestries of unicorns and *faerie* queens. Only the ceiling paintings twenty feet high in Claire's bedchamber remained. Kicking off her shoes, Claire plopped herself down on the cushions, making a soft imprint and, putting her feet on the table, invited her children to do the same.

Slim shook her dyed black bob. "I can't believe you've come all this way up in the world just to want to sink into some middle-class sofa."

"Which you're welcome to jump on anytime. There are no rules here in our private tree house."

"Unless we make them ourselves, right, Mommy?"

Sara joined in, "Fort Claire! That would be a nice name for it, don't you think?" She peeked out her bedroom window to admire the American flag hanging from a long pole over a shiny new set of swings and a jungle gym. "How did you get all this done in a month?"

"By learning perfect Italian, which is what you two are going to do. As well as French. The world is becoming a very small place, and both of you will be ready for it."

Six groaned. "You sound just like Grandfather."

"Why, thank you." Claire tilted her head and smiled with her eyes. "I'm sure he would approve."

That night, with Duccio away, the little family took dinner not in the grand dining room downstairs under the nosy attention of busybody maids and gun-wielding butlers, but rather in the private seclusion of their own little apartment. By the end of the evening, even luxury-loving Slim was disappointed that she had to slip away to a sumptuous bedchamber in one of the noblest palazzos in Italy.

Sara was lying with one knee crossed over the other on the perfectly coifed grass of their high-walled Roman garden, her red hair fanning out over the green lawn. It was late afternoon but the sun was bright enough that she had chosen the shade of a tall poplar to read her long, scolding letter from Grand-mère Ophelia, in which Sara was instructed to begin a list of all the rude and improper misbehavings of her offensive stepfather. Sara looked out over the lawns that were as carefully tended as the exquisitely gowned women who swept in on the arms of important men for one of her mother's dinners. Her eyes followed the trail of a Roman monarch butterfly, but her sharp ears could hear the servants bustling in the downstairs kitchen of Palazzo Duccio. A new American ambassador had been appointed to Italy, and the first formal reception for the new diplomat was being given at her mother and stepfather's house.

A screen door slammed and Sara recognized the quick, light step of her brother.

"Guess who's coming to dinner?"

Sara twisted around and saw Six excitedly waving a telegram in the air.

"President Eisenhower?"

"Nope. Bigger than that."

The dozen or so freckles on Sara's nose crinkled.

"Bigger than Ike?"

"Better."

Who could be better? Along with the letter, Ophelia had sent a stack of *Time* magazines and *Saturday Evening Posts* with interesting stories circled in red ink—in case Sara was getting homesick. She racked her brain, remembering the issues she had scanned.

"Elizabeth Taylor!" She had loved her in *Father of the Bride*. In fact, Sara had liked the whole family. One mother, one father, the sister and brother all under one roof.

"No. Better than that." Six teasingly waved the yellow telegram at his sister. "Guess again."

She caught the twinkle in his eyes. She loved the way he lifted them, shyly at first and then locking them directly on her own.

"Give me a hint."

"Tall, proud, elegant, brilliant . . ." Six paused and then added, "highly respected."

"Grandfather!"

"You win a trip to Charlotte Hall, all expenses paid."

"Phooey on the expenses. When is he coming?"

"Tomorrow. And staying all weekend . . . with us." His perfect teeth were displayed like Chiclets when he widened his grin. His growing broad shoulders and high cheekbones gave significant evidence that he was his mother's son. To Sara had fallen Ophelia's plain looks.

"Is he going to be the new ambassador?" If she couldn't be back in Tuxedo the next best thing would be to have the Harrisons here.

"No, that's Ambassador Luce." He bit his naturally strawberry-colored lips. "Clare Boothe Luce, I think. But she's not staying here. Only Grandfather. And we haven't got much time if we're going to make him a welcome sign and get Cook to whip up his favorite cake."

Sara was so excited she stashed Ophelia's letter in her pocket and hurried after her brother to get out the welcome wagon.

Claire's days ran along in a smooth routine. By seven she was preparing her children's breakfast in the restaurant-sized kitchen downstairs, making French toast and slicing bananas to go with their

berries, and whipping up egg-salad sandwiches for their lunch
boxes. After she had given them each their pep talks and hugged
them off to school, she bathed and then slipped into a lace morning
robe and back into bed so that she could wave good morning to
Duccio. Her maid, Lorenza, arrived promptly at nine with juice and
coffee on a sterling tray along with the *Herald Tribune, Il Corriere,*
and a list of the day's menus to be approved or redone along with
the seating charts if there was to be a dinner. She took her calls on
her private line until ten, and then quickly dressed in her riding
clothes or a Chanel suit, depending on the day's activities. Today
there was a kick in her step and a melody in her head as she went
about making arrangements for tonight's dinner for thirty-six. All
of a sudden she had two guests of honor instead of one: Ambassador
Luce *and* Harrison. Harrison! Just saying his name to herself gave
her a thrill. She'd put him on her right and Clare Luce on Duccio's
right. Even after all her practice charming buffoons and feeding
kings, would she have the presence of mind to continue playing the
cool hostess in front of Harrison—Harrison, who knew everything
about her and every place on her body?

As Claire slipped on her custom-cut riding jodhpurs and jacket,
adding a silk ascot at her throat, she caught a glimpse of an almost
giddy girl in the mirror. But it wasn't until Lorenza pointed it out
that she realized she was singing the same funny tune that her children had been humming this morning. Harrison was coming. And
for different reasons, they were all excited.

All through her morning ride in the park she was breathless.
She had taught herself to be a stylish rider but this was the first
time she could remember ever riding with passion. She rode
faster, trying to outrun the images in her brain of Harrison's long,
subtly muscled limbs and his elegant profile. She rode harder,
quickening the feeling between her own thighs, but she couldn't
put enough horse between her and Harrison; every time she
passed a distinguished-looking rider on the trail she imagined it
was he, only to be disappointed when it wasn't.

Cooled down, showered, and changed, she sat twirling a pencil at the conference table of the weekly meeting of Eleanor House. Tonight she'd ask Ambassador Luce to serve on the board. Claire could barely concentrate on the business at hand as the speeches droned on and sentences evaporated into annoying, insectlike buzzes. She brought her hand to the back of her neck to stop an itch and realized she couldn't scratch it away. It was *that* spot, his spot on her neck that he loved to caress.

Later, she was blithery as a goose girl, fussing over the seating order as if she hadn't already hosted over two hundred formal business dinners in their four lavishly appointed homes. She had to take a headache powder by four P.M., although a worried Lorenza had already brought her three cups of sweetened tea and an Alka-Seltzer. She pressed her fingers against her temples and slowly exhaled to calm herself.

So she was able to appear serene when a hysterical, bathrobe-clad Slim, nearly unrecognizable without her Chanel war paint, was chased into the dining hall by a gun-toting Tutti. The butler was wild-eyed. His master's American bald eagle was on the loose and Tutti was on its trail. He twisted its empty leash menacingly around his wrist.

"You didn't tell me your husband raises goddamn vultures in this crazy house! I found the beast in my bathroom."

"Only one, and it's a national treasure."

"The goddamn bird was in my shower!"

"Fulco will be so upset. What have you done with it?"

"Opened the fucking window and pointed to the Grand Canyon, that's what. That bird must have had a wingspan of twenty feet."

"Eight feet. And it's Duccio's favorite pet. Tutti, we'll just have to find it."

When Duccio had returned from a trip to New York just in time for Easter weekend last year, he had come laden with presents. He had presented Six with a speargun and skin-diving gear for their summer vacation in Capri. There was a pascal lamb for Sara and for Claire a pair of emerald chandelier earrings from Verdura that reached almost to her shoulders. For himself he had purchased a contraband American eagle. The boxed bird's hooded eyes were narrowly awake after an oversedated flight on the plane Duccio had chartered to bring him and his contraband home.

"You know the great bald American eagle is almost distinct," he had told Claire.

"I think you mean extinct, dear. How clever of you to save one."

"I thought it would be a smash addition to our dinners in which we entertain my American clients. It will remind them of the ranges."

"You weren't thinking of using the eagle as a centerpiece, I hope." She had to turn away from Sara and Six, who were helpless with giggles behind the lamb. They all jumped back as the national bird of America awakened and opened its wide wings across the quaking cage.

"You and Tutti figure out the presentation. *Forse*, on my gloved wrist like a falcon. *That* would be very dramatic."

"Or perhaps on a stand like a pirate's parrot," Six said, entirely straight-faced.

"Oh yes, Six. Like that." Duccio threw his small, powerful hands in the air. "Like a pirate." And he stomped happily out of the room.

"Signóre Duccio asked that I arrange for the bald eagle to be present tonight." Tutti walked proudly into the room. The bird had been recovered. Tutti had been with Duccio for sixteen years and had witnessed sights Claire didn't even want to hear about.

"Just keep him tethered in the corner, though, please. I wouldn't want to frighten any of the guests. And the new ambassador is a lady, you know, Tutti, so I'd be sure to keep the bird away from her hairdo."

"Of course, Signóra Claire." And he backed silently out of the room.

"*Mon dieu.* It's like Tarzan and Jane at Greystoke in this place. Are there any other critters you'd like to warn me about?" Slim stuck a Camel into her mouth and lit it with a wooden match.

"Oh, Auntie Slim. I want this to be a fabulous dinner. But you must help me. It's so important to . . . Duccio. I'm just not sure about who sits next to whom." She studied the notebook in which she documented her dinner parties, what she had served and who had sat next to whom.

"Let's see, the elder Agnelli has gout, so it's salt-free and no sauces at his place." Providenzia and Alberto stood at heightened alert behind the mistress of Palazzo Duccio and nodded attentively, as if they were military operatives being briefed by their commanding officer. Their jobs depended on these little details. The headwaiter and his maid followed Claire as she moved down the long table, a pencil in her hand and a spare behind her ear. Slim trailed behind like a smokestack, occasionally backlit by sunlight that floated in through the sheer curtains. Claire had herself selected the crisp, floating fabric that veiled the world outdoors and created an aura of quiet mystery inside her public rooms. Later that evening, lit candles would bathe her guests in a rich golden light. Claire had learned from her European counterparts that the best lighting in the room should be reflected on the guests, making them feel handsome and interesting.

"Ambassador Luce is the reason for the gathering . . ."

"So put her in the centerpiece with the damn eagle and then Duccio can show her off to all his business associates. That's the point of all this, isn't it?" Slim nailed it.

"Precisely. We just don't discuss it."

Slim was only recently learning that in this apparently loveless marriage Claire's loyalty to Duccio was solid. She lit a second Camel with the first, Providenzia holding an ashtray under her hand during the tricky maneuver.

"Ambassador Luce on Duccio's right. And let's give her the Vatican cardinal on *her* right. You know she converted to Catholicism after the death of her daughter." Claire's children, thank goodness, would be present as usual at the cocktail hour, and the thought cheered her. "Mr. Luce is supposed to be a dull conversationalist so Cissy Grant can discuss world events with him over there." She pointed. "Her husband owns half the newspapers in America."

"Yeah, their society columnist runs you weekly in her 'Letter from Abroad.'"

"And you, dear Auntie Slim, get Mr. Grant. You can tell him all the news he doesn't know, you darling."

"What's cooking?"

"Caviar with all the trimmings and quail's eggs in the drawing room—"

"Yum."

"And those not on restricted diets get *pasta portobello,* a soupçon of bouillabaise, *vitello con limone,* and fresh from the sea *pesce spada*—that's grilled sea bass—with *pomodori* and zucchini and then all of Duccio's favorite cheeses and iced pears and pear and lemon sherbets, all homemade, and then all our freshly dipped chocolates from the kitchen with espresso. Good?"

Slim stood back and marveled at this gifted, in-charge hostess.

"I'm going to walk around the front to make sure both the Italian flag and the American flag are displayed properly, and Duccio wants the photograph of FDR and me to be on the hall table next to the official Ike." She rolled her eyes.

"Did you learn all this from us?"

"Every last bit. Well, a few years in the Roosevelt White House and hanging out with your pal the duchess of Windsor helped a little." Claire grinned and slipped her arm through her auntie's. "Come along to Duccio's little gallery. I have to make sure practically every guest coming tonight has his picture hanging in the library." She laughed, yet she knew this was very serious business, and the pictures of the former king of Italy, the head of Fiat, FDR's right-hand man, the publisher of *Time* magazine, all with their arms draped around Duccio, as well as Duccio the family man, all had to be arranged with as much protocol and care as the seating. Claire took such pains because she understood that this particular evening was not about politics and power games but about securing a half-billion-dollar account for her husband's shipping line and another for his South American rubber plant. However, it was the international conversation at the highest level, the most interesting people in the world gathered at her table, that made these dinners so appetizing for the hostess. Having discovered as a young Harrison bride that she moved comfortably in the corridors of power, able to slip in softly a change here and there, she took that element in this artificial marriage to Duccio and nurtured it. All of the people so carefully arranged around her table knew she was equal to any power broker in the smoke-filled rooms back home where presidents were selected and elections won. But her greatest asset was taking the spotlight that shone on her and reflecting it back on her guests. Nobody left Palazzo Duccio without having met somebody they needed to know, enjoying the finest cuisine in Rome, and promising to send a check to Eleanor House. *Con piacere*, with pleasure.

As was her custom, Claire dined with her children at six o'clock before her guests arrived. She never missed a family dinner. Tonight her heart was racing a thousand miles a minute because Harrison was going to join their little group. She couldn't decide whether to dress for her party before or after their separate supper. She wasn't sure how she wanted to look when she saw Harrison. She knew he was coming over just for business matters with Duccio and to see the children, but her entire upper respiratory system was hyperventilating, demanding to know if she and Harrison still loved each other. She took a sip of champagne at her dressing table to quiet her nerves. She couldn't appear rattled, not in front of the children, not in front of Duccio, not in front of her guests, and certainly not in front of Harrison. If only she could stop thinking about him, her hands would stop shaking enough so that she could slip into her white taffeta Balenciaga, pull her hair high off her face with her diamond-and-pearl combs, and fasten the string of pearls, the same pearls she had worn for Harrison, around her neck. She picked up the hand-blown Venetian atomizer from her table and sprayed the scent of vanilla and cocoa beans around her breasts. Her eyes twinkled as the familiar scent wafted up. Let the other ladies wear Chanel No. 5 and Miss Dior tonight. She closed her thick lashes, dangerously imagining what might have been. If, if, and if. Claire's romantic heart was still beating for Harrison, her body heat frozen. For two years now she had slipped her passions into a hidden drawer and only pulled them out when she was alone, free to remember and relive the shared moments; the way he held her hand or stroked her cheek. Italy. Harrison was *her* Italy—Lake Como. Their Isola Bella. Occasionally over the years she had allowed herself to dream. What an asset she could have been to Harrison. If she had been setting *his* table instead, assembling world leaders for *him*, they could have accomplished so much. Together they could have brokered world peace instead of just another Duccio deal.

Opening her eyes, she was startled to see her husband standing behind her. He was never supposed to enter without knocking first. By her startled reaction, he guessed her objection.

"I knocked, my darling, but you obviously have thoughts elsewhere." He held up something big and sparkling. "It would please me if you would wear this tonight. I designed it for you and Verdura made it." His smile was tentative as he tried to read in her eyes if she liked his gift. She smiled, but the demonstration of gratitude was contradicted by the expression in her eyes. He was taken back by the obvious sadness in them. "Don't you like them? They're the biggest turquoises and sapphires I could find."

He touched the back of his hand gently to her cheek. "They're supposed to be my version of raindrops, not teardrops."

"I wasn't crying, Fulco. I was just sitting here thinking how lucky I was and how kind you are to me and my children."

"So it's still gratitude. Someday perhaps."

She took the hand he offered her. "It's a beautiful necklace that I'll wear proudly because you designed it."

"Mention that to the other guests. It's nice for them to know I have an artistic side." He leaned back on his heels and held out a wrist for her to fasten his cuff link. He smelled like vetiver and sandalwood. If she was grateful for his protection, he was grateful for the little gestures that implied they were a couple. And although the rich pirate had his pick of any woman in every port, and had had affairs with some of the world's most beautiful women, he had somehow fallen in love with his elusive wife. He rested his hand on her shoulder as they studied each other in her mirror.

His voice was shaky with desire. "You could show off our necklace better if you put on the blue gown that shows your breasts." She watched his fingers in the mirror as they found their way to her cleavage. She sat motionless as she always did when he touched her. As crude as he was, Duccio had the sensitivity of an exotic blooming plant. He knew he was being frozen out. "*Allora.* The blue dress, my necklace, and you. My table will be magnificent." He turned to her in the mirror before walking out of her apartment. "Perhaps, when all the guests are gone, we can talk about the evening over champagne."

The expression on her mouth never changed as she raised her fingers in the traditional *ciao*. She waited until she could no longer hear his strutting footsteps on the marble before she let the tears she had held back fall down her cheek. She reached for the photograph of her two children to remind herself why she was even there.

*   *   *

When she received Harrison, it was with Sara and Six on either hand and in the blue Christian Dior, wearing Duccio's gaudy gift.

She waited for him to walk toward her down the long, vaulted hall, as if he were just emerging from a tunnel. Partially hidden behind her wide skirt, the children broke loose and ran to the man they loved best in the world. Harrison broke his stern rule of never displaying affection and gathered them up in his arms. Claire was only glad Dior had created cinched waists and voluminous skirts that season; all the better to support her spine and cover her quaking legs. If she felt like leaping into his arms along with her happy children and burying her head in his chest, it was not possible, only imaginable. Her breasts, revealed to their best advantage in the low-cut bodice falling off her shoulders, could barely disguise her palpitating heart. Only a polite handshake marked their greeting as two warm hands grasped each other before reluctantly letting go.

Harrison was relieved he was seated a dozen upscale people down from Claire so he could freely steal a glance or two. Ambassador Luce monopolized the conversation, making it easy for him to enjoy his meal. She was taking credit for the creation of *Life* magazine.

"I said to Harry, 'Let's have a magazine with pictures. Hire me and I'll start it up. He didn't want to hire me, so he married me and got me for free.'" Their end of the table laughed, all except Fenwick Grant, owner of the rival weekly and a dozen or so newspapers, who seemed to be scrutinizing their hostess.

Harrison forked a portobello mushroom and addressed Grant. "I hope you're not planning a story on my daughter-in-law. She really prefers privacy."

"Oh, I'd forgotten your former relationship. She's just the kind of woman my magazines celebrate." The two men looked down the golden table to Claire, who was narrating a witty anecdote in rapid Italian to the rough-edged banker from Naples.

Mrs. Luce observed both of them eyeing their hostess. She returned the energy to her end of the table. "Harrison, don't you remember the night I pleaded with my Harry to kill Hitler? Poison was the plan. That time he flew to Berlin to interview the nasty house painter and Chamberlain? What if my hero had done it then! Only Poland would have been invaded. But Harry resisted me on moral ground, didn't you dear?"

"It was none of my affair. I didn't know how evil the man would become."

"You, Harrison. You shoot and hunt. Would you have killed him?"

"If I had seen the future carnage in a crystal ball, of course." The candlelight shone across his eyes and brow line.

"And Hitler would have become nothing but a historical footnote and the world saved from war." Her eyes and earrings, the same hue in the flattering light, both sparkled.

"I won't ask you, Signóre Ansiano. They say you're in the Mafioso. But how about you, Duccio? Would you have killed to save the world?" She coyly turned her head in his direction.

"I've killed to save my wallet." He twisted his napkin with a snap. "And as a young boy to save my goat. A man does what he must!" Breaking the startled silence in the room, he brought his fist down hard on the table and threw his head back with a crude laugh.

"You can do anything in this world if you're prepared to take the consequences, and consequences depend on character." Clare Boothe Luce clinked Harrison's glass to hers by way of a toast. Suddenly she was bored with murder. "I'm having tea with Claire Duccio tomorrow. I think she has enormous political possibilities. Maybe I can rope her into some embassy position."

"I can speak firsthand that she's an attribute in the political arena. FDR always thought so."

"Franklin," Clare Luce huffed prettily. "He never did give me credit for coining the phrase 'New Deal.'"

The official toasts were gracious. Duccio toasted the new "ambassadress," as he called her, the ambassadress toasted Italy's president, the president toasted his host and hostess, and Claire, on a more personal note, wished luck to her husband's latest acquisition, the SS *Andrea Doria*, the six-hundred-and-ninety-seven-foot Italian luxury liner that was the latest jewel in her husband's growing empire.

"*In bocca al lupo.*" She raised her glass. "In the mouth of the wolf" was Italian slang for "Good luck," she informed Luce.

"Let's dance!" Léonide, the star of Monte Carlo's Ballets Russes, was restless in his chair.

"Shall we adjourn to the ballroom?" Claire rose, signaling that the meal was over. She had long ago eliminated what she regarded as the sexist ritual of cigars in the library for men and ladies' hemline discussions in the *salone*. Dancing brought them all together. And Duccio, who had been taking his lessons diligently, danced like a twirling demon.

The old-fashioned dance rituals were observed at Palazzo Duccio even though the zestful millionaire was a very new member of Roman society. He would dance with Mrs. Luce, one of the guests of honor, while his wife danced with the other, the Honorable William Henry Harrison IV. Claire hesitated, trying to remember which excuse she had decided upon not to have to fold herself into Harrison's waiting arms. Pulled muscle, tennis elbow, eagle bite? She forgot all of them as Harrison moved toward her, put one familiar hand on the small of her back, and with the other clasped her hand in his, setting off a small burst of fireworks whose sparkles impaired her vision. The familiar scents of tweed riding jackets, Washington war briefs in damp leather, and the heady smells of love-soaked sheets in Lake Como accosted her nostrils. It was too much. She couldn't stand there and only dance.

"Excuse me, but I've got to check on the children."

"May I come? I'd like to tell them good night."

Claire looked down at his shoes. Hers were covered by

Christian Dior's New Look billowing out from her well-angled hips.

"Is anyone noticing us?" She didn't want to look up.

"Everyone's dancing."

Summoning her acting skills, Claire picked up her blossoming ballerina skirt and put a gracious smile on her lips. She quasi-danced around the ballroom, checking on everyone else's happiness as she always did. Nothing out of the ordinary. She stopped to speak into her husband's ear, gently touching his forearm. "I'm going to take Harrison up to say good night to his grandchildren. Do you mind?"

"Beautiful party, my dear. Shake hands with my new partner in the *Andrea Doria*. Claire can help us pick the new china and train staff like no one else."

"Thank you, dear." She rustled away, Harrison at her heels. They climbed the seventeenth-century winding staircase.

"This staircase is older than Charlotte Hall," Harrison said to her back.

She turned, both of her hands full of lifted silk taffeta. "Charlotte Hall. The day I arrived there I felt I had come to Manderley."

He looked puzzled.

"You know. Stiff and foreboding, like in *Rebecca*."

"I'm not the romantic-novel type."

"You're not the grandfatherly type, either." She loosened her self-control a notch and gave him a full smile.

"Come along. The children will be thrilled to see you, if they're still awake."

After gently pulling a book from Sara's sleeping hands, Claire and Harrison looked in on Six. He looked like a resting angel, the light from the full moon throwing a filtered beam across his finely chiseled face. One hand lay across his heart as the other fell open across a Winnie the Pooh who had crisscrossed the ocean a dozen times.

"Claire. I want to speak to you about Six's future. Is there somewhere we could speak privately?"

"Here." She arched her worried brows and led him into the darkened sitting room she shared with her children, pushing a football out of the way.

"Ophelia and I have been talking . . ."

She froze. Had he come up here just to talk about his wife? Was Claire only a fuzzy memory to him? Had their great love existed in her heart alone?

"And what have you and Ophelia been speaking about?" Her ironic tone imitated Ambassador Luce's.

"That Six is gifted. That he is too, well . . . special to grow up without a suitable male father figure. He should be raised in America." The words "by us"—meaning Harrison, Ophelia, Harry, and Minnie—were unspoken.

"America?"

"He could be the third Harrison president."

"Your ambition is astonishing." She would not back down from her anger. Claire flew at her former lover like a lioness protecting her cubs, plastering the newly redone room with hurled invectives.

"You invented this arrangement." The teardrop sapphire in her cleavage twisted around backwards. "Honor it, dammit! Do something unselfish! Pretend you have a heart in that bloody blue skeleton of yours. Duccio has more honesty in his stubby finger than in your whole damn elegant hand." The last three words she beat into his chest with her fists.

He caught them, at the same time turning the sapphire around. Her chest was beating hard with anger.

"I don't want your hands on me!" she lied.

"I'm sorry, Claire. I'm so sorry. I tried to be that person I'm supposed to be. But I can't. I love you too much to be away from you. I want you all back." He took her breath away, once with his words and the second time with his lips. Their kiss was as passionate as any from years before but was now fueled by long-pent-up desires, fervent daydreams, and embers that had refused to burn out. Harrison's caress was a great salve for a long-aching wound. Like a smoke of opium for a past addict or a sip of wine for a recovering lush, there was no going back. In one hungry touch of their mouths he had forgotten his practical solution and she her bond and promise. His fingers knitted around her hair and pulled her waist into his groin, and she sighed to the tune of a thousand remembered moans. When he pressed his fingers on that place on her neck, she stopped trying to resist the perilous thing she wanted most.

She sat up alone on the couch well into dawn, hugging her knees and trying to untangle her emotions. She wasn't only playing with her life—Harrison's, her children, even Duccio's life were in her hands. She had to think of the ramifications for them, all of them. She was startled by a soft noise at the hall door. The clock showed five-thirty in the morning. She waited as if in a trance but couldn't seem to move toward the sound. She watched as an envelope was slipped under her door. Numbly she walked on her legs, moving heavily, feeling as if she were stuck in a thick New England fog. Then the American girl who had evolved into such a fine Italian lady knelt down on the floor to read the handwritten note.

Please meet me in Paris at the Ritz a fortnight from today at 8 p.m. I will wait for you in the dining room. If you can't make it I will understand. Please tell the children I'm sorry I had to leave early.

H.

Claire pondered the sun as it came up over her uncommon Italian palazzo. All of the important Harrison communications were laid down in writing, she remembered. She climbed into bed. It was early Sunday and they weren't going to mass until eleven. She lay on her bed watching the nymphs and painted centaurs playing love games on her ceiling. Her eyes circled up to a young Adonis embracing a shy beauty, her long hair covering her nakedness. They seemed so carefree. Did none of them have mother-in-laws and politically ambitious families? Didn't any of them have secrets to hide? She wondered what it would be like if she could will herself up to the fresco and join the careless lovers cavorting on powdery white clouds, the way she and Harrison had carried on in Lake Como. No, she'd rather be earthbound; whatever mistakes she'd made, she'd live with the consequences. She smiled, remembering. And hadn't it been the love begun at Lake Como that had produced her second child? She couldn't imagine life without Six. She settled back in the pillows to nap before Lorenza arrived with her morning tray. Suddenly she was aware of another person in the room.

Rubbing the sleep from his eyes with the back of his hands, Six stood in the open doorway of his mother's room. Claire invited him in with a warm smile.

"Morning, Mommy."

Claire pulled back one corner of her coverlet and Six, wearing a wide grin and carrying his bear, climbed in.

"Good morning, Sweet William." She hugged her son. Surely the silly nymphs overhead didn't know pleasure like this.

She hoped she had made the right decision, choosing between her brain and her heart.

Chapter Thirteen

The Jeweled Collar

Why have we been seduced into abandoning the timeless inner
strength of woman for the temporal outer strength of man?
                                        —*Anne Morrow Lindbergh*
                                        Gift from the Sea

Lorenza brought the most coveted invitation in the world to
Claire on a silver tray. The oversized envelope bore the seal of the
royal house of Grimaldi, so she didn't have to be a detective to
guess what was inside. Ever since it had been announced that
Prince Rainier was marrying a Hollywood goddess, half of titled
Europe had been jockeying for an invitation to the wedding of the
decade. Lorenza was thrilled. Most of the great ladies would be
taking their maids along to Monaco to coif their elaborate hair-
dos and pouf and steam their dresses.

Lorenza was piqued at her lady. Why would she bother to consult her calendar to see if she was free to go? Every lady she knew
would have forgone an emergency appendectomy if it coincided
with Grace Kelly's wedding. The other chambermaids working
for Europe's richest ladies had brayed about how their mistresses
had already sent extravagant engagement gifts as bribes to get
themselves on the guest list. Lorenza honestly adored her mistress, who, she bragged, possessed goodness as well as *la bellezza*.
She had even found fine homes in Chicago, America, for her dead
sister's two youngest babies who otherwise would have gone to a
paupers' state foundling home. Now Lorenza held her breath and

watched as Claire thumbed through her inch-thick 1956 agenda, rifling through her heavily scheduled calendar to make sure there was no conflict on April 18 through 20. It was one of Signóra Duccio's unbendable rules that nothing was allowed to interfere with her Eleanor House duties, or, more important, with Six's soccer schedule.

"We shall be able to make it." She announced, and Lorenza's heartbeat resumed.

At the news of the invitation, Duccio wheeled through the house like he was on roller skates. What a splendid opportunity to seduce his bankers into financing his current costly project, the *Claira Mare*, sister ship to the *Andrea Doria* but even more luxurious. Gone were the days when he had to go to the Mafia for funds. While he kept his Neapolitan friendships intact, Claire had elevated him to a new level of legitimacy. With her seemingly effortless grace she had pulled him up the rungs of the social and financial ladder to a place that held only three or four men on one high, narrow step. And so he pushed her out the door to Paris to be properly coutured for the occasion. Alexandre for her hair, Cartier for the jewels, Balenciaga and Dior for her outfits. It was yet another incarnation of the Aunties before Cilla Pettibone's debut. As Auntie Slim always said, *"Plus ça change, plus c'est la même chose."* Somehow his gruff fussing over her endeared him and his nouveau-riche tastes to Claire, even though she'd have to be careful not to end up looking like his fancy feathered armpiece.

Painful as it was, she'd made the right decision about Harrison. There was no way she could have continued the domestic arrangement at Palazzo Duccio if she had become involved with Harrison again. She wasn't duplicitous enough to have sex with Harrison and dinner with Duccio. She knew she wouldn't be able to conceal her real feelings for him, a love so strong it continued to haunt her dreams, both sleeping and awake. When he had appeared at her dinner for Ambassador Luce two years ago, it became clear that she could barely concentrate with him doing nothing more sensual than standing near her. She hadn't even been able to compose herself enough to dance with him without betraying herself to the whole room. If she were an Oscar-winning performer like Grace Kelly she might be able to convince people she wasn't hanging on his every word or anticipating his next gesture. True, Claire was actress enough to camouflage her dislike of some of her husband's rough habits, but then Duccio was an easy audience. He just needed a little wifely confirmation that he was hot stuff. These days it was only his temper that worried her, especially in front of the children. But he always responded to Claire's calming voice and delicate admonitions. She could soothe away his black outbursts like the careful handler of an untamed dog.

"Do you want the kitchen gossip?" An older but even more handsome Violet primly seated herself on the corner of Claire's map-sized bed. If anything, age had enhanced her mother's natural charms. Watching her, Claire hoped she'd mature as gracefully. Violet reminded her of the timeless lady in the ivory cameo Duccio had given her. She still carried her delicate frame with her perfect posture, her silvery hair only accentuating the violet eyes and creamy skin never weathered by expensive vacations in the sun.

"Oh, here, dear, your husband handed me these to give you." She looked confused. She was used to seeing gifts packaged in pretty boxes, but the wide, clumpy gold and emerald bangle bracelets were just tied together like a bunch of green bananas with a yard of gold string and a dangling notecard. The colored stones were so big Violet mistakenly assumed they must be costume instead of real emeralds, or, as Duccio called them, "the Devil's own stones." The card was written in his wild, speedy scrawl, *Thank you for last night's supper. The Swiss bankers are on board. I salute you—Duccio.*

"This may be none of my business, and I know I'm not as so-phisticated about men as you are, but your wise old mother senses that two married people should spend at least *some* time together."

"We're both happy with the arrangement."

"He seems to want more from you." A single furrow crinkled Violet's brow. "The kitchen staff apparently thinks so, too. With the few Italian phrases I've picked up it seems your husband has a ballerina *and* a singer on the side. I don't want to be indelicate or step out of line, but is your husband a . . . bounder? Do tell me I'm wrong if he's just a great patron of the arts."

"Indeed he is." Claire crossed her legs Indian-style and plunged into her grapefruit. "But he patronizes only female artists." She popped a piece of toast into her mother's open mouth. "Most European men are very different, Mother. They're perfectly content to have a wife who runs their houses and a mistress who sat-isfies their ids."

"Oh." The vowel came out like a soprano's birdcall but it was clear that her mother's insight was as sharp as ever. "Still, I sus-pect your husband is quite in love with you. Surely you must see it. I haven't dressed more than a thousand brides and grooms for nothing. And," she said, a blush suddenly rising from her neck to the tops of her cheeks, "I have more experience than you think."

"Oh, Mother. Picking out china is not the same as under-standing the inner workings of the male psyche."

"Well, I've been keeping company with a widowed gentleman for some time now, and Mr. Zolla's asked me to marry him."

This time it was Claire's mouth that dropped open. She couldn't imagine her mother having anything to do with a man other than sizing him up for a suit. Of course she was happy that her hard-working mother was going to have companionship. It just star-tled her that it was going to be a Mr. Zolla instead of a Labrador. In fact, it almost upset her. Claire had always looked to the Aunties as equal parts of the whole, women doing very nicely without men. There had been enough inner strength in the

Windermere rental to keep them warm in winter, safe at night, and to create a house full of feminine joy. They didn't need the braggadocio strength of a man, which in her mind was always fleeting anyway and accompanied by strength-sapping side effects. The little band of women that had raised her solved their own problems with dignity and marched on like suffragettes espousing the cause of single womanhood. Even Eleanor Roosevelt had taught her it was safer to befriend women than to rely on men as saviors. She had seen enough of the duchess of Windsor up close to know that "keeping the little man happy" was a twenty-four-hour chore and knew from Pam Churchill that looking after even her temporary men was a full-time career. Claire had taken so brilliantly to her profession as Duccio's public wife because she hadn't come to the table with inappropriate expectations. She had never even seen a marriage that was founded on love, and hadn't Violet and the Aunties prepared her for exactly this kind of marriage, a good old financial swap?

In her own way, she was happy without love. Her children were growing up strong and healthy, and she was good at her "job" as Duccio's aide-de-camp cum social secretary (after all, she'd been trained by Harrison for that detailed type of work). She was secure in the knowledge that with Eleanor House she was doing something that mattered in the world. But the main reason she'd been able to keep her calm and equilibrium was that she never thought of Duccio as a man, but rather as her business partner. All this time she had assumed she was emulating her mother, to whom everything was a trade-off or a deal. Now it turned out that her mother wanted the other side of the coin, too, and it confused Claire.

"But, Mother, I thought you didn't need a man."

"I don't, dear. It's just that he's a very fine person, and it's never too late to fall in love." After she took a sip of her morning tea, Violet gave her daughter the 28 Shop look. "You might try it yourself sometime."

Violet's words startled her. She wondered how much evidence of her passion for Harrison was etched in her face. Claire had come to practical terms with the lack of romance in her life a long time ago, pushing those notions out of her thoughts, but somehow hearing her mother's wedding plans tugged at the heartstrings she thought she had clamped off forever.

"Oh, Mother, I thought you were much too practical for romance." She leaned forward to kiss her. It suddenly occurred to Claire that Violet might have sacrificed her own amorous desires to put food on the table.

"Yes, I know what you thought. I brought home the bacon, Wren cooked it, and Slim knew how to serve it to the men. We were three females impersonating one mother."

"But what a mother!" Claire threw her arms up in the air, spilling drops of chamomile tea on the coverlet. She was genuinely happy for her. "All of you gave me the perfect childhood. Every day I call upon one of you to help me say or do the right thing for my children. We didn't need a man around to be happy." But a childhood memory fluttered back to her, causing her to glance sideways. "You know," she said, taking her mother's hand in hers, "I *did* bring Mr. Pettibone home for you."

Her mother tucked a stray hair neatly into place, relieved that she hadn't turned into Pettibone's lifelong mistress and lived a life of disorder.

"Can I give you away to Mr. Zolla? I could have a beautiful wedding here, or at the gardens at Villa Duccio. Zolla. Zolla? Is he Italian? I won't spare any of Duccio's money. You'll have the wedding you've always deserved, better than all of those you planned for all your clients combined."

"Why don't we leave that to Grace Kelly? As a matter of fact, Mr. Zolla, of Lithuanian descent, and I will probably be married very quietly in Scottsdale, Arizona, where we're going to retire. Yes, retire. I deserve a rest. You'll like Max. He's a very decent man. He discovered the Southwest as an executive with the Santa

Fe Railroad. His wife, Edna, was an occasional customer of mine before she passed away."

A widower. Someone older and stable. Claire nodded approvingly.

"Mother, I want you to tell me exactly what I can do. When can I meet the divine Mr. Zolla? Nothing could make me happier than to know someone's finally going to cherish you, even if it is among the cactus. I know what! I'm going to send you that big Tiepolo down in the music room. *The Allegory of Love.* It's pretty racy, though. How's Mr. Zolla's heart? And how tall are the ceilings in your living room in Scottsdale?"

Claire was so used to imagining Harrison's long legs striding around every other corner, only to realize it was her heart playing tricks on her brain, that when she and the duchess of Windsor stepped out of Christian Dior's private salon on the Rue George V in Paris, after having been draped and measured for foodless hours, she chalked up his elegant vision to hunger-induced hallucinations. But when their Rolls-Royce stopped at the traffic light, Léonide Massine, who was eating a chocolate and most decidedly *not* starving himself, pointed out the window to ask Claire if that wasn't her famous father-in-law strolling down the street. Léonide beckoned him over while the two ladies waited in the car.

"Look, I make for you the reunion."

Harrison bent his tall frame to greet the car's occupants through the open window. He recognized the duchess at once. She was clad in a cream bouclé suit with a one-legged flamingo pinned to her lapel and wore a brown ocelot hat on her small head. From deep inside the car and out through the window the duchess extended a taupe kid-gloved hand. Harrison remembered Claire saying that Wallis feared her hands were unfeminine and always kept them covered. He politely shook the gloved hand and was getting ready to rush off when he spied Claire on the far side of the seat. Hatless, her soft hair fell to the shoulders of her camel-colored suit, the slim skirt revealing her silk-stockinged legs. She looked thinner than the last time he had seen her.

Harrison searched for something to say.

"Imagine running into the two of you on George Fifth. I don't suppose I could interest you two in lunch at the Ritz?"

"Oh dear, we're on our way to the hatter's, and you're welcome to join us if you need another bowler or two. Of course we have to hurry. If you keep a hatter waiting long enough he goes mad, you know." Harrison had forgotten how droll the duchess could be.

"Wallis, you go on to the milliner's. I'll faint if I don't get something to eat. Do you mind?"

There was such a look of excitement in Claire's eyes that it caused the duchess's well-drawn eyebrows to rise. She gripped her lizard-skin bag—embossed with the royal insignia she'd made up for herself—tighter to her lap so that Claire could slip past her and out of the car before the light changed.

The two Harrisons felt almost giddy as they requested a table in the back of the Ritz's dining room. The fawning maître d' accommodated them graciously, finding them a place half-hidden behind a palm, although he usually liked to seat the well-known beauties up front and in full view of everybody else, particularly if they were the wives of the spectacularly rich.

Claire didn't look around to see who was in the room like she usually did. All she could think about was the feel of his hand on her back just below her shoulder blades as he steered her to the table. She and Harrison, oblivious to the sideways envious looks and outright stares of recognition they provoked, immediately fell into a discussion of the children, politics, and the past they shared. Their two heads bowed together over their plates, they ordered course after course, although they ate little of the superbly prepared Escoffier meal. Their surprise encounter gave them sustenance enough. Memories of Roosevelt, dinners with Lucy Mercer and Japanese envoys, Six's high grades and exceptional athletic skills, his perfect balance that allowed him to run down a field and side-kick a goal, these were the things they talked about excitedly for over an hour. And who could talk and eat at the same time?

It was Harrison who changed the course of the conversation.

"You know I waited here for you that night until they cleared the tables and then set them again for breakfast. I suspect I got drunk."

"I can't imagine you the least bit out of control." Her voice fell into a hush. "But that was two years ago."

"It evidently made an impression on me. Why didn't you come?" He reached over to lay his hand on hers under a napkin. Coffee was coming.

"It wouldn't have been right. It wouldn't have worked." Claire stopped trying to pretend: "Oh, I wanted to come."

"So this is better if we just meet by accident? What are the odds of another lunch in that lottery?"

"I hope they're in our favor. This is the nicest time I've had in years."

Harrison frowned. "You can't be truly happy in this silly circus you star in." He was convinced of it. "All these ridiculous people." He waved the duke and duchess and French couturiers away with a vanilla cookie.

"I've given up on romantic love. So don't deny me an occasional bit of amusement. At least I get the gossip on other people's love affairs." As she spoke she was struck by how thin the skin at his temples had become and at how deep the purplish blue shadows under his eyes had grown.

"You look tired." She suddenly worried for real that Harrison might not be well.

"It must be the altitudes I travel in. Too much time in airplanes."

Airplanes. Harry. It all tumbled back. "And how is everything at home?" The word still stuck in her throat.

"A total vacuum without you. I spend as little time there as I can manage. I could write my own travel book about Europe: *The Diplomat's Guide to Seven Cities in Seven Days.*"

Claire smiled briefly but as the last of the other lunchers filed out, she allowed her face to show its true feelings. "I know what you're doing is very important, but I wonder if you aren't burning yourself out. It's been three presidents now. Surely there's another brilliant right-hand man out there." She wondered if there was really no one else who had taken *her* place. She had never let anyone else into her heart for a second.

"There's no one else willing to be away from home for months at a time."

"Is there no one . . . ?"

"Only you."

She watched his hands as they grasped his fluted glass, the same hands that had held her breasts and the same mouth that had drunk from them. She shivered.

"Are you cold? Would you like my jacket?"

"No, thanks." A vivid vision of his jacket lying across the same armchair as her dress in their bedroom at Lake Como emerged from her disquieted mind. The good memories seemed to be stored in a more accessible place than the bad ones.

"I'm fine." She lifted her hair to rub a place on the back of her neck in an unconscious gesture. "Really. Fine."

"The finest woman I've ever known, Claire." He knew before she did that she'd shake her head, draw her lips into a Mona Lisa smile, and sit up a little straighter in her chair as if correcting her posture would fix everything. When he leaned over to pick up the bill lying on the table in a leather folder, he caught a whiff of her smells of vanilla and her own sweet juices mixed with the light bouquet of a good French wine.

He picked up her hand instead of the bill and felt her squeeze his fingers back. He was surprised that she wasn't wearing her wedding ring. In fact, she didn't have a single piece of jewelry on, odd for a woman whose husband showered her with everything that shone in a jeweler's light. He lifted her naked fingers to his face, but she plunged them busily into her pocketbook.

When she pushed her sunglasses on it wasn't to keep out the late afternoon light. It was to hide the stubborn tears that wouldn't be willed away. "Let's not do this, Harrison. I'm trying so hard not to want what I can't have." She sighed. "We have the children in common; let's make that enough. And friendship. Perhaps we can handle that." There wasn't a trace of bitterness in her words. She was frantically trying to find a way she could preserve the glow that lit the room when they were in each other's presence. It was a feeling of excitement gilded by calm, that complicated emotion two people could share only when they had been both friends and lovers. And both could remember each other's kindnesses as well as kindled desires as clearly as they could recall favorite passages from childhood poems.

They had shared everything. The birth of Sara, the conception of Six, the war, a bed, and an undying tenderness. Surely she could find a way for them to keep each other company in their secret loneliness without removing so much as a brick from the elaborate facades they each had carefully constructed.

"Six is growing up to be so special. Sometimes I think all of this happened just so we could invent him."

"I'd like to be around him even more. And you. Should we try?"

"As friends?"

"And parents."

"Done."

Two intelligent people, even if they had been in love as much as they, could certainly be "just friends." At least Claire knew it was important to try. Six wouldn't always be a child; it was unthinkable that Harrison wouldn't be his role model. And maybe she could train herself to be satisfied just with Harrison's companionship.

"It's getting late."

"You know I'm going to badger you about Six going to American schools."

"We'll negotiate. Boarding school's still a few years away. We have time."

"I promise to be patient," the diplomat declared.

Outside, the Ritz's black-tuxedoed Hussier arranged for a car to take her to Fiumicino and her return flight to Rome. Smiling at one another, they stood there, uncertain whether to shake hands or kiss each other good-bye on the cheek European-style. The suspense left them motionless. Finally they hugged. A big, warm American hug in which she closed her eyes. In the rush-hour traffic she didn't hear him when he whispered the words, "My love."

There was a decided skip in her step and an enigmatic smile on her face when Claire tiptoed in first to Sara and then to Six's room to kiss her children good night. She checked the safety catch on the spear-gun leaning against Six's stuffed sailfish and knelt on the gaily patterned carpet to roll a football back into his toy chest. Six awakened when her mouth lightly touched his warm bronzed skin.

"Did you have a nice time, Mommy?"

"The nicest. Your grandfather's promised to spend more time with us."

When Six's lashes fluttered shut, he added the figure of his grandfather to his nine-year-old boy's dreams of soccer goals and ski trails. Looking closely at her child, she could see the man he would become. And she could see his father in him. Claire watched maternally as a sleepy smile curled across his still-childish mouth. Claire smiled too as she softly tiptoed out and closed the door to leave Six to slumber peacefully.

There was tension in the car all the way from Nice to Monte Carlo. Lorenza was riding shotgun in front of the Rolls, Claire's

Vuitton travel jewel case sitting squarely in her lap, with Tutti at the wheel. Because of the servants, the Duccios quarreled in English. Claire couldn't quite grasp why her husband was so infuriated. Perhaps it was the unwieldy casino deal he was trying to control in Monaco, pitting himself in a cockfight against Ari Onassis. Or perhaps he was still sulking that Grace Kelly—and the platoon of a hundred reporters trailing her—had sailed over the on SS *Constitution* instead of his ship the *Andrea Doria*. This lost chance at world recognition for his floating investment would explain his bad temper. Claire tried to be accommodating and argued back as pleasantly as possible. The Pirate's black moods got even darker if he had nobody to argue with or nothing to shoot at. As they were sitting in the backseat of a speeding Corniche, driving around hairpin curves overlooking the Mediterranean, she was his only available target. She wished she'd brought along a punching bag for him to abuse. Instead, she tried to distract him with humor.

"Auntie Slim sent me the funniest clipping from the Chicago *Sun-Times*. Irv Kupcinet cracked in his column, 'It isn't the romance that interests Miss Kelly—it's the principality of the thing.'"

"Is that all your Americans think about? Marrying money!"

The arrow went where it was intended, straight to the stone heart of Claire and Duccio's arrangement. It was obvious now that their quarrel was personal. But about what? Claire wondered. She turned away to stare absently out the window at the lush scenery passing by at fifty miles an hour. Too fast for these narrow winding roads, she thought. Pine trees, cactus, cragged vertical rocks, and a vast expanse of flat azure sea commingled happily with fragrant blooms in this fairy-tale land topped off by its pink palace. Surely Duccio should be able to lighten his misdirected anger in such a lovely place. Even before their car officially entered the tiny kingdom of Monaco, all 370 acres of it, nearly the same size

as the original estate grounds of Charlotte Hall, Claire could
sense the joy in the air.

The Monégasques were ecstatic to be able to celebrate not one
but two ceremonies, the civil ceremony in the throne room of the
palace, and the following day a full Cinderella pageant at high
mass in the Cathedral of Saint Nicholas, the church that rose regally out of the rocky coast. At the first wedding, the Duccios
stood at attention by their gold concert chairs, Fulco sullen that
he didn't have a host of medals to display on the left side of his
jacket like the decked-out nobility, Claire a fetching picture in a
cartwheel of a wide-brimmed hat and a floral violet garden dress,
her priceless pearls circling her throat. She found the bride pen-
sive but lovely in a rose lace suit and demure Juliet cap, though
afterwards at the garden reception the new Princess Grace joked
to Claire that now she was only half-married. Claire realized that
she felt the same way about her own marriage. Even if she'd had
a second wedding in a church with a thousand people and *Look*
magazine in attendance, it wouldn't have made her feel otherwise.

At the next day's religious ceremony, the American actress who
had just finished starring in *The Swan,* a fairy-tale film about a
girl who marries a prince, played her part for real. Hollywood designer Helen Rose costumed her in a bridal gown so lovely it had
already launched a thousand copies. As soon as the color photographs appeared in *Look* and *Life,* Violet's department at
Marshall Field's would be besieged by brides who coveted the
twenty-five yards of silk taffeta adorned with Brussels lace and the
translucent veil seeded with tiny pearls. Now, watching from her
ringside seat, even Claire was misty-eyed as Mr. Kelly proudly
walked his daughter down the aisle, her long train trailing behind them like an ivory ocean. It was the only thing about the
bride she envied: that she had a father to give her away. The handsome prince, her very own kingdom, heirloom jewels, even her
own flag to fly . . . Claire had had the equivalent of these and
knew none of it mattered without love.

Claire hoped she hadn't overstepped her bounds when she included a heartfelt handwritten note to the princess-to-be with the six dozen hand-blown Venetian glass goblets emblazoned with the Grimaldi family crest Duccio had insisted they send. She had expressed her welcome from one American woman living abroad to another, and invited her for tea if she ever got homesick. What she didn't say was that they were both married to short Mediterranean men with tall egos, and if Grace wanted marital harmony she'd better get lots of low-heeled shoes. And what she would never hint at was that while Rainier was a prince with a kingdom, Duccio and others like him held Monaco by their purse strings. Claire knew that Duccio held a lien on its banks, if not a mortgage on the palace. Eventually Grace would discover that she was expected to help dig her tiny country out of its debt. Not only was she a brand-new princess, but she had also just become Monaco's vice president of tourism, new business, and casino gambling. CEO, if you will, of Monte Carlo's *Societé des Bains de Mer.* She would have to break bread with starstruck real estate developers from Cleveland, think fast on her feet in both French and Italian, run charity balls when all she wanted was a hamburger, and play gracious hostess to tennis champions, potential investors in Monaco's future, and Greek shipping tycoons . . . all the things Claire now did so effortlessly.

Claire lifted her head, looking around the reception for her husband in this sea of top hats, royal sashes, and organdy bonnets. He was talking to one of those Greek tycoons now, and his complexion was turning royal purple. She hoped Spiros wasn't setting Duccio's trigger off with his outrageous business demands. Not now, in this romantic atmosphere. Let Grace and Rainier enjoy some of the wedding's afterglow, even with the press hounds at their heels. The last time she'd run into Spiros was in front of the Ritz when Harrison was seeing her off. She disliked the troublemaking Greek hellion and had ignored him intentionally that day. She now watched as Duccio suddenly exploded in anger. He turned and stomped toward her, his twisted face a feverish barometer of his rage. Evidently she'd have to soothe whatever *fasaria* Spiros had stirred up. She straightened her posture, bracing herself for the assault, not knowing it would be directed at her.

"*Sgualdrina!*" he hissed into her ear, startling Claire and the multilingual waiter behind her. "You bitch!"

Her eyes widened in shock and her open hands flew up as if to protect herself. "What on earth . . ."

Duccio grabbed a champagne glass from the waiter's tray. She feared he might hurl it at her, hurt her. It was almost as if he were possessed. She had never seen him this out of control.

"I do everything for you, and you dishonor me, you ungrateful whore." He held the glass menacingly, toasting her with his venom.

"Are you drunk?" she whispered. Was he crazy? When he brought the side of his hand down, hitting her hard on the collarbone, it was such a blow that it snapped the string holding her pearls together, sending them flying out and spinning like exquisite white bullets. The pain that shot down the back of her neck was nothing compared to the insult she felt, standing there helpless as the priceless pearls rolled down the front and inside of her lilac Dior suit. Claire bit her lip to stop a tear. She only wished she had on her wide-brimmed hat from yesterday and not the little cloche that left her entire face exposed.

Fortunately for her, the guests' attention and all of the photographers were focused on the far side of the courtyard where at that precise moment, his princess by his side, Prince Rainier III deftly cut the six-tiered wedding cake with his saber.

Claire finally closed her mouth after the shock had escaped. She kneeled to gather the scattered pearls. She shuddered as she saw Duccio's shoe stop a hairline away from her fingers. His words were spoken so quietly she was sure no one but she could hear.

"Pearls before swine."

She lifted her eyes to stare astonished into his for any clue to his anger. She didn't have to wait.

"Spiros and half the world saw you and your unnatural lover. Only Americans would think they could be indiscreet at the Ritz."

"Duccio, I . . . I promise you. I kept my end of the bargain."

"You have never been a wife."

It was true. She had been a wife in name only. But that had been the deal.

From her perspective, kneeling on the stone, he looked like a tall, angry column. She stood, letting the pearls fall like marbles from her fingers. "How dare you. I've kept my end of the bargain."

"You've evidently kept meeting your lover." He shook his head. "I am a man of the street. No finesse. *No gràzia.* Vulgarity is what I know. I know sexual satisfaction on a man's face. That was the look on the father-in-law's face the night I met you in England. Lust. You cannot lie to a liar."

Claire smoothed her fingers down the silk faille of her skirt, carefully putting her characteristic smile back on her face. She rose to her full height. Fueled by her indignation, she spoke clearly, using her best Tuxedo tones to respond.

"While I've lived in your house I have honored your name." No need to throw all of her husband's mistresses and girlfriends into his face; no need to wallow in his mud. She turned on her heel, her skirt swirling around her, and caught a smirking Spiros out of the corner of her eye. Spiros, whose advances she had once laughed away, was clearly enjoying her humiliation. In a flash, Duccio was at her elbow. Claire felt her stomach contort as she shied her face away to divert another blow.

"Where are you going?"

"Home."

"No you're not. You stay here by my side. I might have need of you." He grasped her arm and linked it roughly through his. She cringed at his touch.

He brushed his fingers through his oily hair. The volcano had been momentarily corked. "*Forse* now, you are not so high above me. I may have broken stupid laws, but you have broken morals."

As much as Claire hated him at this moment, she now understood where his anger stemmed from: the most primal feeling in the world. Jealousy. So as Hollywood royalty and European society looked over its shoulder, the elegant Claire Harrison Duccio turned to straighten her husband's tie properly.

He spoke to her through his smiling clenched teeth even as he allowed her wifely gesture. "You should know the stories I learned in Calabria. You can bring a snake into your house, feed, pet, cover it with jeweled collars, but even if you give it a mouse to eat every day, once a month it will bite you. Because it is in the nature of the snake." He shrugged, leaving a quietly trembling Claire to wonder which one of them was the serpent.

Harrison sat smoking a cigar in his office at the American embassy, rereading the letter he'd received from Claire. He had been surprised at her invitation to dine in Paris on August 6. An unimportant trade commission had brought him to the city before he left to pick up the children in Rome to return them to America for their annual Newport holiday. But there was no reason for a fashionable woman like Claire to be in the deserted French capital during the month when even the *boulangere,* the baker's wife, packed up her brood and left for the seashore. There was no reason other than to see him. In the formal letter she clearly indicated "dinner for two," "discussing the children's future," and "possible changes in her life." He was hopeful that this might mean she was leaning toward the reasonable decision of allowing the children to spend more time in the States and receive a quality American education. He put out his cigar and then determinedly pushed the ashtray to the far side of his desk. He had been smoking far too many of these things a day. If he was going to get the chance to be a real father figure—or even a grandfather

figure—to Six, he'd have to get himself back in competitive physical shape. He wouldn't want just to guide the boy, he'd want to
do things, horseback riding, skiing, skin diving, all the things Six
loved, with him. And his mother.

Claire had followed her invitation with a familiar R.S.V.P. ab-
solving him of having to make an immediate decision, ending her
letter with the same words he had used in hers: *If you can't make it
I will understand.* It would take the outbreak of World War III to
keep him away.

He assumed this was to be a very personal discussion, as she
had forgone the traditional Ritz for the tucked-away Chez
Emilon, an excellent restaurant well known for its cuisine but not
frequented by the haute monde of Claire's world. Emilon prepared superb dinners, which he cooked himself for only a dozen
tables generously spaced apart to allow for cozy tête-a-têtes. The
restaurant also served as the dining room for the five or six suites
in the gracious old family home that had been converted into a
first-class inn; its private clientele frequented Emilon as much for
its discreet location hidden away in a residential street on the Left
Bank as for its charm.

The smell of cooking sauces greeted Harrison as he arrived half
an hour early for dinner. There was something pleasantly familiar
in the inviting aromas, and he wondered how he could be reminded of his favorite pot roast in a four-star French restaurant.
Although he couldn't remember ever being there before, the wait
staff called him by name as they took his hat.

He found Claire already seated. She was dressed simply, in a
soft silk blouse the color of tea leaves. The shadows from the real
candles on the wall sconces sent patterns flickering across her
shoulders. She lifted her head to look him straight in the eye. He
thought she still looked young and unspoiled, as if she hadn't
spent the last few years mired in nasty custody lawsuits and
locked into a marriage with a brutish husband—a marriage he
had arranged. She appeared untouched by any of the ugliness that

had swirled around her. As the candlelight illuminated her fresh, heart-shaped face, her eyes shining sincerely beneath dark, full lashes, he thought for a fleeting second that he was back in Lake Como with the young woman he loved. She sat expectantly in the oversized armchair, her fingers resting on a slim little book, Anne Morrow Lindbergh's *Gift from the Sea*.

"Did you bring your reading material along in case I might bore you?"

"No, in case you didn't come. I don't make a good drunk."

"I thought *I* was early." He glanced around the room at the empty tables as he took his seat. Evidently all of Paris had already left for their August holidays. They were the only people in the room.

She picked up a fork, holding it to her pale pink mouth like a big cigar, and cracked in a Groucho Marx voice, "I bought out the whole joint, kiddo." Then, in her normal voice, "So I could be alone with you."

They both held their words until the waiter finished pouring the first glass of wine and presented the appetizer of raw oysters à la Rockefeller, his favorite. He felt flattered and a little embarrassed at finding himself in the middle of what looked like a classic seduction scene. He glanced around the room, on the lookout for a strolling violinist playing "La Vie en Rose." But the way Claire kept nervously rubbing her shoulder implied that this wasn't about romance, and the resolute set of her mouth told him she had something weighty to discuss. They both knew each other's little habits too well for games.

"I feel like I'm on the receiving end of that old Washington strategy. First you feed 'em, then you hit 'em up for the favor. What's the favor? What's wrong?"

"I want to come home."

The diplomat in Harrison knew he had to reflect a few moments before he responded. He took a sip of wine.

Claire practically impaled him with her unblinking gaze, waiting for his response.

"That's a pretty loaded request. Exactly where *home?*"

"Chicago, Washington . . . anywhere America. I want to get . . . I mean . . ." The words tumbled out as fast as a child's list of Christmas wishes. "I want to divorce Duccio, move back home, raise our children, have you in our lives. I wasn't going to ask you until I plied you with a delicious dinner—they're making your favorite pot roast—but I need to know. Is it possible? Can I? Do I bring harm on you if I break the arrangement? My so-called marriage. Is Duccio such an important financial part of your life that I need to stay? I will if I have to. If I come home, will Ophelia sue me for custody?" Her entire face was a question mark.

"Hold on. What's happened?"

"It's time I make a life, not just run away from one."

"Has he hurt you?"

She shook her head no, rubbing her hand across the slope of her shoulder.

"Let's take this step by step. What is it you really want to know?"

"Will Ophelia file a custody suit if I go back to America?"

"The minute your foot touches the shore."

"Can't you stop it?"

He didn't even flinch. "No. The papers are already prepared in case you ever returned for a visit or if one of your aunts died and you came home for the funeral."

"Why does it still matter so much to her? She has the children Christmas and August."

"Ophelia, Harry, and Minnie . . . the Harrisons, on the legal document, have filed for full custody, on the grounds that you are an unfit mother, a European party girl, a Communist sympathizer and"—he hated to say this—"illegitimate."

Claire picked up the small fork like she was going to charge the Bastille instead of her oysters on the half shell. Those accusations were crazy. "And you'd let that happen."

"After I saw you and the children in Rome two years ago I hired the best team of lawyers to see if I could personally become their guardian. But according to custodial law"—he almost choked on these words—"I have no rights as a grandfather. And Harry is . . . their legal father."

She looked down, pushing a slippery oyster around in its shell with her fork, as if she were looking for its pearl.

"I'm only with Duccio because *you* sent me." She pushed her plate away.

The diplomat laid both hands on the table. "I think I'd better explain the situation to you. I've become an unwelcome guest in my own home. Ophelia and I don't speak. We have nothing to say to one another. She asks nothing of me but that I appear on the family Christmas card, and I expect nothing of her except to forward my mail. I live at the Waldorf when I do business in New York, but, louse that I am, I do go home for Christmas and August."

"To see the children." She understood. She had just returned from a tense holiday with Duccio off the coast of Corsica, where they had been spearfishing. The children were tanned and sun-kissed, and fit. At least she could take some strange pride in sending them back to Ophelia almost heroically beautiful. "But you could've come to us."

"As what? The man who came to dinner? Duccio can be very hot-tempered and play a ruthless hand in business when he's crossed. I would never want to put you in the way of his jealous nature. I've seen a side of him you haven't."

Claire held her fingers against her lips as if she were trying to keep something from escaping.

It suddenly occurred to him that he had put her in jeopardy simply by sending her away from him and into Duccio's lethal arms. He felt old and pathetic. Why hadn't he been man enough to stand up to his wrathful wife to protect Claire and his second son?

"How obligated are you to Duccio? Would I mess up your finances if I left?" Having been a Harrison, she was taking the practical approach to the problem.

"Of course not. Excuse me for insulting your husband, but I do more for him than he's done for me."

Both of them looked lost in thought as the pot roast, a plume of steam curling from its ceramic platter, was placed before them. Ordinarily he would have been delighted at seeing his favorite food so perfectly prepared, but his appetite was dulled by the battle between love and duty that was being waged in his honorable head. He had been awarded every plaque, title, and honor due a man who tripled a family fortune and channeled his passion into public service. And if Claire had never walked into his house, perhaps that would have been enough. But ever since he had tasted the simple riches of unselfish love and love unselfishly returned, it made all his accomplishments appear like the monogrammed silver bowls that lined his mantel: empty vessels of self-aggrandizement. Now sitting across the table from him was his last hope for happiness.

"Would you be offended if I held your hand?"

She had to lean forward to hear his words, they were so quietly spoken. She observed that their fingers were already only inches apart. When their hands finally touched, all the old feelings rushed through her veins, making it harder to decide what really mattered. No, she *always* remembered what was important to her: her children and Harrison.

"Claire, I want you to consider something very carefully. Would you and the children live with me, marry me if you could consider it? I'm going to fly home in the morning and demand Ophelia give me a divorce."

For years she had waited to hear these words.

*   *   *

When they walked through the narrow hall to the room she had taken for the night, Claire and Harrison left Tuxedo, Washington, and Rome behind them. Traveling light, they brought along only the memories of their fingerprints on one another's bodies. To Harrison, Claire was a mythic land to be returned to at any cost, and to save himself he would cross any bridge to get there. The valleys of her body, the deep gorge below her neck, the smooth terrain of her thighs, were the familiar places he pined for. She was simply his world. When he embraced her, his emotions were as sea-pitched as hers. Would he be able to please her as much he had before? He pressed the anxious warmth of his mouth against the soft fullness of hers and laid his hand to rest on that spot on the back of her neck, the center of her sensuality, his Isle of Capri. When he put his lips there where they had wandered so many times before and cupped her breasts with his hands, he felt he had come home after a long journey during which jealous gods had conspired against them.

Why shouldn't they be in love? Theirs was neither a sin nor unnatural, just a divergence from a steel, rigid norm. The hard facts of their situation turned evanescent and drifted away as Claire and Harrison were filled with longings as soft as Claire's tea-colored blouse. They both knew they could never return to the notion of traditional Home ever again; no, they had committed themselves, breaking ties, burning bridges, and from now they would be welcome only in one another's arms and in the love they would engender. They could breathe life into their own "Italy," making a geography of their own, leaving behind those who had blown gales in their direction and stirred up tempests. He promised her they would create their own Sardinia by the sea, or Isola Bella in Lake Como, an island of their own to harbor them and the children.

Claire did not relinquish her heart to Harrison. Instead, she shared it with him, a much richer gift, presented by a worldly woman, than the total surrender of an impressionable young girl. She whispered words to him on the tip of her tongue and then pushed its moistness into his mouth. She tangled her fingers in his silver hair, marveling at the silkiness of it, inhaling the smells of him she had so crazily craved for so long.

She arched her neck, exposing her throat's lovely hollow to him, leaning back to gather all his kisses. She lavished her willingness on him and invited his advances. He was astonished at how much more powerful love was when it was shared by a man and a mature woman instead of a dominant male and his devoted young admirer. Then, he had been the only man she knew. Now, out of all the men in her glittering world, she wanted him. It made him feel more potent to be chosen.

As she shuddered little kisses down the strong ridge of his chest and then the lean gully of his stomach, she lifted her head to survey the corporeal muscle and sinew that was Harrison, to make sure he was not just some erotic imagining of hers. When she sweetly pulled him into her mouth, she was sated by the familiar tastes of oysters seasoned with the briny juices of Courvoisier and salt. It didn't matter to Claire as they lay comforting each other, catching their breath in the four-poster bed, that they could never go home again.

They made love for the third time as the dawn rolled in over the Seine and across the low rooftops. It discovered them in their secret lovers' chamber, their faces hidden, buried as they were in one another's flesh. With the morning sun rising in a brilliant blue sky, Harrison bent over the bed to kiss her, then forced himself out the door to catch his plane.

Feeling warm and powerful, she sank back into the feather-filled mattress for a few more hours of dreams. They had climaxed together with such frenzy in the early hours of the morning that she'd thought her heart would surely burst and her breaths stop coming. Now he had gone home to extricate himself from Ophelia, flying out on the 9 A.M. from Paris to New York. He was like a man on a one-directive mission: to make a clean break and disentangle the nasty loose ends. Claire would return to Rome by train where she would gather her children and her things and stay in Harrison's Ritz Hotel apartment until domestic arrangements could be made.

She drifted into the little parlor and picked up the newspaper that lay on the wood floor, not bothering to read it. All her news was happy. Why spoil it with the world's worries?

In the bathroom she splashed cold water all over herself in the hopes of toning down the warm glow radiating from her face. A night of passion with the man she loved had brightened her complexion, even her eyes lighting up at a higher voltage than the low they'd been dimmed to over these lonely years. But all that was about to change. Her hope and exhilaration were written all over her face.

She wondered how she would be able to disguise the happiness from Duccio's streetwise suspicions. She sighed, remembering how he always bragged he could gauge which way a punch was being thrown at him by just reading his opponent's eyes, whether in a brawl from his rough past or in the sparring he engaged in for exercise. A chill snaked down her spine as she imagined her next conversation with Duccio.

She pushed on her prescription sunglasses before picking up the phone to dial Rome. She called the private line that only she or Lorenza answered. Lorenza picked up with a cheery *"Pronto."* All was well. Six and Sara were out horseback riding with Tutti as chaperone, but they would be packed and ready for their trip to America with Grandfather in the morning. Signóre Duccio hadn't left the house all day but was still at home in his first-floor office. There had been noisy meetings all morning long, Lorenza reported, with lots of men and lots of screaming. Hardly unusual.

Claire pulled on her silk shirt, wrapped an orange and tan Hermès scarf over her head, tying it twice around her neck, and stepped into her low-heeled Italian shoes and traveling trousers.

She wondered if Lorenza was the loyal friend she seemed to be or if she only treated Claire so well because she was the wife of the vastly powerful Fulco Duccio. She'd need to enlist Lorenza's deft hands in packing up her belongings and helping her with the rest of the preparations without letting the rest of the household staff know. Secrecy was crucial. Instinctively Claire knew that the best way to handle her hot-tempered husband was to announce her intentions to divorce him only after she and her children were safely settled in Harrison's Paris suite.

She stopped by the lobby to pay her bill and was just a little surprised to discover that Harrison had settled the account. How very like him, with his old-fashioned good manners. Even if the lady had rented out the joint and provided the love nest, he had picked up the tab. She smiled as she stepped out into the street to hail a taxi and was almost knocked over by a newsboy carrying a load of papers and crying out the morning's headlines. Her thoughts were on the stars and her head in the clouds.

She saw the three-inch headline and heard the horrible news at the same precise moment: ANDREA DORIA SINKS, 25 DEAD, 17 MISSING.

She stood speechless with her heart throbbing in her throat, coming out of her lover's daze with the same frenzied speed in which hundreds of sleeping passengers onboard had jerked awake as the liner *Stockholm* had rammed her husband's luxury ship. Her eyes hurriedly scanned the story, her mind switching to French as she read the lurid account.

On her last night out before docking in New York Harbor, the *Andrea Doria* had been walled in by a thick North Atlantic fog. The mists closed in around the late diners eating off plates Claire had helped design beneath chandeliers grand enough for even Duccio's liking. Some of the passengers had been enjoying a movie in one of the ship's four theaters while stylish dancers swayed to the rhythms of the orchestra's last song, *Arrivedérci, Roma*.

Lulled by the soothing roll and the sea sounds, they were unprepared for the crunching roar of the *Stockholm*'s knife-sharp prow (reinforced for cutting through ice in Sweden's ports) grinding thirty feet deep into the starboard side of *Andrea Doria*. They were also unprepared for its aftermath. Claire's breathing was ragged. Her children had sailed to the States twice on the grand luxury liner, always in the company of Violet or one of the Aunties. She shuddered, not able even to imagine the horrid possibilities. She said a quick prayer for all those souls aboard and then rushed on to the station to get back to her children. She thanked God Sara and Six hadn't sailed. Luckily, they were waiting to return with Grandfather Harrison. And now even that had changed.

And then her thoughts turned to the crazy rage Duccio must be in. *Big meetings all morning, lots of screaming.* He would be violently possessed, angrily pitching ashtrays against walls, screaming in eight different languages at the top of his lungs, hurling explosive epithets at whichever unlucky person happened to be nearest, deranged at the news that his most expensive trophy, all six hundred and ninety-seven feet of her, was lying belly-up at the bottom of the sea.

It was that strange time of day at the four-hundred-year-old palazzo when the fading light of dusk fooled the eye. It often spooked Six and Sara, who frequently giggled and swore to their mother that a stone statue had just moved his arm or waved his sword, for a fleeting second coming alive. As Claire opened the heavy palazzo door, she looked down the long, tunnel-like corridor, darkened by shimmering afternoon shadows. She entered the house quietly, hoping she would have time to climb the stairs to see the children before having to calm Duccio's wrath. She tilted her head in surprise. It occurred to her that Duccio must have added to his ever-expanding art collection in her absence. In the darkness she could just make out an unfamiliar marble statue holding an offering in its arms. She wondered why no one had thought to turn the lights on. Not even a spotlight on the statue, as Duccio usually arranged to light his newest prize treasures. With its broad shoulders and long, shapeless legs, she wondered if this was the valuable Greek kouros that Duccio had been trying to outbid Onassis for. She was momentarily stunned when, from her perspective fifty feet down the vaulted entry, which had always reminded her of a tomb, the Greek statue breathed. But that was the spell this hall held over everyone's imagination, Claire told herself as she turned on one of the entranceway torchères. She moved forward only a few steps before she froze. In the light, she could clearly see that the statue was Tutti, and the lifeless bundle in his arms her son.

Claire shrieked. As she ran down the hall in the slow-motion gait of a person trapped in a nightmare, there was time for her to imagine a thousand explanations: Six had fallen off his horse and sprained his ankle; he had just fallen asleep and Tutti was carrying him up to bed; they were all playing a game of swinging statues and Six was "it." But the other side of her brain had only to see the unnatural angle at which Six's neck and head hung from his shoulders. His eyes rolled back in his head. His boy-child's curled fingers were more rigid than limp. Her ears were deaf to her own screams. She fell to her knees in what she thought was silence as Tutti handed Claire the body of her dead son.

Chapter Fourteen

Into the Tunnel

Grief fills the room up of my absent child,
Lies in his bed, walks up and down with me,
Puts on his pretty looks, repeats his words,
Remembers me of all his gracious parts,
Stuffs out his vacant garments with his form:
Then have I reason to be fond of grief.

—*Shakespeare*
King John

Six's baseball cap still hung from the rump of the onyx centaur guarding the entry hall of Palazzo Duccio, as if he might grab it in his hurry to run out and play. No one had the courage or heart to remove it, least of all Lorenza, who passed it, crossing her heart and dabbing her eyes with her black cotton gloves, each time she answered the doorbell. The festive chimes rang out almost incessantly, and in this somber house on the morning after death, whoever was the nearest—butler, chambermaid, or cook—bustled to the door to stop the sound. Lorenza knew that Tutti had been ordered to kill the bell's gay melody and replace it with a more respectful toll. Duccio had also instructed the help to wear crepe-soled shoes to keep a silence in the house and to hang black bunting from all the balconies. Even the dogs and cats had been ordered into mourning; they, along with the canaries in Duccio's library, wore crepe bows around their necks. Lorenza wondered if this elaborate display of grief could hide what had really happened in the house.

An accident, they were saying. A terrible freak accident, so unfortunate and doubly tragic coming on the heels of the *Andrea Doria* disaster. The Neapolitan banker was unembarrassed to weep real tears, saying that God had blessed Duccio with so much and was now extracting payment. The bishop shook his head and knew out loud that Six was certainly at peace in heaven. Though the boy was not a Catholic, last rites had been administered by the Vatican's secretary of the treasury, Archbishop D'Agostini, who happened to be in the house at the time. Surely he was with the angels now, this child as beautiful as a seraphim. What a misfortune that the child was as reckless as he was golden, falling to death from the top of the marble balcony, balancing like a circus ropewalker on the narrow ledge until something distracted him. He had slipped and then toppled off, breaking his neck either when he hit the staircase railing or when he finally landed on the marble floor.

Lorenza turned her back on Duccio and his men, afraid to meet their eyes. She rushed upstairs to hold Signóra Duccio's bloodless hand. She'd been very surprised to see that her refined lady mourned her child with the same naked grief as the simple people from her village. She had wailed with the same banshee voice, thrashing feverishly around on the floor, flagellating her body with her arms like the bent black-shawled peasant women wailing their dead off to heaven. But now her lady sat staring out a window in Six's room upstairs. The signóra was in a pill-induced stupor, the remedy prescribed by Duccio's doctor to quiet the animal howl emanating from deep inside her. Lorenza's tears flowed freely as she knelt by Claire's side. Signóra's normally translucent skin had turned paler than porcelain. The bones in her face protruded as sharp as knives, cutting through the sunken hollows of her cheeks. Her mouth continued to quiver as it opened and shut like an unlatched window in a storm. Each time Lorenza expected a glass-shattering scream to come out of the wide-open mouth, but each time only an anguished whisper escaped Claire's trembling lips. Rocking in the yellow and gold armchair in which she had read Six his stories, tears streaming down her cheeks, Claire's fingers gripped his soccer jersey, twisting it around and around her wrist, making it impossible for anyone to take it away from her. His smells still filled the jersey, and the sweet perspiration of the young athletic boy permeated his uniform; she could conjure him up just by holding his shirt to her face. Lorenza laid her hands lightly over Claire's and rocked with her. She decided that the next time the doctor came in with his needles and jelly-bean bags of pills she'd keep him away. She'd stand guard until Violet and Harrison arrived to protect her. She'd already covered Sara with a blanket, as the child had billeted herself on Six's bed and just lay there as if she had died, too. It worried her even more than Claire's very human unraveling, the kind she had seen too often as a child during the war, that Sara had gone rigid and frozen.

When the child had heard Lorenza's screams the day before, she'd come flying out of her room. When she saw her brother's body lying at the bottom of the stairs, a thick hedge of kneeling men around him, she urged him to get up and tried to shake him awake.

"Don't tease me, Six," she'd cried. "This isn't a game. Get up, get up!" And for the first time in his life, Six didn't wink back and jump up gaily from one of his practical jokes. When Duccio ordered her out, she'd fought him with her small angry fists until two men dragged her away, her shoes leaving lines of black scuff marks on the floor as she flailed the air with her arms.

"Too bad it was the golden one and not the ugly little Puritan who fell from the balcony." Duccio's cruel words were in Italian, but Sara understood. *She* should have been the one who died. She was supposed to have been Six's protector. She had promised her mother. And Grand-mère Ophelia. She had let them all down. Six was gone, it was her fault, and there was nothing more to say.

Lorenza had watched, horrified, as the child stiffened and turned icy-eyed, as if her feelings were being carried away by Tutti along with her brother's body down the long, darkening hall. One of the dark men in gray suits tucked Sara under his arm like one of her mute Madame Alexander dolls and carted her up the stairs to her room. The little girl, *poverina ragazza,* hadn't uttered a word since.

Lorenza thanked all her special saints—Maria, Teresa, and Santa Lucia—when Violet finally arrived with the morning. Now she wouldn't be the only one standing sentry, protecting Sara and Claire from only she knew what. The proper lady in the quiet suit could organize the commotion taking place downstairs, throwing out the florists who wove insincere garlands around the small coffin and sending the publicity hounds packing. Lorenza took Violet's hat and apologized repeatedly for her own disheveled appearance. She had lost her apron and her bun had come undone sometime during the long night, which she had spent kneeling on the floor, holding hands with Claire and rubbing a comforting arm on Sara's shoulder. She hadn't allowed herself to doze off for a second, all the while keeping her watchful eyes on the door. Now Lorenza heaved her first sigh of relief in hours and let her aching shoulders fall. Relief had come in the shape of a diminutive lady with a brooch that matched the piercing color of her eyes.

Violet was anguished to see the tragic little scene that she discovered in Claire's private apartment. Her own broken heart and exhaustion from traveling fourteen hours were forgotten when she saw her daughter rocking stone-eyed in Six's chair, but the picture that sucked the air out of her lungs was of her granddaughter guarding a ghost. Sara had curled herself around the imprint Six's sleeping body had made on the bed linens only two mornings ago, so that the child looked as if she were sleeping next to her brother, her arm thrown protectively over the hollow left by his young boy's body.

Violet swung into grim action. There would be time for her own tears later. The best way to help her daughter was to be the person she'd always been: the one who dealt with the necessary details. A casual observer would have mistaken her efficient reserve for lack of feeling; in reality Violet was conducting herself in the only way she knew, burying the ache in her own heart to allow everyone else their sorrow. Grief for Violet had always been a luxury, a private indulgence she could allow herself only when everyone else had been consoled. She asked Lorenza for Claire's agenda, the phone numbers of her closest friends, a washcloth for her daughter's face, and instructed the anxious woman to try to coax some soup or juice into Sara's tightly clenched mouth.

She blinked away the mist from her own eyes as Claire dug her fingers into her arm to tell her with a weak smile what bright thing Six had said only two days ago. Violet purposely distanced herself from this pitiful little scene in Six's bedroom. Three generations of women swallowed up in sorrow. She knew that as always they would be left to their own devices to comfort each other out of tragedy. What the lioness in her felt intuitively was the need to show strength and gather them close together; otherwise Duccio and Ophelia would mark them as vulnerable prey.

The watchful den mother took a moment to lick her cub's wounds. Taking Claire's peaked face between her palms, she listened as Claire begged her to explain why Six was gone. She rubbed her daughter's shoulders as Claire wondered aloud what God could have been thinking. Had he been away from his desk? They'd taken the wrong boy. Violet clasped their hands together, making a double church steeple with their fingers as Claire fretted that Six wouldn't know anyone else in heaven. Who would look after him or show him the way? She wouldn't want him to get in the wrong line with the lost souls.

"Sara, my first baby Sara, why weren't you watching out for your brother? Why did you let him down? Why?"

Violet leaped to Sara's defense and held her grandchild in her arms. All the warmth had left her body. "Hush, Sara, don't listen. Your mother's very upset. An accident isn't anybody's fault."

Then Claire turned the blame upon herself. "Why wasn't I at home?" She let her face fall into her hands. It was all her fault. She'd been making love to Harrison while Six tumbled off the railing. "Harrison. Harrison."

Violet patted Sara's hair and tiptoed into Claire's room, a few feet away, where she apprehensively telephoned Charlotte Hall to inquire what time their plane was due to arrive. She was surprised to hear Ophelia's clipped, businesslike tones informing her that Six's burial site and stone were being prepared for interment in the family plot in Tuxedo Park and they would hold the funeral when her grandson arrived home next week. She hoped that the Duccios wouldn't allow Six's Roman memorial service to take on the flavor of one of their over-the-top dinner affairs. She and Harrison would appreciate it if Claire would remember that out of her own neglect she had lost William Henry Harrison VI, the heir to one of America's oldest and most important families, and perhaps out of respect for the rest of the Harrisons, who stood united, she could try to conduct herself with a modicum of good taste.

Violet was flabbergasted, her dark intuitions proving true. It was obvious that, in the moment when Claire was the most defenseless, Ophelia would strike. Like well-bred vultures, Ophelia and her lawyers were already circling over the carcass of Claire's life. Ophelia would seize the death of her grandson, the light of Claire's life, as an opportunity to renew her custody suit for Sara, the child whom she considered her own. With a shudder, Violet realized she'd have to put the steel back in Claire's spine if she didn't want to lose her daughter, too. But why wasn't Harrison helping? She'd long suspected there were deep feelings between the two of them. Where was he now?

*　　*　　*

One day earlier in Tuxedo Park, Harrison had shifted his jaw into the stiff diplomatic expression he wore for his most difficult negotiations. He adjusted the four-in-hand knot of his English silk rep tie, lying against the precise fit of his formal chalk-striped suit. Ending his marriage to an increasingly embittered Ophelia rated right up there with persuading Emperor Hirohito to deny his birthright as the Sun God. He had left his travel bags at the Waldorf Towers and driven out to Tuxedo Park to deliver the news in person.

He didn't expect histrionics from Ophelia, whose sense of superiority was sustained by never stooping to middle-class emotions. They had lived like a divorced couple for years anyway. She had only to give her legal consent on a piece of paper that Tom had already drawn up. The whole thing would be very civilized. No announcements of divorce in absentia over hash at "21," in full view of every gossipmonger in town. His code of honor dictated that he conduct this distasteful business himself, in private. He was tired from his long flight, but, more important, he realized that he was truly exhausted from sleepless years spent shuttling between Europe's capitals on presidential whims and missions. Claire was right. Now was the time for him to find some peace and harmony in his life. Most of all, he was bone-tired of the domestic lie he lived. Now all that would change with a few flourishes of Ophelia's boarding-school penmanship from her pearl-handled pen.

Her voice was polite, but anger flashed in her eyes. Even the coolly independent Ophelia was affronted that Harrison had been gone for five wordless months. And now here he was, walking in the door with that damn diplomat look on his face. She looked past him, hoping to see Sara and Six dancing around a mountain of traveling trunks. He never showed up at Charlotte Hall anymore unless he was with the children.

"I came early to have a word with you." A leaden civility edged his voice.

Little alarm bells rang inside Ophelia's head. If he was going to tell her he wouldn't be escorting her to the Slocums' ball in Newport next weekend, she was definitely not going to let him off the hook. There were appearances to keep up.

"You could have at least telegrammed that you were coming." She glanced crisply at her wristwatch, as if he were two hours late instead of two days early. "You look like you haven't slept properly for a week. Don't tell me you just washed up from the *Andrea Doria*. Terrible about that leaky boat. Boots Hollingsworth was on the bloody vessel. Broke her arm. Well, where are Sara and Six? Are the children still arriving on Wednesday?" She was at his heels as he walked into the drawing room.

"You know I prefer to stay out of those arrangements. You should consult Claire about the matter of the children's schedules." He politely gestured for her to sit down in her favorite chair, the Queen Anne that had belonged to her mother.

The heavy hoods of Ophelia's lids blinked while her eyes remained in trigger focus. "I shall not have a conversation about that woman in my house."

"*That* woman, as you call Claire, is very dear to me."

Ophelia was startled: Harrison was behaving too badly for words. She tsked-tsked her disapproval and quietly told him to remember his manners in her house. There was only a trace of irritation in her unexcitable facade. She would express her disdain for Claire, but she wouldn't be drawn into an argument about the international tart.

"You know, I've asked the lawyers if they can't do something about her using our good name as if it belonged to her. Sandwiching 'Harrison' between 'Claire' and 'Duccio' is totally unacceptable. It's as if we put our family's seal of approval on that little upstart and her troll of a husband. Why, over at Perkins and Williams the other day—"

"Have the decency to drop the lawsuit, Ophelia. I'm afraid she'll never return if you keep on hounding her. She could prevent you from seeing the children."

"She cannot break the agreement. I have Sara and Six August and Christmas, and as soon as one of those silly aunts dies and she plants one of her tangoing feet back on American soil, I'll have her hauled into court." Ophelia was still aghast that her former daughter-in-law had entertained Evita Perón during her Italian visit, even giving a well-publicized dinner dance for the Argentinean call girl turned politician. She'd been furious that Sara and Six had been photographed with the bleached blond dictatoress. How she'd been able to live that down at Bailey's was a testament to her self-control and breeding.

"You'll do no such thing."

"Don't speak to me in that tone, Harrison. My people have been living in Fifth Avenue mansions for generations and are just as good as all your family's public servants." One unplucked eyebrow went in the direction of the rock crystal chandelier hanging from the domed ceiling.

She was unintentionally making this very easy for him. "I told you I came out today to discuss something quite important with you. Face to face. I've given the matter a great deal of thought and serious reflection." He smoothed the crease of his double-pleated trousers as he sat down in the Salem side chair.

Ophelia had an unpleasant déjà-vu moment, remembering how Claire had sat in that same straight-backed chair when Ophelia had interviewed her for the position of Harry's bride and found her unsuitable.

"I've decided we should end our marriage."

He searched her eyes for a reaction, but found none. Instead, she turned and rang for the servants. "Bring some water, Agnes," she called. "I believe Mr. Harrison's blood pressure's got away from him." She wheeled around to address her husband. "Have you lost your mind? Is your blood sugar elevated? Divorce! A well-arranged marriage like ours will never end on a piece of paper. Can you imagine Franklin divorcing Eleanor?" That was the ticket; Ophelia always knew when to haul out FDR. "I think your leash is quite long enough as it is. You've no *idea* the lame excuses I've had to invent for your rude absences." To control the unwelcome anger she felt rising, she plucked a cigarette from a silver eggcup and waited for Harrison to light it. It was always helpful to do something busy with one's hands when emotions started to stir.

"Divorce!" This time the word huskily issued from both sides of her mouth. "Out of the question. And there's simply no way you could afford it. Perkins and Williams has every zero and decimal point in your entire portfolio. The two of us are, quite simply, attached at the pocketbook."

"Then I give it all to you. Everything I have in the States."

"Madame, you rang?"

"I'll have some aspirin, Agnes, please." Harrison was suddenly feeling light-headed.

"He'll have no such thing. Leave us alone now." Ophelia shooed her away.

Harrison put his fingers to his temples.

"What do you mean, everything in the States? Oh, I see. You've stashed your fortune all over Europe. That's why you've been in Paris and Rome and Switzerland, deceiving me that you were on hush-hush diplomatic duties when you were just squirreling away our assets."

Harrison rubbed his forehead. The negotiations with Hirohito and even Stalin had been less taxing. "I can assure you, my dear, and Perkins and Williams will back me up, that there's a sizable fortune at your fingertips. I have just kept capital I've accumulated in Europe the last few years, where it was earned."

He opened his cigar case as he closed his argument. "I would like that glass of water, though." As far as he was concerned, it was over, done, civilized. There was only one small detail. Better to hear it from him.

"Claire is leaving Duccio." He spoke in a muted voice.

"So? There's no one I know who would be even remotely interested in her." She hated it when she had to lean over to hear him.

"Only me."

The silver eggcup toppled from her fingers.

"I plan to live very quietly with Claire and the children in Europe. I'm sorry if this comes as a shock to you, but I think you've probably known for a long time. Both Claire and I long to step out of the spotlight, so you needn't worry that we'll be a glaring embarrassment to you. Everything should remain pretty much the same for you."

Before the image of him lying dead with his letter opener through his heart flashed through her mind, there was a fleeting vision of Eleanor Roosevelt's mantel with a Tiffany Christmas card from Ophelia, Harry, and Minnie next to a tasteless holiday photograph of Harrison, Claire, and the children. Ophelia clenched her jaw—she was desperate to save her situation. She would not lose her standing or Sara, whom she had raised as her own. The girl had belonged to her from the minute she was born. No. Divorce would be fought on every front. Harry would help her bring his father to his lost senses, and never, *never* would Harrison be allowed to marry Claire. The usual extraordinary allowances could be made. But there would never be another Mrs. Harrison IV.

She summoned up fifty years of good breeding. "You can have any size or color mistress you like. That way you can hold on to all your club memberships and share in our hefty financial bundle. You can keep the respect of our friends and your presidents." Her smile was chilling. "Otherwise, you lose everything."

"I'll lose nothing I care about. You don't seem to understand."

"Then surely you've lost your marbles, Harrison. I understand you've been under a great deal of strain. Perhaps we could get you into a good institution? The Paine-Whitney, perhaps."

"I'm just getting out of one."

Her next words came out in a hiss. "Then things will get very ugly." And with her sapphire ring pointing to their ancestors on the walls, she broke her cardinal rule of never raising her voice.

"We won't let you get away with this!" she shrieked. "I'll have you in a straitjacket!"

Over the years, the diplomat had heard every threat and histrionic hurled at him in every language. "I hope in time we can be friends. I have the highest regard for you, but I plan to take some happiness while I can."

Ophelia waved him away with her handkerchief. If there was even a remote chance that she could get away with it, she would have preferred him dead to seeing him alive with Claire.

"I'm going to my study to collect a few things, and then I'll be leaving." He walked into his favorite room in the house, the room where he had first met Claire. He checked his pocket watch. It would be seven hours later in Rome. She should be leaving for Paris with the children about now. He decided to check on them.

The first sharp pain seemed to come out of the telephone and shoot into his ear. It traveled down the left side of his arm with such severity he thought Ophelia might have shot him. He looked startled before he went slack-jawed. The water he had just been drinking dribbled down his chin, although he couldn't feel it on his face, and the telephone receiver fell from his suddenly useless fingers. The transatlantic call had delivered its devastating blow. Lorenza's trembling voice and the devastating message it conveyed came across the copper wires almost static-free. Six was dead. His cherished son.

In her dressing room, Ophelia had sat and composed herself until she was able to muster up the courage to negotiate again with Harrison. Surely they could come to terms. Her status in society depended on it—why, she might even be drummed out of the Social Register. Everyone welcomed a woman with an absent diplomatic husband, but nobody appreciated one abandoned for her daughter-in-law. The scandal would ruin all of their lives; none of them, including the children, would ever be received anywhere again. How could he be so selfish? She'd make him see.

She stopped in the doorwell, afraid to enter the room. Within a matter of minutes, Harrison had aged twenty-five years, white as a sheet of his Smythson's stationery, his face a ragged road map of ditches and lines. With one hand he clutched his forehead and with the other he tried to reach out to her for help. She stood there, composed, her narrow eyes squinting at him as he struggled to get his words out. His words were hard to make out, but it sounded something like "Oh my God, not my son. Tell her I'm coming." Before Ophelia hung up the dangling phone, she heard enough of Lorenza's hysterical ravings to know that Six was dead.

As it was cocktail hour in Tuxedo, and Ophelia never liked to impose on her professional friends, she waited several hours before she telephoned Dr. Fawcett. As she told the elderly doctor afterwards, she would have called earlier, but she thought her husband was just having a nap on the floor after his long flight home. No, no, she explained, he often did that sort of thing, lying on the hard floor to support his back. And Dr. Fawcett would never think of second-guessing Mrs. William Henry Harrison IV. The doctor assured her that the stroke appeared to be a mild one but ordered absolute quiet and bed rest for a couple of weeks. The good wife obligingly complied, ordering the drapes drawn in his darkened bedroom, even having the telephone removed. She added a prescription of her own: No visitors and no newspapers, nothing that would upset her husband. "Don't worry," she told the doctor, "I'll make sure he doesn't even listen to a radio, or do anything that might excite him. People will just have to get along without him." And then she helped old Dr. Fawcett, who had been her mother's doctor, put his antique stethoscope back in his pocket.

Taking Dr. Fawcett's arm as she led him into the living room for a highball, she persuaded him that loving home care in the bosom of his family would be better than the latest advances of medical science in an unfriendly hospital. Dr. Fawcett, who'd received every Harrison Christmas card for the last forty years, nodded in absolute agreement.

"I'll protect him from the outside world. If someone wants to get to Harrison, they'll have to go through me."

Later, when a bad dream awoke Claire from a restless nap, she called for Harrison again even before sipping some water to wet her parched lips. In the nightmare Six was laughing, his arms outstretched as if to embrace his mother happily, but he seemed to be moving away from her at the same time, so that no matter how fast she ran, he was always just out of her grasp. She awakened soaked with sweat, as if she really had been running. Violet was there to mop her brow.

All she wanted to do was get her daughter and granddaughter out of this pirate's hellish palace. She sensed something strange and off-kilter in this "memorial service" Duccio was conducting for his stepson. Duccio hadn't been in once to see Claire or Sara. Instead, he was downstairs receiving voluptuous opera singers in black capes, film stars with lace handkerchiefs, and other business tycoons come to pay their respects to the financier. Lorenza served as their fourth pair of eyes, running back up and down the stairs, bringing condolence notes for Claire and news of all the glitterati arriving. Each time Lorenza breathlessly flew in with a "Maria Callas is here" or "a Mr. Agnelli's just arrived," Violet, who had arranged all kinds of gatherings for her Field's customers, some with just a day's notice, couldn't imagine who was getting out the news. Could it be that he was actually inviting these people to his stepson's service, people who had never even met Six? Was he holding a farewell party? Why were there society reporters and photographers downstairs? In her own mind she agreed with what Ophelia had warned them against, the ruthless tycoon might turn her stepson's fall from the stairs into a media event designed to garner sympathy for his next lucrative deal.

"Mother, is Harrison here yet?"

"The Harrisons are waiting for you to bring Six back to Charlotte Hall so they can bury him with family. The Aunties will meet us there. It is time to go. Sara needs you, Claire. We can take Sweet William home with us. Right after Duccio's service." Violet frowned. She didn't have the strength to take on Duccio. If she interfered, he might hold up the body with paperwork. He had the connections and the power. They'd just have to suffer through the service and then depart swiftly.

"We'll leave Italy behind us." She wished they could leave Tuxedo Park behind, too. Ophelia had sounded so cold about Six's death. She was his grandmother but was behaving as if she weren't even related to Six. They were a strange lot, those Harrisons. Violet couldn't understand people who prided themselves on such stiff decorum that they couldn't even express emotion at a time like this.

"Look, Claire. A shooting star. Our Six is in those little stars.

" 'He will make the face of heaven so fine

" 'That all the world will be in love with night,

" 'And pay no worship to the garish sun.' "

Violet softly quoted the lines from *Romeo and Juliet* that she had always loved but never understood until now. Her daughter mumbled the words along with her. Only Sara remained silent.

Violet tried to coax some response from Sara, even an angry word or a sob. But Sara couldn't be persuaded to speak or even move from the enclosure of Six's room.

Violet massaged her daughter's temples, until her skin was warmer for the rubbing and pinker for the increased circulation. She spoke simple words of comfort culled from all the churches they had attended during Claire's childhood, reminding Claire how all living things had a life beyond the temporal, that Six would live forever in the river beyond Charlotte Hall, the rock he loved to climb, the tree in which he'd carved the number six, in the hearts of all who loved him. That he'd only been on loan to Claire and, being too perfect for this world of ours, was invited back to Heaven. That she would negate all the goodness he had spread around like apple seeds if she wouldn't roust herself to keep his spirit alive. And Sara needed her. She needed Claire to let her know none of this was her fault.

Claire, seated numbly at her dressing table, listened to her mother. She *did* blame Sara. She couldn't help it—Six was the only joy both mother and daughter had shared, and through careless watchkeeping Sara had allowed that one joy to be dimmed forever. But mostly she blamed herself for not being there, for being with Harrison instead. She wondered what Harrison was feeling and when he was coming. Violet peered over her daughter's shoulder in the mirror and smoothed her hair. Lorenza entered carrying a sheer black veil from the house of Dior that Duccio had ordered. She laid it on the chaise next to the streamlined suit by Givenchy he had instructed her to steam for Six's service. Claire didn't give either item a glance. Her attention was drawn to her daughter, who was still curled up on Six's bed, her knees pulled up to her waist. Claire wanted to curl up in a ball like Sara and retreat from the world, too, but her mother was right: She had to hold herself together for her daughter's sake. Sara was hurting as much as she was, and now that she was Claire's only child, Sara was doubly deserving of Claire's maternal love and guidance.

"Oh, God, help me for her," she pleaded.

Lorenza tiptoed in again to deliver a tray laden with condolence notes, and Claire seized upon the distraction.

"Look, Sara. Somebody's sent us a note with Princess Grace as a postage stamp. Come and see. They've written such nice things about your brother." Even though Sara didn't speak, Claire was relieved that she got up from the bed and pulled Six's stamp collection down from the shelf. Claire walked over to hold her daughter, but Sara resisted, choosing to hug the stamp portfolio instead. How like a Harrison her daughter was, looking for comfort in an object instead of a human being. She vowed to bring the child back to the world of emotion before it was too late. Claire pulled Sara close in spite of the girl's resistance and rocked her only child, their separate tears running into a single river of sorrow.

The fragile trio moved hesitantly like a band of lost orphans into the palazzo's stone chapel. Claire and Violet flinched as lightbulbs flashed inches from their faces. For one terrible moment Claire thought she had blundered into a cocktail party. Scores of overdressed people swiveled around to gawk at her walking down the aisle. Were they there to see how a fashion plate mourned her child? She wished she could make them all go away and let her grieve in peace. If she had had her wits about her, she would have turned around and run, but she was too stricken to do anything but follow the service. And she wouldn't leave Six, beautiful Six, there alone in his casket. She took some solace in knowing the veil covered her face so that the strangers couldn't see her private grief.

Suddenly Duccio was at her side, as if Violet and Lorenza were giving the bride away to the waiting groom. He embraced her in a bold gesture, leaving something heavy, a large black cross, hanging around her neck. She started to fidget it away, but both her hands were taken from her as Duccio's brother and the archbishop, closing in on either side, supported her shaking elbows. She watched numbly as Duccio lifted the cross and turned it around almost proudly before he signaled the current diva from La Scala to begin her mournful aria. Claire succumbed to the soprano's beautiful dirge, in her secret heart hoping that the notes echoing off the apse might be heard by the angels ushering Six into heaven. A small smile came to her lips at the thought of angels as lovely as the *putti* on the chapel walls keeping Six company on his cloud, listening with him to Verdi's exquisite requiem. Perhaps they were accompanying the soprano on the lyre or a flute. This vision gladdened her, and her smile widened.

A second series of flashbulbs went off, catching Claire with a look on her face that was almost beatific. What was Duccio thinking, to have allowed photographers into the chapel? She brought a hand up to hide her face and snagged her glove on something sharp. She looked down for the first time since Duccio had hung the heavy cross on her. It was not one of the simple wood crucifixes from the chapel shelf, like she'd thought. With a wave of nausea she realized she was wearing a nearly priceless Romanesque treasure, part of Duccio's collection of religious icons, that had belonged to Catherine de' Medici. The thirteenth-century enamel cross was gaudily set with rubies and emeralds on the horizontal beam, an enormous polished diamond at its center. She flipped the cross back over to its plain black side and flashed a dark look at Duccio. How could he be turning a simple service for her son into an opportunity to display his wealth? She leaned over the stout belly of Duccio's brother to hold Sara's hand. They both needed to hold on to each other as they listened to the archbishop's eulogy to Six's ten short years on this earth. Harrison decorum or no, Sara folded her fingers over her mother's as she listened to a happy anecdote from Six's last month, retold by Archbishop D'Agostini, who had been charmed by the boy ever since he had entered Duccio's home.

Claire was lulled into a lapse of calm even as she sank onto the hard bench. Maybe Duccio had been right to insist upon having more than just immediate family present. The trio of schoolboys, classmates of Six, who recalled their friend with short stories of his athletic prowess and leadership, brought a twinge of pride to Claire's heart. Soon the remembered glories broke away, however, with the bitter realization that all the promise that Six had within him would never be fulfilled. She would never sit in a school chapel to listen proudly to his graduation speech or hear him take his wedding vows. She bowed her head, her shoulders shaking, wondering to what authority she could speak to to bring him back. Surely people like Harrison and Duccio were powerful enough to broker any deal. She held Sara's hand harder even as she wondered why, if one of her children had to be taken away, it had to be Six. She was immediately sorry for this thought and, her eyes resting on the sorrowful silhouette of her daughter, silently apologized to Sara for even thinking such a thing. Claire knew that even though Sara wasn't an easy child, she would have willingly given her life to save her brother. There was no blame there. If anyone was guilty, it was she and Harrison, who out of love had conceived a child in sin. Did God punish you for such a thing? Is that why Harrison hadn't come? Was he pushing her away along with his guilt? Oh, beautiful Six. Her golden child with his puckish laugh and big easy smile. Who had melted frozen hearts in Tuxedo Park and soothed troubled ones across the ocean.

My special child. Gone away forever. The tears that fell from Claire's eyes blurred everything else that happened. The rest of the day went on behind a grim waterfall.

While the cocktail party continued all afternoon in the grand *salone,* upstairs Lorenza insisted that the mourners—Six's mother, sister, and grandmother—take their first nourishment of the day. They sat on a couch in Claire's private quarters, the still unspeaking Sara rigid between them, as they tried to get Sara to eat, though neither could swallow food herself.

Finally, Violet nudged them into motion. The sense of dread she felt propelled her with a strange energy. She knew she had to take her chicks and fly away. She pulled Claire into the dressing room to pack the few things that mattered and asked Sara, who wordlessly complied, to ready her traveling trunk. She instructed Lorenza to close up Six's belongings, reminding her to place school prizes and photos carefully into a separate case.

Lorenza rushed into Claire's closet, its Savonnerie rug littered with dozens of discarded Diors and tissue-stuffed Jacques Faths lying like well-dressed headless corpses amidst the open drawers and half-filled steamer trunks. Empty padded hangers swung wildly from the clothes rods overhead and one-of-a-kind jewels spilled out of the open vault. Lorenza threw herself at the signóra's feet, her arms around Claire's knees, and sobbed as she pled with her to take her with them. To America where she could look after her lady. Away from here so she could be safe.

"Safe from what?" Violet, a curtain of silk scarves hanging from her arm, stopped dead in her tracks.

"Safe from the dangers here." Lorenza nervously scanned the satin-quilted walls as if they were hiding enemy eyes and ears.

"What dangers? What do you mean?" The delicate-boned Violet shook the big-shouldered peasant girl.

Lorenza, shuddering and quaking with emotion, told them what she knew to be true, so help her Holy Mary. Claire and Violet, wondering how their tragedy could get any blacker, didn't see Sara as she stepped silently into the dressing room. While Lorenza swore on the sacred souls of her dead mother and unborn babies that everything she said was true, Sara stood unseen behind a billowing New Look gown, its velvet-bowed satin skirt large enough to hide ten children, and listened wild-eyed.

Lorenza told them how she had heard the children laughing as they arrived home from riding in the park. Tutti was with them. She heard their happy voices and started down the stairs where she had been folding and packing their summer things for Newport. She'd passed a sulking Sara, who told her Six was teasing her nonstop because she had lost their horse race by a nose and she'd find a way to tease him back. He was laughing right behind her, wearing the smile that got him out of any mischief. Almost as an afterthought he turned and bounded back down the stairs, taking two at a time. Lorenza heard his voice clearly; she had followed just a dozen feet behind. He politely knocked on the library door and entered in that authoritative way he had—you know—like his grandfather. Poor Six walked straight into a shouting match, all the partners of the *Andrea Doria* were there loudly hurling blame at each other and frantically calculating up their losses. Duccio's brother's voice was the loudest after Duccio's, and they were both raising holy hell. When Six inquired as to what time you would be home, signóra—Lorenza nodded to a stricken Claire—Duccio had exploded.

Lorenza apologized for repeating what she'd overheard. "That whore!" he'd cried. "That unfit wife, that woman is not here when I want her!"

Six had shaken his boy's fist at Duccio. "Don't you dare speak about my mother like that!"

Claire could envision the scene clearly. Sir Six riding to her rescue.

"If I ever hear you speak against my mother again you'll have me to fight! She's better than you any day!"

At first, Duccio had only laughed. And then he'd struck the fatal blow.

"Signóra," Lorenza said, "I saw it standing in the doorway. It was like a chop to the neck with the side of his hand." She illustrated. But Claire already knew about those hands.

Lorenza wept as she told how she had heard the crack of bones as she saw Six fall onto the floor. And then she'd backed away on her crepe-soled shoes and run silently across the marble.

She ran afraid for her own life. She feared that Duccio's brother, Zio Duccio, saw her.

What could she have done? What should she do? Whom should she tell? Lorenza pleaded. Zio Duccio had already given her a tip of fifty thousand lire just for bringing him a ginger caramel. She held the paper money, two months' wages, in her outstretched hand.

"Signóra, take me with you, please."

Claire slowly looked from the money to the girl, replaying the horrible scene in her head. She looked around the closet for a weapon, anything sharp she could use to drive through the heart of her son's killer. Her eyes landed on a silver shoehorn. She picked it up, then dropped it. If she killed Duccio, who would take care of Sara? No, she needed to rescue them, not make matters worse. She could avenge her son's death some other way. Later. But he would be avenged. "Mother, we're leaving now. Get Sara. I'll call a hearse to bring Six's coffin with us. Lorenza, after you've shipped our bags you'll join us. We're getting out of this godforsaken house now." She turned so fast in every direction that the heavy cross around her neck swung like a hangman's noose.

Violet looked very faint. She couldn't find Sara anywhere in Claire's apartment, the little rooms that were supposed to have been the family's sanctuary. She sank into Claire's Recamier couch, her face the same green as the grapes on the table, her breath coming in erratic spasms.

"Find Sara," she gasped, but Claire was already out the door.

It was like running into a tunnel. The long arched passageway connecting the rest of the palace to Duccio's wing was only vaguely illuminated by the courtyard clerestory. It was that strange time of late afternoon once again. The sounds of the well-dressed condolence callers drifted up the stairs and followed her down the tunnel. One of the iron double doors to Duccio's private quarters was open. Wide enough for a child to slip through, Claire thought, her heart pounding in her head. She could hear her own high heels click against the terrazzo as she passed his reading room, his sitting room, his guest room, and ran breathless into his bedroom suite. She was too late.

Duccio lay sprawled on his bloodied turquoise rug with the yellow stars. One arrow pierced his heart, another had torn open his jugular. He looked crooked and angry lying there and Claire was glad he was dead. He deserved a violent end. But it was Sara standing over him with Six's speargun in her hand.

Sara's tongue wagged silently, trying to coax the barely audible word, the first she'd spoken in days, out of her contorted mouth.

"Mommy."

Finding her voice at last, she shrieked again. "Mommy!"

It should have been me, Claire thought. If I couldn't have been there to save my son I could have at least avenged him. I should have killed Duccio. I should have been there first. Sara, so devastated by Six's death it had taken days for her to utter a single word, would never survive the stigma of being Duccio's murderer. At age thirteen, in America, they might put her under psychiatric care, in a clinic endowed by the Harrisons. But here in Italy, with all of Duccio's powerful family against her, God knows what would happen to the child. Claire had only seconds to think before Lorenza's piercing screams broke the silence, bringing with them a stampede of the curious up the stairs.

"Oh, signóra, hurry! The chief of police is here, the archbishop is coming!" She crossed and recrossed her heart, jumping up and down on her rubber-soled shoes as if she were stamping out a fire. "You must not be in the room when they come. They will blame you! *La Poverina* is small; soon she will be forgiven."

Claire turned gently to Sara, who still gripped the speargun with all her might. The child's eyes were whirlpools of fear and hatred. Only a mother could read in them a quiet plea for help. If I couldn't have been there to save my son I should at least save my daughter, Claire told herself. She didn't hesitate a moment more. Pushing Sara hard out of the way, she grabbed the speargun from her so that she was the one standing there with the weapon in her hand when the archbishop and Zio Duccio rushed into the room, a swirl of black and scarlet.

Chapter Fifteen

Notorious

In spite of even the archenemy sorrow, one can remain alive long past the usual date of disintegration if one is unafraid of change, insatiable in intellectual curiosity, interested in big things and happy in small ways.

—Edith Wharton

I want the one with the handcuffs." Ophelia Harrison, who had never mixed with the people before, let alone had anything to do with the people's press, had taken Anita Lace, former war correspondent for Grant Publications and now its society editor, to her bosom. Anita was serving up lurid details of Claire and the Duccio murder to America in her weekly column and making Claire as unpopular as Lizzie Borden.

Magnifying lens in hand, Ophelia studied the photographs of Claire wearing the Medici cross at her son's funeral.

"Over the top," Miss Lace purred.

"Oh, use this one. She's practically grinning." Ophelia thought the pictures of the smiling, veiled murderess most suitable for her public relations campaign. Almost as good as Claire in cuffs. In her plot to save her marriage and gain legal custody of Sara, she didn't mind a few ugly mentions of the family in order to throw Claire to the dogs. She almost had what she wanted. The still-feeble Harrison was in his bedroom under the watchful eye of Rudy, his physical therapist, learning to squeeze a tennis ball with his left hand. Sara was on the terrace, silently working on her remedial math at an iron garden table. Ophelia had declared her Italian schooling inferior to Miss Westcott's of Tuxedo Park and had arranged for an army of elbow-patched tutors so Sara would be up to snuff for the fall semester. They, along with the psychiatrists and grief counselors, were smuggled up the back stairs of Charlotte Hall, so as not to encourage any rumors that Sara had gone a bit "off" since her brother's fatal accident. Sara was certainly allowed to be sad. Ophelia had told her as much. However, she also let Sara know that she was behaving in the best Harrison tradition, buttoning up her sorrow and keeping a stiff upper lip. Even though some of the more Freudian child psychiatrists warned Ophelia that an overheated vortex was bubbling beneath the thirteen-year-old's quiet facade, Ophelia took their advice with a grain of salt. Most of these shrinks were Jewish, she reasoned, and what could they possibly know about upper-class WASP behavior?

In Italy, passions were unashamedly worn on everyone's sleeves. There was a great communal wail across the boot at the loss of Europe's most colorful financial pirate. The city of Rome hired a seaplane to drop a thousand white carnations and gladioli, a thunderstorm of petals, over Palazzo Duccio, and the mayor decreed an official day of mourning. Even Italy's president attended the funeral, whose pageantry rivaled that of *Aida*. Duccio's bereft mistress, the opera soprano, refused to perform for two nights, standing up SRO audiences, and when she did go on, she performed Desdemona in Verdi's *Otello* dressed head to toe in black. The crowds cheered her for it. Duccio was hailed as a mythic god of riches and eulogized as the man—no matter what means he used—who gave Italy back its pride. Other Europeans hadn't dared joke about Italy's pathetic behavior during the war, not when Duccio was around to buy and sell them.

Once Fulco Duccio was properly canonized, attention turned to Claire, the white-gloved murderess. Here was a real Greek tragedy, better than any opera at La Scala. The beautiful lady's son had died, and two days later she was found standing in dumb shock over Duccio's corpse. Even the murder weapon, a speargun from Abercrombie and Fitch, could have been an operatic prop. Had she gone mad? Had there been an unseen murderer in the house, an enemy of Duccio's? Was she the beleaguered heroine in a mythological tragedy? It was like watching *Madame Butterfly* performed in modern costume. Would the thin lady sing and then plunge a dagger into her own heart?

Full-page photos in *Oggi, Paris Match,* and Grant Publications' *U.S. Week,* of a magnificently coutured Claire and jaunty Duccio in a conga line with a laughing duke and duchess of Windsor, toasting Ambassador Luce at Palazzo Duccio, and christening the *Andrea Doria* with champagne, were all passed around at every barbershop and ladies' *parrucchiere.* Recirculated pictures of the murderess and her children posing with Evita Perón, and even a color photo of Claire and Duccio kissing the ring of Pope Pius XII only fed the frenzy. The Italians gobbled up every picture of the refined Claire with their nightly cappuccino and then queued up at the magazine stands in the morning in case there was a new slant on the big story. Perhaps there would be a picture of Claire they hadn't seen before, one of her in a different Dior or with a new hairdo they could copy or in an expensively decorated room in one of her houses. And if there was a photo of her with an arm around her almost preternaturally beautiful son, teary housewives bought two or three of the glossy rags from the newsstands. There was nothing more fascinating to the hordes hungry for gossip than to see one of the untouchable rich toppled from her pink marble pedestal.

As the frenzy built, the fact that she wouldn't deny or confirm or even confess to the obvious reduced the press to repeating rapidly spreading rumors and writing sensational fiction. If she had just said he'd beaten her, or that it was a terrible accident, they could have turned her into a tragic martyr and sold millions more papers in the continuing weeks. Even Grant Publications' American newspapers had a hefty rise in sales whenever they put that photograph of Claire Harrison Duccio, the one of her curiously smiling under her veil, on their front page. His news editors salivated at the thought of increased circulation once the lady started talking. But Ophelia didn't want Claire to talk. She only needed her to sign on the dotted line. She dispatched Tom Brewster and his briefcase to put an end to the story.

The windowless cell stank of hundreds of years of criminals, its chipped green paint thinly disguising limestone walls damp for the last century. Only the faintest trace of Claire's own vanilla-tinged scent kept Tom from putting his handkerchief over his nose as he entered the place where Claire had been held for five anguished days.

She momentarily brightened, straining her eyes in the dimness to make sure it was he, relieved to see any face from home. As she shakily stood to embrace him, he noticed how thin she'd grown since even the latest pictures he'd seen of her, her arms swinging like taut sticks from her sagging shoulders.

Claire managed a wan smile as she spoke. "At last. A face from home. Harrison's emissary, I presume." Finally he had rallied to unmire the mess.

She looked startled when he backed off from her embrace and shyly retreated to the splintering cot, the only piece of furniture in the dank room. He didn't have the heart to hold her or lie to her. He was Ophelia's emissary, not Harrison's. And he'd been given specific instructions.

"Are you here to help?" She was a little taken aback by Tom's correct coolness and the rigid way he kept his hands on his briefcase, refusing even to shake her hand.

"It's so damn hot in here. Must be a hundred degrees!"

"I haven't been paying much attention to the weather."

He wiped the sweat off his forehead and saw that her dress was stained with perspiration. The dress. It was the same funeral suit, without the jacket, that he had seen in all the papers for the last three days.

Claire suddenly felt very afraid. She lowered her eyes and focused on the black flies that swarmed around the opposite wall of the cell. She had been rushed from the scene of the crime straight to this room with only Italian interrogators for company; she had a thousand questions to ask Tom.

"Have you seen Sara?"

"Yes." He would try to be kind. "We had her removed from that house immediately after you were jailed."

A sign of life sparkled in her dead eyes. "Where did you take her?" Her voice was suddenly stronger.

"To her grandparents. Back to her father. There's not much you can do for her from here." He waved his hand around the grimy little cell with the lawyerly gesture he used to grandstand a jury. "She's in pretty bad shape. Even Violet has agreed it was for the best." He felt like a traitor, but Ophelia's instructions had been as clear as they were brutal. Claire was to be sufficiently maligned so that any court would find her an unfit mother, but she was not to be actually charged with anything more than bad manners. Ophelia wouldn't allow her granddaughter to be known as the child of a convicted felon; then Sara would be ineligible for New York's debutante presentation ball or a listing in the Social Register. It would be like the time society swain Harry Thaw had murdered the noted architect Stanford White and all the young Thaw ladies had to flee New York's cold, snubbing shoulders for distant European outposts to find husbands, none of their own set wanting anything to do with the scandal-tainted family. Ophelia would have none of that.

Instead, she would take advantage of Harrison's illness and the multiple tragedies of the past week to secure her heart's desire:

her granddaughter's custody. As Tom's bread was lavishly buttered by the Harrison holdings, all he could do was follow orders.

"I have papers for you to sign."

"What kind of papers?" She cocked her head to one side. Tom thought that without any makeup she looked like a very tired little girl. "Papers drawn up by whom? Who are you representing here, Tom? I thought it might be *me.*" It suddenly occurred to her that he was the same family friend and lawyer who had encouraged her to sign the divorce papers over lunch at the 21 Club. The deal that had forced her out of the country—to this place—in order to keep her children.

"Where's Harrison?"

"Claire . . ." He tried to soften the blow. Their love affair had never been a secret to him. "Harrison is still recovering. He's suffered a stroke."

"A stroke?" She was confused. How could he have had a stroke? She had made love to him barely a week ago. She looked down at her watch, but it wasn't on her wrist. Then she remembered that she had traded it for a stale cup of coffee from one of her dead-eyed jailers.

"Ophelia says . . ."

"What stroke?" She rose weakly. "Tell me what happened!" Her high-pitched hysteria brought two alert guards armed with carbine guns to the bars.

Tom felt he could no longer suppress his impulse to protect the fragile figure before him. He took her in his arms and felt the light weight of her body collapse against his. She sobbed into his chest.

"He's not dead, too, is he? Oh, no, he's not gone, tell me! Oh, please!"

"No. No. He's had some speech impairment. That's all. His arm, his leg, some mild paralysis. But he's resting and in therapy. It'll all come back. Eventually. It was just a small stroke."

"A stroke." They had all had quite a stroke of bad luck. She wiped her tears away. She didn't want Tom Brewster's sympathy. She wanted to know what was in his briefcase.

He translated the document from legalese. In exchange for them dropping all charges against her, Duccio's brothers and sisters demanded that she relinquish all claims to his fortune, his houses, paintings, her jewels, even her own clothes. The stocks he held in her name and her own personal fortune, everything that Duccio had overseen, was to become part of his estate. On Italy's legal books the death would be classified as accidental—like her son's. She was to leave Italy at once with just her funeral suit and her handbag.

Tom did not reveal how he had arrived at Palazzo Duccio to find the plump sisters, sisters-in-law, and cousins from Calabria decked out in Claire's necklaces and fur stoles, using her dainty, custom-made underwear for handkerchiefs as they sat around in the stifling heat and mourned their loss, the women as well as the men puffing on Duccio's fat cigars. Pictures of Claire had been torn from the walls and spat upon, although some of the relatives hotly argued in a southern Italian dialect over who would be the one to get the picture of Claire hugging a radiant Princess Grace. A confused lot, they had loved Claire from afar for her dignified pulchritude—like a Venus de Milo in couture—while detesting their brother for his selfish arrogance and the tightfisted way he mistreated them. Now they glorified his memory and publicly booed Claire the villainess, although in reality they were grateful to the long-lashed American for bumping off their brother and leaving them flush. Besides, what good would it have done to have a trial in which some of Duccio's *real* deals might be exposed as well, not to mention some of his illegal business practices? The state could demand heavier taxes. At the very least, his former partners might file lawsuits that would erode their inherited fortune, perhaps tying up their money in the courts for years. And what, saints preserve them, if the lovely lady with the face of an angel and those lilac eyes was found innocent? All Duccio's fortunes would then be inherited by her. No, get her out of the country and quietly count their lira. The lawyer from New York was right. Run with the money. And let Claire go.

"Go where?"

"Paris." He wiped the sweat from his face and neck with his starched handkerchief, the moisture staining the burgundy monogram. He pulled the one-way ticket from his inside pocket and handed it to her.

"Paris?" There was a picture of the Eiffel Tower on the ticket cover.

"It's the only place I could think of where you don't have enemies. But you have lots of friends, I'm told." He spoke in a polite, careful voice, but his message was clear, just as it had been years ago. *You have no choice.*

He pulled out a stack of documents from his bulging briefcase. As soon as Claire signed, the chief of police, the magistrate, everyone would follow like falling dominoes. He would personally escort her to the airport, he assured her. In Paris she could stay at Harrison's apartment at the Ritz. It had already been paid for in advance.

"Yes." She had been planning to go there with Sara and Six to join Harrison and begin their life together. A lifetime ago. Two lifetimes.

"Three months. You'll have three months at the Ritz." He smiled gently at her. "It isn't prison, you know?"

She wondered if it wasn't. "Sara. How soon can Sara join me? She needs me."

"I'm afraid you've lost Sara, Claire. You're a murderess. You're front-page headlines everywhere. In the eyes of the world you're quite unfit to be a mother."

"I was just protecting my children. My child. Oh Tom, you've got to help me. You don't know what's happened. Sara's going to need so much love. And not the Harrison kind." She stood more erect as she grew stronger.

"It's out of my control." The words were icy, but beneath them

Tom was melting. Claire's sober responses were confirming his suspicions. Something about Six's death followed by Duccio's sudden murder was darker than it seemed. If he were Claire's lawyer, he would suspect that his client was protecting someone. But the bright attorney had made his pact with power a long time ago. His wagon was hitched to the Harrisons' star, not to this young woman who had just fallen out of the sky.

"You're right," Tom continued. "Sara does need help, expensive professional treatments. The kind the Harrisons can provide." He had seen the girl and found her strangely damaged. And without saying it, he guessed she'd had her child's hand in all this.

"Frankly, Claire, you don't have two nickels to rub together. Not anymore. You couldn't even provide food or clothes for her, let alone battle Ophelia in court. But at least when you sign these papers Sara won't be the daughter of a murderer."

A murderer. She looked around her filthy cell. This was how the world treated a killer. She would never be sorry she had saved her daughter from spending even one night in a place like this.

Even in her anguish she knew just how much help Sara needed. More help than she could now afford. And what was her alternative? Stay in jail and lose Sara anyway? The irony was inescapable. By protecting her daughter she had lost her.

"Where have they taken Six?" Claire spoke in whispery surrender.

"The family plot at Charlotte Hall. Someday"—Claire caught a glimpse of compassion in his eyes—"someday you'll be able to visit him. It's my other grim duty to bring him home." He delivered the line that would guarantee her signature. "The Duccios will release his body after these documents are official."

The idea that her son hadn't been laid to rest yet caused Claire's hands to tremble. She would sign any piece of paper. She struggled to hang on to any rational thoughts.

"Then take Violet with you. I want her to go along." She shakily took his hands in both of hers and fought back the tears. Only

after he promised that Violet would accompany Six on his journey back home did she sign the stack of documents that set her
free—free from the physical walls of her jail cell but not from the
limitless expanse of grief that lay before her, a far more bitter sentence than any prison term.

The concierge tried not to stare as he handed her a dog-eared copy
of the *Herald Tribune* along with the brass room key. The newspaper ran Anita Lace's column on page one along with the same
photograph that had stared back at her from every kiosk in both
airports. Damn Duccio. He had garbed her in the sheer veil that
concealed nothing, that only highlighted the grief in her eyes and
the otherworldly smile on her full lips. She had been thinking
about Six on his cloud to heaven at the time, but in the grainy
black-and-white photo that was cropped just below the huge jeweled cross around her neck, she looked guilty of everything from
murder to bad taste.

She tried to read the paper again, her vision clouded. Her
tragedy was being covered as thoroughly as the war. Anita Lace,
the official megaphone of international gossip, was keeping Claire
on the front burner:

> Suicide by speargun seems to be the verdict of the Roman
> Magistrate. Claire Harrison Duccio was set free today after a
> week of interrogation in a Rome jailhouse. The stylish lady
> was charged with nothing worse than you and I have done:
> a speeding ticket for leaving Italy in record time. But you
> and I have never left a husband lying on the floor with a
> spear in his chest. Turns out the fabulously rich Fulco
> Duccio evidently had his own domestic suspicions. He left
> the big zero to the black widow. Most of that vast booty of
> his went to his understated brothers and sisters, who live
> quietly in Calabria, and a charitable chunk of it to the
> Roman Catholic Church. Meanwhile, my sources hear the

lady in question has gone to that Holy Mecca of the famous and infamous: the Ritz in Paris. *Arrivedérci,* Claire.

At the manager's suggestion, she was discreetly whisked up the back elevator along with a Pomeranian and his walker. Claire wasn't certain whether this was to protect her or the hotel's reputation. It was also suggested to her that she might feel more comfortable dining in the privacy of her suite. And where last week she might have tipped Jean-Luc or Monsieur Gireau, now she just whispered *"Merci,"* knowing all she had in the world was the five hundred dollars Tom had slipped into her Hermès handbag. She wasn't going to waste it.

She was sitting in the dark on the silken bedspread, clutching her bag to her chest and rocking, trying to clear her head. The insistently ringing buzzer wasn't helping. Finally the determined banging on the door roused her from her trance. She tried to focus her mind. Who could it be? Sara run away from Ophelia so they could grieve together and share their secret truth? Harrison, once again robust and strong enough for both of them? Perhaps it could be Six, all apple-cheeked and sun bronzed, back to awaken her from a very bad dream. Just the thought brought a smile. Or was it just the dinner she had no appetite for? But the room service cart would offer her a choice of knives and crystal goblets sharp enough to sever a vein. She stared at her thin white wrist, a blue artery pumping blood to her broken heart. If only she were a priceless piece of cracked porcelain, or shattered Baccarat glass, she could be sent to the third-floor fix-it shop at Marshall Field's, where the man with special glue could put her back together.

She moved like a zombie to the door. If it was the Angel of Death come for her she would gladly usher him in.

She stepped back to let the crazy escapee from the flea market waddle into her rooms. In her exhaustion something close to a laugh tumbled out of her mouth. She let the portly lady hug her before she realized it was Lorenza underneath six layers of dresses and one taffeta petticoat heisted from Claire's closet.

"Oh, signóra. I took what I can. They are *tróppo* vulgar, that Duccio lot. They go barefoot and smoke bad smell cigars even at breakfast table. Holy Maria."

Claire's Dior cocktail hat was balanced on top of her chiffon-and-straw Ascot boater, both plunked devil-may-care over Lorenza's long, dark tresses, the whole of her body padded two feet deep with Chanel, Fath, and Givenchy.

"How in the world did the Ritz guards let you up to the suite?"

"I told them I was with my lady Signóra Duccio, and they took me right up. *Subito!* In the baggage elevator. My cousin is the assistant to the breadmaker chef in the kitchen so it wasn't a problem to find you. Everyone knows you are here!"

She tottered on Claire's purloined pumps as she looked around the rooms as if scouting for spies.

"Wait until signóra sees what I sew into the hem of my bottom dress." She had been allowed one suitcase when she left Palazzo Duccio so she had piled as much as she could on herself like a packmule and joined her lady. Lorenza turned a dozen different shades as she shed layer after layer of colorful clothing. Claire looked on in amazement.

Finally, the one-woman fashion show stopped at Claire's favorite wasp-waisted black day dress. Lorenza waved a pair of manicure scissors from her purse and began to snip open the hem.

"Signóra, here. I did not know what was your favorite and all the Duccio sisters have got the *importante* things from the safes. I hope I did okay." With almost human exuberance out tumbled a pair of Verdura's chandelier earrings and the godforsaken cross.

"Oh, Lorenza. This is the kindest thing anyone's ever done for me." Although she would have preferred never to see these hated reminders of Duccio again, Claire was grateful for the girl's loyalty.

"More, signóra." Lorenza's moistened eyes twinkled. She was glad to please her lady, who looked so haggard and sad. Claire's dead eyes sparkled too, for just an instant, when she saw the booty, wrapped in towels, that filled the entire suitcase. Lorenza had smuggled out all the framed photographs that had sat on Claire's dressing table. Six in his soccer uniform, Sara on horseback, the three of them holding hands, Claire and Harrison gazing adoringly at Six. The photographs gave her a reason to bathe, have a little supper, and live at least one more day to gaze at the memories that were her life.

Lorenza indulged her broken lady in every way. She applied old folk remedies to soothe her body: a warm poultice of rosemary herbs and chamomile leaves for her chest and a cold compress soaked in violet water for her forehead. To feed the ache in both their hearts, they shared stories of Six, even quietly laughing together when they remembered how at six o'clock one morning he had used his easy charms to convince Cook to make waffles with raspberries and homemade gelato for him and his entire soccer team. They never tired of retelling one another the funny things he had said or done, and never had enough reasons to look at her photographs and remember the pleasant moments right before the picture was snapped. The lady and her unpaid maid prayed together at the candles Lorenza lit at the little shrine she had arranged, and Claire read from the Bible as well as her Emily Dickinson. She invoked Protestant and Catholic rituals as well as some of Lorenza's country saints with their folklorish magic. But Claire's favorite pastime was making up pictures of Six in heaven, using their imaginations to decorate a room for him there. First Claire put a leather armchair in his bedroom, with a cozy comforter to keep him warm, and then a table wide enough for his jigsaw puzzles. Lorenza added a bowl of fresh fruit, his favorite pears and sweet mangoes in an inexhaustible supply. They installed a wide picture window looking out onto all his favorite places: the oak tree outside his bedroom at Charlotte

Hall, the soccer field in Rome, with his pony, GI Joe, saddled up and tethered to a tree. It was heaven, after all, so they could pick Six's favorite place for each season. Italy's seacoast in the summer, Rome in spring, Christmas at Charlotte Hall. For his shelves, they painstakingly selected his favorite books by Jack London and his baseball cards and of course his prize stamps. Finally, they inserted Six himself, bursting with energy and wearing his irrepressible smile. Now when Claire pictured her son, she could always find him in the "room" they had decorated for him Upstairs.

By the third week in Paris, Claire felt strong enough to take her first walk outside. Wearing sunglasses, scarves, and holding one another's arms, the two women crept along the still-asleep streets to a six A.M. service at Sacre Coeur, where they lit candles for Six. By the fourth week they discovered a tiny church near Chez Emilon where the priest welcomed them. Indeed, he greeted them each morning, expecting them when he opened the creaking iron doors. Claire always returned to the Ritz at the service entrance, walking the same path each day through the kitchen and to her room. It was a routine she welcomed. But time was running out, and so was money.

In early October, when Violet and her husband Mr. Zolla surprised her on their honeymoon visit, Claire nervously joined them at a belated wedding breakfast for three at L'Espadon in the Ritz. It was her first time out in public. Inevitably, Violet turned the conversation to pressing practical matters.

"Where do you go from here?" Violet asked. She and Mr. Zolla could live very comfortably on his retirement savings and Sante Fe pension, but Claire was living in a four-figure-a-day luxury suite that was only paid for through the month.

"Have you made a plan yet? Do you know where you want to live? Of course you're welcome to come stay with us." Violet took a sip from the bubbly champagne her husband had ordered. She had grieved for Six and then tucked her sorrow away in a drawer with life's other disappointments.

"I think I'll stay here." She eyed her mother's champagne glass, resenting her return to life. "I'll start looking for a place I can afford." The square set of Claire's jaw was determined, and the full mouth, just a quiver away from tears, resigned. It was obvious she wasn't ready to go home, wherever that was now.

"Here. I have a little something for you." Violet pulled an envelope out of her pocketbook and pushed it across the table to her daughter.

"But it's I who should be giving you a wedding gift." A deep blush traveled up from her neck. For five years running she had been on the International Best Dressed List, the mistress of luxurious homes, a two-fisted philanthropist, and here she was, at age thirty-two, on the receiving end of a cash envelope from her hard-working mother.

Violet was glad to see some pink replacing Claire's pallor, even if it was just the flush of embarrassment. "No. No, dear. Your wedding gift already came and went, the way of the unwanted lamp shade or your least favorite cousin's brass candlesticks. Returned."

"Quite the little businesslady." Mr. Zolla gently ribbed his bride with his elbow. "Couldn't sell the hot Tiepolo, so she swapped."

"Well, that's not exactly how it was, Max." Violet scolded sweetly. "We didn't want to stir up a fuss, what with your late husband's estate laying claim to your underwear. And I checked with the Art Institute, but one can't just go around selling Italian masterpieces that have been shipped out of the country willy-nilly."

"Swapped it to a Sante Fe art dealer for two genuine oil paintings and some cash. That's my Violet." Max was clearly besotted with his resourceful wife.

"Yes. Two Georgia O'Keeffe paintings. *Blooms in the Desert.* One for you, the cow's skull with the white flower, and one for us." She patted Mr. Zolla's sun-reddened hand. "So you've given us a magnificent wedding gift. Only this fits a lot nicer in our Santa Fe living room than Tiepolo's rather vast *Allegory of Love.*" She smiled, nudging Claire to smile back.

Claire couldn't help it. The tears streamed with a mind of their own, over her chiseled cheeks and into the frosting of her mille-feuille. Not until she examined the envelope and found in it enough for a year's rent in something a little more sensible than the Ritz did she realize the extent of her mother's love.

"Why don't you come out to us for a while? Or back to Chicago?"

"No, not yet." She was pleased for her mother but couldn't help feeling resentful that she could find joy in a world without Six. She put a brave smile on her lips. "I'll come back when I'm more on my feet. It will be soon." Her voice was full of false vibrato when she lifted her champagne flute and with a deep gulp toasted the kindly Mr. and Mrs. Zolla. A gossipy diner turned to observe the notorious Claire Duccio seated behind a leafy palm at a "Siberia" table in the hotel's dining room. Celebrating.

Eleanor House, Claire Duccio's personal charity for sending European orphans Stateside, is going belly-up. The foundling home and placement center for kiddies with accents was always funded big-time by two noble families that no longer speak to Madame Ex: the rich, rich Duccio clan of Italy and the quietly rich, distinguished, and close-knit Harrison family of Tuxedo Park, Washington, and Newport. They raise ambassadors like other families raise rabbits. Seems the questionable lady who once raised eyebrows for her Communist liberal-leaning tendencies won't foot the foundlings' bills. Tsk, tsk, Claire. Is it because you were half a foundling yourself? Mrs. Duccio of the long lashes and longer gams has been seen celebrating around Paris while still in widow's weeds. Born in a department store—literally, folks—in Better Dresses and Lingerie, Claire could easily sell *one* earring and keep Eleanor House alive.

Lèonide was swinging Anita's column in a wide port de bras, as befitted a dancer from the Ballets Russes.

"Of course Anita's column is accompanied by da picture of you in about two centimeters of rubies and emeralds like da czarina's. What did become of dat necklace?"

"I'm going to sell the damn cross. And keep Eleanor House going." Infuriated by the columnist's words, Claire was stalking the room like a cornered tigress. The orphans' placement center she had founded had grown into an important institution that had found homes for more than six thousand children. It was equipped with a legal department and a health center, and was a sterling role model for other foundations like it. And if it wasn't exactly a full-time career for Claire, it was her song to the world. If the critics were going to boo her off the stage, she at least had to make sure the music lived on. How dare they make hundreds of children suffer just because she had become notorious! She walked faster, remembering the agreement she had signed with the "help" of Tom. She had only just recently bothered to read the damn document. Anything she still retained from the marriage that had a value of over five thousand dollars immediately reverted back to Duccio's estate. It was the "Cross Clause." No one had been able to find it after Claire had been carted off to jail. Apparently, she had torn it off and flung it on the floor at the dead Duccio. Lorenza, resourceful even in a panic, had kicked the multimillion-dollar relic under Duccio's silk chair and retrieved it when everyone else's attention was on the corpse. For four frightened days and nights, the ladies' maid had worn it under her uniform, along with a garlic clove to keep the devilishly curious away. Then she gave notice to her new employers, was given a week's salary without a letter of recommendation, and mule-packed herself off to join the beleaguered signóra once she knew where to find her.

"I'll give it to Eleanor House anonymously. *They* can be the ones to sell it. Let them think it came from Duccio, and he can get his posthumous honor in hell. And don't think I'm not going to fire off a letter to that lousy Grant character who owns this vicious columnist. Anita Lace, my foot. Arsenic and lace is more like it. And if she tries to dish up dirt on those little two-year-olds, I'll kill her!"

Léonide put his hands to his ears in horror. "No, no, Claire! Don't ever use dat word! If dey find her with da speargun in her heart, Léonide may be called to testify!"

Claire ignored him. "How do you suppose Sara feels when she reads trash like this? And how about my orphans? Where will they go? What now? Anita Arsenic Lace is destroying much more than me. If I'm supposed to be a crazy murderer, then let me at Lace and Fenwick Grant!"

Léonide hoped that Claire was only venting her rage, like a hot-blooded Russian *artiste*. But with the anger a light started to burn in her dull eyes.

"Ah, anger. It ees a very good sign. Ees part of da healing."

If Claire thought that perhaps another woman might show her the way out of the tunnel, it wasn't going to be Pamela Churchill. The two women had been friends for years, but it was a friendship based on shallow reciprocity and not the depth of a true female bond.

"Well, why don't you just find some rich man? That's what I would do." After several telephone calls, Pam had agreed to see her. "Just not in public. Why don't you come up for tea?"

They were seated on the perfectly proportioned Louis XVI divan, a gift from Baron Elie de Rothschild, in Pam's Paris apartment, which was paid for by Gianni Agnelli. Pam had targeted and chosen her lovers carefully. "And you mustn't go 'round so mopey. That's how I got Elie. His wife kept grieving for her sister Theresa. Men *hate* grief."

Claire bristled. But she reined in her feelings, for the good of her newly devised plan. She had come to ask the woman who had houseguested months at a time with her at Palazzo Duccio for the loan of her apartment until her own little place was ready in a few weeks.

"I'll be gone by the time you return from the south of France. You won't even know I was here."

"Frankly, darling, it's not *that* I'm worried about. It's that you've become so infamous, and I have to guard my reputation."

Claire laughed aloud. The infamous Pam worried about reputations?

"But Pam, you always said you were *above* the bourgeois business of morals." Hadn't Pam just generously loaned the Bentley to Louise de Vilmorin for a tryst with Orson Welles? And she wasn't a bit perturbed when it had come back with cigar holes in the leather seats. But then again, Louise's social credentials were impeccable.

"A little adultery isn't the same as a shooting. If you had just winged him, he would have gotten the point and you wouldn't have lost your caché." Coming from the woman who kept the world's richest husbands keeping her, Pam's rejection bordered on the comical, but as this was just the most minor in a series of grave disappointments, Claire squared her shoulders and put down her teacup. She knew now that any hopes of counting on old friends were as far-fetched as a shop girl's daydream.

Some mornings were better than others. One day she had fight and resolve. Others she could barely climb out of bed. Today was one of the dark days. Gloriously bright and sunny, the sky was like an artist's bright blue canvas before he had introduced the realism of a cloud. It was the worst kind of day for Claire, because it reminded her of all of Six's unrealized days. All morning long she had seen him impishly exiting a revolving door, hurrying around a bend, out of the corner of her eye the way a widow might see her husband standing beside her or someone who has lost his leg feels his missing limb. Twice today she sensed Six beside her. Was he beckoning her to follow him or encouraging her to stay? She was by herself for the first time in weeks. Lorenza was off on a picnic with her cousin, the sous pastry chef, and his eligible friend, the meat chef. After all, Lorenza hadn't lost her life or misplaced her loved ones. She was very young, only twenty-three. Her life was ahead of her. She shouldn't have to baby-sit Claire.

At thirty-two, Claire felt she'd seen too much. One child dead, another stolen away. She'd spent the whole day wandering around the city of light and had waited until dusk to take the long solitary walk across the bridge. She stopped to search into the dark water, but the Seine only stared back at her, cold and uninviting, not even throwing back her own reflection. She continued on over the Seine toward the little chapel on the Left Bank where the priest always welcomed her. The fall wind blew and she quickened her step, squaring her shoulders against each heavy gust of wind. The smell of chestnuts in the air, dinner wines being uncorked, different mixtures of hot fish stews and braised meats filled her nostrils. She walked past low houses that afforded her a view of a low-slung moon in the blue sky while daylight still danced around the darker, orange-streaked twilight. She missed Six. She felt more alone than ever as she listened to her solitary footsteps on the cold cobblestones. Claire hesitated in front of the old church, so small that most people missed it as they hurried by. But she was in no hurry. Vesper services were just beginning.

She lit her candles and walked heavily to her spot, a hard, wobbly bench on the aisle. She always went to the same pew. She recognized the same disheveled man who always hogged the pew in front of her; out of habit she nodded to him and he grunted back.

She smelled the lady behind her before she turned around. Her sense of smell had been so keen lately. The woman smelled good, like autumns in Maine and warm clothes that had been in the closet all summer and just pulled from their cedarwood storage for their first chilly outing.

When she finally turned to put a picture with the friendly smells, she had to smile back, as the woman was already smiling at her. She was suntanned and weathered, with tousled hair and bright teeth. Claire knew at once she was an adventurer. She looked more closely as the services began in the candlelit church. Was it Amelia Earhart? Her heroine, who by just a casual contact in the store, taught her independence and inspired her to go places? The flying lady's shining spirit had seen her through two births, both times Claire hallucinating that Amelia was flying her to safety. Maybe she had returned to wing Claire far away, to take her to Six. Claire turned back to the altar but the lady leaned over her shoulder to speak into her ear.

"Claire, I'd like to talk to you."

The words were spoken so calmly that she had to listen. She couldn't be real. Not with a lovely voice like that.

"Claire. Perhaps I can help you through this." Claire knew she must be dreaming, but she gave herself up to this gentle hallucination.

"How? Have you suffered too?"

"Oh yes." The soft voice had a twang, but was somehow privileged. "I lost a little boy, too. He was killed. Murdered. But I didn't have him as long as you."

Claire turned to face the woman.

"Do you still miss him?"

"Every day."

"And the pain . . ."

"It never goes away. But somehow you shutter it away inside you. Pretty soon it's just your private sorrow and no one comes around to pay condolences. The world likes to remember glory, not loss."

The woman tossed her head, her short hair different dusty colors in the candlelight.

"Stay alive, Claire, and live well. Only you can keep his real memory alive. You mustn't lose his glory."

Together they prayed from the little French service book. Prayed for Six and her lost boy. The woman put her hand on

Claire's shoulder and she could feel its weight. It struck Claire that no one had ever touched her in a dream before.

"I sensed you were in trouble. Steer by your own stars, Claire, and take this time to carve out another life for yourself. You can't have the same one back again. It won't be easy, but it will be worthwhile. You'll try, won't you?"

"I will. How did you know I was in trouble?"

"I was there. A long time ago. This is the hardest part now. When part of you wants to go on and the other part wants to hang on to the past. And when your face is flashed around the world it makes it hard to find a quiet place to heal." The woman reached into her pocket. "You can call me sometime. To talk, if you like."

"I didn't know angels had telephone numbers."

"I'm just a woman who lost a child. I felt you might want another person nearby who's suffered that way too. For a long time I was jealous of women who hadn't known my kind of sorrow. It's easier to swallow compassion from someone who's been there. But it's always a bitter taste."

The woman pulled up the hood of her jacket. Evidently the dream was over.

They shook hands at the church door, not quickly, but holding each other's hand the way women friends do.

"Good night, Claire."

Claire stopped under a street lamp to read the card. If it hadn't been her, if it had been just an ordinary woman, it would have had the same impact on Claire. She would have been equally grateful. But she was touched nonetheless that it was a woman world-famous and yet invisible who had reached out to her. She turned and watched Anne Morrow Lindbergh retreat into the shadows.

Slim, spruce in a yellow linen suit, gustily threw open the heavy draperies.

"Up, up! *Vite!* It's noon, a bit warm, but a lovely day." Slim was thrilled to be living the bohemian life in Paris. At last. She put her hands on her boyish hips and surveyed the sun poking around the vegetable garden in the courtyard of Hotel Emilon.

"It's Sunday." Claire pulled the sheets over her head. She had negotiated an affordable rate on a furnished apartment on the fifth floor of Emilon's hotel, in the less desirable back rooms facing the courtyard. The only decor she had added were her framed photographs and the Georgia O'Keeffe. In her bones she knew her situation was temporary. This little warren of rooms was just a cocoon from which she would reemerge a different Claire.

"We've got to get you ready." Slim, not even a little out of breath from the five-story climb up the hotel's ancient stairs, threw open the armoire where Lorenza had neatly hung all the pretty things Claire never wore. "Get up. We're gainfully employed."

"As what?" Claire lifted her tousled head from the pillow. For the last two months she had been working at a private antique shop on the Pont du Carousel, for the trade only. So far no former dinner guests of hers had barged in to demand she be fired. But Pamela Churchill, antiques consultant in tow, trooped into the shop weekly. She bought exquisite Louis XVI bureau *plats* and eighteenth-century doorknobs, letting Claire have the commission as long as she got a kickback on all the pieces Baron de Rothschild purchased for her.

"We're going to be costume consultants! You're going to show a young actress how to walk like a great lady. It's Hollywood in Paris!" Slim fanned herself with a copy *Vogue,* a panoply of fashion whizzing by as the colorful pages whirred into a homemade cartoon. "I'm so excited. They're making a film of Colette's novella *Gigi.*"

"The one about the young French girl raised by her auntie to be a courtesan? I think I've seen that movie." Or lived it, she thought.

"Oh, it's going to be so romantic. Maurice Chevalier is starring. Did I tell you it's a musical? Put this one on. It's gray. You've been in black for a year."

"What are we supposed to do? Are they paying us?" She swung her feet over the side of the rumpled bed. Violet's daughter was ever mindful of her lack of money.

"Gobs. Sacks of francs." Slim tossed a slip and two silk stockings over her shoulder like a striptease artist. "Cecil Beaton is designing the sets and costumes. And guess who's directing?"

"No idea." Claire pulled a stocking onto one of her long legs. The silk felt odd against her bare skin. She hadn't bothered to dress since she got off work on Friday. Paris was sweltering. The hottest spring in years had segued into the steamiest summer in decades.

"Oh, come on. Play along. Guess who's directing *Gigi*. I'll give you a hint." She pointed to the window, from which Claire could see the spire of Notre Dame.

"Quasimodo?"

"Vincente Minnelli."

"Uncle Vin?" All the male visitors to the Windermere had been Uncle Something or Other, but the name Vincente Minnelli brought a smile to even Claire's rigid lips. He had been the clever young window display designer at Field's, the one who had made the custom canopy with the fairy-tale trappings for Claire's bed. Now he was directing musicals. And movies.

"Hurry up. *Dépêche.* It's the month of *Août.* The antique shop is closed for three weeks. What else did you have planned for today?"

"Write Sara letter number seventy-six."

"You can do that when we get home. Who knows what will happen? After all, it *is* Paris."

The opening and closing shots of *Gigi* had been set up in the leafy Bois de Boulogne. The twenty-four hundred acres of city park in the sixteenth Arrondissement, with its shimmering ponds and well-mannered gardens, were abuzz with activity in the mid-day sun. The mood was fun and fast-paced. There was a festive frenzy around these creative folks making a fairy tale come alive with their zoom lenses and melting extras. And it was a fairy tale Claire could relate to: the story of a poor, fatherless girl who was trained to be a rich man's companion and hostess. Admittedly she knew a thing or two about the process of going from schoolgirl to society doyenne in the space of a week. At any rate, it was good to hear English spoken again, along with a peppering of French, as Claire led the way through hammering and construction in the quiet gray Dior dress that Lorenza had, as Slim put it, "saved from the fire." They wound their way in the stifling heat through the crew of actors, technicians, and carpenters, and giggled like schoolgirls as costumed cocottes, strapped into their constraining corsets, fainted dead away in the heat, fake trees collapsed, and Maurice Chevalier without his glasses mistook Claire for Her Serene Highness Princess Grace and congratulated her on win-ning last year's Oscar for *The Country Girl*. Claire, suddenly feel-ing very lighthearted, nodded regally to the famous French singer rather than explain. Lorenza joined the game, following behind Claire as if she were her lady-in-waiting. The world of make-believe and Hollywood—even on the Seine—felt very free and inviting to Claire.

And the scandalous Claire Harrison Duccio held some appeal for these movie folk. She was greeted with more respect than cu-riosity by both the director and producer, the latter grateful that at last now there was someone on set who could teach Leslie Caron ladylike deportment and "real regal posture." And Minnelli, after eyeing her cool brand of pale beauty, inquired if she would like to play an extra, one of the turn-of-the-century aristocrats in the Maxim's scene. Claire politely declined—she couldn't even imagine what Anita Lace would write about her if she appeared in Technicolor décolletage—but certainly she'd help in the scene where the auntie teaches Gigi how to tell a fine jewel from a bad stone.

Lorenza was dispatched to sew black feathers on a white ball gown and Slim was assigned to Cecil Beaton's costume trailer. They would all be paid for their work. They felt neither their heat fatigue nor the weariness when ten hours later they all trooped home, humming "Gigi, la-la-la-la, do-do-do-do, la-la-la, Gigi," and Claire finally had something fun to put in her letter to Sara.

On the set over the next week Claire was completely distracted from any thoughts of her own circumstances as she instructed Leslie Caron, showing her how she should balance books on her head in the good posture scene, holding out her hands the way she had been instructed as a child in order to acquire aristocratic carriage along with a gliding walk. Delight shone on her face as she remembered how the Field's models and salesladies had applauded her so long ago when she finally got it right.

She held the lighting men and several costume ladies captive when she charmingly demonstrated to the young actress how to choose a cigar for a gentleman, holding it up to her ear to listen for the moist sound of freshness, lightly waving it under her nose for a whiff of its age and tobacco blends, just as she'd learned in Field's cigar shop and had done for Harrison. She showed her how to shake her head coquettishly as she refused one, putting it back in its box, saving the man from a cigar that hadn't been properly kept in a humidor, and say, "No, no. I wouldn't let you smoke that one, dear. It's all dried out and won't draw well." And both the actress and Claire burst out laughing.

But she drew a larger audience, Chevalier, Minnelli, and some of the studio's executives among them, as she taught Gigi how to hold a sapphire up to the light to read it for star quality, examine a string of pearls for matched opalescence, and turn a white diamond around in her fingers, revolving it in natural light to make sure it had clarity and a blue cast. As she played with the millions of dollars' worth of jewels borrowed for the scene, Claire behaved as naturally as a housewife checking for cracked eggs in the carton. She casually held stones up to Caron's ears and neck, and then laid them carelessly aside as if a million-dollar necklace held no special charm for her.

One of the visiting MGM vice presidents, Bernie Thal, whispered to his pal, Hollywood agent Lefty Lefkowitz. "The dame shits diamonds, she's had so many." But Lefty was much more impressed when one of the security guards from Cartier shyly tapped Claire on the shoulder. His offer to shake the famous lady's hand was greeted instead with a warm hug and amiable conversation. The guard had made dozens of trips to Rome to carry pieces for Signóra Duccio to try on at her husband's insistence and had despised the cruel man who treated him like dirt. Mrs. Duccio had always offered him a drink, a chair, dinner if it got late, and introduced him to her children. He was all for her, no matter what she was supposed to have done. Out of earshot of this conversation, Lefty saw only one classy dame greeting a regular guy like a king.

"Some broad. That's real refinement." He nudged Thal. And both denizens of Hollywood agreed, because back there under the movieland stars it wasn't what you did as much as how you acted.

Lefty Lefkowitz had a reputation in Hollywood. If he wasn't the most successful agent in town, he was one of the nicest, a real hand-holder. And while the stars at the top signed on with Swifty Lazar or William Morris, Lefty had them on their way up or their way back down. He was on location with the more-than-middle-aged Hermione Gingold, who was making a Lefty-staged comeback in this picture that was being dubbed "My Fair Lady Goes to Paris" at his favorite haunts back home, the Brown Derby and the Polo Lounge.

Lefty's dark coal eyes were blinkless, due to an inherited infirmity, so he skimmed the world like a sea ray scouting the bottom of the sea. His eyes being sensitive to the sun, he kept them shielded by Coke-bottle sunglasses from under which he scrutinized the pallor of Claire's powdered skin and admired the inaccessibility of the cool lady who even in this heat wave looked a tiny bit chilled. She was a knockout. She made all the babes he dated and both his ex-wives look like bimbos. But the eyes, those purple eyes, were utter Hollywood. They had a vulnerability in them, like they had just witnessed a terrible train wreck, and he impulsively felt very protective of her. And being a film-noir fan, he couldn't help being also a little bit titillated by the fact that she might have bumped off a bad guy. Lefty had heard from reliable sources that Duccio supplied the Nazis with gun parts and rubber during the war, so if she had shot a Nazi, well, that made her a hero in his book.

Her second week on the set, he decided to follow her. He had developed a crush on Claire, and although he knew a woman like her would never bother with a guy like him except to be exceedingly polite, he could certainly dream.

She had a great walk, more of a glide, and moved slowly but purposefully down the streets, like early Garbo or Grace in *The Swan*. Lefty was barely five five and stretched for every inch, but Claire was tall and willowy even when she stooped to retrieve a child's fallen franc from the sidewalk and gently fold it into the child's palm.

He loved to watch her, and one morning set out to follow her as she moved in that unhurried way she had to, of all places, a jewelry store. "What else is new?" he said to himself, and then, "Why bother? You could never afford her."

Out of curiosity he entered the shop. She went toward the back of the store, looking down not at the jewelry but the carpet, and just stood there waiting. When the mustachioed salesman came to the counter he just held out his hand. She gave him a large velvet box. As he held the contents up to the light, he could see they were as colorful as a Coney Island carousel and swung like chandeliers. He watched as after much discussion the salesman handed her a wad of bills and she put it into her purse, leaving the fancy earrings behind. If he hadn't witnessed the transaction with his own myopic eyes, he would never have guessed that Claire Harrison Duccio was a lady in distress. Lefty suddenly had an impulse to own a pair of big dangling earrings. He marched over to do his Hollywood agent shtick and negotiate the best deal. That he was good at. But the hard part would be to approach her and ask her to dinner so he could have occasion to be a big shot and deliver his gift.

He invited her to a little bistro. Nothing fancy. With his streetwise instincts he knew better than to take her to Ledoyen or La Tour d'Argent, restaurants he had seen her photographed at, nibbling on foie gras or black truffles. Surely they would invoke memories of her other life, which he was gathering hadn't been such a good deal. Lefty felt he had so little going for him in his pursuit of Claire that his only chance was to be different. They went by taxi to Palais-Royal, where Colette had lived, to a casual spot named after the writer's first husband, Willi. It was a cozy wine bar with a simple menu. That way she wouldn't feel pressured that this was a night on the town, or that they even had to make it more than a drink. If it happened, it happened.

Lefty knew from years as an agent to the famous and wounded that you didn't entice a golden bird with force.

He loved the way her pretty hands played with her wineglass and how she kept her eyes riveted on his when he talked. He was enchanted by the lift of her mouth whenever she spoke of her children or how she laughed out loud at his jokes about the *Gigi* set. She seemed so interested in his Hollywood stories, those luminous purple eyes growing as big as her butter plate. He thought she might have been genuinely impressed when he told her that during the war he had been in the First Motion Picture Unit, a "Hollywood Commando," with Ronnie Reagan and his other pals. Dinner went without a hitch. And when they finally walked out together, relaxed, it was like he had bribed the mayor of Paris to create a Hollywood movie moment just for them. The street lanterns suddenly glowed dimmer, and at exactly one minute to ten, the fountains stopped playing and all they could hear were the birds. He took her elbow and she let him.

Dinner became a habit. They always dined alone, somewhere quiet and out of the way. After their third meal, she knew precisely what he liked, had guessed about his ulcer, would order foods that didn't aggravate his hiatal hernia, and then ask for a deliciously forbidden dessert to be brought to the table with two spoons, allowing him "just a taste." She made him feel taller, more important, and coddled, just by the way she shone her eyes on him. And he found her glamorous. He wanted nothing more than to keep her around him forever.

One evening, Lefty just blurted it out. "I need you."

"For what? I bet back home you have everything you want."

"I don't have you. You'd make a better man out of me. Every time I'm around you I just feel great. *Gigi*'s packing up and moving to Hollywood for the last scenes. Why don't you come too?"

"But what would I do there?"

"Well, you could be my business partner. Yeah. That'd be good."

Claire hesitated. What good would it do to travel ten thousand miles with the same infamous name and unflattering baggage? It was as if Lefty read her thoughts and answered her prayers.

"You know, everyone in Hollywood changes their names. Marilyn Monroe was Norma Jean Baker and Lana Turner used to be Julia Jean Mildred Frances Turner."

"And if you were my agent, Lefty, what would you change my name to?

"Claire Harrison Lefkowitz, whaddya think?" His unblinking eyes darkened with excitement. "And you wouldn't have to worry about the press, either. Guys like me in Hollywood, we tell the gossip columnists what to write."

*   *   *

"Oh, Lefty Lefkowitz. He doesn't have any money. Just a job."
Pamela, back from a failed holiday with one man, was repacking
her bags to go off with another. "Why would you take up with
him?" She dusted the silver frame holding a picture of her son,
young Winston Churchill, with her tea napkin.

"Honestly, Claire, all you get from men like that are love letters and a little kindness. Look, do you think this frame is too ornate? Napoleon gave it to Josephine and Elie's given it to me."

Claire thanked her for tea and hurried out of Pam's overstuffed
apartment. Suddenly a cup of kindness sounded very good.

Sara had finally telephoned Claire. It was the anniversary of
Six's death and, although Sara hadn't said anything personal, she
let Claire know she had saved up her allowance and added it to
the William Henry Harrison VI Endowment at Eleanor House.
Claire had begun the fund with the money from the sale of the
chandelier earrings. Nothing was firmed up, but Sara let it be
known that if they weren't so far apart it might be nice to see each
other once in a while. Claire knew enough geography to realize if
it were just a county and not an ocean between them it might be
possible to see her. She also knew she couldn't negotiate with
Harry and Ophelia over visitation rights without a mediator, perhaps a tough-talking agent with her best interests at heart. But
more than anything, Claire realized that she couldn't keep the
name Duccio anymore, not with all the scandalous associations it
evoked. If she was to be permitted to see Sara again, return to
America, and rebuild Eleanor House with new and larger fund-
ing, she would have to reinvent herself. Again.

It was time.

Chapter Sixteen

Julia and Norma Jean

In Hollywood a girl's virtue is much less important than her hairdo.
— *Marilyn Monroe*

The new Goodyear tires rumbled along faux French cobblestones as they pulled into the driveway. Lefty drove the Caddie into the turnaround of the rented house, and the mixed fragrances of eucalyptus, orange blossom, and bougainvillea enveloped them. The sun that shone on their faces felt fresh and safe, and suddenly the smells of baked Italian bread, olive oil, the mold of centuries-old buildings crumbling in elegance, and unpasteurized heavy crème fraîche seemed to disappear into a side compartment of Claire's brain.

She was in Los Angeles, America. The land of light and second chances. Lefty jumped out of the convertible to open Claire's door.

"Oh, Lefty, it's so brand-new!" The newness smelled wonderful to Claire. Certainly houses that had been built only a year ago couldn't carry dark whispers in their walls. Or other people's haughty ancestors. Or ghosts.

"It's heaven." Slim was thrilled. She pushed on a pair of sunglasses in the shape of sequined cat's eyes as she slinked out of the backseat. Slim had been reading *Screenland* and *Movieweek* aloud to Claire since she was a baby. Now here she was in movieland wondering if it wasn't too late to be discovered. She certainly wasn't a has-been. She'd never even been a "was."

"Where's the guest room?" Slim called out.

"The fanciest one is in the pool house," Lefty yelled after her.

"But it's all glass!" Slim had swiftly moved around the back and was poking around the kidney-shaped swimming pool, her high heels leaving puncture wounds in the freshly clipped grass. The glass pavilion was a boxy rectangle, four glass walls revealing contemporary leather-and-chrome couches and glass tables, partitioned his and her changing rooms, and a stark kitchen wrapping around the sleeping area. All in clear view of everyone. A Calder mobile in primary colors swung from the ceiling like a sleek set of wind chimes. It was way too modern for Slim's taste and reminded her of store windows designed to display the merchandise. "This place needs curtains!" she shouted back.

"Perhaps just a woman's touch." Claire laughed softly. While the others were loopy with travel fatigue, the yellow ball of sun sitting in the blue sky acted like a vitamin pill on Claire. She excitedly surveyed the house's interior. How fine it was to be in a place without heavy damask draperies or dark shadows, where one room spilled over into another and tall uncovered windows ran from floor to ceiling. Right off the bat, she'd replace the tight-panted matador painted on black velvet hanging over the fireplace with her Georgia O'Keeffe. The *Cow's Skull with Flowers* would be perfect there, and she'd find a few good antiques in light woods to pull the room together.

She could feel the adrenaline start to pump through her system, pushing out old poisons. Claire was determined that this thing with Lefty was not going to be temporary. There was too much at stake. It was here that she could make a home for herself and her daughter.

She stood in the double-story sunken living room, the California sun streaming in like an unfiltered ray of hope. It warmed her, and she pulled her black cardigan off her shoulders as if she were shedding a layer of old skin. Summoning up all her decorating skills, she set about putting her Bel Air house in order.

She put a finger to her chin, mentally rearranging the room, as Lorenza, panting like a stevedore, heaved in the O'Keeffe and uncovered the painting from its nubby wool blanket. She had lugged it herself all the way from Paris, never letting the signóra's favorite, and now only, possession out of her eyesight.

The O'Keeffe held a private message for Claire. Somehow, within the feminine brushstrokes, inside the painted southwestern sky with its calm, unmoving clouds, the cow's skull with its intimation of mortality, and the white bloom bursting with its promise of life, all the members of her little family were depicted. Including Six. And Sara. Claire planned to fix up a special room for her daughter. Something fresh and gay. She imagined eyelet curtains in pastel colors blowing in at the open windows.

This was a place for fresh starts. She could heal herself and Sara here, applying lush garden balms to their psychic wounds the way these Californians cured their cuts and burns with the juice from their backyard aloe plants. After all, Claire was in Hollywood now. Wasn't this the place where people started over? Reinventing yourself was the name of the game here.

Claire had promised Lefty she would marry him just as soon as he could figure out how to spring Sara from Ophelia's upper-crust prison. The wedding itself was small, just a handful of Lefty's friends in the backyard. Bernie Thal and his wife, Lena Horne and her husband, Violet with Mr. Zolla, and Slim and Wren stood around the pool as Lefty and Claire exchanged vows and trampled their glasses under the bougainvillea-draped chuppah. Gardenias on plastic lily pads floated on the surface of the swimming pool. The liberal Hollywood rabbi they had found to marry the Jew to the notorious shiksa loudly bestowed blessings on them. The bride's face shone radiant with respect and gratitude for Lefty, the sun pinking her cheeks and pulling golden streaks through her hair. She beamed at him for all the goodness he had arranged. He had negotiated with Tom for a hard couple of weeks so Sara could stand at her mother's side as the flower girl, clutching a lace doily with tea roses to her chest. Only Sara wasn't exactly playing the part the way her mother had envisioned.

When Violet had brought Six back to Charlotte Hall to be buried, she had opened her unquestioning arms to Sara. It was the only place the damaged child found any emotional refuge. After Sara lived through a devastating seventy-two hours that began with discovering her brother dead at the bottom of the stairs and ended with watching her mother hauled off in handcuffs for a crime Sara herself had committed, Ophelia had simply put her in a burgundy party dress and told her to greet the guests arriving at Charlotte Hall to pay their respects. And asked her to remember that Harrisons kept their troubles to themselves. In the days following the funeral, Ophelia expected either uncomplaining silence or pleasant table talk from her granddaughter. Violet, however, expected nothing, and simply offered a warm lap to climb into or a hug. She would sit for hours softly stroking her hand on Sara's quivering cheek. And while Claire became an unmentionable in the Harrison house, referred to only as "her" or "she," Violet assumed her grandmotherly duties, training her lioness's eye on the shattered Sara. She trooped over, rain or shine, from her room at the Tuxedo Park Inn, where she stayed for two months. Violet seemed to be the only one able to soothe the smileless child's daytime nightmares. It terrified her that the hollowness in Sara's eyes was growing deeper and the pale skin beneath the unruly red hair turning to chalk. Even Ophelia became alarmed, and, for the first time in the tidy agenda of her life, had to admit to herself that here was a problem too big for her to solve or sweep under the Oriental rugs. Ophelia still considered Sara entirely hers, but as Sara's numbness and remoteness grew more impenetrable and the "black moods" turned into deep depressions, Ophelia allowed Sara to take the occasional holiday out West with her now respectably married maternal grandmother.

So Sara was permitted to accompany Violet to *"Her's* next marriage," as it was referred to around the breakfast table at Charlotte Hall.

All during the vows, spoken in English and Hebrew, Sara stood closer to Violet than to her mother, but after kissing husband number three, Claire turned to her only child.

"Sara," she whispered into her ear. "I will always love you." She spoke as sincerely and tenderly as if she were making her second sacred pledge of the day.

And while she didn't say "Mother" or "Mommy," as she'd cried out an anguished year ago in Rome, Claire thought there was a glint—faint, but still a spark of some affection—in the fourteen-year-old's cold eyes. Claire promised herself she'd find a way to break through the stiff politeness that stood like a seawall against her daughter's storm of memories.

"It's like she's grown a protective shell around her, retreating in and out like a snapping turtle," Slim whispered to Violet.

Lena Horne decided to sing, and Violet danced with Mr. Zolla to a different tune that was humming in his head. A happy Lefty made toast after toast, trying hard to get Sara to break a smile.

"She's a tough nut to crack. Maybe I shoulda invited Lucille Ball," he said to Bernie before strutting over in his quick, jerky steps to get the kid at least to grin.

"I'd bet a young lady like you would like a backstage pass to the Elvis Presley concert. How 'bout it?"

"No, thank you, Mr. Lefkowitz." Sara affected the tone of Grand-mère Ophelia.

"Call me Lefty. Do you like concerts?"

"We hold season's tickets to Carnegie Hall and the Metropolitan Opera, Mr. Lefty. My family has had them for ages."

He shrugged away her bratty disdain and unnerving gaze. "Well, maybe a smart kid like you might want to come with your mother and me to see the *$64,000 Question.* You get to use your brains."

"That would be nice." Sara smoothed the front of her skirt, looking very Eastern Seaboard in her navy Sunday suit.

Claire glanced over at Sara and Lefty—they seemed to be getting along—and then at her mother and the Aunties, and smiled to herself. She felt thankful to be alive and in the company of her newly extended family. Maybe one day they could all be happy again. Auntie Wren threw rice that stuck to Claire's ice-blue sheath, but it didn't matter, since they were all going to stay at the house for their honeymoon.

"Why would anyone want to leave paradise?" Claire asked Lefty after they'd cut the wedding cake sweetened with honey for good luck.

"I wouldn't dream of asking you to leave your family while they're all here together. Those Aunties are terrific—characters straight out of an old screenplay. *The Aunties of Heavenly Falls.*" He held out his hands as if he were seeing it on a marquee. "Sort of a Frank Capra–esque thing." He winked at her. "And Sara, well, she's already quite the little character actress."

"Oh, Lefty. How could I have gotten so lucky to have you fix everything in my life?"

"Hold on, Toots. I'm the one that should be thanking whoever fixes these kinds of things. Sending buckets of orchids to the big director in the sky."

When Perry Como's mellow voice came on over the poolside speaker, Lefty asked Claire Harrison Lefkowitz—he loved the sound of the names together—to dance. She swayed with him, following his offbeat tilt, like Anna with the king of Siam. Claire, posture-perfect and balletic, Lefty with two eponymous feet, his bald head bobbing with vim, both of them completely contented with their happy two-step. If it couldn't be love, Claire thought, who was she to argue with contentment? After a trio of "I do"s a desire for normality seemed very, well, normal.

Out of the corner of her eye she saw Sara slip away by herself. She excused herself and followed her to the back of the pool where she found her sitting straight-backed on a drainpipe cover.

"You'll soil that pretty suit," Claire tentatively said.

"I don't care."

"Then neither do I." Claire plopped herself next to her daughter, Bel Air mud staining her sheath.

"I thought clothes were all you ever cared about."

"It's a little luxury. Not on my ten-most-important list."

"Grand-mère Ophelia says—"

"Ophelia isn't my problem anymore. *You're* my concern, and I care very much about you." Claire slipped her arm around Sara's shoulder. The girl stiffened like a cat who had been kicked.

Claire retreated. She wanted to hold Sara or smooth her hair. She wanted to touch that part of her that reminded her of Six, of the good times they'd shared along with the color of their eyes. Claire was so willing to love her, to help her through all her obvious rage and confusion. She could muster up the patience. But she couldn't help being repelled by those Ophelia-like mannerisms, that same speech, the arrogant looks that brought to mind a knuckle-rapping teacher who suspected Claire of cheating on her homework. She squashed the feelings welling up inside of her.

"I didn't know they were allowed to make such ugly houses." Sara pointed her chin in the air toward the fake mansard roof. "And I've never seen plastic water lilies before."

"It's Hollywood. There's fake snow for Christmas and rabbits that talk. I can't wait to take you to the studios to see all the magic."

"You didn't really expect that I'd be comfortable in a place like this, did you?" The challenge in her voice was chilling.

"No." Claire hugged her own knees to her chest in lieu of her daughter. "I just wanted you to know that there's one other person in the world who understands how bad you feel. And that she's always there for you."

"*She.* That's what we call you at home. No one refers to you by any of your names at home anymore."

"Not even Grandfather? How is he doing?"

"Just grand. Almost fully recovered." Sara wasn't about to tell Mrs. Lefty Lefkowitz that Grandfather Harrison still defended her to the rest of the family and insisted on keeping a little photo on his study desk of himself with Sara, Six, and Claire taken a few weeks before the tragedy.

"No. No one ever speaks of you. As you know, we only discuss people of accomplishment and who excel in public service."

Claire was glad Lefty was calling her in his small, nasal voice. She didn't feel like having her heart broken on her wedding day.

A look that could have been construed as contrite softened Sara's stormy eyes. "What are you going to call this house?" asked the child who had grown up in houses with names instead of numbers.

"I was thinking of calling it home." Claire stood on her high heels and went back to the music.

Lefty had saved her, repotted her in fresh soil so that she could survive, so in return Claire set about smoothing the texture of Lefty's life. She made sure their home on Alamedo Drive was always filled with plumped pillows and flowers. Suddenly it was if an outdoor garden had moved indoors. Apricots, peaches, and lemon-colored draperies and cushions covered the chairs, and sectional couches were arranged like avant-garde fruit.

And the blooms could be expense-accounted, the once-again-thrifty Claire was pleased to note, because the agency's offices were on the newly decorated first floor. With the house now refurbished, Claire Harrison Lefkowitz invited the A-list clients to join Lefty's roster. First they came out of curiosity, to meet the society dame who had murdered her husband, killing him with a speargun for sharks, but as Lefty's PR people massaged the story, her legend became more intriguing. This beautiful friend of the restrained Princess Grace as well as a wild Evita, with the same liberal leanings as Hollywood's "in" crowd, had killed a Nazi. So what? She only did what Sam Goldwyn had ordered and John Wayne had carried out a hundred times on the screen. The stars came to gawk at the lady who had killed her husband and lunched with the pope, but they stayed when the hardworking, well-connected Lefkowitzes got them the juiciest parts. They also got them the best press. Claire became a stickler for this part of the business. She protected her clients with a mother hen's ferocity, and woe to the gossip columnist who back-stabbed one of Lefty and Claire's clients. Anita Lace was banned from all film openings and any star's news that Lefty had anything to do with. If possible, Grant Publications always received the studio press release a day later than anyone else.

"*Tant pis* for you," Lefty hollered into the phone at *U.S. Week*'s editor in chief. He had picked up a little French from his wife.

Throughout the first year, Claire threw herself into Lefty's business with relish. He had thrown her a life raft, and she would return the favor by saving the agency that had been more loss than profit when she'd become his bride. Once she learned Lefty's craft, being an agent was easy labor for Claire. It wasn't unlike the work she'd done as the hostess of Palazzo Duccio. Introducing the players, bolstering their egos, and closing the deal—Claire had been doing that for Duccio in three different languages. Here everyone spoke English, more or less. Plus she got paid. Claire had tasted poverty and had felt the helplessness of a woman alone without a job title or even the means to support her child. This time, Violet's daughter turned around her husband's business and then took fifty percent for herself. It was so much more satisfying than being the decorative dinner-giver and jewelry model.

Still, her hostess skills came in handy. An invitation to Lefty and Claire's was considered a social coup. After all, their living room was now where Judy Garland belted out her songs at the piano, where Lauren Bacall and Bogey stayed up till three A.M. talking politics in a haze of their own cigarette smoke, and Fred Astaire danced on the terrace with Auntie Slim, who declared herself a "Hollywood extra" after a few deftly executed spins around the flagstones. The only guarantee that you'd be on this coveted list was to sign a Lefkowitz contract. Claire even took Ingrid Bergman to lunch at Chasen's, where they girl-talked over chili about Rossellini, whom Claire had known in Italy, just so that everyone who mattered could see her with the elusive actress. That lunch alone attracted three more clients to the firm.

Building up Lefty's business was part of the package, and although bringing people to the table for movie deals was fun, Claire itched to recapture the feeling that she was truly achieving a goal close to her heart, as she had with Eleanor House.

The idea for the documentary came to her one evening after dinner while she was reading a *McCall's* story on Eleanor Roosevelt's life. Her bare feet were propped on Lefty's lap. Husband and wife both in their matching Sulka robes, their Sunday-dinner trays arranged in front of the TV. Ed Sullivan's show was turned on low.

"This is so unfair!" Claire railed into Lefty's good ear. "Millions of women who read this fluff are going to think Eleanor was just a busybody housewife who charged around the world uninvited. She revolutionized domestic policy at home. She *invented* the issues. Day care, civil rights, equality in education—that all came from her!"

Lefty loved it when she talked like this, as if exposing her liberal sentiments were akin to talking dirty. He egged her on. "Yeah, fix it, Toots. And get me a buttermilk while you're up."

"Seriously, dear. I want to shake everyone by the shoulders so they'll understand this wonderful woman. Franklin won the war but Eleanor reformed this country. She was the one who opened the military to minorities, gave women jobs with real pay, fought against child labor."

Lefty looked up from Sullivan. "You got my attention. If you could take the passion you feel and put it on the screen, you'd have something. And you *were* there . . ." He ran his tongue over his lower lip. "Go for it. Call up Eleanor and negotiate the film rights. Go for greatness." His eyes shot her an adrenaline hit through his windowpane lenses.

"Do you think I could? Could *I* rescue *her* reputation?" For a moment Claire wondered if someday someone would do the same for her. She asked Lefty her own sixty-four-thousand-dollar question. "Lefty, will this town take me seriously? Eleanor Roosevelt as remembered by me? People may not even want to work with Claire Harrison Lefkowitz." A blush colored her high cheeks.

"Well, it won't be easy. But this town loves a comeback. It won't be the first time somebody came to town and changed their reputation. Norma Jean was just a pretty girl with a lot of problems, but Marilyn Monroe's a big star. You won't know unless you try. But give the audience a break, Claire, and bring Max Factor into the movie. I know she's a hell of a dame, but Mrs. Roosevelt could use a little mascara." Lefty toasted her with his buttermilk.

Truth be known, Claire liked him even better on their first anniversary than on their wedding day. She gazed fondly at the cross-hatched lines etched on the road map that was his face, as if a chicken had run across it in a panic. She wondered why she hadn't noticed how handsome he was before now.

Certainly, he was pint-sized. But then again, so were most of the leading Hollywood players. Claire towered over the likes of a petite Liz Taylor, and even the voluptuous Marilyn Monroe, who liked to kick around without her shoes, came up only to Claire's clavicle. Claire often wore Capezio flats to client dinners once she realized that she was like a skyscraper over Spencer Tracy, young Paul Newman, and Eddie Fisher in the buffet line.

Eleanor, on the other hand, was a towering figure, larger than life, and Claire knew it wouldn't be a simple task to bring her to the big screen. Or to do her justice. The project was ambitious, but in her new California can-do environment, and with Lefty's encouragement, so was Claire.

She assembled a list of all of the people she would need to contact: Anna; wounded soldiers whom Eleanor had visited in the hospitals; Mary McLeod Bethune, the director of NYA's Division of Negro Affairs; Secretary of State Stimson; and all the grandchildren. She didn't dare contact Harrison. As she reviewed the old newsreels, though, she discovered that now she had an opportunity to play the black-and-white movies costarring the man she loved. She hadn't seen him in two years, but when she caught her first glimpse of Harrison on the news footage, her pulse raced as if it had been only yesterday. She felt a secret thrill each time she saw him climb the steps of the *Sacred Cow* to fly away with Franklin, or trim the sails with Eleanor at Campobello, his shirt open at his tanned throat.

Violet, however, had reservations. There was a note of concern in her voice as she expressed her doubts about the Eleanor project to her daughter.

"You can't spend all day sitting in a dark projection room. You already have two full-time jobs."

Claire was fidgety. Her fingers tapped on the turquoise poolside phone as she waited for a potential documentary director to call back.

"You are helping run your husband's agency, and doing a fine job, dear." Violet paused, then plunged ahead. "And then there is your real job. Raising your child."

Claire turned to look at her daughter. Sara was standing poised on the edge of the diving board. The lanky fifteen-year-old kept racing out on the board and then back as if she couldn't decide whether or not to jump. Sara hung her toes over the edge, swinging her skinny arms out over her head, and then abruptly caught herself before pacing back again. The springboard bounced over and over. It made Claire nervous. But she had been tense ever since her mother and Sara arrived in L.A. for Easter break.

"Sara, come over here and I'll put some lotion on you. You're getting too dark!" Claire called through the old-fashioned megaphone Lefty had bought for her. PRODUCER was painted on it in big bold letters.

Sara ignored her mother.

Claire turned to Violet. "Honestly, Mother, I don't know what to do. She never listens to me. Look at her skin. She's as dark as the yardman!"

Violet cleared her throat as she continued pulling the thread through her needlepoint. "Sara's suntan is the least of your worries. She's on the edge, you know, and I don't mean of the diving board."

Both women turned to look as the young girl finally sprang from the board and expertly jackknifed into the water, setting off a series of rippling circles in the cold, smooth surface.

"Claire, your daughter needs you."

Without seeing, Claire could tell that her mother's eyes were leveled directly at her own.

"But they've only let me see her a few times this year."

"Look at her. She's wound up as tight as a mummy. Each time one of her wounds has started to open and ooze, Ophelia has just slapped on another bandage and told her people of their class don't display emotion. I fear that one day soon it will all be too much to hold inside and she'll just unravel."

"But what can I do if they don't let me near her? I can't mother her by mail!" The word brought back memories of her own childhood and a father who existed only in a handful of postcards. "It practically takes an act of Congress just to arrange these little visits."

"I know you do your best, and I know you had to sign away your rights in Rome. But with you out here in make-believe land, as nice as it is, dear"—Violet coaxed all the honey she could into her worried voice—"and Sara living in Wuthering Heights"—Violet had adopted Sara's nickname for Charlotte Hall—"she's not getting the old-fashioned graham-cracker-and-milk kind of parental love and stability she craves."

A flood of guilt squeezed Claire's gut. "Ever since Six died—"

Violet held up her hand. "Sara's the only one who truly needs you now. We just have to arrange it so Sara insists on visiting you. Lefty's a good man. He'll share you with your daughter."

Claire nodded. One of the main reasons she had married Lefty was so she could bring Sara back into her life. She tried to imagine luring her daughter the way she had reeled in recalcitrant generals to the table in the war years or coaxed skittish actors to the Lefkowitz Talent Agency.

"Lefty and I filed for custody the day after we married. It's impossible to fight Ophelia Harrison, even in the California courts. Mother, help me. If Sara doesn't conform to Ophelia's ways, she'll banish her to some mental institution. And the stupid laws are on her side. I knew I wouldn't have a chance without a husband, but now . . ." Her voice trailed off.

It was ironic, she reflected, that her untraditional, cash-poor family had raised her beautifully without the benefit of husbands or a father. They had given her values, self-confidence, and unconditional love—all the things Claire was failing to provide for her daughter. Even with the head start of high social position and untold wealth.

"Is it my fault, Mother? Did I do this to her?" Claire's eyes glistened with real tears. "I abandoned her, didn't I?"

"No, dear. Sara's the child you were never allowed to mother. Ophelia stole those early years. Now you must do everything you can to rescue her." Violet's warning was spoken in kindness.

"But how?"

"Sara loves you, Claire. It's just buried in all the confusion. What's happened to Sara has happened. If she is going to survive what's already fallen across her path, it will depend on her own strong will and her support team. Us."

Sara climbed out of the pool, shaking herself like a rude Irish setter, sprays of water beads flying off her wet red hair.

Claire brightened. Finally, the guilt was being replaced with a plan. Dodging the water spout, she stood to hold out a dry beach towel for Sara. She'd been world famous for catering to the desires of all sorts of difficult folks, persuading people who wouldn't even speak to one another to dine together at her table; surely she could convince her daughter to accept an invitation to lunch. To some, an egg-salad sandwich with the crusts cut off was a dull prospect, but for Sara it was a comfort food that brought back the best of times. Only Claire would serve it up in a place where they could begin to make new memories.

Claire pitched the idea to Sara as enthusiastically as she had proposed her Eleanor film to the studio. "Why don't we all go out for egg salad?" Honey to catch the bear, live bait to lure the sailfish, and a sandwich to reel Sara back in. "Three generations at the Brown Derby could be fun."

"Sounds like purgatory to me. A bunch of old farts and has-beens talking about their old movies and eating dead animals, medium rare." Sara groaned. "I'd puke."

"Now, now, we're talking about eating lunch, not spoiling everyone's appetite." Violet managed a laugh and a stern look at the same time.

"Mine's already spoiled. I'm going into the kitchen to 'lunch' with Lorenza. Don't worry, I won't play with any sharp knives. That was what you two were talking about, wasn't it? Gram, look at my tan lines." She snapped her bathing-suit straps to show her grandmother.

"I'll be so black they won't let me in the Tuxedo Club." When Sara smiled, which was rarely, she displayed a prominent overbite, a physical characteristic she shared with Ophelia.

Claire sighed. MGM was an easier sell than this subversive fifteen-year-old. She'd just have to try harder, matching each of Sara's insults with a forgiving hug. As Claire watched her sullen daughter enter the house through a sliding glass door, she wondered to herself if she would have loved her flesh-and-blood offshoot better if she resembled Harrison and not her paternal grandmother.

When Harrison's invitation for lunch arrived, Claire assumed it must be about Sara. Or related to the documentary. Probably in response to the dozens of letters she had sent out in request for home movies of the Roosevelt White House years. As connected as Harrison was, she was sure he'd heard about the project.

She immediately recognized the handwriting on his imposing stationery with a World Bank address, and for a moment before opening it she felt as giddy as a schoolgirl finally receiving a note from the football captain she'd had a secret crush on for years. His letter curtly informed her that he'd be stopping off in Los Angeles for two days before his aid mission left for Hong Kong, and asked that if the date coincided with her calendar she might join him for lunch at the Bel Air at 12:30 on the fifteenth of the month. And then came the little phrase that stirred her heart: *No reply necessary.*

As the date approached, Claire found herself getting leaden fingers while she practiced Lefty's favorite show tunes at the piano and unable to concentrate while she read over new properties for her clients. She figured if she went to a psychoanalyst like everyone else in town, or even to an advice-giving hairdresser instead of doing up her own French roll, they would have advised her to attend this reunion and just get it out of her system. After all, she had been contentedly married for over a year.

The morning of the lunch she felt like a fourteen-year-old. Lorenza couldn't understand why her lady had to try on everything in her closet just to meet a former father-in-law. Hats, gloves, sweaters, even some of the Dior suits that hadn't seen the light of day for ages were strewn around her dressing area like when one of those Hollywood wives got a divorce and held a luxury garage sale. The final choice was pretty boring, according to Lorenza's point of view: feet first, a pair of open-toed pumps; a slim white linen skirt with a subtle kick-flair; and a plain-necked cashmere sweater set.

Lorenza shook her head in the mirror behind Claire. "The signóra looks like she was just in a stick-up."

"You think so? I look too naked without any jewelry?" On a scale of one to ten, her nerves were jittering at a twelve.

"*Forse,* the signóre's secretary dresses this much"—she held her forefinger and thumb a good two inches apart—"more exciting."

"Oh, it's noon already. I haven't got time to change. I'll be late. Harrison hates late." She had already spent two hours trying to get herself together. While Claire breathlessly ran into her bath to spray a last whiff of vanilla around her shoulders and then hurriedly brush out her hair, pins flying everywhere, Lorenza scurried to her own room and dashed back with her prized pop beads from Woolworth's. She snapped the fake pearls together at the back of Claire's neck, and assured the signóra that now she looked like the lady she was. In her rush, Claire barely noticed the bubble-gum-machine quality of her borrowed jewelry.

She parked her sports car beneath the bell-shaped leaves of a ginkgo tree and, pulling the scarf off her head, she quickly stepped under the Bel Air Hotel canopy and then over the winding pathway past the quaint stucco cottages and white-picketed rosebeds, as casually as she could.

Harrison was already seated. He stood when he saw her enter the restaurant and waited for her to walk over to their table. She was struck by how out of place he looked out here in Southern California, with his formal manners and aristocratic bearing. It was almost as if he had stepped off the set of a period film, a graying Gregory Peck immaculately tailored for his role as the distinguished ambassador in a war movie.

It had been almost two years since she'd seen him. And so many ruined lives ago. She was so apprehensive she was trembling, but she lifted her head and tried to disguise it. She might have pulled it off, too, if he hadn't taken her hand. Suddenly, every day, every hour away from him, the man she was destined to love, lifted away like an early-morning L.A. fog. The last time they'd been together, he had asked her to run away with him. He held her hand in both of his for a long moment and she left it there, confused and lost in remembrance, before she took her chair.

Their table for three was placed at the end of the room, far enough away from the others for privacy and overlooking a deep bay window. The empty chair seemed to symbolize that someone was missing. Their son. Claire bit her lip, not acting at all.

"You're looking well, Claire. I'm glad you agreed to see me."

"I'm just glad you're feeling better. I was worried." She was trying to remember what part she was playing: jilted fiancée, notorious murderess, or happily married Hollywood wife. She knew she was sitting a breath away from the only man she had ever loved, but she didn't have one clue how to behave. She needed direction. When the waiter came, she studied the oversized menu as if it might hold her next line.

"Smoked salmon, please, and the cold artichoke."

"You won't mind if I have something heartier?" He smiled that sideways smile of his and suddenly she remembered her role. She watched him, mesmerized as he methodically sliced his tomatoes and precisely peppered his lettuce leaves, patting his napkin to the side of his chin. She couldn't detect any sign of a stroke. He appeared as in control as ever.

"Are you just passing through?" She was willing herself not to care.

"I've taken the chairmanship of the World Bank and am leaving in two days for Hong Kong and New Delhi. I shall be traveling about a month. We're putting together a new industrial program for emerging nations."

Claire's eyes lit up. Of course he knew this would interest her.

"How exciting, Harrison. Building self-help infrastructure."

"Exactly. Foreign aid by itself isn't enough. We only create enemies by giving starving people bottled water. We need to have them build their own wells. And then create jobs. Self-reliance is where I plan to take this project."

"I couldn't agree more. How brilliant of you." Claire was right at home. She didn't even need a cue card. She was already seduced by his humanitarian endeavors.

"You know, we have a representative from Eleanor House along on the trip. You've done a fine job there, Claire." He reached across the table to pat her hand and then let his fingers tighten their grip. "Darling."

Darling. She knew she should have winced at the word, but coming from Harrison's soft lips it sounded natural to her ears. But so did "Toots" now.

"Why don't you come along and supervise the children's part? You could, you know, as founder of Eleanor House." The invitation hung in the air.

Claire was amazed. Here in Hollywood she had won a hard-earned respect. To the rest of the world, however, she was still a fortune-hunting murderess. Had he conveniently forgotten, or was he just being polite?

"I've only just been put back on the letterhead."

"Yes, I saw. It was noble of you to resign when things weren't going well."

When things weren't going well. The euphemism for what had happened unsettled her. An artichoke leaf dropped from her fingertips onto the tablecloth.

"But I knew it was you who gave them the endowment that allowed them to continue. I matched it, you know. In Six's name." His skin went sallow.

Claire couldn't help it. She wasn't a good enough actress. The tears welled up in her eyes. Hurt and anger exploded inside of her. "Where were you? I needed you." Her shoulders started to shake.

"He killed Six." It was the first time she had uttered the truth. But she wanted him to know. "And you sent me there." A year in Hollywood had taught her to reach down into the quick of her pain as if she were a method actress drawing on her own, very real, emotions. Except that she wasn't acting. "Everything in my life was in shambles and you never came." She didn't care that her tears were falling like hailstones into her artichoke heart. The waiter headed in their direction did a quick military maneuver to skirt around their table. Whether it was a rich woman sobbing to her investment banker or an actress auditioning for a part, he decided to give table twenty-seven a wide berth.

Claire's eyes were livid with anger. "How could you just casually invite me for April in India or Pakistan after you left me penniless in an Italian jail cell? I wasn't even allowed to see my son buried."

"Our son." His skin was the color of ash. "It was out of my control."

Claire bristled. Those were the exact words Tom had used when he'd ordered her to catch the next plane out of Rome, leaving everything, everyone, behind.

"But I can make it up to you now. Truly, Claire. I've got my health back. It was hearing about Six that caused my stroke." He looked ashamed, as if by falling sick he had broken his code of honor along with her heart. "Allow me to take care of both of us now."

"It's just too late."

"I'm free now. It's inevitable you'll hear about it, but I've tried to handle it as discreetly as possible. I've divorced Ophelia. I'm yours if you'll have me."

She was frozen. Harrison was free. But what was she supposed to do? Drop Lefty? Fly away with a song in her heart? The man she had loved since she was eighteen, the minute she had laid eyes on him—no, before, that, the man who had materialized out of

her Field's catalog dream book—was back again, pleading for her
hand. And she had just given it to another.

"I understand if you need some time, darling. If you won't
come now, we can be together in two months when I return."

The waiter thought the Seberg look-alike must have got the
part from the way she turned off the tears and determinedly attacked her peach melba.

"No, Harrison. It's too late for us. If only you could have come
sooner." She wouldn't leave Lefty. He might not be the one she
loved, but he had been the one who was there when her life died.
And sometimes being there was more important than love.

Lana Turner was coming to dinner. A very excited Lefty was trying to behave as if the star of *The Bad and the Beautiful* wasn't currently testifying in the L.A. courthouse in defense of her
daughter, who was on trial for fatally stabbing hoodlum Johnny
Stompanato. And Claire was trying to pretend that the man she
loved hadn't just asked her to run away with him two days ago.
And that her brain didn't have to shut off her heart to prevent her
from following after him.

Baskets of fruit and flowers had been arriving at three-minute
intervals from hopeful attendees. But Claire insisted that Lana be
protected, so only the film star's most loyal friends and the cream
of Hollywood society were invited. All day long the phones had
been ringing off the hook. Everyone wanted to come to the
Lefkowitzes' dinner. The murder of Stompanato, Lana's lover, was
making headlines all over the country, and this was Lana's first
outing.

Lana was a client, and the film studio had insisted on this little dinner to show she wasn't being shunned by her peers, a real
career-killer. So Lefty had arranged for supper under the flattering
light of the Chinese lanterns around the kidney-shaped pool.
Claire understood only too well the importance of making sure
the lady felt welcome at the best table in town. She also felt the

need to protect her guest of honor from the sharp pen of the press and any party crashers—and she felt the need to try to quell her own resurfacing emotions. The buzz in town was that Lana had stabbed her jealous lover in a knock-down-drag-out fight and that her fifteen-year-old daughter had taken the blame when the police stormed in, a loyal gesture to save her mother. Claire shivered in the warm air and wondered if Lana Turner's daughter had taken the blame to protect her. Dear God, she whispered, don't let someone else live the same nightmare I have.

The whole movie colony was desperate to witness this meeting. Would Claire and Lana embrace as sisters in violence? Would they tell one another the truth? The hand-picked guests included only one columnist—a friendly one—from the *Hollywood Reporter* who always spun out his column as Lefty dictated. So the little group was suddenly thrown off balance when Mrs. Cecile Juarez, descendant of one of the first families of Los Angeles and widowed owner of the *L.A. Mirror,* showed up with Fenwick Grant instead of her nephew as her escort.

Grant saw Claire before she spotted him. He stood off to one side in the shadow of the pool house, studying his hostess, the woman who had sent the circulation of his papers soaring, the one whom his attack-dog columnist Anita Lace had ruined. But somehow she had risen, Phoenix-like, out of her own ashes. She was moving gracefully among her guests, whispering a word here, lightly touching another on his arm, finishing one sentence as she moved on to the next person. Like a butterfly, he thought, only more interesting. She made all the other women look overdressed. She wore a slim black sheath that covered her obviously ample cleavage all the way to the collarbone but must have been designed by a superior architect, as it had no back at all. He had little time to wonder at anything else before Lefty tapped him on his elbow, Fenwick Grant's six-three shoulder being out of Lefty's reach.

"Hit the road, bub. You got a big set of balls showing up here."

Grant, who combined a Harvard education with street smarts, wasn't easily intimidated. "I'm here with Cecile Juarez."

"You're outta here. Listen, Grant, maybe someday I'll forgive you for what you did to my wife, but tonight isn't it." Lefty practiced his own smooth brand of diplomacy. He was anxious to usher Grant out before Claire could be upset by his intrusion.

Grant turned to comply a moment too late. Claire saw him and walked straight over to one of the two people she despised most on the face of the earth. Somebody had to be blamed for all her tragedy, and tonight the fellow who broadcast the news, milking the story and getting rich off her troubles, was it. By now she knew enough about the newspaper business to know that Anita Lace had been working under his skillful direction.

In her high heels Claire was more of a vertical match for him than Lefty. Her haughty aquiline nose was just inches from his face.

"I assume you've blundered in by mistake and you're not a trespasser."

Lefty brought his hands to his ulcer, hoping she wouldn't finish her thought.

"In case you don't bother to read your own newspapers, trespassers can be shot in this neighborhood. Happens all the time. When I moved to Bel Air, I think it was your Anita Lace who dubbed this street Murderer's Row. Are you leaving now, or would you like one last drink? How do you take your poison?"

If Fenwick Grant hadn't been so bedazzled by her, so mesmerized by the sound of her elegantly impassioned voice as she squelched him, light-years away from the cool, bored hostess he'd met at Duccio's table, he might have actually been frightened by this soft-spoken, tough-talking woman. If he wasn't mistaken there was real passion beneath the surface. But had he known about the scene that was about to take place, the newspaperman would have risked his life and stayed.

"My apologies." He was cavalier about the effect his chiseled features and charms had on all the others; he gave the impression that if his good looks evaporated in the morning, he wouldn't give a damn. The Hollywood men who made their livings with their faces were glad to see him go, though the ladies felt the sexual energy of the cocktail hour drop when he raised his hand in surrender to Claire and left.

Lana Turner swept in late, a vision of angelic innocence mixed with devilish sensuality in a short white cocktail dress that exposed three-fourths of her bosom. Her high heels, reinforced with gold taps, clicked like a sound track on the flagstone patio. Claire and Lana maneuvered their way through the cocktail crowd, ignoring everyone else until they came face-to-face. Silently, they reached out and hugged each other tightly.

The guests stilled the ice in their drinks and stopped speaking in order to hear every word. They stared at the two women. Both were pale, one with an inch of William Tuttle on her face, the other with a soft dusting of powder; one with platinum hair poured out of a bottle, the other with sleek brown mane lightly sunstreaked; one encased, sausagelike, in a white vavoom number, a transparent chiffon scarf blowing around her neck; the other sleekly aristocratic in backless basic black. The guests were breathless waiting for the two beautiful women to speak.

But the odd couple decided to offer the curious gapers nothing more than a silent movie tonight. Claire ushered Lana into the glass pool house, closing the sliding door behind her. For the next two hours the guests sipped their cocktails and nibbled their shrimp, all the while feverishly trying to read the ladies' lips as they played the best scene of the year on their brightly lit stage.

Esther Hoffman, married to the head of MGM, couldn't take it any longer. "Look, they're hugging! What do you think they're hugging about?"

Manny Moses put on his glasses. "I think that's a tear rolling out of Lana's eye. I didn't know she could do tears without glycerin drops."

"Can't we get any sound?" The studio czar was beside himself. "I didn't come here to play charades!"

Cecile Juarez lifted her lorgnette from her evening bag. She could regale her bridge club with this scene for months. "They both look innocent to me. Mothers protecting children. There ought to be a law against police harassing women."

"Or mobsters beating up movie stars."

"*Mildred Pierce!*" Esther Hoffman shouted, recalling the Joan Crawford classic that had been big box office. "Just imagine Lana in a remake where the mother sacrifices everything for her daughter. It'll be a smash! I'll have the studio get right on it."

"Oh my God." Cecil Mulholland was beside himself. "I think she's confessing."

"Which one? I can't see from here."

"Sit down! I used to read lips. I think they're *both* confessing."

"Confessing?"

"Confessing to covering up. You know, the noble gesture."

"I'm going to weep. Look at them. Holding hands. I'd kill to have women like that kill for me."

"If *I* were on the jury"—the actor moonlighting as a waiter and serving the beef tenderloin couldn't restrain himself—"I'd find them both innocent. They're *gor*-jus."

"Well, for my money, but don't let it leave this table"—Esther Hoffman pointed her finger like she was betting on black at the roulette table—"Turner's guilty and Lefkowitz is innocent."

"I'd bet on it."

They watched as attentively as if they were in a darkened movie house until Lefty broke up the silent movie.

"Come on, you voyeurs. Let's change the subject. So what else is new?" Watching the two women, it dawned on Lefty that the stories about his wife were as mired in mystery as Lana's alibi.

Then he knew it in his gut. Now he understood why Sara wouldn't accept her mother's affection. Sara was guilty.

*   *   *

Sara showed up unexpectedly at the back door. It was almost a year to the day after Lana Turner's morose daughter had been acquitted and three tense visits later from Claire's edgy teenager. Usually Sara's appearances were preceded by three-way calls between Tom, Lefty, and the doctors at Wolford, the high-priced country club of mental institutions where behind hewn hedges the problem heirs of the very rich were sent for warm baths and electroshocks whenever their behavior crossed the line between eccentric and embarrassing. Ophelia had insisted on Wolford, although Claire despised the sanatorium, where Sara's behavior vacillated from cold detachment to aggressive boldness. After her therapy sessions began, Claire never knew which Sara was coming: the quiet, moody one, or the brat who packed a wallop.

Sara's little holidays were big letdowns for Claire. She offered egg-salad sandwiches and open arms while Sara responded with sneers and icy stares. And when Sara defied her mother with her bad behavior, Claire swallowed her pride and covered it up.

"I don't think the inmates in *The Snake Pit* had worse manners than your little darling." Lefty seemed to be the only one who could tell the difference between Sara's real pain and her cool manipulation of all the adults around her. Like the time they had all had a family barbecue around the pool and Sara had watched in silence, arms folded across her chest, as her mother's Hermès scarf blew over the grill and caught fire. After Lefty had stamped out the flames, he turned to Sara.

"Why didn't you pull your mother's scarf out of the barbecue?"

"*She* doesn't care about material things. *She* told me."

Tonight Sara showed up unexpectedly with a look in her eye that implied she had much more to throw on the fire. Lefty thought she resembled a teenage mutant from a sci-fi movie, her face a phantasmagoria of white against a backdrop of unruly red hair.

"I hitchhiked all the way from Wolford," she bragged. Claire wasn't expecting her for her hard-won half of Sara's summer vacation for at least another week. With her tank top embedded with dirt and a leather jacket hanging loose from her shoulders, Sara hardly looked like the sweet sixteen-year-old the Aunties carefully shopped for.

"I just blew out of there with this suicide psycho. We went over the wall."

"The fuzz on your tail?" Lefty had cast enough B prison movies to play along.

Sara laughed. That was a good sign. Real nutcases couldn't laugh at themselves.

"The wife having another party?" Sara sounded more like mumbly James Dean in *Rebel Without a Cause* than herself.

"You on drugs?"

"Only antidepressants and some Di-Seds to sleep. All the regular junk the doctors pump into me. Why? You got some?"

"Just my Bromo-Seltzers and phenobarbital. Ulcer's kicking up again." He rubbed his tummy.

Straight talk from Lefty always seemed to summon up Sara's saner side. A grin curled her mouth as she peeked over his shoulder into the living room, where Lucille Ball was leading the guests in a spirited game of charades. "Hey, are deaf and dumb actors *her* newest cause?"

"We're having a fund-raiser for Eleanor House. They're playing charades for money."

"I'm good at that. Play it all the time in the nuthouse."

"C'mon in. Your mother will be thrilled to see you."

"Yeah. I bet. If I walk in looking like this I'll probably embarrass her in front of her friends. But she'll pretend not to notice as usual and just give me one of those precious hugs."

"Well, you do look kind of creepy. What's with the hair under the arms?"

Lefty wondered if he should invite some of Hollywood's equally crazy offspring to soften the effect of Sara. He hoped he had convinced Claire that what Sara needed now was a swift kick in the rump.

The minute Claire saw her daughter, she put down a platter of guacamole and ran to hug her. Her usual gesture. Sara eluded her embrace, leaving Claire alone with empty open arms. Grabbing a beer from the bar, the swaggering escapee arranged herself cross-legged on the arm of a banana leaf–covered couch and stared down her mother's guests with an "I-dare-you" look.

Lefty walked into Claire's hug. She let her arms rest on his shoulders as he whispered into her hair. "It's time for a tougher kind of love, Toots. You took the rap for the murder. Why should she get all the sympathy?"

He could feel every vertebra in her spine stiffen. "I never said—"

"Yeah, yeah, so my street-smarts intuition is pretty damned good. I didn't get where I am by my looks, you know. I think the kid wants you to put up your dukes. For Pete's sake, Claire, she's pushing you into the ring."

Claire was speechless for a long moment. Her fingers fell from Lefty's shoulders and grasped his hands.

"But she just got here. If I push too hard, she'll vanish again." Claire was terrified of Sara's moods. If she challenged her daughter tonight there might not be any vacation to enjoy together. She had looked forward to it for months. Only Lefty knew the toll these visits took on her. Claire smiled gratefully at her husband and put her lips to his ear. "No one's ever cared for me the way you do." She took Lefty's face in her hands and kissed him even as she watched Sara blowing smoke rings at the guests.

Lucille Ball's charades team was silently acting out movie titles. The loser would donate five thousand dollars to Eleanor House. The leggy comedienne with hair the hybrid color of strawberries and oranges was wildly acting out one of her own comedies, *The Long, Long Trailer.* Determined not to lose, she bawled out her Latin husband when he ruined her team's chances by confusing "trailer" with "tailor."

"But on da piece of paper I didn't see da *rrrr*!" He spoke with the same mambo beat that accompanied the bandleader's singing. "I am da man here. Only a bimbo shouts at her husband!"

The former showgirl and current head of Desilu Productions, one of the most powerful women in Hollywood, belted her husband with a Swedish meatball. "Yeah, and I got confused because I'm the breadwinner in this family. Why don't you go home and beat your bongos!"

Desi's retort eluded the crowd, as it was fired off in rapid Spanish. Lefty's team was next.

Just as he reached his hand into the hat to read the name of the movie a member of his team would act out, Sara stood. She raised one arm high over her head, like in school, asking for permission to join his team and exposing a tuft of red hair almost the color of Lucy's under her arm. Lefty explained to a horrified Lana Turner, to whom body hair was more repellent than murder, that all the rich people in New York were going beatnik this season. But he was visibly unnerved as he read the title of the Alfred Hitchcock film they were pantomiming before Sara snatched it out of his hands.

She went for the second word first, drawing a rectangle in the air with her dirty fingers and pretending to peer out.

"Close up!"

"Mirror!" The actors tried to guess.

Sara now unlocked the invisible square and lifted it.

"*The Postman Always Rings Twice!*" Lana's only frame of reference was her own movies.

"Window!" Someone cried out, and Sara signaled with a gnawed finger that the guess was correct.

Now she was going for the first word. By the time Lefty gauged what she was doing, it was too late. The meatball he was holding was too small to cover her scrawny derriere as she turned her behind to the room and dropped her jeans, exposing her naked rear.

"*Rearrr Window!*" Desi cried out, winning for his side. And in the startled living room, with Sara's jeans bunched around her ankles, Lucy and Desi jumped up and down and hugged. "I love you, you adorable Latin lover!" She pinched his cheeks. "No buts about it!" she cracked. And she pursed her overblown red lips and kissed him madly as Lorenza hurriedly pulled Sara's jeans up to cover her nakedness and dragged her out to the kitchen.

A very controlled Claire simply put her hands together as if to applaud the winning stunt, but couldn't quite make a sound.

"Hey Claire. Your kid's got a great sense of timing. And a great tuchis!" Lucy bellowed.

It hadn't escaped Claire's notice that Lucy had drawn the line when Desi had fired off an insult. She'd set off a fiery, name-calling blowout, but five minutes later they were in one another's arms. Claire had tried to give her troubled daughter what she wanted—her favorite foods, the permission to hate her if that was what she needed, the leeway to keep jackknifing into the swimming pool, purposely keeping them all on edge—when maybe what Sara really wanted was to be rudely awakened from her own nightmare. Maybe Lefty was right.

Claire's hands finally made a loud, sharp sound as she slapped them together, almost as if they had made a decision without her. Jaw set, she marched after Sara into the kitchen.

It wasn't with gentle understanding that she swung Sara around by her bony shoulders.

"How dare you walk in my home and plant your poison!" Her broad shoulders brushed against the kitchen's miniature ferns, setting them swinging.

"Oh, playing out our anger at last, are we? Oh, goody. We do this all the time at Wolford. It's a great game. You'll love it. At Wolford, if you're good enough at anger, the doctors let you sit down and be the fourth at their game of bridge."

"I've fought so hard not to let the Charlotte Hall crowd put you in straitjackets and on drugs. But maybe that's what you want. Then you don't have to think about the past."

"That's all I think about. Six is dead, and you're not." The pallor that had dulled Sara's features was replaced by a vivid shade of red. It was almost as if someone had defibrillated her dead heart.

"I can see you're very good at anger therapy."

"And you're a very good actress. You've got to be the best Lady Macbeth in La-La Land."

Claire thrust her hands within an inch of Sara's face. "I wish these hands *had* murdered Duccio. I'm guilty, too. Of wanting to kill him. It could have been me. I was only seconds away from doing the deed. And then you would have been the one to make the decision. Would you have protected me?"

The blood pulsing through Sara's face swelled the veins at her temple. This game wasn't as much fun as bridge or anger therapy. "But *I* was the one who killed him."

"And I was proud you did."

"Then why didn't you let me have the credit? You took the only courageous thing I ever did away from me." There was ice in her voice. "You get to be a celebrity murderess"—she laughed bitterly—"and I just get to be crazy."

For a moment Claire lost her balance. The scene in the guest house between Lana and herself whirled through her head. Would Sara be better off now if Claire had let her be hauled away in handcuffs and tried for murder? Seconds. She had had only seconds to make the decision. Maybe Ophelia wouldn't have even wanted Sara if she knew she was a killer. Then her daughter would have been freed from one of her prisons.

"I thought I was saving you."

"Some life raft."

"Well, you're still here."

"Sort of."

The tears welling up in Claire's eyes were almost on the surface of her irises, but she strengthened her resolve and pushed them back. Along with her compassion. She knew she had to tough this out. Be as bad as Ophelia had said she was. Maybe if Sara disliked her enough, her daughter could shut this swinging door that led back to Rome and open a new door to her future. Claire was jeopardizing everything she had with Sara in order to set her free. Did she love her enough to let her go?

"I'm sending you away."

"Where? Back to Wuthering Heights? Or Sing-Sing?" Beneath her sneer Sara's body was trembling.

"Away from all of us." Claire's voice was dead calm. "Someplace where you have to start over. Like I did in that Roman jail cell. Like Grandma Violet did as a shop girl when her husband left her penniless and pregnant with me. She composed a life for herself and she did it with grace and dignity, not thrashing around like a vulgar brat like you. I've tried to compose a life that includes you, but I can't force you to participate. There are other people who have suffered, too, Sara. If you're not a murderess, and not crazy, who are you, Sara?" Claire's tongue almost swallowed her words. "Maybe it's time you seek yourself out. All you're doing right now is bumping around like a car in an amusement park, trying to collide with the rest of us. Get on the road that's going to take you someplace. Replace the people who have disappointed you with people who won't." Claire hoped she wasn't slamming the door on herself. "Go as who you are to this place and don't take the baggage of the rest of us with you."

"I don't like walking through doors if I don't know what's behind them."

"Leave it ajar in case you want to come back."

"And I wouldn't have to see any of you?"

"You don't even have to use your real last name if you don't want to. Just think of it as your summer vacation away from all of us." She paused. She was sending Sara away, and maybe she wouldn't return. "I'm sending you to work at Eleanor House."

*   *   *

"No word from Sara?"

"Sorry, Toots. But here's something from Val-Kill."

Claire took the long envelope from Lefty's hand. The tidy cursive was definitely Eleanor's. Claire had to smile at the stamp, a purple rendering of Franklin's head in profile.

In her letter, Eleanor complained that there had been too much "misguided historical fiction" about her achievements as well as her personal life and embraced the opportunity to work with an old friend she could trust to set the record straight for posterity. And what Claire thought might have worked against her—her glaring past notoriety—Eleanor saw as an empathetic experience that enabled Claire to understand how misconceptions and character slander could chip away at important accomplishments, particularly controversial social reform like hers. Claire didn't have to be told how Eleanor had been maligned when in fact her enemies were really undermining her civil rights efforts and battles for women's equality.

When Claire finished reading the letter, she hugged Lefty and threw herself into her film at an even more fevered pitch. The project snowballed, and as the documentary grew, more and more people were attracted to it. Marian Anderson agreed to sing in the film and relive the historic event when Mrs. Roosevelt, who had resigned from the Daughters of the American Revolution in protest at their refusal to let the Negro American contralto sing at Constitution Hall, arranged for her to perform at a massive outdoor concert on the steps of the Lincoln Memorial. The rushes of Ms. Anderson's memories and voice on the screen were emotional and stirring.

When Eleanor and Anna decided they would attend the Washington opening of Claire's documentary, Claire anguished over whether she could turn the opening into a gala benefit for Eleanor House.

"Go for it, Toots. Shine the floodlight on the old lady. She deserves the applause. But so do you."

After the scandal, she had taken her name off the organization's letterhead and kept her participation secret, so as not to damage further the organization's chances of surviving, even after she had endowed it anonymously with the sizable sum from the sale of the de' Medici cross. Eventually, though, she had resumed her rightful place as founder and now was its most vocal spokesperson. She had even added Princess Grace to her board. In a bold move engineered by herself and carefully controlled by Lefty, she allowed a women's page feature on herself, the making of *The Eleanor Years,* and the twelve thriving Eleanor Houses to run in the *Los Angeles Times.* Claire was careful to protect Sara from the reporter working on the piece. Evidently Sara was surviving, if not exactly thriving, at the Eleanor House in New York. Teaching poetry, of all things, and helping place the older, less wanted orphans in homes. Although it disturbed Claire that she hadn't heard a word from Sara herself—it was the home's director who kept her informed—she busied herself in her film in order to do what she had promised her daughter. Leave her alone.

After the *Times* article appeared, Claire started to receive weekly mea culpa letters from Fenwick Grant himself, whose company owned the rival *L.A. Spectator* and four other California newspapers, calling for a truce. She paid no heed to his condescending requests for her to be generous and leave the past behind them, even going so far as to offer to run an apology on his editorial pages.

"What is he, fucking nuts?" asked Lefty. "You can only call a truce when one guy recognizes the other as an equal."

In his next letter Grant offered her the cover of *Sunday News Magazine,* which was inserted into all twenty-five of his newspapers. Along with "her version" of the Duccio murder. Was this abominable man never going to get the point?

"The nerve of him!" Claire tossed Grant's latest letter onto her husband's desk. "His papers branded me a murderess. I was never officially charged."

"Yeah, you could *show* him how you did it, using him as the next victim." Even though Lefty knew the truth, and even through they shared everything, including his socks when her feet got cold and the scrambled eggs she whipped up for Sunday supper, Claire would never betray Sara's actions that day to another living soul. And so Sara's role in the murder was never again discussed. Not even with dear old Lefty, who had a heart as big as all Bel-Air.

There was only one other part of her life she didn't share with him—Harrison's poignant letters, the ones she read privately and then refolded, placing them in her only locked drawer.

The Washington premiere of *The Eleanor Years* on September 25, 1962, was a heady assemblage of reigning politicians, Hollywood royalty, a real Kennedy roundup, and a gathering of the Roosevelt clan. Every living member of the Roosevelt family and all surviving members of Franklin's White House still standing showed up at the black-tie salute to "Our Lady of the New Deal." Claire was particularly excited because Harrison was supposed to be coming as part of Eleanor's party. Anna had told her. So she paid extra attention to her appearance, trying on outfit after outfit until Lefty assured her she looked like an entirely different Claire: Claire Lefkowitz, Producer. Her shiny hair was swept off her face in a bouffant. On her white satin dinner suit, the short skirt emphasizing her long-stemmed legs, she had pinned an *Eleanor for President* button.

Pam Churchill arrived arm-in-arm with Broadway producer Leland Hayward, her new husband and her former friend Slim Hayward's old one. When Harrison showed up, proud as punch, with his old friends Archibald and Starling Fillmore, Claire felt his eyes on her and blushed the shade of the theater curtain. She stole a few glances at him. She wondered how much she had changed in the five years since she had seen him—would he still find her desirable?—but when their eyes locked, her question was answered. The Aunties sat in a balcony box next to the one reserved for President and Mrs. Kennedy, his red plush seat replaced by a waiting rocking chair.

As much as Auntie Slim loved Claire, she forgot all about the film once the first lady and the president arrived. Kennedy had forgone the closed-circuit television heavyweight boxing match between Floyd Patterson and Sonny Liston to attend.

"You see, Jack," Slim overheard Jackie gaily whisper into the president's ear, "all the heavyweights are *here.*"

But Sara wasn't, although her seat remained empty, just in case she changed her mind and came after all. There was no telling with Sara. There were signs, though, and Claire cherished every one of them, that her daughter was making a tentative place for herself in the world, one set apart from both Hollywood and Tuxedo Park. When Sara adamantly refused to join the other debutantes in what would have been her own coming-out season, Ophelia had come to the realization that maybe Sara really was crazy. She agreed to let Sara leave her first semester at Vassar and move into the New York City branch of Eleanor House, where she was now a resident teacher to the younger children. To the ladies of her clubs, Ophelia passed off her granddaughter's decision to choose social work over high society as proof of the Harrisons' outstanding philanthropic spirit.

Claire anxiously watched the back of E.R.'s head for her response, and was conscious of exhaling for the first time since the lights had dimmed when the former first lady patted her eyes with Anna's handkerchief. She pointed and laughed at the earnest young girl she was on the screen, clutching her diary as her voice-over said, "I wasn't really sure that I would have anything interesting to record." The audience loved being in on the joke and laughed with her. There had been enough interesting times to fill volumes.

"Did you notice the Kennedys and the Roosevelts have the same kind of teeth?" Lefty elbowed Claire like it was some sort of astute political observation as the audience applauded and rose to its feet. *The Eleanor Years* was a hit, a critical success among the people whose approval mattered to Claire.

Claire was able by now to do several things at once, so she smiled head-on for the cameras, accepted her kudos with grace, kept an eye out for Sara and another out for Harrison as she double-checked out the place cards at her table. The incorrigible Fenwick Grant had somehow connived his way into the seat next to hers. By now, her actions were rote. She simply took his place card and moved it down to the far end of the long table.

Too exhilarated to eat, she just watched the others. She was enchanted by the way Jackie held the rapt attention of both her dinner partners with her little-girl voice and grown-up wit. She admired how Eleanor held up her end of the table with anecdotes about Franklin, often making herself the butt of her own jokes. She observed with some interest when Starling Fillmore dropped three lumps of sugar into her husband's coffee and then two into Harrison's without bothering to ask. How very cozy, Claire thought, and wondered why the little scene rattled her. She shifted her gaze to Mrs. Archibald Vanderbilt Fillmore, analyzing her like an actress the Lefkowitz Talent Agency might sign up. If Claire had included the Lucy Mercer chapter in her documentary, Starling Fillmore could have played the part on a moment's notice. Well into her fifties, she still possessed the unruffled calm of a woman who had never had a truly troubling thought startle the neurons of her brain.

Long-lashed, longer-necked, she prettily wore a slightly puzzled look on her delicate features as if she were constantly wondering, Two lumps or three? There was something even more familiar about Harrison's friend's wife, but Claire couldn't quite put her finger on it.

It wasn't until the after-dinner brandy and bonbons were served that Claire caught Harrison's eye. He rose to move to her side of the table, wearing the expectant look of a man with a promise to deliver. But as President and Mrs. Kennedy decided to leave at the same time that Mrs. Roosevelt stood, the whole table was suddenly hindered by a phalanx of burly Secret Service men. So Harrison and Claire's words together went unspoken and the moment vanished. Later at the curb as the limousines and taxi cabs queued up, Claire caught a closer glimpse of Mrs. Fillmore and her two escorts. The slight woman daintily sidestepped a puddle even as she pointed it out for both of them to avoid. She spoke quietly, first into one's ear and then the other's, informing the men who the approaching senator from Virginia was with or what Ethel Kennedy right behind them had named her last child.

It suddenly dawned on Claire who Mrs. Fillmore reminded her of. Herself. The young, adoring Claire who had worked as Harrison's assistant, anticipating all his needs, smoothing out the wrinkles. She wondered if the soft-spoken Mrs. Fillmore lit Harrison's cigar before or after she lit her husband's. As one more photograph of Claire was snapped with Eleanor and the political editor of the *Washington Post* blocked her path to the departing Harrison and promised her she'd love tomorrow's coverage for a change, she felt an onrush of sadness. How many Claires ago was that unquestioning girl whom Harrison had fallen in love with? How many reinventions was she removed from that Claire, protected by the strong shoulders of her mentor and all-consumed with pleasing him? She wondered if that trusting innocent to whom no harm had yet been done was still visible beneath the dazzling disguise of the fiercely independent working wife with a smash movie up her sleeve. She hoped so, but she knew it was out of necessity that she had changed her outside colors. In order to survive.

*   *   *

With the success of *The Eleanor Years* came invitations to speak at
Democratic lunches, teas, and women's groups of every size.
Often she tossed aside her notes on Eleanor, using them only as a
jumping-off point, and addressed the very modern issues that
were close to her heart: children's education and mental health,
and women's rights. Claire brightened when the question-and-
answer period after her speeches began to focus on requests for her
to talk about Eleanor House or even enter politics herself rather
than the infamous de' Medici cross and her days as a "party girl."
But when, after a few years of hard work on state party commissions and children's welfare reforms, that phrase appeared in a
piece in the *Los Angeles Times,* it was referring not to her hostessing skills, but to her effectiveness in the party of Roosevelt and
Kennedy.

It was curious how, in the age of jet planes and telephones,
Claire's contact with the two people she loved most was through
the mail. Harrison's letters from his new home on Lake Como
were a precise recounting of his progress on a three-volume mem-
oir of the war years that he had finally begun. But between the
lines she could read his unwritten message: Italy wasn't the same
without her. He complained that he couldn't find a satisfactory
researcher, firing one after another. He listed the things they
couldn't do: organize his notes, relive the historical past with
him, plan his day, inspire him. "Indeed, all the things you, my
dear Claire, do so well." He described the lake, its sunsets and
scents, but it was all unnecessary. Claire had already etched every
detail of their lake idyll in her mind. She stared out in her Bel Air
garden at the silk floss tree with its pink blossoms and dreamed
of Italian olive trees. She wondered how much more damage
would be done if she followed her girlish heart instead of her
grown woman's obligations.

She answered his letters on her Claire Harrison Lefkowitz stationery, the blue sheets from I. Magnin. Although she kept her news breezy and her sentiments to herself, she'd usually mail them with rare stamps from her collection, knowing they would speak volumes to Harrison, who understood their priceless value.

When Sara made contact it was with terse messages scribbled on file cards and stuffed into Eleanor House envelopes. Sometimes she forgot to stamp them, and when they arrived it was with postage due. They were like telegrams, just enough words to express Sara's outrage when an adopting couple wanted to exchange their orphan for one who was younger or whose eyes were a brighter color, or her quiet pride in one of her young pupils. Claire was glad her daughter shared her social conscience, gladder still that she shared anything at all with her. Occasionally her brief notes would mention a young poetry professor "with the kindest voice" who volunteered with her on weekends, and Claire thought she was finally starting to detect the normal stirrings of a young woman in Sara. Claire had to read between the lines wherever she could before Sara's communication cut off sharply with a quick "Gotta go."

Over the following years, she made arrangements twice to meet Harrison. But once Sara surprised her with a weekend visit, and the next time, she tried to steal a quick moment to meet him for lunch when she and Lefty were in New York for the opening of his new production of the play *A Hole in the Heart,* but had been literally turned around in the lobby. Lefty whirled her full circle in the hotel's revolving door as he was arriving with Wildenstein the art dealer and an enormous Chagall between them. He'd bought the painting with his anticipated proceeds from the play.

After that, Harrison's letters turned more formal, but they evoked just as much emotion. Particularly when he sent her a set of architect's drawings. Did she remember Isola Bella? It was the one they could see from their bed during the days of their Italian idyll. He'd purchased the villa and was modernizing it, complete with American plumbing. How like Harrison to expect precision in paradise, Claire mused, but her eyes were moist as she put the plans in her drawer along with his other letters.

The day Harrison telephoned, Lefty had gone to the doctor's office to get something stronger for the nagging pain in his gut. He kept a veritable pharmacy in a special locked lizard briefcase as it was. It had a secret combination because they didn't want Sara helping herself on one of her drop-ins to his stash of Tuinal, Seconal, phenobarbital, and Tums, mixing some sort of pharmaceutical cocktail. Although Sara seemed to be on the road to composing a quiet life for herself, there were still occasional disturbing U-turns and detours.

Harrison's voice over the phone sounded the way Claire felt. Distressed. His voice carried all the suppressed emotion it had conveyed the day she had picked him up at the airport after FDR had died. Now he had lost his second best friend, Archibald Fillmore, who, though Harrison's senior by a mere seven years, was the first contemporary of his to die. Back in New York to serve as pallbearer and trustee for the estate, he was dismally glum, not just over the lost companionship, he told Claire, but because it reminded him that his life was speeding on by, and couldn't she . . .

No matter how she longed to up and sail away with him, to love him on their private island instead of only in her secret heart, Lefty's car horn honking in the driveway and Sara's scribbled postcard on the kitchen counter reminded Claire of her commitments and obligations. She forced herself to cut the phone call short, almost choking as she repeated the message from Sara in front of her: "Gotta go."

If she threw herself into her political speeches, lobbied Congress for mothers' rights in cases of divorce, preoccupied herself with her and Lefty's clients, all the time keeping tabs on Sara, there were moments in the day when she didn't think about Harrison and all the might-have-beens. She made a stirring speech for child advocacy in front of a clearly moved state legislature in Sacramento, but the throaty catch in her voice was already there for another reason.

She even started preparing elaborate suppers, cooking fancy recipes herself so that she wouldn't have any free time at all for regrets, not that Lefty was eating much more these days than custard and chicken hash seasoned with Alka-Seltzer. He explained that if he ate only things that were the color white, he had fewer knots in his stomach.

One night Dr. Sax came to dinner—clear broth, white chicken, white toast, and tapioca—to break the news to them. Lefty was suffering from stomach cancer and there was "trouble in the colon" as well.

"She's the best goddamned nurse on the face of the planet," Lefty boasted to Dr. Sax after several months of surgeries and chemotherapy. "She can change a catheter better than anyone at Cedars-Sinai and look cute doing it. Neither one of us minds my baldness, Doc, because I've been bald since my bar mitzvah," Lefty joked. His spirits were unfailing.

The Lefkowitzes kept Lefty's sickness secret, Hollywood being the kind of town that would have him buried with the "Big C" before he was done with lunch. No, better to keep up appearances. The success of *A Hole in the Heart* had paid for Lefty's Chagall and a strand of real pearls for Claire. But it couldn't carry them through constant surgeries and expensive doctors if they both stopped working. So Claire shouldered the extra responsibilities of running the agency, entertaining clients at early dinners before Lefty got too tired, sometimes staging his appearance at a visible event so he could be photographed and the pictures strategically run for weeks. Like when Ronald Reagan became Governor of California and appointed Claire to oversee the California Commission on Child Welfare—their old Hollywood friend picking the girl and not her party. Before her induction, they had Sid the tailor over to the house to pad one of Lefty's suits so he would look like he had some meat on his bones after eighteen months of sickness and weeks of ingesting liquid meals through a tube.

"Think quarterback, Sid. Stuff me. And make Claire something, too. She deserves it."

And so she held her head high and wore Lefty's pearls around her neck, medical bills mounting, and dreamed of Lake Como as she and Lorenza carried him from bedroom to living room so that he could welcome his visitors like a gentleman in his BarcaLounger, under the Chagall painting of an upside-down groom and his bride dancing in front of a laughing cow.

"See that, Toots? It's my favorite picture. But when I'm gone, sell it and buy something interesting."

"Oh, Lefty, don't talk like that. You're not going—"

"Yeah, I am, Toots, and since you're not coming with—not for a long time—promise me you'll sell the picture and get something terrific for yourself."

"Like what?"

"Something important . . . like a political career."

Claire laughed. She'd hardly laughed in the last few months. There'd been dozens of emergency rides to the hospital, so many that Lefty had memorized the ambulance drivers' names and kibbitzed with them even as they untangled his life-support tubes. She hadn't even answered her mail or opened Harrison's last five or six letters. She didn't think she could bear to hear about Italy right now. Romantic Lake Como. She didn't want to feel guilty betraying Lefty, even if it was only in her thoughts. If she didn't open Harrison's letters she wouldn't be tempted to long for him. But once in a while it was nice to close her eyes and dream, momentarily wiping out the smells of rubber sheets and isopropyl alcohol.

Eventually, Lefty grew too weak to be helped down the stairs, so before his oldest clients and friends began arriving for the cocktail hour, Lorenza and she helped fold a shrunken Lefty into the dumbwaiter so he could ride down.

"I'm coming down with the lamb shanks and the matzo balls," he quipped. "Just make sure I'm riding with the good silver."

After that he zoned in and out of consciousness. So when he told Claire that Sara had been to see him, she chalked it up to the effects of medication. But the nurse confirmed that her daughter with the wild red mane of hair had come and gone.

"What? She was here? Why didn't she stay to see me?" Claire felt betrayed. After a year of nursing Lefty in a fluorescent room filled with whirring machines and IV tubes, she needed someone to talk to.

"Listen, Toots, it was my deathbed scene. What you should be proud of is that she came. Maybe she never will be your best buddy. But the point is, there's a good person inside your demon daughter."

Turning away her tear-stained face, she gathered up the Sunday *New York Times*. He loved it when she read to him.

"And don't forget, Toots, if I check out on some Wednesday I want you back on the block by Friday. You've been sitting shiva for a year now. Enough."

Claire smiled and turned to Section One to read the political news. Her heart stopped as she saw the picture and read the story.

Ambassador William Henry Harrison IV of New York and Washington wed Starling Millbrook Fillmore of Tuxedo Park and Newport in the ambassador's home on Lake Como, where he is at work on Volume II of his series *The Roosevelt Years.*

Claire let out such an anguished sigh while her muscles shook visibly out of control that Lefty asked Lorenza to help him up to hold his wife.

"Somebody has to console her in her grief. Might as well be me." He rocked her gently in his arms. "C'mon, Toots. Don't lose it now. We're in the home stretch."

She nodded through her tears. "Did I ever tell you that I love you, Lefty?"

His smile was broad. "No, but I kinda figgered. You coulda left with the big tweedy guy anytime, but you always stayed. I never did understand why. I'm sure you get points for that."

And they held each other, giving each other the gentle comfort they had always reserved only for one another.

After Lefty was buried at Hillside Memorial Park, Claire sat shiva for two nights, hosting Lefty's friends and serving his favorite deli platters from Nate 'n' Al's. On the third night, however, even as the guests were arriving to read prayers and pay their condolences, Claire was out the door and winging her way to Washington with a long gown in a garment bag thrown over her arms. She was headed to the black-tie Chagall retrospective at the National Gallery of Art to rearrange the place cards.

She was going to seat herself next to Fenwick Grant.

Chapter Seventeen

Party Girl

A woman's life can really be a succession of lives, each revolving around some emotionally compelling situation or challenge.
—*Wallis, Duchess of Windsor*

The caviar canapés and sturgeon-lined baskets of quail's eggs were floating around the room on silver trays held aloft by white-gloved waiters. Quite a contrast, Claire thought, to the hospital food and gray uniformed orderlies of the past year. In the marble galleries of the museum, Claire turned heads as she beelined her way to his table. In Washington, apparently, black-gowned widows didn't barge uninvited into gala affairs.

Fenwick Grant raised one eyebrow as she deftly purloined the place card next to his and replaced it with the one in her hand.

"I figured I'd be hearing from you. Just not so soon. Sorry about Lefty." He squared his shoulders. Grant was a hard-boiled newspaperman, and Lefty had died three days ago—yesterday's news, as far as he was concerned. He watched her as she re-arranged the seating as if the National Gallery of Art were her private dining room, putting herself on Grant's left.

"I always knew you were crazy about me."

"Don't flatter yourself. I have to file in two days if I run for Hathaway's vacant congressional seat. I want to know if I have your support. Pass the butter."

Grant handed her his butter plate. Apparently Lefty had willed her his chutzpah.

He liked her style, the notorious air that she breezily carried around like an expensive accessory, the vanilla-like smell mixed with something musky, and her softly delivered tough talk. He noticed, though, that she was a good ten pounds thinner than the last time he'd seen her, and there were faint blue shadows under her eyes.

"I was wondering if I could meet your editorial staff in your office tomorrow morning? The from-the-horse's-mouth sort of thing—just so nothing gets lost in the translation when I plead my platform. You have fifty-six or fifty-seven papers in your news empire? How about if your California dailies endorse me and cover me favorably and the others print good national coverage? Sorry to hurry you, Grant, but I need to know before dessert."

He thought the expectant look on her face was delicious. "Why not just give me until the chicken à la king gets cold? Don't stand on ceremony or be shy. Just say what's on your mind." His newspaperman's eyes reappraised her. "You won't quite fit in, Claire. You're too attractive. You know what I've always said: Politics is Hollywood for ugly people."

Claire covered her laugh with a black handkerchief.

"Careful, Claire, you've got a new reputation to uphold. Congressional politics is a different game. And Washington's a pretty stodgy town."

"That reminds me. I'd like you to fire Anita Lace in the morning. I'll be in at nine-thirty A.M., so why don't you break the news to the little darling at nine-fifteen?"

Grant was intrigued. "And precisely what does Grant Publications get in return?"

"Lefty's deathbed forgiveness. You'll be back in the Hollywood inner circle. Your entertainment reporters will be back in the loop. Deal?"

"Ax Lace at nine-fifteen. Smoke the peace pipe with you at nine thirty."

Fenwick Grant felt he was being railroaded, but it promised to be an interesting ride. Each time this lady reinvented herself to fit into the changing terrain, she went all out. First a socialite, then a murderess, then a Hollywood power broker. Writing about Claire as candidate would certainly be a circulation booster. And an endorsement now, he thought to himself, didn't mean he couldn't do an exposé later.

He grinned widely, smile lines extending all the way to his ears, as they shook on it.

"Do you actually have a platform, or is this some California analyst's therapy for getting over Lefty?"

"We can go over my platform point by point tomorrow in your office." The reporter in him sensed her intentions. She would not tell him more news tonight. He shifted gears.

"Did you happen to see the Chagall exhibit as you walked in?"

"It's extraordinary. Lefty loved Chagall."

"Winthrop Pauling underwrote the show. He and his wife are major collectors. They convinced the lender of the huge blue-and-yellow painting to sell to them. It's in the arts and style feature in Sunday's paper. Anita Lace did the story." Grant waited for her reaction to the name. Out of all the publications in his tightly run empire he was most proud of the Washington *Herald.* Even more than *U.S. Week,* which was number two, just behind *Time* magazine. Grant leveled his gaze at this woman who had been news in the "People" section of both of them, a half-smirk on his ruggedly handsome face.

Claire smirked back. She had her own plan for dealing with her poison-pen nemesis. Now she was merely wondering if the Paulings had an early Chagall in deep reds, yellows, and blues of a bride and groom and a cow in their collection.

"Where are the Paulings?" Claire turned and craned her neck.

"Two tables over, with your Senator and Mrs. Bostwick, and Averell Harriman and his wife." He angled his lantern jaw in the Paulings' direction.

"Thank you, Mr. Grant. See you in the morning." And Claire picked up her place card and moved toward the Paulings' table.

"Oh, and let your date know, I only ate her roll. I didn't touch her silverware. I'll have the waiter tell her your 'emergency interview' is over." She flashed him her best diplomatic smile, tinged with just enough Hollywood to make it interesting. "What's her name again?"

Suddenly Fenwick Grant couldn't remember.

"Patience," he called after her. "I just remembered. Her name is Patience." There was a wolfish grin on his lips as he watched the way her back curved into her narrow hips.

But Claire was already on her way. She had lovingly nursed dear Lefty night and day for two years. She was forty-two years old and there was an open seat in Congress for which she had two days left to file and announce. Now she had neither time nor patience.

On her way early the next morning to the chrome-and-green-glass headquarters of Grant Publications, Claire thought how proud Lefty would be of her. She whirled herself through the revolving doors of the imposingly ugly building. Last night she had made her pact with power, brokered a calculated peace with the press, sold the Chagall for her campaign chest, and scheduled a lunch with California's influential Senator Bostwick. All between cocktails and dessert. She had one thing left to do. Her high heels resonated with authority on the speckled marble floor. In an effort to blend in with the Washington crowd, she hadn't accessorized her severely cut business suit with anything except white gloves and Lefty's pearls. Still, she could tell from the newsroom stares that her demeanor was still more Bel Air than Beltway, as if her shiny Hollywood veneer couldn't be scrubbed away overnight.

She followed the explicit directions Grant's secretary had given her to the labyrinthine newsroom with its vast expanse of desks all topped by ringing telephones and whirring typewriters. There in the center of it all she found a red-faced Anita Lace angrily emptying out the messy contents of her desk drawers and muttering under her breath. Her short gray-and-brown hair bristled around her square head. She wore half-glasses hanging from her neck on a plastic lavaliere, and was skinny everywhere except around her ankles. Claire was reminded of the loyal battalions of humorless, thick-necked women in Eleanor's army. When Anita looked up and saw Claire standing over her she hurled a few spicy expletives before she went back to collecting her clutter.

"Come to gloat, have you?"

"No. Actually, I hear you might be in the market for a job. I thought I might employ you."

"You bitch. I don't do social secretary stuff. I ought to thank you. Maybe now I can go back to politics," she mumbled, a cigarette dangling from her dry lips.

"That's exactly what I had in mind. I'm running for the House of Representatives. Hathaway's seat. And I need the savviest press secretary around. Someone who's not afraid to talk back to me."

"After what I've done to you?"

Lefty's words rumbled through Claire's mind: "Get the press, Toots, before they get you. Bring out your own skeletons—they're less interesting if you clean out your own closet!"

"Yes, Anita. You know the facts. You certainly know how to misrepresent them. And you were the best war reporter around until you started your social skullduggery."

It was hard to tell if the red flush on Anita's face was from embarrassment or some oxygen deprivation caused by trying to light a fresh cigarette while hanging her head down in a deep drawer to remove her things.

"But I butchered you."

"So you can butcher my opponent. Furthermore, you'll be able to anticipate the worst they could print about me and deflect it. But I shall expect and demand absolute loyalty from you." She leaned down to ignite Anita's dangling cigarette. "We'll play war, Anita, but we can win and make a difference. I never took what you wrote about me personally. You only put Ophelia's vitriol into colorful sentences." A fleeting look of remembered sorrow crossed Claire's face.

"I want to make sure divorced mothers don't lose custody of their children just because they're poor. Like I almost did before I moved to Italy. Anita, I want to make children's rights a real issue. Along with day care and affordable health care for families with catastrophic illnesses. Like cancer." An impassioned Claire continued even as she brought her voice to a lower pitch. "You know, the feminists are just discovering what my aunties have always known. That women pulling together leads to women's power."

Anita perked up. She had been born a liberal Democrat.

And then Claire closed her deal with what she hoped would be the clincher. "I want to make certain women get equal pay for equal work. And I'll make damn sure good writers don't get demoted just because they're women." She watched as the thought sparked Anita's attention. "Of course, you'll be my speechwriter, too. Let's take on the big boys."

It was as if Anita were a middle-aged Cinderella finally getting invited to the palace. "My gawd. You're the glam Eleanor."

She stretched out her nail-bitten hand to Claire, her fingers black with typewriter ribbon. "So if we get you elected I'll be press secretary. Right?"

"Absolutely."

Anita slammed the desk drawer. She wouldn't be needing the phone numbers of chatty hotel concierges and maître d's, her trusty spies for her social column, anymore. If Claire won, Anita could call her own shots from the hallowed marbled halls on Capitol Hill. As Congressman Glam's press secretary. Or chief of staff. Who knew where this thing might go?

"So, Mrs. Lefkowitz, where do we begin?"

"We're going to write my announcement speech. It will be televised throughout the state. The power of television is politically underutilized. I think I understand the medium." She linked her arm through Anita's as she led the elfin woman down the hall to Grant's office and caused a commotion, shutting down the Smith Coronas in the city newsroom. The Poison Pen and her most maligned victim nodded in sync, separated by a good five inches in height but somehow with their heads huddled together.

"Incidentally, I'm going back to my Washington roots."

The social scribe, caught off balance, crankily pointed a finger toward Claire's scalp. "What roots?"

"Oh, not my hair." Claire caught her drift. "Just my name. I'm Claire Harrison again. It's simpler to remember."

"And it's probably the most famous political name in America." Anita marveled at both Claire's political savvy and her guts.

"It's the name I share with my daughter."

"Oh, right. Will she come out for you?" Anita vividly remembered being instructed by Ophelia not to cover Sara's electroshock treatments and Claire's constant efforts to get help for her daughter, who had been relegated to the side shadows by the grandmother. She hadn't spoken to the old witch in years, but she'd heard that Ophelia had gone nuts herself when Sara had refused to attend the Tuxedo Hunt Ball on the arm of Edward Langley. Young Langley, of the Baltimore Langleys, had been in Sara's "class" at Wolford for shooting the family's house cats. "Is she still bonkers?"

Claire bristled at the question.

"Thought so. See? That's your weak spot. We'll have to work on your reaction. Reporters will ask you that." She tugged on an unadorned earlobe. "Will Sara be campaigning for you?"

Claire composed herself. "Well, she's busy with her own life. She's getting married."

"What?" Anita's rubber soles skidded to a stop. She had

thought the kid was too crazy to marry. "Oh. I get it. Something you arranged. Some blue-blood schnook who wants to marry into the family. And Sara gets a love life. Good idea. America loves weddings."

"Then they'll be disappointed. The young man is a poetry teacher. He's very nice. But the baby will be born soon after the wedding."

She delivered the line calmly, but the hawk-eyed Anita could see her distress.

"Yeah, I get it. Maybe she should just work the phone bank. Any more surprises?"

"Just me."

Anita wondered if the family thing might be a campaign obstacle. This certainly wasn't Beaver and Mrs. Cleaver. Not to mention those damn good looks of Claire's.

"How do you get along with Mrs. Average America? You know, will other gals vote for you?"

"I'm a gal."

Amazed, Anita scratched some dandruff out of her hair and wondered what kind of speech would catapult Claire Harrison— "Why don't you all just forget about the Duccio years and leave out the Lefkowitz?"—into the hearts of the California voters.

"When is this speech scheduled?"

"Sunday. Right after *The Wonderful World of Disney.*"

"How the hell did you get the Sunday prime spot?"

"Oh, I called a friend at Desilu."

Anita smiled. The glam Eleanor knew how to play with power. She had come a long way since Anita had been hired to hack away at the victimized fashion plate.

"Well, your family *has* to be there. American women without families on the podium are suspect."

"But I've just been widowed."

"In that case, people will expect you to stay at home."

"I can't. I want to run. I promised Lefty."

"Shit." Anita coughed. "Divorced, double widow, with an off-the-wall kid, running for your United States Representative. Just what middle America is pining for."

"I've got my war years record. The State Department liaison work under Harrison. Eleanor House. Co-owner of a film and television agency. Two state educational review boards—"

Speargun murderer, thought Anita. Had *that* been analyzed in a poll? "Well, it's not exactly like you won the Purple Heart."

"Trust me, Anita. We can do it. You're the toughest and the best. Why don't you go pack up your things and be ready by four?" She called over her slim shoulder, "We're flying back to L.A. and getting down to work. How do you like that slogan? 'Women getting down to work.' Oh, it reminds me. While I'm in with Grant, why don't you get that new group, the National Organization for Women, to endorse me. Good idea?" And then Claire threw in the Lefty clincher, Lefty-style: "Right, Toots? We're all broads under the skin."

Anita stood in the hall, shaking her head and wondering if trying to get Claire Harrison elected was some sort of divine punishment for having ground the woman into the mud. But she liked the smooth way Claire had reeled her in. Not demoting top gun reporters to the society beat just because they were women. Anita was hooked.

"Yeah, sure, I'm in," she snapped. She stood there in her mannish, putty-colored suit and ground a cigarette into the elevator ash can with her fist. Power to the broads.

Anita couldn't believe it when Shirley Temple Black, who had been appointed U.N. ambassador earlier in the year, agreed to stand beside Claire on the podium. The gruff press secretary pedaled her feet as fast as she could to keep up with Claire, quizzing her as she ran alongside.

"How were you able to pull that off?"

Claire simply grinned and whispered, "Marshall Field's and Company," as if it had been a clearinghouse for the world's most powerful women instead of a giant department store.

"Well, other than the fact that she's a Republican and tap-danced on film with a man who played her black slave, it's peachy."

Anita still couldn't figure what to do with the fashion part of Claire's life. There were so many portraits of her still reprinted in *Vogue* and *Town and Country* wearing haute couture creations and far-away expressions that it was as if Claire were running not against her opponent, but her old image. "For God's sake, if they ask you about Johnson's Great Society remember it's not some big bash you attended.

"And watch you don't tumble on the q-and-a. Good God, there are so many questions the reporters could trip you up on. We're not ready yet!" They were only a few yards from the podium and the plunge into public scrutiny.

"Gracious, Anita, I'm only running for Congress, not the pope's wife."

"But that's just the point. You've been *everybody's* wife."

"Not everybody's." Anita Lace, ace reporter, thought she heard a twinge of regret in the candidate's voice just before it deepened into a bell-like ring of distinction and she ascended the platform. "I am running as my own woman. Now."

Shirley Temple Black delivered a bright-eyed introduction, and Claire, remembering to sparkle, threw her Halston hat into the ring.

It didn't hurt when her Republican opponent, Bill Strudel, was labeled by Grant's Los Angeles newspaper as "Mr. Milquetoast," but Claire still was trailing him miserably in the polls. In newspapers other than Grant's she was still relegated to the entertainment pages or society news—one photo of Claire opening a preschool day-care center in central L.A. where hot lunches would be served ran in the food section—while, as state's attorney, Bill Strudel's daily pronouncements on parking meters or redwood trees were reported on page one. She needed to break out of her old mold, become a tough political chameleon, one who could survive the land-mined terrain of electoral politics and fit in with the good old boys.

She worked her "small crowds," as Anita referred to the handful of women who turned out to meet the candidate at high teas and shopping centers. She'd stand at a bus stop for hours, speaking through a megaphone or shaking hands with passersby. Occasionally someone asked her if she was waiting for the uptown express.

But little by little she started to do better in the shopping centers. As a child reared in the do-without Depression, a former shop girl, and an enforced penny-pincher during the nonworking years as Lefty's nurse, she knew the price of milk and eggs, medicines, as well as Tide detergent and Dial soap.

"Hey, Claire, ever been in a grocery store like the rest of us?" one loudmouthed heckler shouted out to her in front of Claire's station wagon while they were passing out buttons and pamphlets from the tailgate. These were always the ones who asked her to autograph a veiled Claire Duccio photo or her Irving Penn portrait from *U.S. Week* or *Life.*

"You bet. I do all my own grocery shopping."

"Well, how much does caviar cost these days?" The heckler leaned back on her sandals and let her words carry into the group, causing a stirring of giggles.

The bored *L.A. Times* cub political reporter grudgingly sent out to cover Claire that day poised his pen over his pad and started listening. He already had his headline: "Claire on Caviar: The Party Girl's Campaign for Congress." He waited for her to flesh out his comic-relief story.

"Never touch the stuff myself. But if its to your liking, I hope you buy the California kind. It'll keep our dollars in our local economy." She shot the reporter a Lefty look. "Cut, wrap, end of story."

And women started to like her. There was always the gossipy fringe group that came to press the flesh of someone they had read about in the glossies for years, and to please them Claire might tell a light anecdote or two. If a little tip about the La Leche mothers' breast-feeding method from the lovely princess of Monaco or Eleanor Roosevelt's recipes for scrambled eggs following her speech on financial parity for women or children's advocacy programs garnered her additional votes, she could handle it. After all, she had been trained to read a room and cater to it. Slowly her popularity was growing.

From her mother and, later, the duchess of Windsor, Claire had picked up the uncanny knack for making everyone else around her feel important. She locked her violet eyes on someone's face and just listened, listened like their opinion was the single solution to the cold war or would settle the Cuban problem once and for all. She cocked her head at an angle and listened until her target was exhausted from being listened to. Anyone who came under Claire's listening spell became her devoted supporter, but Claire couldn't go eye-to-eye with everyone in her congressional district, so she utilized her other skills.

She was always the first to write a thank-you note—the Aunties had taught her this courtesy—to the man who sent her five dollars as well as the lady who sent in five hundred. Sometimes she'd just pick up the telephone and call them to thank them—and sometimes reel them in as a volunteer or for an even bigger donation. Her Italian and smattering of Spanish stood her well in the California ethnic communities, and Lefty's Hollywood crowd threw star-studded political cocktail parties for her. But even with all that and Anita's bright, smart speeches, she couldn't reach the people in the middle. The ones who lived in one house with one husband and squeaky-clean children who hadn't shot their Italian stepfathers or been electroshocked at

Wolford. People who quietly went about their conventional lives—the ones who had never quite accepted her—and the ones who voted.

As much as Claire would have liked to have her daughter by her side, she refused to push Sara into the searing spotlight of the press. Sara had made dramatic headway in her private world at Eleanor House. And the sensitive young professor she had married treated her as delicately as he treated his prized first edition of T. S. Eliot. When one of Claire's campaign consultants booked a newspaper interview for Claire and her daughter, Claire vetoed it.

"Pictures are fine. But Sara's not running. I am. The voters should understand that. Cancel it." Claire had worked too hard to bring Sara to even the low end of normalcy to let anything—even her fierce desire to sit in Congress—undermine what was even more important to her: her fragile daughter's mental health.

Anita was ecstatic that the girl wouldn't be participating. She thought Sara's unpredictability was a dangerous liability and wanted her visible only as a quiet young woman waving from a distance, hard evidence that Claire was a real woman with a womb who had given birth and was a good grandmother, but clearly out of reach of snooping reporters.

Claire insisted just as fervently on buttons and bumper stickers that simply proclaimed, HARRISON FOR CONGRESS, with CLAIRE printed in small letters at the top. If the name evoked a hundred years of patriotic Harrisons, Harrisons who had already served their country proudly with a dozen special envoys, eight ambassadors, four-star generals, and two American presidents, Claire considered it her earned right to use it, sort of a belated divorce settlement from Ophelia and Harry. It wasn't important to Claire how she got to Congress, just that she got there.

Fenwick Grant started to appear on Claire's doorstep on his drop-ins to his Los Angeles paper with almost punctual spontaneity.

There they would have little strategy suppers like the new friends they were becoming. He would sit across the table from her and lift her spirits when they were sapped by events of the hard day. And she would listen intelligently, absorbing his advice. His ego needed no bolstering, but sometimes she could flatter another pro-Claire editorial out of him. If Anita was joining them, her head usually fell into her dessert of cigarettes and coffee by 10 P.M., and Claire had to shake her awake before leading her upstairs and tucking her in.

Tonight Grant was waiting, jacket off, shirtsleeves rolled up newsroom-style, when Claire hurried back down the stairs of the house she had shared with Lefty. On the dimly lit landing she caught her breath as she realized how much this man, with his foot rakishly posed on the stairs, his old school tie loosened, silver streaking his hair, resembled Harrison.

"Do you mind if I smoke a cigar?" He threw a flirtatious glance up the stairs. His Harvard-educated accent was polite, but the arrogant way he was already lighting his illegal Havana was pure chauvinistic Grant.

"You look very comfortable." She came down the last three steps in the same time she had taken to descend the rest of the staircase.

He had dozens of young women at his beck and call, but increasingly it was Claire's power and intellect that he could cozy up with.

"I've taken the liberty."

"I've been in so many smoke-filled rooms today I feel like some air. Would you mind?"

"What a terrific idea. I just happen to have a convertible parked in your driveway. Top down okay? I wouldn't want to muss the candidate's hair." His grin was appealingly boyish and matched his vulpine green-gray eyes. He left his jacket on the newel post to be retrieved later.

"Oh, I forgot to turn the outside lights on." Fortunately Claire was blushing in the dark, where no one could see.

"I'm like one of those nocturnal predators. My vision improves at night. Here, lean on me." His arm was tennis-server taut, his bare forearm firm and steady to her touch. Suddenly it felt comfortable to Claire to have someone to lean on again, even if it was only for the few steps to his racy car. As he opened the door for her, she caught a whiff of his unsubtle masculine smells: cigars, commingled with California sea air and a spicy aftershave.

Once in the creamy leather bucket seats, the Santa Monica mountain breezes rushing past her cheek, she felt almost girlish again. Sitting next to her, fiddling with the radio dials, was this tall and athletically built man, quite handsome in his blue and white broad-striped Turnbull and Asser shirt. It was odd how she had never once before felt the pull of his good looks. His full head of hair blew back neatly in the light wind, as if he had taken two Brylcreem-ed fingers and pushed the hair in that direction.

She let her head fall back and closed her eyes, not caring where the car was pointed.

Instinctively he knew he shouldn't talk politics with her tonight. "Claire, do you know how attractive you look when you're relaxed?"

Her peal of laughter was effervescent. "No, tell me. I need some positive editorial."

"Like I'd like to stop the car and take you in my arms."

"I'm running for Congress, Grant. And I'm a grandmother. Now what would a Washington A-list bachelor do with a grandmother?"

"Just off the top of my head? I could think of about fifty things to do with you." In the moonlight supplemented by passing street lamps, she caught a flash of his polished teeth and the flecks of warmth in his eyes. He took one large hand off the steering wheel and placed it on her knee.

"It's too soon, Grant." Claire's voice was soft but steady.

"It's been a year."

"Just seven months. Lefty and I shared a very happy decade. Ten years of closeness and continual gladness that is very rare. And it all just rushed by."

"You were a very good wife to him."

"He was a very dear husband."

"Well, I'm a rogue. But a charming one."

"I've noticed." The laughter was back in her voice.

"I'll try again, you realize." He put both hands back on the wheel.

"I'd be bloody furious with you if you didn't keep trying."

An hour later, they pulled into the darkened house on Alamedo Drive. She started to say good night in the car, but he reminded her that he had left his jacket in the foyer.

As they approached the door, the jangle of the telephone pierced the night. Lorenza hadn't spent nights at the house since Lefty died, and surely Anita was gone in an exhausted heap upstairs, probably with a cigarette stuck in her fingers. Claire frowned and picked up the phone. It was 1 A.M. Nothing good ever came from a telephone call at 1 A.M.

"Calling from where?" Claire raised her voice in response to the faraway static on the line. "Khartoum?"

"The Middle East." There was trouble in the Middle East, the publisher knew, and pricked up his ears.

"What kind of mission? Harrison, can you hear me?" Grant watched her as he folded his long arms across his chest and leaned impatiently against the lemon-tree-wallpapered foyer.

"Oh, dear. Yes. Quite the delicacy in Saudi Arabia. Oh no. No. Well, I hope she's better soon." Claire brought one delicate hand slowly down the front of her body, almost as if she were in a lover's embrace.

"But that was so dear of you. Yes, your luck matters to me. Hellooo. Hello? Harrison?" She looked both excited and disappointed as she put down the receiver.

"That was Ambassador Harrison calling from Cairo. I think. He's taken poor fragile Starling down the Nile, through Damascus and Beirut, and had her be guest of honor at the palace of the king of Saudi Arabia. You know what that means."

The media mogul didn't know, and he didn't like not knowing.

"The guest of honor—and his escort—gets served the delicacy du jour. In this case, sheep's eyes. And Harrison's wife is suffering some intestinal distress for it." She shook her head. "To travel that part of the world, you have to have a constitution like Harrison's." She paused, and then with just a hint of something—was it female rivalry?—in her voice, added, "Or mine."

Grant nodded with even more knowing than Claire.

"But mainly he called to wish me luck in the last debate on Tuesday. May we all have luck of the Nile gods."

Anita blew smoke out of her ears and shuffled the pollsters' papers. "No chance." She shook her head. "No chance in hell. We're done for."

"Don't polls ever lie? Surely people lie when they're polled, just to be polite." Auntie Wren was trying to make sunshine out of gloomy statistics.

"Nope. Turns out the citizens of this district want Harriet Nelson."

"Maybe they're not ready for a strong woman."

"Well, dear, maybe you could pretend to be more helpless. Men don't like pushy women. You could faint or something. Don't they have the sympathy vote out here?" Auntie Slim had become a political strategist.

Sara listened silently from her cushion on the floor as she combed young Violet's strawberry shock of hair.

"The margins are just too wide. I guess if Strudel falls down drunk in Tuesday's televised debate or Claire manages to bring the World Series home, or maybe put caviar on every table in California, we might see a turnaround."

"Never mind. However things turn out, it's been a good run. Sara, will you help prep me for the debate?"

"Can't. I have somewhere I have to go," Sara said, but continued to stare vaguely out the window as she fussed with her daughter's silky hair.

Claire wondered, not for the first time, if the campaign had put too much strain on her daughter. Every time she thought she'd made some headway in their delicate relationship, Sara would get skittish and retreat inside herself again or, worse, turn off her phone and shut her mother out again. "All right, dear. Auntie Slim, how about you?"

"Well, I hate to take the man's part but since your debate is only three nights away, I'll just have to play along. Imagine. *Moi.* A man!" At sixty-nine years old, Slim was slimmer than ever. "When Cyrus was alive, he used to say, 'Slim, if it's one thing you'll never be, it's a man.' " Since his death, their relationship had taken on a historical legitimacy.

The night of the debate, Claire's all-girl family turned out in force. Aunties Slim and Wren sat in the front row wearing crisp linen dresses in red, white, and blue. The ladies, both of whom collected Social Security checks, were still looking peppy and held small American flags on gold sticks in their laps, ready for the wave.

Violet and Mr. Zolla sat on the aisle. Violet's composed face hid her concern over her daughter's foray into a televised debate.

"I wish Claire had worn her white gloves. To show everyone she's a real lady," she whispered to Anita.

Anita Lace was enveloped in a fog of Pall Mall smoke even though she had just put out her last cigarette seconds before. "She'd be better off with a pair of Everlast boxing gloves. Bill Strudel is no gentleman."

"Oh, dear." Violet bit her lip as she gave Claire an encouraging

V-for-victory salute. She nervously wondered how long she should keep Sara's waiting chair empty.

She didn't have to wait more than a few minutes. Lana Turner tiptoed down the aisle in her dark glasses and a full-length white beaver coat, looking for any open seat, and pushed past the starstruck usher when she spied one up front and center. Anita saw the pure platinum actress wiggling down the sloped stairs of the Los Angeles P.S. 27 high school auditorium and hoped Lana was just lost. She couldn't really be walking toward Sara's seat.

"Holy shit. Let's pray the lights dim before she sits down." Anita felt her diverticulitis acting up.

Violet graciously extended her white-gloved hand to Lana's tan leather one trimmed in turkey feathers as they pressed the fabric.

The head of the League of Women Voters cleared her thin voice and introduced the state's attorney and his Democratic challenger. Bill Strudel won the toss of the coin and began his opening speech.

"Since the age of Washington, voting for our congressional representatives, deciding who is going to speak for you good folks at home has been a sacred American ritual. One that requires soul searching and serious reflection to find the right man"—he paused for emphasis—"to represent you." On cue, his hands went out to all the "you"s in the audience.

"This isn't about bumper stickers, bake-offs, or the price of fish eggs. Let's not let the little things distract us. This is about the big issues. Big business, big economies, big decisions. No, Mrs. Harrison, it's not about the price of eggs—it's about winning a war, victory in Vietnam! It's about fueling a nation, knowing about the big cogs and wheels that turn this world. Big-boy battles. Congress is no dinner party, Mrs. Harrison; it's not about chicken and eggs, whichever came first." He paused for a laugh. "I concede the kitchen to you, Mrs. Harrison. Leave Congress to me. In terms you can appreciate, Bill Strudel is as American as apple pie!"

Slim leaned in on Violet's right. "If he's so American, why is he wearing a Brioni suit? Hand-cut in Italy."

"Whaddaya say!" Anita gave a whistle.

"Oh, yes. That's the kind Johnny used to wear." Lana agreed.

After Anita rummaged for a scrap of paper and finally found the pencil stuck behind her ear, the note was written and passed up to Claire. Strudel was just concluding his opening speech.

"Quite a monologue," Lana remarked during his applause. "Are Claire's lines as good?"

Anita nodded and swallowed a diarrhea pill. Where was Sara? Somewhere along, Strudel would introduce his wife and the five little Strudels. What was Claire going to do? Introduce the Aunties and Lana?

Strudel shook hands with his slim opponent like a welter-weight in the ring and said into the stand-up mike, "You look terrific, Claire. Doesn't she, folks?"

"That was nice of him." Wren beamed back.

"Condescending little twerp," Slim said under her breath.

Claire stood elegantly poised, her hands straight by her side.

"Ladies and gentlemen, fellow registered voters of California, members of the free press, thank you for allowing me to join the best working political system in the world and to address you in the most democratic institution of its kind, the open town forum, in a public debate. I have traveled the world. I have seen up front and in person the other systems. After the war I served as an aide on the economic recovery mission in Europe and saw the darkness and destruction left by fascism and the strangling of free voices by a spreading communism, and let me tell you, ladies and gentlemen, it is good to be an American. Democracy is a good thing. It is good to live in a place where education is free and excellent, where medical care is available and unsurpassed, where fresh food is plentiful and affordable. I beg to differ, Mr. Strudel, but the price of eggs *does* matter. A thriving nation needs nurturing. And food, affordable food at fair prices, is one of our unassailable rights, along with a free press, free to criticize us, free to throw those same eggs at us when our leaders lose sight of the small issues that drive this big, wonderful country to greatness. Men and women, women and men, gainfully employed, earning equally, raising their families, families of every kind. We can be an even greater America if we try.

"Mr. Strudel has graciously complimented me on looking nice. Thank you, Mr. Strudel, you look nice, too. We both wanted to appear presentable at a televised event in which we both seek to represent this important district made up of good men and women, people who have worked in this great country for fifty years, like my mother over there, never missing an opportunity to vote, and people who were naturalized yesterday and are voting in their first election, all of us good Americans. To speak to you tonight I chose to wear this nice suit sewn by the garment workers of America, under the union label. See? The American union workers have my vote of confidence. They have my business. Mr. Strudel complimented me tonight on my appearance. I compliment him on his. But it worries me that he wants to represent you wearing a suit made not in American but in Italy. I wholeheartedly endorse free trade, but I also wholeheartedly support the American worker. Little things do matter, Mr. Strudel. Like buying American suits. And knowing the price of eggs."

Little bursts of applause punctuated Claire's speech, and as the debate rolled on, Claire picked up both momentum and the audience. She was winning over the television audience in even bigger numbers. She knew from all the Lefkowitz Talent Agency years the power of the impact and the rules of television. She knew her message was in how she looked as well as what she said. After all, it hadn't been so many years ago that Kennedy had won his televised debate against Nixon because he'd powdered down properly and had a tan.

So Claire stood before the voters with a softly powdered face, composed, her autumn brown hair swept off her fine features into a smoothly organized chignon. Her pale blue suit could have been one that Jackie Kennedy would have worn a few years back. Lefty's pearls graced her long neck and the cadence of her speech was unhurried midwestern with no trace of geography other than that unchartered place: well-bred, upper-crust America, the land of Grace Kelly, Katharine Hepburn, and, as the wider audience got used to listening to her soft, well-chosen words, Claire Harrison.

The Gordian knots in Anita's digestive tract actually started to untwist as the debate proceeded. It wasn't until Strudel did his "family finale" that she clenched again.

"My friends, I want you to see what America really stands for: the traditional family. And I'd like for you to meet mine. Would all you Strudels stand and come up here on the podium with your father? C'mon. My pretty wife, Susie; my sons Kevin, quarterback at UCLA, Peter, All-American at Miami, and John, high school soccer star . . ."

"Can you imagine what that poor woman's laundry hamper smells like when they're all home? All those jocks." Slim whispered to Anita even as she politely applauded each child's athletic abilities.

Then she saw the look on Claire's face. Soccer. That had been the word that had done it. Six and soccer. Claire looked like she was going to cry. The long hours campaigning, sleepless weeks, Sara's absence—at this moment, it was all taking its toll on the candidate. Violet saw it coming, and had to restrain herself from rushing up to take her daughter in her arms. What was she doing up there? What was she trying to prove? Why didn't she just stop trying so hard?

". . . my girls, Stacy and Jane. We're just that all-American family, I guess. Claire, I don't want to hog the spotlight. C'mon, introduce us to whomever."

He turned toward Claire, who looked like a woman in line for the guillotine. The sorrow she felt daily for her son was heightened by standing in this high school, the place another reminder of Six's interrupted life. The silence in the auditorium was deafening. The tears she wouldn't release rolled down the Aunties' cheeks instead. For one long moment she didn't want to be in the spotlight, but when she saw Sara walking toward her, holding little Violet in her arms, she lifted her chin in pride. The look was enough to turn the attention of the press and their pack of cameras on the heretofore unavailable daughter.

A panicked Anita pushed another pill under her tongue. It probably wasn't the right remedy, she mused, for a trailing candidate's cuckoo daughter to have a crack-up at the height of a televised debate. Christ, the girl had unbelievable timing.

Anita watched as Claire extended her hand to her daughter as if this were a rehearsed emotional moment. She wasn't sure why Sara was ascending the platform, and she waited as apprehensively as the rest of the audience. The story of Sara's little *Rear Window* pantomime raced through her mind. Sara, her wispy flower-child hair pulled back into a curly Alice in Wonderland nimbus, stood in the center of the stage beneath the mike the women's league mediator had used and introduced herself in a clear, unaffected voice. The voice, amplified, echoed through the expectant audience.

"My name is Sara Harrison, and I am one of Claire Harrison's children." Her quiet introduction set off a craning of necks to see the mother's famous face in the offspring. Her next words captivated them completely. "My mother has so much love and energy to give that it has spilled over to nurture hundreds of others. I want you to meet some of my mother's other children."

Anita was perched on the edge of her seat as the parade of young adults and teenagers began. No one, not even Claire Organ Harrison Duccio Lefkowitz, could possibly have produced this many illegitimate children. And such colorful ones.

"Hello. My name is Maria Fasano Perkins. I am one of Claire Harrison's children. After the war in Italy I was a frightened, starving orphan, alone. Claire was the one who brought me here to Eleanor House to feed me, teach me, and love me. Even after she found a permanent home for me with a good family in New Jersey, she helped me with homework and, later, with entrance into college. Today I am married, a mother of two"—she paused, looking directly into the blinding glare of the flashbulbs—"and I am a teacher in this high school."

The Aunties waved to Maria with their dampened handkerchiefs as she beamed back and made way for the next clean-cut young person.

"Hello, my name is Tony Fuller." He looked over his shoulder, shooting Claire a big toothy grin. "I was born in L.A. and left on nobody's doorstep. I was adopted by Eleanor House and Claire. Now I'm a sophomore at UCLA on the William Henry Harrison VI scholarship—that was Claire's son, who died too early—and"—there was pride in his voice—"I'm a big brother for two little fellas at Eleanor House."

Claire opened her arms to give him a hug.

One by one, dozens of grown children joined them, including the now-grown Korean children who'd actually lived with her in the early days at Charlotte Hall as well as teenagers recently arrived from Vietnam and some born here who had just fallen through the cracks of New York or Chicago welfare systems. They all warmly referred to the candidate as "Claire." Even the most cynical reporter in the room—even Anita—could feel the mood lift as real people, speaking from the heart, acknowledged Claire as a woman who mattered. A world-changing mother, untraditional to be sure, but someone who had zeroed in on an enormous problem and then taken a stand to fix it. The twenty or so of "Claire's children" who stood on the stage were only representatives of countless kids across the country who'd been helped through Claire's unselfish efforts. While Bill Strudel was father to the same five freckled faces whose teeth were fixed by the same rigorous orthodontist, Claire was "mother" to thousands of children from all over the world and had maternally helped tend to their universal growing pains. She was a woman to be reckoned with. The American viewers at home started to wonder why the press had shown them only the woman's warts—they all had those—and had left out her goodness. And judging from the looks of these young adults, she had done her part efficiently and well—not a bad sort to have in Congress.

Fenwick Grant watched the debate, which on the East Coast aired late in the evening, from his Washington *Herald* office. He viewed it on the customized three-screen television panel built into the burled-oak bookcases that housed his year-by-year bound copies of *U.S. Week* and a couple of Pulitzer Prizes. It was ten o'clock at night inside the Beltway, and his offices were relatively quiet. It was the time of his day he liked best. Reflection time. As he was married to his newspaper and no one else, he was, at this hour and still at work, cheating only on his mistresses.

For most of the debate he watched out of the corner of his eye, a scotch at his elbow, his Gucci loafers propped on the aircraft-carrier-sized desk that filled his enormous office, reading tomorrow's editorial on Vietnam. Bea, his longtime secretary, glanced up occasionally to see how Mrs. Harrison was doing, salting her seasoned political observations with a female's response to Claire's clothes.

"She reminds me of Jackie Kennedy before she married that Greek. She wears blue well." Bea handed him a batch of letters to the editor and a copy of tomorrow morning's *London Times*.

They both stopped working for a moment to hear Bill Strudel's sanctimonious windup in which he denigrated Claire as a lousy mother.

"Uh-oh. He's moving in for the kill. It's all over now." He could smell defeat with his unerring political nose, even through a television screen airing a California debate on a one-hour delay.

"I hate to look. It's like watching a car wreck."

"Shards of glass and twisted metal. The price of politics."

They both went back to more pressing matters, but pricked up their trained ears when Sara's polite voice rang out with the soon-to-be-famous words.

"I am one of Claire Harrison's children." It was said in such a way that both hard-boiled news junkies respectively put down their Dictaphone and pen.

"We have a history-making handkerchief moment here."

"A captioned picture at the very least." Grant hit a button that would alert the presses to a change in format.

"Oh, look at that dear Italian girl and the way she's looking at Claire. And Claire, why, she looks so proud of her. Like a real mother."

Moved to the point of distraction, Bea took a swig of her boss's scotch. She pointed to Claire on the screen. She looked so sincerely proud, her head tilted off to one side, the half-smile quivering on her lips, a hint of real tears clouding her lovely eyes.

"Oh, it's so wonderful." Bea patted her own tear away with Grant's linen coaster. As far as he could remember, she hadn't shed a tear since her dog Mamie had died in '59.

"I smell victory."

"She'd have my vote."

"Looks like she'll be coming to town, eh?"

Bea picked up her pad. "What kind of flowers shall I send?"

"Victory flowers. A dozen roses. No. Two dozen."

"What kind?"

"Red ones. The All-American rose."

"And the card?"

" 'Congrats on going from party girl to the Democratic Party's best girl. Yours, Grant.' "

The move to Washington was swift. The rented house on Alamedo Drive was substituted for an efficiency apartment off Wilshire Boulevard to keep her California residency in order and a two-bedroom apartment in the Watergate complex to run a smooth daily life in Washington.

Grant was a frequent visitor to Claire's apartment and an escort to National Gallery dinners, the opera, and small insider suppers in Georgetown, where he maintained a weathered Federal period four-story brick house. Lately, the congresswoman from California had been invited to the more private weekend gatherings at HurryUp, his horse farm in Virginia, but so far the lady had declined.

Ambassador Harrison arrived before his telegram. He stood, all ramrod-postured six feet of him, gray derby and gloves in hand, in the congresswoman's outside office. The two young aides tripped over one another in the anteroom trying to find a chair good enough for the distinguished statesman.

"I'm sure Representative Harrison"—his mind did a quick cartwheel, remembering that they had the same famous name for a reason—"will be back in ten minutes. She just went to the floor for a vote. Can I get you something, sir?"

Harrison thanked them, but no. The earnest eager-beavers tried to find something to offer the waiting legend who had set the foreign policy for five presidents, Republicans and Democrats both. A Coke, a candy bar? The diplomat declined.

There was a distinguished air about him and an aloofness that was more than presidential. When Anita Lace stomped in a full two minutes before Claire's high heels echoed on the marble floor, she had just enough time to marvel that the powers that be had forged an alloy out of iron and oak. Proof positive was standing before her.

The smile on his face was for Claire, directed behind Anita and high over her head. Like the man, the smile was the real article.

"Harrison. How wonderful. I had no idea . . ." Her startled hands went to her already smooth chignon.

Then the two Harrisons intertwined fingers as they greeted one another, pressing their cheeks together one at a time, Claire closing her eyes. It almost made Anita want to throw rice.

Awkward introductions were made all around until aide number two waved the telegram of arrival that had gone missing.

"Well, now that you're officially here, may I usher you into my
office?"

Harrison dropped his gloves into the bowl of his hat and followed her into her inner office. A fireplace flanked by two deep
red leather chairs and the flags of the United States and California
gave the room authority. A worn burled desk, covered with family pictures of granddaughter Violet, Sara, and Six, and photographs of Eleanor House children and Eleanor Roosevelt
herself—one with the young Claire standing shyly at her side,
which was still ingrained in Harrison's mind—lent the room its
personal aura.

"This desk belonged to Eleanor, you know. Anna let me have
it when I won. As a gift."

"Eleanor would have been proud of you."

"I like to think so."

"But not as proud as I am."

And Claire blushed, a ripened peach blush like the Claire of so
many Washingtons ago.

"May I take you to dinner, dear?"

The word softened her. Claire glanced at her agenda. He was
here for a presidential briefing. She was scheduled for three
California reception "stop-ins" and a late dinner meeting with her
staff.

"Yes. I'm surprisingly free."

"Shall we be sentimentalists and have dinner at the Willard?"

"Heavens no! It's home to hobos now."

"Nostalgia is a bitter pill sometimes, isn't it?"

"Why not the Congressional Club?"

"Done." Even after they shook hands good-bye, she walked
him out of her office past the starstruck staff and down the long
hall to the elevator, her arm still on his sleeve.

"I think I'll take the stairs."

"Of course. Until dinner, then."

And as she watched him briskly take the steps like she had watched him do a hundred times before, so many years ago, she realized she'd forgotten to ask about Starling.

Anita was strangely silent when Claire breezed back in, her press secretary assessing her with unblinking fish eyes.

Aide number one handed her the six urgent messages and told her of two personal calls that had come in during the last five minutes.

"I'll take personal first. Sara and then Fenwick Grant."

Grant was leaving for the country, where he had thrown together a quick dinner at HurryUp—quick in Grant's lexicon meant news-breaking—for Kissinger, a well-known Chinese dissident, Madame Chiang Kai-shek, *U.S. Week*'s foreign desk editor, and the captain of the U.S. Ping-Pong team. Would Claire be his hostess? It sounded intriguing, but thank you, no. Grant sounded miffed and hung up without ceremony. Over the last few months he had actually started referring to them as a couple, as in, "I guess we're becoming a power couple." In his unsuccessful attempt to bed her, he had even suggested matrimony—the wolf's response to a bruised ego.

Claire slipped away early to bathe and change from one tailored suit to another and be on time for Harrison. She smiled to herself in the mirror as she brushed her still-lustrous hair. As many times as she had reinvented herself, as many reincarnations of Claire as had attracted the critical attention of the world and its scrutiny, there were some things in life that never changed.

They were ushered to a corner table in the club's green-leather-and-brass-tack dining room. Nothing had changed in the Old Guard decor in twenty-five years.

There was so much to catch up on they had to take turns to keep from jumping into each other's news. They became happily alive in one another's company. Sara was expecting again, and the young English professor had turned out to be a kind soul and good husband and was willing to relocate to Georgetown. So Claire could see more of her "girls." Harrison was going to spend time with his granddaughter at the end of the week before he returned to Italy. Claire was thrilled to learn that his three-volume tome on Franklin was short-listed for the Pulitzer Prize, but they both were puzzled by Harry and Minnie's decision at this stage of life to adopt a child.

"I don't suppose they'll go through Eleanor House." Claire sipped from her second glass of wine. ·

"Why not? I don't think—"

"Harrison. Really."

"No, dear. Time closes a lot of open wounds." He touched her hand.

The feel of his skin next to hers elicited a rush of past memories. All the other times. All the other touches.

There was so much history between the two of them. Memories engraved on her heart, in which the love outweighed the disappointments. She felt so intimately connected to him that she could even commiserate when he told her about the rare form of amoebic enteritis that was wasting Starling's delicate constitution and often left her partially bedridden. She had picked it up on their trip down the Nile.

"She's quite uncomplaining. She cheerfully does all her correspondence and runs the house from her bedroom and sitting room upstairs. And you know how beautiful the views are overlooking Lake Como."

Claire nodded, remembering.

"It was my error to try to make a globe-trotting adventuress out of such a refined little bird. Before we married, her entire world had been Tuxedo Park, Palm Beach, and Newport. I had the audacity to drag her around to places like Damascus and Cairo on my trade missions."

"What do the doctors say?"

"That she's more delicate than before but with a quiet routine she could have a good many years."

"I hope she can improve. She's so lovely." Claire lowered her eyes and hoped he didn't notice the catch in her voice. She glanced at the same leather-strapped tank watch he'd always worn. Three hours had flown by as they had renewed a friendship and reignited familiar feelings.

It was almost midnight when Harrison's car and driver took them back to the Watergate, but, reluctant to say good-bye, she asked him up for a brandy. He accepted.

"Come look, Harrison." She leaned her arms on the balustrade. "The same moon. The same Washington Monument. The Lincoln Memorial." She pointed. "You can see all of our old Washington from my terrace. Come out. It's not so chilly."

He stepped out onto the balcony into the crisp January air and stood behind her for a few moments before he brought his hands to her shoulders and they looked out at their Washington together. At this hour the city was so still it could have been 1942 again.

"It's like it always was." He wrapped one arm around her body, his elbow brushing against her breasts. "Those are probably Buicks and Hudsons down there and FDR's still at work in the Oval Office." They both laughed.

So many memories flooded every corner of her mind. When he turned her around to embrace her, she was surprised at the passion that traveled between them, like an electrical current passing through wires that had suddenly been reconnected.

The kiss was the same kiss that had happened a hundred times before. Their familiar fragrances inviting the personal invasion of one another, long-dammed-up juices starting to flow freely. He took her in his arms and covered her mouth with his own hungry one, transporting her to a place she'd thought she would never see again.

"Oh, Harrison. It's only ever been you."

A tear of his fell onto her cheek, commingled with one of her own, and traveled with it together down the slope of her face. She didn't know when her tender feelings for him had been so intense.

She wanted him.

Together again, they were the same Harrison and Claire.

"I love you," she whispered. But you're still unavailable, she thought. "It's Nixon in the Oval Office, not FDR, dear. The presidents may have changed, but the fact that you're married hasn't." Her heart was racing like a young girl's.

He held out his hand. "Stop filibustering and come to bed with me. We keep starting things and then letting others interfere."

"Others matter," she said, but when he took her in his arms again, nothing mattered but the sound of his next breath and the next place on her body that his hands would touch.

Already they were aroused as sensually as if she were his naked lover, waiting for him. He lifted her hair so he could caress the place on the back of her neck. Her shoulders shivered in the cold and he brought her close to warm her, her ivory satin slip exposing her hardened nipples through the soft folds of fabric. He pulled the slip down to her waist and brought his lips to her breasts, firm and round, just as he remembered. Remembered every sleepless night he had spent away from her.

She let her head fall back and wrapped the cloth of his shirt around her knuckles as he traced moist circles across her breasts with his mouth. The moistness surged through her body like an ancient river.

We belong to each other, she thought.

His fingers pressed into her rib cage with proprietary strength. As if his hands were aware that he owned her.

"You're mine, Claire. You've always been mine." And then he pushed her lace underthings away so she was entirely naked. Every part of her body wanted her lover, safely returned from the land of the Pyramids, from which her father had never returned.

"Be mine now, Claire." He put his virility into words as his fingers moved to the softness of her thighs.

It took every rational cell and whatever threads of common sense still clung to the tangled fustian in her brain to push him away.

"But you can't be mine. Harrison, when will you ever remember that you're . . . you're always married. I don't want to be the sick wife's substitute." She brought her slip to her still smooth belly. "For heaven's sake, be mine or just go away. I won't love you in secret. Not anymore." She took several steps back, putting a love seat between them.

Harrison struggled to come to grips with his conflicting emotions. "Oh, Claire. I was free for you once, but I'm not now. Please. We can give each other love. But there are duties we need—"

"Your duties." She pulled the slip on in one movement. It was like a suit of armor against temptation.

"I don't know where I was going. It only felt like it was right." He was always the gentleman, even in lust.

"I was going there too. But it isn't right. Harrison"—her violet eyes locked onto his—"you and I are the strong ones. We're not allowed to be weak."

"Yes." Harrison's voice came out of a hollow tunnel. "So many people depend on us."

"I love you, Harrison." The words hung there in the silence. Claire had to break it somehow, and uttered softly, "Please go."

He turned to leave. Every mixed thought she was having rose like a cloud of confusion between them. Desire, duty, love, hurt, the exhilarated way this forbidden encounter made her feel.

"Maybe I need more time." Her eyes were misted with memory.

"Time is the one thing we don't have anymore, dear."

And he leaned over to take the derby with the gray gloves lying inside from her outstretched arm, leaving a kiss on her naked shoulder.

The congresswoman from California stood in her darkened living room in her bare feet, shifting her weight, trying to figure out what to do next. If she were voting for a ban on nuclear proliferation or for ending the war in Southeast Asia, it would be easy. But having to decide whether or not to follow her heart back to the unavailable man she loved, perhaps jeopardizing the eggshell path to recovery she had paved for her daughter, his granddaughter, plunging them all into some defenseless, damaging place, shattering the life Harrison had built with Starling, this was, all of this was too much for her to decide.

She pulled on the leather boots in the foyer, wrapped a fur over her slip, and grabbed her handbag as she flew out the door, taking the elevator straight to the garage. She floored the pedal all the way to HurryUp, hoping the highway patrol from Virginia wouldn't stop the junior congresswoman for speeding.

She switched on the radio to distract her and turned it off again when it couldn't. All of her important memories were intertwined with Harrison. But tonight she was determined to invent new ones. If she didn't find a new place to put her emotions, she'd be destined to dwell only in the vacant slots Harrison could offer her. She pulled off the highway at Middleburg and onto the blacktop road leading to HurryUp past the darkened barns and pitch-black meadows. She plowed the car past winterized oaks and boxwood protected with tarpaulins. She sped past the dirt intersection that would bring her to Willow Oaks, the country house that Pamela Churchill Hayward Harriman was negotiating to purchase for herself and Averell, her latest, oldest husband. She had married him a few months after he had been widowed, rekindling a thirty-year-old affair with her longtime married lover. Marriage was on Claire's mind. She brought her Lincoln to an abrupt stop in the gravel driveway, inches from Grant's Mercedes. She pounded on the door, rousing one of the servants and pushing past the surprised butler in his nightclothes. She wasn't sure where Grant's bedroom was, but using her woman's intuition, she walked right to it. A pair of man's boxer shorts, one silk stocking, and a pair of dyed-to-match slingbacks on the floor impeded her progress. Focused as she was, she hurdled over the sartorial evidence of the evening's earlier diversions.

"Grant." All the unspent passion and sexual energy of the hours with Harrison underscored her greeting. "We must talk."

Her fur flew open as she put one hand on her waist, revealing her well-kept body beneath her skimpy slip. In one gesture, Grant switched on the lamp and sat upright. Anger, embarrassment, and amusement rippled through his expression.

"Are you nuts, Claire? What's happened? China's invaded us while I was sleeping? What? What?"

"I think we should get married."

"What?" There was still sleep to be rubbed out of his eyes. It was three o'clock in the morning.

"Weren't you proposing last week when you said we were the perfect power couple?"

"Yes, but—"

"Move over. I accept."

Chapter Eighteen

HurryUp

Of any stopping place in life, it is good to ask whether it will be a good place from which to go on as well as a good place to remain.

—*Mary Catherine Bateson*

Overnight, Claire stopped being perceived as a sightseeing tourist and became a bona fide Beltway player. After two years of hard work legislating social reform and harder work opening the doors to Washington's all-boy inner sanctum, Claire's foray into politics was instantly legitimized with a pair of "I do"s. Claire was now one-half of this company town's hottest power couple, prominent enough to rate editorial page punditry. The *Congressional Record* depicted her in its political cartoons as a women's-libbing bulldog, while the *Post's* cartoonist had satirically drawn her as Grant's "pet poodle."

Claire and Grant laughed at the high-level gossip they sparked over the late fireside suppers they shared.

"I'd understand all the curiosity if I were a cabinet member or spying for Russia." She dropped two sugar lumps into his coffee. "But all this commotion just for being a lowly congresswoman? What is the fascination in two mature, ordinary people settling down together?"

Grant grinned lopsidedly at his bride. "We're neither ordinary nor particularly mature. If I weren't sleeping with you, I'd be rooting through your garbage looking for gossip to print about you." He leaned over to kiss the inside of her wrist, a grin as wide as the Potomac reshaping his mouth.

Claire winced. Some of the past was just too raw to be re-minded of.

"No you wouldn't. You're a gentleman. And becoming quite a good husband."

"A rank amateur at it. I'm a newspaper fellow first. You just understand me so well. That's what's so terrific about you. You never sulk when I stand you up for Kissinger." He winked at her, half closing a flirty eye. "I feel as if I just joined the most elite men's club in the world: the Husbands of Claire Club."

Claire put down her fork in mock protest. This man who pos-sessed fistfuls of power and smarts could sometimes have the ma-turity level of a boastful teenager. Somehow, though, they were making it all work out very nicely. She raised her wrist to meet his lips.

Amazing, Claire thought, how since she had taken not just her second congressional oath but her fourth marital vow, how much faster her phone calls got returned these days and how she sud-denly rated a choicer hook in the Capitol cloakroom. All this in the bra-burning age of feminism. She sighed. Even old Senator Pines, the bigoted octogenarian who chaired the Committee on Child and Welfare Reforms, had stopped greeting her with a booming "Helloooo, Congresslady Hollywooood. Don't our gams look gooood today!"—at least to her face. As the Hollywood Widow she'd usually cringed whenever she found herself sharing the Russell Building's dinner mint–sized elevator with the south-ern senator and his vexing prejudices. "A hundred years behind the times," she'd exclaimed to Grant. "He belongs in a curio shop, not Congress!" Pines and Claire had crossed sharp swords with unendearing regularity. But now she suddenly rated a hearty handshake—and a fair hearing on her Head Start and hot-lunch programs, one of which had just passed the Senate. And it was simply because Claire shared a pillow with the owner of the most influential paper in the senator's home state.

Yes, marrying Grant had been the correct career move. Her union with the owner of the country's second most influential newspaper was a good one in her mind, even if with their busy schedules and her frequent trips to California to visit her constituents it wasn't always a toe-warmer. Being Harrison's mistress—a second time—well, that would have been unthinkable. Though those pretty thoughts still danced through her brain when she wasn't careful. Probably they always would. This husband she had was a handful. Dashingly handsome, self-absorbed, the one-man think tank sitting across from her each morning over orange juice and seven newspapers ground his teeth in his sleep and often awakened with a guilty look on his face. As if he, too, might have been dreaming about someone else.

Will you never stop marrying men you don't love? Harrison had written to her on the stationery, which bore his name as a head, that accompanied her wedding gift. But the problem was, if it was love, it could be only Harrison. And if it couldn't be Harrison, it would always be somebody almost like him. In her matrimonial laundry list there was the boyish soldier with the same name, followed by the Italian pirate who shared Harrison's financial acumen, succeeded by the kind man who shared his insight, and now Fenwick Grant, who simply looked like him, all their shortcomings coming out in the wash. Claire was careful not to ascribe too many Harrison-like qualities to her cocky newspaperman husband. If she were back in Hollywood, she would never have cast him in the Harrison part. It would be like Cary Grant playing Moses. She giggled at the thought.

Claire reined in her horse. She was out riding the trails at HurryUp. After four years of marriage, she and Grant had settled into a pleasant routine. It was only when she was alone or in the company of an old friend like Pam that she allowed Harrison into the conversation.

Always Harrison. She sighed to the lace frost on the December trees that lined the path.

"Harrison's always the same," Pamela Harriman, Claire's red-haired riding companion, echoed. "You'd think the man would have a bald spot like Averell by now or use a cane. Even have a cataract. But no, he's a silver-haired Adonis. We saw him out in New York at the Whitneys'. Starling was home with that ridiculous Nile fever, ailing as usual. Creatures like her have no genetic stamina. If she was a horse, they'd shoot her." It was obvious that Pam had no patience for sickness. "He was quite elegant in his English bespoke suit. Dark blue with a wide chalk stripe. So very Harrison."

Pamela sat perfectly straight astride her horse, the top of her velvet helmet peeking over her horse's ears. She looked handsome in her tan jodhpurs, polished J. Lobb black boots that came to just below the knee, and a tweed riding coat cut to accommodate her ample bosom—the bosom that Slim half-joked had been pointed like a Holland and Holland big-game hunting rifle at the world's richest men.

Her red flame of hair was cupped around ears that listened only selectively, and a line of freckles stubbornly crossed the delicate bridge of her nose. Some indication of the lady's own tenacity. At fifty-four, she still possessed a girlishness that glimmered through her cool, hard shell. Claire still considered Pam more of a fellow traveler than a friend, as they had very little in common except for the number of old skins they had shed.

"Averell's putting me on the board of Braniff. He thinks I should know more about the business of money."

"I think you've managed very well without an M.B.A.," Claire deadpanned, wishing that someone with a sense of irony, Auntie Slim perhaps, were along for the ride.

Pam possessed a vague air of disconnectedness, seeming to suffer separation anxiety whenever she was even more than a foot or two away from her husband. Having finally landed her married lover from thirty years before, she held on to him as tightly as if he were a young stallion from her stables instead of a hard-of-hearing eighty-two-year-old geezer. She had practically rescued him from the grave, Claire marveled, reviving him into marriage where, in a growing collection of homes, she took such good care of him that he was miraculously invigorated and revitalized. Like an old oak that had suddenly sprouted a new branch. Pam often referred to Averell as "the Governor," as if bestowing his old title on him elevated *her* a step up in the life she'd built on borrowed prestige.

The two horses halted at a fallen tree on the trail.

"Women with important husbands have so many hurdles to jump." Pamela Churchill Hayward Harriman spoke from experience. She led the way over the dead wood with her high-stepping horse. She had brought her own costly thoroughbred with her for the weekend. Even though she was now married to a vastly wealthy political emissary, she still referred to herself as Winston Churchill's daughter-in-law, glowing in the reflection of history's giant hero the way other women clipped on a pair of bright earrings.

"You're so clever, Pammie. You should write a book. Sort of a survival manual." *Advice for the Other Woman,* Claire thought as she posted expertly. Claire sat as lightly in her saddle as if she had been born to it. With each new success of her own, her confidence grew.

It amazed Claire that this woman, who had been surrounded by so many great men, had never ventured out with a career agenda of her own or been bitten by her own bug of ambition. She had settled instead for spousal or mistress duty serving gift-bearing titans of all sorts.

"What is Grant giving you for your birthday? Averell gave me a plane," Pam said flatly, as if receiving an aircraft was like getting a toaster. "You know, dear, you really have nothing to show for all your marriages."

"I have my daughter. And my politics. Not to mention my adorable grandbabies. And a very bright future." Claire brushed off Pam's remarks like evaporating snowflakes.

"But where are your financial assets?"

"Oh, Pam. I don't think like you."

"Well, you should. Money matters." Pam pondered this needlepoint-pillow philosophy for a minute. "A woman with property is twice as enticing. Especially as she gets a little age on her." Pamela cleared her throat like a prim schoolteacher. "Remember the last three times you entrusted your finances to your husbands? You can't add up zeros! Put some property in your name. Especially since you're married to such a handsome scoundrel. You thought you were well off with young Harry. Not to mention Duccio. And this is a big birthday. You should become a woman of property now. You're turning fifty." She punched the number out as if she were keeping score.

"Thank you, Pam. I have two whole days to go before I have to deal with being half a century old." She had winced this morning when she'd combed six new silvery hairs into her chignon.

"You should be in crisis *now*. Then you'll be over it by the party." Pragmatic Pam was humorless, but she always made Claire laugh, even if she had to giggle behind her gloved hand.

The party was set for Saturday, and all of the Washington establishment elite was invited. Claire was using her birthday as an occasion to bronze their social status the way Sara had bronzed Dylan's baby shoes, solidifying political and journalistic alliances. The crowd was going to be stellar.

"I'm doing the seating tomorrow. Any preferences?"

"Just seat me with Averell. At the head table. By the way, are you having Charity Foxley?" There was a gossipy glint in Pam's eyes.

"Why, yes. She's a neighbor out here. Grant rides with her. She's the best jumper in the country." There was no jealousy in Claire's velvet voice.

"So I've heard."

"She's an Olympic equestrienne."

"How patriotic of you. A ribbon winner. You're more broad-minded than I." Pam ran her horse's reins firmly through her fingers. "Young women who hang around stables too long get very frisky. You can't have that much horse flesh between your legs all day without getting aroused."

"What are you trying to tell me?" Claire's baser instincts raced to the surface.

"I wouldn't have her to my house. Or on my horse." She raised an auburn-tinted eyebrow. "Even if Averell were a hundred and two years old. Well, I must canter off, dear, back to your guest-house. The Governor will be awakening from his nap in a few minutes and I like to be the first thing he sees when he opens his eyes." Her smile was quick and crisp.

With an expert if graceless movement of her custom-booted foot, she turned her mount back to HurryUp's stables, maintaining her peculiar warmthless smile and leaving Claire alone with new doubts to add to her sudden terror about turning fifty. Claire was glad to see her go. Until Claire had had this little trail talk with Pam, she thought she and Grant were having a perfectly adequate marriage. So why should she let Pam plant a dirty seed of doubt? From where she sat, her domestic garden was all abloom.

She made a mental list of their exterior good points.

The Fenwick Grants were lionized by the East Coast establishment. The recklessly handsome publisher and his glamorous congresswoman wife had become the darlings of the political, social, and journalistic set in the same short time it took the Watergate burglars to bumble into Democratic National Committee headquarters. In no time at all, Claire had skillfully passed two school integration votes and co-authored a bill on affirmative action.

Grant's newspapers had come in a close second to Kay Graham's *Washington Post* on the Watergate coverage, hard on the heels of Kay's foot soldiers Bob Woodward and Carl Bernstein. They had both excelled in their worlds, even though Grant was growing obsessively preoccupied with catching up to the competition, often forgetting he had another wife besides his work. But that was the price of power, Claire knew. Her husband spent longer and longer hours toiling in his office, often arriving at one of their famous Georgetown suppers on Q Street, coat in hand, like a tardy guest. At 10:45, when Grant lifted his glass to toast his guest of honor, he usually had one eye on his Cartier tank watch. As everyone inside the Beltway knew, official Washington dinner parties ended promptly at 11 P.M.

"Power gets up early." Grant winked and clinked his glass with those people important enough to be gathered around the four tables of ten that filled the dining room and spilled over into the trellised garden room. "And we newspaper fellows have to be up even earlier to cover it."

His guests always laughed at this same joke. Clever Washington insiders would never jeopardize their public careers with a snub to the capital's press lord.

At the eleventh stroke of the Adams clock in the hall, he would kiss his wife good-bye and jump into his car for the ride back to the office. There he returned to the horrors of Hanoi, the glut of deaths in the Gulf of Tonkin, the bloody massacre at Kent State, and the wiretapped mess of the DNC Watergate offices—all Shangri-las to him. As were the unattainable guests whom he would have preferred to have had at his carefully Claire-tended round tables that night: Mao Tse-tung, Patty Hearst with the Symbionese Liberation Army, General Westmoreland, Jackie O., and Deep Throat, the unnameable source who had fed the *Post* reporters tips about the Watergate break-in. Congressman Claire's and Publisher Grant's lives were so full of bean-spilling sources, daily disgraced Nixon revelations, and Claire's demanding

California constituency that the mere fact that the Fenwick Grants' marriage was held together more by politics than passion went unobserved. Except by Harrison. His chatty hand-scripted notes arrived regularly from exotic places, all bearing colorful postage stamps.

In her professional life Claire had decided to remain Claire Harrison. No poll had been taken as yet on the matter of women politicians giving up their last names for their new husbands, but she instinctively felt that the Zeitgeist demanded she hang on to her own identity. It was 1974, and Germaine Greer and Gloria Steinem had replaced Betty Grable and Jane Russell as pin-up girls since the last time Claire had lived in Washington. A more modern Claire had been one of the first investors in Gloria Steinem's new magazine, *Ms*, along with the *Washington Post*'s chairman, Kay Graham. Together they lent an air of white-gloved, dignified accomplishment to the marching, miniskirted missionaries. The times had changed, and adaptable Claire changed along with them.

Claire pulled her horse, a ladylike palfrey, away from the trail and across the back fields of HurryUp. She loved this place. She surveyed it now with eyes framed by thick lashes wetted with snow. This country house had become home. Maybe Pam was right. It was time to become a woman of property. She had always lived in her husbands' houses, running perfect showplaces for the men of the moment, and had never been mistress of her own.

Not so different from Pam, Claire thought as her mare jerked her head up stubbornly, trying to get her shod hooves back on the beaten trail.

Claire pulled her horse around, steering Tooker to a clearing with an unobstructed view of HurryUp. From here she could see the white frame and fieldstone house sitting atop a rolling bluff. It wasn't as imposing as Charlotte Hall with its foreboding Gothic vastness, and while not as richly ornate and baroque as Palazzo Duccio with its centuries-old splendor and gold woven tapestries, HurryUp held a charm for Claire that no other pile of bricks or stone had ever inspired.

She had been comfortable enough in Lefty's rented Bel Air house all done up in Hollywood moderne decor and accented in colors like avocado and peach. And while life with the Aunties had been delicious, it had been lived in a residential hotel, inside rooms with weekly rates on the doors. No, she had never really had a home of her own. Not until now.

She lifted her eyes from the base of the great oak tree shading the property to the house it protected. Perhaps home was where you finally realized it was. She felt secure in the notion that her daughter's Volkswagen bus, rocking with the laughter of Claire's grandchildren, Violet, Billy, and Dylan, each blessed with the high spirits of Six, would be arriving for the weekend party in a matter of hours. The steady predictability of Seth and the responsibility of raising three healthy, demanding children—a task Sara refused to share with nannies or maids—had done more for her daughter's well-being than all the years of psychoanalysis. It was Thursday afternoon, and they would have plenty of family time before the "Big 5-0" party. It filled her with a sense of peace to know that Violet and Mr. Zolla and Auntie Slim were noisily unpacking in the upstairs guest rooms in their usual dramatic fashion. And that even Auntie Wren, who had a year ago been laid to her final rest in HurryUp's old circle cemetery, or "the Pie" as it was referred to, was present in spirit.

A shadow crossed Claire's forehead as she ducked a low, bare branch. She wanted to bring Six home, too, and bury him lovingly in the center of the Pie. The thought had been gnawing at her. Finally there was a home to bring him to. She would have the old plot weeded and beautifully replanted. She could turn it into a garden of tranquillity.

She'd have to battle Ophelia finally to have her child back, she thought. But the wheels of fortune had turned full circle for

Claire. Suddenly she had all the clout in the world with which to fight her bitter foe.

With resolution she pulled the reins to ride Tooker closer to the elevated bluff cradling the Pie. Warm tears stung her eyes. She feared and despised Ophelia. But she loved the memory of Six more. A picture of him, always unchanged, sitting on a white cloud, always filled part of her thoughts. She, Six, Sara, and Harrison. Could it have ever worked out for them? Was it ever even an attainable possibility?

Claire finally gave her horse its head and let Tooker lead her away from the eighteenth-century burial plot and onto the frozen mud path curving around the back of HurryUp.

The house before her had grown up over one hundred fifty years and changed, accommodating its inhabitants, surviving— like herself. It was a home that had evolved, sprawling in its added-on foundation that comfortably combined three types of American architecture. The kitchen and heart of the house, on a low rise, sloped to accommodate the view, had been built in 1803 with wood from the surrounding forests. The later foundation and bedrooms were laid with local fieldstone, and the whole hodge-podged facade had been pulled together from bricks molded and fired on the property. By 1897, the broad, tall facade of red brick and fieldstone had a second floor from which its inhabitants could watch out for forest fires, its windows and the gabled ones on the third floor trimmed in polished sandstone. In the 1920s the house had been sold to the founder of the *Washington Post*, Grant's competition, and when he had purchased it for a whistle in the late fifties it had been known as the Post House. Grant, who had used it only to bed underage girl grooms or married Middleburg equestriennes, renamed it HurryUp, as he had usually used it from a rushed late-Saturday-night seduction supper until a rumpled Sunday brunch.

Claire chose to ignore the house's most recent history, appreciating it instead for its ability to encompass many different styles yet retain its own integrity. It reminded Claire of herself.

She'd never liked the gazebo, though, a wooden relic from the Victorian period built for high tea and low romantic assignations. Her head in the snowy clouds, Claire barely noticed that Tooker was taking her directly to that paint-faded structure now.

She was mildly surprised when Tooker dropped her off right in front of the gazebo, as if it were a destination. The gazebo sat on the rim of a duck pond, and the worn brick path was strewn with untended reeds. She was startled to hear little grunts and moaning quacks from the fowl. She hadn't realized ducks were so noisy or that enough of them to make that kind of commotion hadn't gone farther south for the winter. The sensible part of her brain, all caught up in her reverie, hadn't prepared her for the raw scene of libido that smacked her squarely in the face. She was speechless, but her widened eyes spoke for her.

Grant, caught with his pants down, was unapologetic.

Even with his charismatic personality, he couldn't disguise two naked bodies in flagrante delicto in the gazebo.

"Oh. Claire. You startled me. You know Charity Foxley here."

Charity. In her shock Claire made a mental list: first Patience, now Charity. Charity in the raw.

"Yes. I know all your virtues," she snapped.

Grant covered his penis with his ascot. Claire turned to face Charity.

Charity's thoroughbred body rippled as she rose to her full height, turning herself sideways almost for Claire's appraisal.

Claire watched, agonized, as Charity took her time covering her bare breasts and bottom in the nippy air with Tooker's plaid blanket.

Grant was as debonair and sophisticated as a lead actor in one of Lefty's light comedies. As a man who had spent his career documenting the extremes of human behavior, gratifying his own baser carnal pleasures was to him, well, ordinary. Still naked, he

leaned, arms folded, against the gazebo wall, his lip curled as if
he might crack a rakish joke. After all, he could always make the
argument that she had had to walk over another woman's lingerie
the night she had proposed to him. "So what did you expect?" he
asked. "Fidelity?" Fidelity certainly wasn't one of his virtues. Or
was there a girl somewhere, Claire angrily wondered, with that
name who knew her husband's weakness for firm young flesh?
Preferably from fine old families. It suddenly occurred to her that
Grant might be pursuing a perverse hobby of bedding all the
virtues in Virginia.

"Have you no scruples at all?" Tears lessened the impact of her
shouted words. Claire's eyes looked off toward the sky, as if visu-
alizing another place with another man was a balm for the tacky
scene she had stumbled upon.

"You knew what you were getting into when you married me,"
Grant said matter-of-factly.

"I thought we respected each other."

"As much as people like you and I can. Nobody puts chains
around me. Or restrictions on my comings and goings."

"But this is our home."

"My home."

Claire was furious. She was mad at Grant less for being un-
faithful than for making her feel like Eleanor to Charity's Lucy.
Like the blind-eyed do-gooder wife cheated on with her own
White House china, crystal, and sheets while she was away on her
missions. Mad as hell that if he were going to betray her he had
the nerve to do it at HurryUp. Furious he was jay naked wearing
only a wide grin of "So what?" nonchalance and his Cartier tank
watch and his smooth Jack Kennedy coif. Madder still that
Charity's twenty-eight-year-old thighs were slimmer than her
own and that her childless belly was as taut and flat as a drum
skin. And that her face bore a sneer that told Claire clearly she
was challenging her openly for her husband. Charity was a
modern-day Lucy Mercer.

"Excuse me, Congressman Harrison." Bare-breasted and with her tight breeches cupping her firm ass, Charity languidly pulled on her jacket as she breezed past Claire in the doorway.

"See you at the party, Grant," she called over her shoulder, casually carrying her sweater and underwear in her hand.

"Happy birthday, Senator."

Claire felt like she'd been kicked in the chest by her horse, knocking all the wind out of her.

"Damn you, Grant." The color had fled Claire's face and drained her lips, leaving them a milky white.

"Grow up, Claire. There are three hundred guests coming on Saturday. If you want a menopausal drama, do it for an audience."

"You're such an impossible prick."

Grant groaned, irritated only that he had been caught. "This"—he pointed his chin toward Charity's retreating figure— "isn't about us. It's about sex. So I'm attracted to youth and beauty. Get over it."

Youth and beauty. She had once been youth and beauty to Harrison's power and intellect. Maybe that was the perennial payoff, the same drama being recycled time and again. What did an older, wiser woman have to trade? Was power a marketable commodity for her as well?

"I want a divorce."

She said it with quiet fury, but what she really wanted was to wail, "I don't want a divorce. I want a home and someone to share it with. Why are you mucking it up, you selfish bastard! Can't you keep your penis in your jodhpurs?"

She swung out at him with her riding crop. He grabbed her wrists before it hit his shoulder.

"No divorce. I haven't got the time. And a respected congresswoman would never survive the public scrutiny. You know, Claire, you're beginning to bore me. All your do-goodness consumes you. A few close huddles with Senator Pines and you think you're the belle of the capital. Although God knows you spend more time there than you do at home."

Home. Her family was there now, unpacking their dresses for her big birthday bash. She had already seen Sara and Seth's van pull up from the clearing. So her grandchildren were home, too.

"I don't want your naked equestriennes on this property."

"Don't get so emotional. It doesn't suit you."

"Of course I'm emotional. How can you make love to another woman right under my nose? It's so contemptible." Claire's voice startled any ducks that had hung around for the mild winter, skipping Arkansas or Georgia. "How can you be so insensitive?"

"Hey, I'm an insensitive kind of guy."

"Then let's get a divorce."

"Why bother? I don't want to marry again anytime soon. If I'm saddled with you, I have a good excuse not to marry my horsey girlfriends, as you call them." His grin was wide, almost appealing if you couldn't hear what he was saying. Even when he was being a lout he exuded an irrepressible charm. He moved toward her as if he wanted to finish with her what he had started with Fidelity or Chastity or whatever her name was. In his own mind he was forgiven.

Claire was shaken.

He smiled at her. "No divorce, all right? Just when I have Vietnam exploding and no access to Gerald Ford, I don't need to be distracted. I need to spend my time on big stuff like the Nixon tapes, or whether Jackie is leaving Ari." His gray eyes sparkled, and she was appalled at herself for finding him appealing.

Claire could feel all the dignity leave her face. Her anger fumed into degradation. "I need to think."

"About what? Neither one of us has time for unrealistic emotions. Claire, give me some space. There are enough bedrooms here for all of us."

Suddenly, Claire wanted to live up to her old reputation as a

hot-tempered murderess. Instead, she stormed out the screen
door with a revised goal.

I want HurryUp, she thought. I want a home of my own. I'll
pay the taxes, I'll fix it up, I'll restore it. And as long as he be-
haves, he'll be welcome to stay here. But he'll have to take his
"virtues" somewhere else.

Stomping up to the house, she tried to compose herself. Her riding boots left deeper than usual imprints on the sloped winter
lawn. Little Violet and Billy were on her like playful puppies, and
she was glad for all their genuine hugs and kisses. Billy was Six's
double, and Claire gave him an extra squeeze. Looking at his dimples and clear, sky-blue eyes framed by a halo of flaxen curls made
her smile. His physical likeness to Six and his quick intelligence
far beyond his four years made Claire feel there was continuity in
this life. Or even that Billy had been touched in heaven by Uncle
Six, as Sara's children had been taught to remember her brother.

Sara looked serious. She walked up to Claire in that fey, defiant
way of hers. Her husband, Seth, was holding Dylan, who, as far
as Claire could determine, resembled Harry more than any one of
the three. The whiny voice of a free-wheeling folk singer sang out
loudly from the van's tape deck.

"Claire." Sara hadn't called her "Mother" since Rome. "We
need to talk."

There was a confrontational tone in her voice, as if her latest
shrink had advised her to have it out with her mother on this
birthday weekend. "We need to hash something out." Claire
thought she heard more spirit than usual in her daughter's small,
high voice.

"If you want an argument, Sara, go to the gazebo," she
snapped. She was usually more careful with Sara's fragile feelings.
"I'm going to my room."

Grant never returned for the six o'clock family supper, and
Claire was glad of it. She had only to say "Patty Hearst" or "Deep

Throat" and everyone nodded knowingly, impressed. A busy press lord had to stay on top of these things and was expected to be absent from time to time. In this year of Nixon's resignation, no one in the newspaper business ever had a quiet day. Was Ford going to pardon the disgraced president or not? Would Nixon's chief of staff go to the slammer? Was Ford up to the job?

She was relieved when he failed to arrive and removed his plate after soup. She wouldn't have wanted to spoil her mellow mood at her happy dinner table with the grandchildren, the Aunties, the Harrimans, and a few editorial page journalists all happily mixed together like jellybeans in a candy dish. They talked, interrupting each other, for hours. There was political gossip and children's prattle. Claire's country tables were always flexible: There was always room for one more and a no-show was never missed.

After the meal, Pam tugged Claire's elbow as the adults wandered into the living room filled with overstuffed armchairs and cluttered coffee tables stacked with periodicals and bird porcelains.

"Ave wants to know if Grant really knows who Deep Throat is."

Claire, annoyed to the backbone, shot back conspiratorially, "As a matter of fact, I think Grant had a tête-à-tête with Deep Throat this afternoon. It's what waylaid him."

"Oooh," Pam trilled. As the anonymous source who had caused a president to resign, Deep Throat was the number one celebrity of the year. "Why don't you invite Mr. Deep Throat to your party? That would endear you to Grant. He'd be indebted to you forever."

A lightbulb went on in Claire's brain.

Harrison's gift arrived that night by parcel from Italy: a small watercolor by John Singer Sargent, the American painter who had lived abroad. Evidently that was how Harrison had begun to see himself. An American in exile. The sentiment inside was not the traditional birthday greeting but rather one cursory line:

Another year we're not together . . .

W.H.H. IV

Claire was still tossing in bed when she heard footsteps outside on the old floorboards.

"Claire, are you awake?" Sara rapped softly on her mother's door after everyone else had gone to sleep.

Claire's "Come in" was weary.

Sara, her face scrubbed, and wearing a blue quilted bathrobe with its looped belt missing, looked like the troubled teenager she had once been.

"Do you want to talk, Sara?" Even Claire's top-notch acting skills couldn't disguise the melancholy in her voice.

"Funny. That's what I was going to ask you. I didn't go through twenty years of psychoanalysis not to recognize a fellow soul in conflict. I knew that something wasn't right from the way you walked up the hill. Want to hash it out?" She wore her inherited lopsided grin. "I might be able to help."

"Come over here." Claire opened her arms to her daughter, and for once Sara stepped into them.

"You shouldn't stay away. I love you, you know." Claire lifted her daughter's chin delicately with her fingers.

"My children love Grand Claire more than the world." Claire had to smile. Somewhere along the line "Grandma" had been shortened to just "Grand."

"And you?"

"Consider me the lost generation. But I'm working on it." There was a glimmer of warmth in Sara's voice.

"May I hug you, then?"

"Of course. Mother."

They rocked together, and suddenly whether Grant or a thousand Grants ever came back seemed utterly unimportant. *Mother.* She hadn't heard that word spoken to her since Six had died. She tried to disguise her joy. Maybe Sara had said it by accident.

"Billy's so bright, you know. He seems to grasp everything. You're doing a nice job with him. You're a good mother, Sara."

"Thank you. All the kids are bright. But Billy tests right off the charts. Top of his class."

"Does he remind you of Six, too?"

"Every day."

"Seth is a good husband to you, isn't he?"

"He's like the Roman Colosseum. He's always there." They both laughed. "Of course, he'd never be good enough for you. Poetry professors don't get to be stamps."

Claire hugged her daughter tighter.

"Being there is important." Her eyes traveled far away.

"I often think about that terrible time." A hundred hollows filled Claire's face.

"Do you know what I remember about that day?"

"What, Sara?" The anguish was evident in Claire's voice. "What do you remember about that day?"

"Your ice-blue satin Christian Dior and pink raspberries." She said the words into her mother's breast like she was sharing a clue-filled secret.

Claire was confused. Why would Six's death remind her of blue couture and pink fruit?

"I was hiding in your closet that day behind that voluminous big shiny gown of yours. The one Six always walked behind, completely covered up, whenever he crashed one of your fancy dress parties."

Mother and daughter laughed softly together, both of them remembering how Six worked the party room, invisible behind the blue billowy width of his mother's skirt.

"But what about the pink raspberries?"

"I stood there shaking in your big closet, cowering behind the Dior, listening to Lorenza tell about how Duccio had struck Six in a rage. Killing him." Years of explosive anger still stuck in her throat. And guilt undiluted by years of therapy. Claire shared her daughter's complicated emotions. All these years and they had never spoken about Six's murder. There was a silence in the room so powerful it hung there, a tangible physical presence.

"I don't remember anything else until I heard you calling my name over and over." Sara ran the words together. *Overandover.*

"It was like I was asleep and awake at the same time. Your voice awakened me from a nightmare and there was the dead man on the floor and I tried to scream but I couldn't so I just watched as a deep stain of blood, shaped like a spreading raspberry, kept oozing from his chest. Growing bigger in horrible slow motion, the juice spilling across his shirt. I just watched it and then you as you performed your unselfish act of heroism." Her pupils were pinwheels of stormy colors. "You let them think you did it."

"I didn't want you to have to suffer, Sara."

Sara's cheeks turned the hue of mottled red beets. "I did suffer. And I thought about it until my brain wouldn't think anymore. But if it were one of my children in trouble, I'd do the same thing you did." Her lip was quivering, as if she couldn't decide whether to say more or to stop.

"Oh, Sara." Claire's emotions were too deep for tears.

"Grand-mère Ophelia tried to tell me we were to consider you dead, but every school I went to, girls were reading magazines with pictures of you in party dresses, icy blue dresses, and I had to defend you." There was no stopping her now. The dam was opened. Tears and pent-up emotions tumbled out like water over a dangerous fall. "I hated you for everything!"

"I'm so sorry, baby. I'm so sorry." For the first time Claire mourned the lost years with Sara as well as with Six.

"At Charlotte Hall, Six's ghost walked with all the other heroic Harrisons. I knew it was my fault. I should have been protecting my little brother." Sara's jeremiad was directed at herself. "Lorenza overheard everything. Six was so brave and he was defending your honor to the Pirate." Sara spit out the words. Her red hair looked as if it were on fire.

"Six was destined to fight for one of us. He always defended the underdog. Even against bigger and stronger opponents. It wasn't your fault." Claire's voice was full of uncried tears. "My dear Sara. Were there really so many ghosts at Charlotte Hall?"

"But you haunted me the most. Mother." Sara stood and choked out the words that had to come. "You were the worst ghost because you so nobly sacrificed yourself for me, the most worthless of us all. I always had to pretend I didn't, but I loved you so much."

"Oh, Sara. Please, baby. Don't let angry what-ifs stand between us anymore."

Sara's head fell against Claire's body, whose breasts had stayed full of milk for this child long beyond their natural use, Ophelia having torn Sara from her mother's nurturing nipples. Instead Claire had offered them to Harrison. So many what-ifs.

She smoothed Sara's unruly waves of hair and brushed the tears away with her cool hands.

"There, Sara, there."

"I want you to know the rest."

"I'm not sure I can take hearing any more." Now Claire's voice was childishly vulnerable.

"Grandpa and I defended you. But in secret. We had to whisper happy stories about you to each other in order to keep our spirits up. Whenever Grand-mère overheard us she would send me to some horrible predebutante etiquette lesson and take Grandpa's stroke therapist away. She liked him unable to speak, or walk, I think. It put her in charge of everything. It was very hard for him. We both loved you so much and yet for different reasons we were paralyzed."

Claire closed her eyes in silent understanding.

"And neither one of us could help you when you were in Paris."

"There was Lefty." Claire brightened.

"I liked him," Sara admitted.

"Me too. But I'm going to have bags under my eyes for my birthday party if we don't stop this. People will say I *look* fifty!"

Sara leveled one of the X-ray psychoanalyst looks she'd learned at her mother. "Do you want to keep Grant?" There was a trace of contempt when she said his name. "Anita says the Beltway scuttlebutt is that Charity Foxley is telling everyone that tomorrow night is going to be your going-away party. That's why you're glum, isn't it? Do you want to save your marriage?"

Claire sighed. "I suppose. Why?"

"Then fight for him. Dr. Newman always says that if you find out what makes a person tick, they can't hurt you."

"All right, Dr. Sara. What do you think makes Grant tick?"

"Shower him with power."

Claire laughed.

"Run for the Senate. The seat's open. You heard the dinner talk tonight. Piersall's retiring. I'll help. Like I did before."

"You certainly did. You put me right over the top, you brilliant political strategist." They hugged a last time.

"We'll talk again, won't we?"

"Of course, Mother."

For the first time, Claire knew that everything would be all right on this home front. A great worry lifted away from her shoulders, which had been bent low from all the day's drama. She slept dreamlessly, but somehow even in an exhausted sleep she heard the light breathing of her daughter on the four-poster bed beside her. And it soothed her to her core. In the first hours of morning, years of agony had been suddenly erased from Claire's face, her eyes brighter, and there was a genuine lift to her smile.

Sunday morning, Claire surveyed her closet critically before pulling out a dress.

"You can't wear that!" Auntie Slim had one bright cherry fingernail pointed at Claire's black sheath. "Wear something gay. It's your birthday."

"Hush," Violet scolded. "Have you heard from Grant, dear? He *is* coming?"

"Oh, yes. He called this morning. I think Pam was listening in on the receiver. I heard those British gasps of hers."

"Where's Grant?" Slim, all done up in head-to-toe pistachio green Chanel, was pacing the floor under her own white cloud of smoke. "You can't have a birthday party without a host. Gotta have a man."

"He'll be here, dears. He telephoned." Claire spoke to all three female reflections in her mirror. The skirted dressing table she was seated at was both a cosmetics counter and a gallery—dainty bottles of replenishing creams and perfumes shared the space with an array of pictures of Six, Sara, and herself with dozens of important world leaders, and one with Grant. Suddenly she knew what was the matter with all these high-powered pictures. She was always at the *elbow* of influence.

"Thank God." Slim breathed a sigh of relief and plopped into a chintz armchair emblazoned with delicate Chinese ladies holding fans. She could use a fan herself, she thought. "Let me tell you, I had a fiftieth birthday without a husband and it was no picnic. Did I ever tell you about the time Cyrus—"

"Shush, Slim. Cyrus has been dead a decade." Violet nervously carried her daughter's dark sheath over to the dressing table, where Claire, still in her slip, was powdering her nose far too slowly for a renowned hostess whose guests were already assembling downstairs.

"Let's help get her ready."

Once again Claire was back at the 28 Shop, getting dressed for Cilla Pettibone's deb party. With one pleasant addition: her daughter.

"Don't rush her. I don't want Mother to look harried." Sara

poked her unruly red curls out of the closet. Both older women picked up their heads at the word "Mother." Slim even knocked Violet with a feather-light elbow to her ribs.

"Careful, dear. Evidently some unpleasant business has resolved itself overnight," Violet whispered.

"Indeed!" Slim pronounced.

"I think you should descend the stairs like a swan, head up, after everyone's already gathered, and just make your announcement at the bottom of the landing," Sara told her mother.

"What announcement?" Violet and Slim's voices chimed in.

"Does Grant know about this announcement?" Violet was the voice of caution.

"No, it's really for him. Something Mother and I cooked up."

"I don't know if that's how you keep a husband happy. With an announcement."

"I think it's how you keep this one." Claire spoke through pinched lips as she applied her bright pink lipstick.

"Here, Mother. Try the aquamarine sheath. It's more festive."

"All right, dear." The smile on Claire's partially painted lips made Violet and Slim breathe a collective sigh of relief. If Claire was this happy, they would be happy too. If she was making announcements on a husbandless happy birthday, she must have her reasons.

"Oh, my God!" Slim shouted from her seat by the window. "It's Jackie O.! She's arriving with Senator Kennedy. How did you get Jacqueline Kennedy Onassis to come?"

"Pam Harriman arranged it. Mother wanted someone really interesting to put on Grant's right."

"I think she hit the jackpot," Slim crowed.

"You sure it isn't *Grant's* birthday?" Claire winked. "Has Grant arrived yet, Sara?" She slipped on the shoulder straps of her gown with the dramatic train that Sara had selected, a relic from the Hollywood days. She had worn it to the Oscars.

"About five minutes ago." Sara was getting minute-by-minute updates from the security person on the foyer phone.

"Alone?"

"No. He arrived with Charity Foxley and her ex-husband."

"How civilized." Claire was pleased the six-year-old dress still fit. "Figure's still good?" She lifted her eyes expectantly.

Three heads bobbed enthusiastically.

"I think I'm a nervous wreck. I'm too old for these dress-up parties." Violet was smoothing the back of Claire's satin train and mopping her brow with a scarf.

"Nonsense. Don't be an old hen. This is fun. Just like old times." Slim brought up the slack.

"Did you rearrange the place cards?"

"Yep. Jacqueline Kennedy Onassis is on Grant's right. Coretta Scott King is across the table and Betty Ford is on his left. I put ol' Charity at the end with her ex."

"Good girl."

"The first lady Mrs. Ford?" Violet asked. "Am I missing something here?" She had been trying to follow the exchange between her daughter and granddaughter. "I thought you were the Democratic congressperson."

"I am. Incidentally, I've decided to run for the Senate. Sara's brainstorm. But Grant runs a bipartisan newspaper, so Sara and I padded the guest list yesterday and today to make it more interesting for him. Didn't we, dear?"

"You bet."

"Maybe, if he's good, we'll even give him the scoop on my candidacy."

"Oh, Claire, you look beautiful." There were tears of joy in Violet's lovely eyes—for a variety of reasons. But mainly because Claire and her daughter seemed to have pulled open the heavy curtain between them.

"Go on, you dears. I'll be down in a second." Claire's voice was exquisitely calm.

"Oh, I love it. It's like we're the bridesmaids." Slim gaily patted her black-and-gray bob, her sheared bangs worn long to cover any forehead wrinkles. "This is so much fun. It's like flying in the eye of a hurricane!"

"Sara, will you come with me?" Claire asked over her shoulder on the threshold of the bedroom door, one bare arm stretched behind her to hold her daughter's hand.

"No. It's your spotlight." Sara clasped a triple-stranded pearl bracelet with a narrow diamond clasp around her mother's wrist. And she added to her mother's ensemble a pair of diamond-and-turquoise earrings borrowed from Pam.

"Don't you think it's too much?" A little upside-down V furrowed its way onto Claire's brow.

"Not for a lady who has to wow them. And him. Go for greatness." She gave her mother's narrow wrist a little squeeze.

"Thank you, dear. Whatever happens tonight, it's already the best birthday I've ever had."

"Hurry." Sara shooed her out. "I'm right behind you."

Spotting Claire at the top of the stairs, Peter Duchin lifted his fingers from the piano keys and signaled his band to pause and then begin anew. A twelve-piece orchestra, including one trombone, rolled out a musical fanfare. And Claire began her studied descent, shoulders back, head high, as she glided down the curved staircase that rose thirty feet in to the incongruous hodgepodge of a house that Claire had fallen in love with.

Every eye lifted as the crowd below strained to get a look at Claire without her traditional day-to-dinner suit. And jewelry. There was a sense of anticipation swelling from the cocktail party that had already been going on for an hour without the legendary hostess. An audible sigh of approval rose as they appraised the elegantly transformed Claire. She could feel everyone's eyes riveted upon her.

She sized up the crowd and assessed the room like the astute politician she had become and decided to wait until after dinner for her speech. A sideways glance at Grant from the corner of her eye told her savvy antennas to wait until he'd drunk a glass of champagne to her health and been thoroughly Jackie O'd and Betty Ford-ized at dinner.

She moved gracefully through her guest list of the mighty like a barn dancer swinging around the room, handing off one partner even as she do-si-doed to the next. She avoided Grant on purpose, for Charity was boldly annexed to his sleeve. She'd put distance between them at dinner, too. At the one rectangular table set under the green-and-white tent erected behind the house for dinner, she'd put herself at one head, separated by twenty-two bold-faced names from his seat at the opposite end.

The party was lavish by Washington standards. The tent was heated, the dinner catered by the Jockey Club, whose waiters were attired in scarlet riding coats. And as a last-minute homage to her husband, the side panels of the tent's canvas interior had been hung with *U.S. Week*'s magazine covers, a project that had taken three *Washington Herald* staffers and Anita Lace all afternoon to assemble. With the brightly burning silver candelabras, the boxwood dotted with silver and white roses hand-tied to the hedge's green branches ringing the dance floor, and long, skirted white tablecloths trimmed with holly leaves and berries, the tented space was visibly exciting. But the biggest decorative coup of all was draping the room with Washington and New York A-list celebrities and then topping it with Jackie O., the beguiling mystery guest who had hardly set a foot in Washington since she had departed years before under the glare of a thousand flash-bulbs, fleeing doe-like from unrelenting attention with her two young children. The picture of the young Jackie in her pink suit stained by her husband's blood was etched on the collective memory of everyone in the room—pink raspberries. Claire wondered at how much grief this woman had had to suffer. She had done it privately and with dignity. Now here she was, the most pho-tographed woman in history, charmingly whispering into Grant's ear, the candlelight illuminating the irises of her dark eyes, her animated face glowing. The grin on Grant's face grew wider as her voice, a breathless hush of excitement, parlayed international items of gossip and news in an unhurried roll. She had come on the arm of her brother-in-law Senator Edward Kennedy, with whom Claire had conferred only this morning. Claire spoke to all the extra invitees she had added, starting early the day before. As quickly and gaily as Sara, Anita, and Pam could dial their unlisted numbers, Claire had corraled them in. A Herculean effort, all to rearouse Grant's interest. It had been a surprise coup that Jackie was visiting in Middleburg on a private hunt weekend with Polly Sully, her millionaire husband left behind.

Practically all the other A-listers shone brighter and elevated their conversations a notch up in the presence of Jackie, America's eternal first lady. The current first lady was almost giddy to be in her company and, emboldened by good wine and champagne, managed to glimmer herself. The rest of the awed guests were impressed with themselves simply for being invited.

"Wall-to-wall legends." The news editor of the *New York Times* practically panted.

But Grant was the most intrigued of all. He had to hand it to his clever wife. She was one in a billion. At one meal she had fed him a loquacious Jackie as well as direct access to the president. Claire noticed with some satisfaction that he hadn't given a glance to a peevish Charity Foxley all through dinner. The hostess took the unhappy expression on this guest's face as a good indicator of how her party was going.

"When did Sara, you, and Claire cook all this up? If Patty Hearst jumps out of the birthday cake I'll just collapse," Slim prattled to Anita from her front-row seat at their round table adjoining Claire's, and Coretta's, and Jackie's, and Betty's, and Grant's, and Charity's, and the Harrimans', and the Kennedys', and Kay Graham's as well.

"I worked like a bat outta hell to change every damn detail that had been set in stone. My feet are hurting like crazy. Even my bunions are exhausted." The two women spoke behind a thick cover of unfiltered cigarette smoke.

"Damned if this ground isn't levitating with all the power sitting on it." Slim's excitement at being at this social altitude was unbridled.

"Yeah, it'll fertilize the crops." Mouth opened, Anita chewed and spoke at the same time.

At the other table, flanking Claire's back so she could listen to their merry prattle, were her other prized guests, cutting hungrily into their glazed slices of Virginia honey-baked ham and butterscotched sweet potatoes. Grand Claire's grandchildren were here, colorfully dressed in trust-fund hippie style, and so were Lorenza, her husband, and their two children, who were dressed like foreign princes in velvet suits, along with some of the youngsters from the Virginia chapter of Eleanor House.

"So is it doing the trick? Does Grant look impressed?" Slim craned her neck to see. Grant was engrossed by the mesmerizing Jackie, who was complimenting him on a recent editorial, calling it "litra-cheur," stretching out the word in her heavy Bouvier accent. The ladies watched as he melted into putty. With every breathy whisper she uttered, he fell further under Jackie's spell. As the table's candlelight shone on her bare shoulders and reflected off the gold cuffs worn at her wrists, Grant too felt fired by her flame. Occasionally he turned to the present first lady, only to return as quickly as he could to the living legend beguiling him with shared secrets.

"Really, I don't see why Claire wants to keep the priapic fool around. She's turning fifty and he's the one having a midlife crisis," Slim snapped.

"Oh, Claire's doing it for us. She always wanted us to have a man in our lives since she was a small girl." Violet sighed.

"Frankly, if you ask me, her only romance is a secret one—"

Slim was unceremoniously silenced by Anita Lace, former ace reporter, always wary that another paper's spy might be planted at a nearby table. In this age of wiretapping and peeping-Tom pranksters, Anita was convinced the day would come when no secrets would be safe in Washington.

"We all suspect the same secret. Let's keep it that way—a suspicion." She peeked under the tablecloth to make sure. "I was called at six this morning to hightail it over here to learn I'm running her senatorial campaign! Honestly, you'd think we women could learn to plan our lives better. A fine woman like Claire still rotating her life around a man's. When will the Claires of the world realize they can address the issues of the day without a lump of testosterone in their beds? Who needs 'em?"

"But look at her!" Violet said proudly. "She's so happy."

Anita snorted and dipped a stumpy finger in the centerpiece, one of the frosted gingerbread houses designed in the shape of HurryUp that were placed in the center of each table.

"It's delicious," Anita croaked.

"Isn't it all?" Slim crowed back.

When she felt the timing was right and after Senator Kennedy, as prearranged, had toasted the "life of his Party, the Democratic one," Claire stood. Averell Harriman poured her champagne flute full as she in turn toasted the illustrious persons in the room, singling out her mother and her daughter.

"I want to thank my generous husband for giving me the best gift of all. No, it's not an editorial endorsement." She waited until her happy guests stopped laughing. "It's this house. HurryUp." She beamed proudly.

"I want to thank my husband for giving me the most precious gift any woman can have"—only Sara could see that she was nervously pulling on her pearl bracelet—"a place to hang her hat."

She lifted her eyes to meet his. "To my husband. And my home. HurryUp." She raised her glass to Grant and let the guests' gushes fill the tent, toasting Grant's generosity. He was sitting undeniably frozen, even as a big-time lawyer like Edward Bennett Williams, counsel to presidents, legal defender of Jimmy Hoffa and Mafia godfather Frank Costello, and who had just won an acquittal for Texas governor John Connally, nodded his lawyerly head. Williams's witnessing of the bargain without vocal objection from Grant was as good as a signed deed in Claire's mind.

She held her breath, wondering to herself what Grant would do even as she continued with her after-dinner toasts.

Inebriated not by the medley of fine California Sonoma wines served at dinner but by the rich-bodied presence of his two dinner companions, Grant was well mellowed. If only, the Washington hostess in Claire mused to herself as she watched him, more people understood the power of the place card. She cleared her throat as Grant stood to his full height of over six feet. Would he toast her and take the house back? In front of all these people?

Sensing nervousness on the part of her normally composed mother, Sara patted Billy on the behind and shooed him up to stand beside his grandmother.

"Go to Grand Claire, Billy. Go on!"

Claire showered him with hugs, to the delight of her guests, and then lifted him up in her arms. Anita, on her feet and right behind her, quickly removed the champagne glass from Claire's hand in case *Newsview* and the *New York Times* took advantage of this photo opportunity. No sense seeing the candidate from California with a drink in her hand, even if it was made from grapes from her own state.

The beautiful woman with the high cheekbones, flawless complexion, and lithe figure didn't resemble an ordinary grandmother any more than the prim Pam Harriman looked like one of the great courtesans of history or Jackie O. with her feathery voice and wide saucer eyes brought to mind a public relations wizard who knew better than Madison Avenue how to guard a legend and keep it alive. Then Claire's gaze fell upon the unimposing woman who had saved her in person and time and time again with her written words, Anne Morrow Lindbergh. She may have faded from the public eye, but Claire would never forget the way her heroine's words helped her to live through her grief over Six.

What did these women all have in common? Why were they all sisters to Claire under the skin? The answer would be written in their biographies. These were women, like it or not, who had the boldness to reinvent themselves, time and time again, in order to survive, protecting themselves and their children. They had done it by shedding an old life to pick up a new one when the promise of the old had been shattered.

Claire scanned the tent full of so many faces that mattered to her and others to whom she mattered not at all. She spoke slowly, Billy in her arms, Anita's mechanically prepped microphone at her freshly lipsticked mouth.

"Being half a century old is very heady stuff, let me tell you. It makes you reflect on where you have been and, furthermore, where you are going. I am a very blessed woman. I have family, my mother, my auntie, my two generations of children." Her broad smile was directed at Sara. "And a talented husband who puts up with me.

"I have decided the Senate is a good forum from which I can be an effective thorn in the side of people who feel that issues pertaining to children and sexism and racism matter less than other issues. I see none bigger. When as a young bride I sat at the feet of Eleanor Roosevelt, I would listen to her tell us that if we were all equally fighting World War Two for peace in the world, we had better make sure we had jobs and equality at home. Being a woman and a new homeowner"—Claire's eyes twinkled—"I think I will spend a few more years tidying up some of the mess in our House on the Hill. Grant, I hope I have your support." She reached out her arm. But how was he going to react?

At the other end of the table, Jackie applauded with her large hands and pointed them in Grant's direction. Her full lips were a breath away from Grant's earlobe as she stood to salute Claire. "I think that's your cue, Grant." When she said his name, it sounded like an enchantress's invitation. Her voice was accompanied by the tinkling sound of her wind-chime earrings. "Nothing makes a strong man look even more important than when he is helping a good woman, Graaant. Incidentally, I'd like to be a quiet helper in Claire's campaign. Would that be all right?" Jackie's beguiling magic, the Sonoma wine, and the womanly beauty radiating from Claire tonight suddenly made Charity Foxley a forgotten hiccup.

Grant moved proudly to Claire's side to validate his gift of a home to her. After everything she had done for him tonight, he felt proud and manly being able to add something as simple as a house to her gift list. He stood there handsome in his custom-cut tuxedo, his windburned face in masculine contrast to Claire's pale beauty. Even he noticed how her differences complemented him. He effused to the hushed crowd, "I can only regret that journalist's ethics keep me from putting my talented wife on the cover of all my periodicals. As you know, a good-looking woman on the cover always sells.

"I give you, esteemed ladies and gentleman"—Grant lifted his glass, prodding Anita to shrug—it was okay for a newspaperman to be photographed with a drink in his hand; they were supposed to be boozy anyhow—"the next senator from California, Claire Harrison, my wife."

"And a woman of property at last," Pam whispered loudly into her Governor's ear.

The Senate race was a shoo-in. California loved Claire for her high-level Washington access and voted her in by a wide majority. She could pass job bills and highway budgets and build new schools and raise teacher salaries—and did. Since the working girl in her never forgot about weekly wages, she rewarded California coastal cities with naval bases and landlocked towns with air force sites.

As a representative, she had stood at Coretta King's shoulder as she muscled in segregation reforms. Now, as a senator in the Ford administration, Claire increased her zeal. She followed Coretta's lead in ensuring that Dr. King's initiatives be continued through equalizing education and creating job opportunities rather than merely erecting statues and issuing plaques. As Claire played the Washington game by following the rules and adding a little finesse, her influence became increasingly powerful.

And, while never a love match, her relationship with Grant gradually developed into one of mutual respect, one based on domestic courtesy and civilized consideration. He highlighted passages in his papers for her in yellow marker that he knew she would find interesting, and with her knack for mimicry, she repeated for him the floor speeches of his least favorite senators with all the humor and drama of Lucy and Lana. After some minor household reforms, Fenwick Grant became the ideal husband for Claire, the politician. This marriage made her feel grounded and attached to something solid; if passion wasn't part of the equation, still it all added up to a mature complement of progress and power. After all, Grant loved the scent of power. And Claire now wore it behind her ears, on her wrists, and at her pulse points.

When spring returned to HurryUp after the long winter of 1975, with its jonquils, dogwood, and forsythia and Easter egg–colored blooms limning the newly landscaped Pie, Claire pushed her other business to one side and recommitted herself to bringing her son home finally, now that she had a place of her own to gather all her loved ones in. It had been over a year and a half since she'd won her Senate seat, and it gnawed at her like an old wound in her heart that Six lay in a long, anonymous row with Ophelia's ancestors, whom he had never known, in a rectangular plot behind a house in which only Ophelia lived and which she had reliably heard was never visited by Harry, not even to lay flowers across his grave. She was denied visitation under the legal document she had been forced to sign in Italy, and Ophelia held her to every word of its terms. After all, Six's grave was on her property, and Ophelia had threatened to shoot if the "murderess" stepped a foot onto her soil.

Whether it was the passage of time or the fact that she was now a U.S. Senator who was married to a media mogul able to protect her from the kind of damage Ophelia had heaped upon her before, or whether it was because she had proselytized Ophelia's hench-man into her loyal press secretary, or merely the fact that she was over half a century old, Claire felt she was of a mind and age to confront Ophelia.

Claire commissioned a sculptor who worked in marble, whose chiseled work encircled the rotunda of the Senate Building, his latest piece a marble bust of Robert Kennedy, which he had sculpted from photographs and memories. She put Sara in charge of the likeness, and her daughter thanked her for her confidence.

Then she attempted Six's exhumation. There was no dealing with Ophelia. She wouldn't keep her lawyers' appointments or come to the phone, and she lied to her fellow members at the Tuxedo Club that grave robbers had tried to desecrate her family's remains. She even hired private security police for her ancestors' bones. Claire finally realized that the only way to kill an old witch was to drop a house on her. And in her case, probably the House *and* the Senate.

Age hadn't softened Ophelia's hardness. Her nasty disposition and prejudices only magnified with the accumulation of years. Sara still dutifully visited her grand-mère with her children, but they always cried before the visits and complained to Claire about stomachaches before and nightmares later. Fit as a fiddle, Ophelia still enjoyed a strict daily regimen of diet and exercise, walking briskly around the grounds of Charlotte Hall and nourishing her-self with its home-grown vegetables and their supernatural vitamins. She had taken to keeping bees on the grounds to harvest her own honey and in the winter months retired to her "cottage" in Hobe Sound, adding grapefruits from her grove to her menu.

She still kept her sharp wits about her, and her mean streak focused principally on "Senator Strumpet," as she referred to Claire. Even the formidable Edward Bennett Williams, who had advised feisty presidents and defended mobsters, found Ophelia "terrorizing."

"My God, Claire. I think I've met the devil and she's your former mother-in-law. I swear she was going to spit up green bile while we were having tea. I went to mass as soon as I got outta there."

"Well, what's your best legal advice on this?" Senator Harrison asked.

"Hire a hit man and I'll defend you." He was joking, of course, but he also was telling her that legally pursuing this thing was out of the question. Clout was what was required.

"What's the most important thing to her? Cut her off from it and she'll come around."

What was important enough for Ophelia to fear losing? What was worth a trade of buried bones to her, bones that were like the Holy Grail to Claire?

Ophelia had stocks and bonds and houses and Harry and Minnie and their adopted child, William Henry Harrison the Sixth. Number Six. Again. Claire had heard from Williams what he had unearthed through the legal grapevine: Ophelia Harrison had purchased this child just to hurt Claire. But Claire suspected it was really a clinical effort to give the Harrisons a direct male heir, a hysterical attempt to entice Harrison back. Claire despised her for using her son's name in an unconscionable game of one-upmanship.

When Ophelia had learned from Tom that Six was really the child of Harrison and Claire, she had become demonic, allowing her darker side to rule both her left and right hands.

Tom was CEO of Harrison, Harrison and Pettibone, the commodities exchange that Harrison had relinquished per his divorce agreement. The youthful CEO wanted stock and voting control as a reward for the long hours he put in; although Harry was the firm's chairman and president, he held these titles in name only, spending more time on the links than in the office. Yet it was not Tom's work ethic that allowed him to prevail in his fight for control. Instead, he won through social blackmail, threatening to go public to the papers with the ugly facts of Ophelia's former husband's and former daughter-in-law's affair. It was a sordid enough scandal to excise Ophelia from her social circles in Tuxedo Park, New York, Hobe Sound, and Newport. And to remove her from the best chair in all her clubs where she sat on the membership committees, Brahmin-style, deciding who was good enough to join and who wasn't. But Ophelia couldn't stand to have any mud smeared on her own hem. She'd lose her finger-pointing status. According to Williams, Tom had emerged with basically sixty percent of the company, all to preserve Ophelia's pristine reputation.

Surely Claire could get the silly woman, who had swapped a company for her unsullied name, to return her child's remains under the same conditions. And so the deal had been worked out. She left only the final details to her lawyers.

Claire had thought about the war of the two Mrs. Harrisons for some time before she had acted on it. She would use her connections and even the foot trail of Tom to trade Six for Ophelia's social standing. At first, she hated the thought of undermining an old lady. But then she reasoned that age was relative, and, besides, Ophelia was no lady.

Claire herself flew up to New York to retrieve Six. She borrowed the Harrimans' plane so she could ride back with the coffin. Her heart was weighted in anticipation of the sad journey she was finally taking and at the same time exhilarated that she would finally be bringing him home. Forever.

* * *

If heavenly spirits and souls could be comforted by down-to-earth displays of loving remembrance, Claire would tend to it. In her own mind's eye, Six was the beautiful seraphim, eternally an adolescent angel dwelling in the room in the clouds she and Lorenza had long ago decorated for him with all his favorite things. But somehow she needed to have his earthly remains at rest in the garden of tranquillity she had created for him in the Pie. Where she could tend to the flowers on his grave of velvety green grass and have a place to pray, keeping him remembered by his family.

It stung her to the core that she had never seen him again or been allowed to say words over his little body since that day of Duccio's memorial-service circus. Now he would be buried in the Pie in which Auntie Wren already lay and where places were reserved for Slim, Violet, and even Claire herself. Death was part of the circle of life as much as birth and should be planned for, she had reasoned in her increasingly pragmatic way.

She had tried to stifle any desire to confront Ophelia on her own turf. The prearranged plan was for Claire to collect her son's remains from Charlotte Hall's private burial plot and leave. Ophelia had promised to absent herself from the property or, if indisposed, to stay inside the house. What was the point of meeting again?

"This has been the oddest custody case I've ever been involved with, Senator." Sam, the young attorney who was already considered a preeminent Supreme Court advocate, had smacked his lips over his Perrier and shaken his head on the flight over. Odd indeed.

Ophelia had finally been defeated, but only by the clout of the mighty, one of whom Claire had now undeniably become. This time Claire had the press on her side and the strength that came from "under the table" influence. But still she felt uneasy.

The ride from the airfield was interminable. Claire could hear her heart thumping in her ears, feeling as nervous as the first time

Harry had brought her here as his young bride, three weddings ago. She felt beads of perspiration forming at the wings of her brown-and-silver chignon, the widely imitated Claire Harrison coiffure. She took a deep breath and asked one of the attorneys to turn up the air conditioning in the sedan. As her face returned to its usual look of composed serenity, she glanced down at her dark Chanel suit and peeled off one of her trademark white gloves, laying it over the handle of the cognac crocodile handbag that rested perfectly centered in her lap. Only a simple gold wedding band adorned her hand. She had dressed carefully for this occasion. Ophelia was so devious. She might make a last-ditch effort to stand in her way. She wanted to be impeccably groomed so as not to arch even an undertaker's eyebrow. Suddenly she felt as ill prepared as the schoolgirl she had been on that first visit to Charlotte Hall. As they turned down the long driveway, she imagined a pair of eyes behind every tree.

When they pulled into the courtyard, Claire was sure she saw one of the stone lions move. It was Ophelia, standing on the threshold of her house as if to turn them away.

"Jesus, Senator Harrison," one of the young lawyers piped up. "You didn't tell us we were serving papers on Medusa."

A decade of ferocity was etched on Ophelia's face. Her creased chins jutted out like a ski jump from the glum valley of her downturned mouth. The meanness and hatred that had been part of her features for so long had been petrified on her face. The narrowing, rheumy eyes and protruding lower lip dropped to reveal a line of brownish bottom teeth.

"God, Senator. Does she wear a muzzle?"

Claire steeled herself and stepped out of the car. What was the old Medusa myth? If she looked you in the eye you turned to stone. Claire wondered if she should push on her sunglasses. One granite monument to the past was enough.

She shook off the chill that even on this summer day shivered down her spine and willed herself to picture something pleasant.

Ah, the Aunties. She saw them young, as they used to be. Their goodness and love were the perfect antidote to Ophelia.

She wanted to get this business over with as quickly as possible. She mounted the flagstone steps with determination, marching up the stair entry, chin thrust up, white gloves concealing her clenched fists. Ophelia's walking stick, a heavy black pole topped with a silver dog's head, missed her foot by less than an inch.

"Don't come any farther. You're a trespasser here, Senator Strumpet. And your bastard isn't ready." She moved her eyes up and down Claire's clothing until Claire felt naked and exposed. She sneered at Claire, her eyes flashing with yellow specks. "His grave is the one with the shallow stone. Food for worms. Dig him up yourself, if you will." Ophelia showed the rest of her teeth as she tilted her hand back toward a servant wearing a carnation and holding a shovel.

Claire looked momentarily frightened as she turned to her legal team for answers. It wasn't supposed to have been like this. Six was supposed to be ready.

Young turk number one was already on the car phone, yelling about the whereabouts of the exhumation crew. He turned to Claire, relieved.

"She kept them out all morning but they're at the grave site now, with some guys from the sheriff's office. She's just bluffing."

There was an instant look of dislike on his young face for the bad witch guarding her Tudor dungeon. Both men moved in as if to protect Claire from some dark force of evil.

"You can't take him. He's mine. He belongs with the ancestors." Ophelia raised her stick.

"He was never yours," Claire said quietly. "He was only Harrison's." She watched as the look of understanding spread over Ophelia's twisted features. She backed off and Claire moved in.

"Ophelia, you're an ugly fool. Once you had everything. Now you are like a foul-smelling puddle. Just something we have to step over on our way home." The word "home" gave her courage.

"You're just a living illustration of a snaggle-toothed witch from one of Harry's old nursery books. You haven't changed at all. Go back to hell."

Both the chauffeur and lawyers were startled to hear the lady-like senator with the aristocratic bearing haul off at the mouth. The tips of Ophelia's ears brightened to an unhealthy pink. The younger attorney glanced at his Perrier bottle in the car and vaguely wondered whether it was true that if you poured water on a witch she would melt.

Her venom exhausted, Claire turned on her low heel, giving Ophelia nothing but her back as she eased her way into the car, the doors still expectantly open. Her shoulders trembled with rage. Under her shaky directions, the limousine pulled into the plotted ground that housed Charlotte Hall's mausoleum and the few mathematically arranged lesser stones planted around the outside perimeter marked by two massive granite urns. The site was cold and impersonal, closer in proximity to Harry's house than Ophelia's. Six's undistinguished flat stone was off to one side, its grave open as two men in overalls and a hydraulic iron lift pulled the child-sized casket into the air.

Claire's breath momentarily left her body, and her knees weakened at the sudden lightness. Still she managed to hang on. She would not crumble in front of Ophelia, who stood rooted to her spot watching. As the bronze casket was removed and pushed into the Cadillac hearse, Claire caught a glimpse of two petty, living ghosts. Harry and Minnie were peering from behind a curtain at her bold action of taking home her own. Claire turned to confront them full face. But then she softened. How pathetic these pale remnants from her past appeared now. Harry's fly-boy handsome features had been ravaged by quarts of Boodles gin and decades of self-loathing. Minnie's face, pinched next to his, wore the expression of a cranky governess. And to think she had even lived in that poor excuse for a home, decorated with silk snobbery and sterling-silver prejudice. How little had changed here. Claire noticed that even the crewelworked curtains were the same pattern Ophelia had ordered for her and Harry thirty-five years ago. How far away and long ago it all seemed. What if she had stayed? In Washington she lived in a world of power and action, where everyone was in perpetual motion. But here everyone was like figures painted on an expensive antique vase, forever frozen, doomed to go on repeating the same useless activity.

She didn't breathe normally or even sigh until Six's casket was loaded onto the plane and she and her admiring attorneys, their faces bursting with adulation, were onboard. By now they would have fought battalions for Claire.

"Senator Harrison, I would have gladly bopped that old witch in her crooked nose. It would have been worth sixty days in jail!" Sam slapped a cocky backhand on his gray flannel thigh.

"I could get you a reduced sentence. Thirty days," Robb boasted.

"Yeah, Claire. Excuse me, Senator. I just feel like we're pals now that we've been in the trenches together. You know."

"I know."

"Why didn't you just haul off and hit the dragon lady? I wouldn't have told. I would have perjured myself for you." There was a look of fealty on the earnest face of Williams's brightest protégé.

How like youth, even my own, she thought. To want to feed evil with anger.

"Because, son, it wasn't necessary. I'm leaving with what we came for. We've won. Now we can go home."

Claire leaned her head back on the gray leather seat. The Gulfstream jet taxied down the runway and pulled into its take-off slot. Soon they would be away from here. She closed her eyes. Six was safe and she was protected by her two by-now doggedly faithful guardians.

"Senator. Senator Harrison!" The Harrimans' pilot was standing over her. "Excuse me, Senator." He cleared his throat and

Claire could smell the coffee on his breath. In her anxiety, her adrenaline level had jumped, making all her senses more vivid.

"I'm sorry to disturb you, Senator."

She had been dreaming. Italy. Six. Sara. And always Harrison. "Yes. What's the matter?" Her efficient Senator side was awakened.

"A big summer storm with gale-force winds has moved in over the mid-Atlantic states. National Airport and Dulles are both closed. We can try to make it into BWI if you want, but it's risky. It's the inland turbulence from Hurricane Nan. We'd like to wait it out until morning."

"Hurricane Nan? L-M-N-O-P, she played out the alphabetical order in which hurricanes were named. N. The next would be O. It could be Hurricane Ophelia.

"Yes, of course." She didn't want to put Six's remains in jeopardy. "We'll wait until it's safe."

"Probably not until morning, ma'am. I'll make some hotel reservations."

Claire thought about Six, alone in the cargo hold. "I'll sleep onboard if you don't mind. I'll just need some tea and a blanket."

The Harrimans' pilot looked doubtful. Mrs. Harriman would never have slept aboard unless they squeezed in a four-poster draped in Porthault linens.

"Please. I don't want to leave my son's remains unguarded." She leveled her violet eyes at him.

The former air force lieutenant snapped to attention. He would never leave a fellow soldier returning in a wood box alone, either. "Yes, ma'am. We'll all wait it out. I'll have sandwiches brought aboard."

By seven A.M., the storm had dissipated and the still crisply uniformed captain informed Claire that they would soon be ready for takeoff. They were checking the fuel now. Robb went into the small private terminal for doughnuts and newspapers. He came back as white as a sheet. He leaned down toward Claire almost in apology.

"There was a terrible automobile accident last night." He slipped to one knee. "The radio is reporting that Fenwick Grant was seriously injured . . . another report says he was killed in the storm on the Eastern Shore. And—this is none of my business, I guess, but I think you should know this, too. They're saying he was with that TV journalist Prudence Savage. She died too." He held out his hand for her to hold.

She didn't need the comfort.

"My husband. And Prudence Savage. Killed? Together?"

Robb respected the way she held herself together.

"Could there be a mistake?" Did it have to be one of Grant's virtues?

"Not according to the early news reports." His admiration for this remarkably strong woman was growing. She was beautiful in her composed, quiet way. Even in the hard glare of morning, after a night spent sitting on an airplane seat with her long legs folded under her. Why, half the gals he knew would have looked like hell. And been going to pieces.

"Are we going to be able to take off now?" she asked softly. She folded her hands and readied herself for what lay ahead.

The sun spilled onto the Pie, brighter after the series of roiling thunderstorms. Today the light was shining undiluted onto the freshly clustered beds of summer roses, black-eyed Susans, peonies, and sweet William that encircled HurryUp's garden of tranquillity like a charm bracelet. The waist-tall boxwood and carefully planted burst of Virginia wildflowers separated the clearing from the surrounding blue grass and the steep elderly trees whose leafy arches folded over them.

She listened as Sara read her poem and watched as little Violet and Dylan each showered a little shovelful of red clay over Uncle Six's grave. And Slim and Violet threw handfuls of sweet William and white rose petals. Claire felt a great wave of relief, content to let the others take the lead celebrating his memory and pouring their love upon the fresh grave at the top of the east corner of the Pie. Six's statue stood in the center of the circle like a heavenly imp, as much the handiwork of Sara as of the sculptor. The marble likeness was astonishing even down to the dimple in his cheek and the wink of mischief in the eye. What Sara had added to the body of the sculpture was the best of her flower-child whimsy. And the personality of Six, with sisterly love.

She had given him wings the spread size of Icarus's, only folded, the carved feathers acting as an eternal umbrella to shield the body of Six from the vicissitudes of the elements. She had found a way to protect him.

Finally, it was Claire's turn to approach Six's resting place.

"You are home, my darling." She patted the headstone with one hand and Sara's shoulders with the other. The wind blew up, stirring yellow pollen from the golden sycamore tree under which they stood, fluttering down upon them like gold caviar. The private little band of Six's celebrants—they numbered less than a dozen—formed a circle in the clearing and gave up a moment of silence. She wished Harrison had been able to attend. It would have meant so much to her. But Starling was seriously ill again—hospitalized in London—and Harrison was unable to leave her bedside. He had made sure to send the pocket watch that Six had always admired, however, the one Harrison had promised him when he was older. Claire laid it in the ground beside the blossoms. Finally the family clasped hands and sang Six's favorite hymn as they filed out of the garden.

Two days later, Claire trooped up to the Pie again, only this time shoulder to shoulder with the East Coast establishment and an assortment of Kennedys, journalists, the current president and several hopefuls, both political parties well represented. There were about two hundred folks in all, including the entire first string of the Washington Redskins. As it was still uncertain as to

whom the childless Grant had left his empire, no one in the running wanted to snub the publisher's widow. She didn't bother
with a veil, opting for a black Chanel and sunglasses, her official
mourning suit that she wore to all the State funerals she was invited to attend.

She listened respectfully to the words of praise heaped upon her
husband by the powerful and didn't mind when an uninvited
photographer snapped her picture as she tossed her wedding ring
into the ground after Grant's empty casket, a composed look of
respect across her features. It wasn't anybody's business but hers
and Anita's that only Grant's impressive public reputation was in
the box being buried and that his ashes were sitting in a comely
green spice jar between the fresh mint and oregano on her kitchen
windowsill—where she could keep her eye on him.

Prudence Savage's funeral in her Ohio hometown was receiving
a lot of ink, too. Every paper but Grant's was printing stories
questioning what Grant was doing in the middle of the night on
the Eastern Shore with the leggy young political star of television's *24 Hours.*

Grant's papers all ran the single short quote from Claire delivered by her press secretary, Anita Lace.

"Senator Harrison deeply mourns the loss of her husband as
well as her friend Prudence Savage. The two of them were hurrying to Claire's home from a meeting to welcome her back from a
family business trip in New York." When asked "What kind of
meeting goes on with two people until two A.M. in an empty
beach house?" Anita simply echoed Claire and uttered "Deep
Throat" in her "Get it now, buddy?" confidential way.

"Who the hell is going to come forward and deny it? Deep
Throat? What is he going to do? Jump out from behind his cover
and identify himself to protect his reputation?" Anita argued.
The "Deep Throat" spin on the matter of Grant and Prudence
gave some color to the old story of a man caught cheating on his
wife.

"Anyway, a lot of Democrats turned up at the Pie to mourn him." Anita wiped a single tear away.

"He certainly was popular." Slim wore a perky pillbox hat on her head.

Claire buried the empty casket with all the dignity she could muster. She presided over a postburial tea-and-bourbon reception back at the house, where she was overheard to say to a reporter, "I've been to a lot of teas in my day so I know a tempest in a teapot when I see one." Cut. Wrap. Lefty would have been proud of her. Rumors laid to rest.

In all the commotion she hadn't seen the *New York Times* obituary with its accompanying profile of the elegant older woman. Starling Endicott Fillmore Harrison of Newport, Rhode Island; Lake Como, Italy; and Tuxedo Park, New York, philanthropist and staunch supporter of the decorative arts and gardening, had died at her Italian villa after a long illness.

After the reading of the eighth draft of Grant's last will and testament, Claire discovered that she was rich. Not Harrison rich, but rich enough to name a wing for special diseases at Cedars-Sinai Hospital in L.A. for Lefty. This she did with pride. She carefully oversaw the building of a new airport in Loudoun County named for her latest late husband, Pulitzer Prize–winning publisher Fenwick Grant, out of the trust she presided over with his appointed board. She also picked out a distinguished drawing, a three-quarter profile, for the U.S. Postal Department when it issued a commemorative stamp in his honor. Violet, Billy, and Dylan got a kick out of sending their letters with Uncle Grant's picture on them. She sent a condolence note to Harrison and mailed it with the stamp. And after Claire added the first issue of the Grant stamp to her famous stamp collection, she closed the book on him.

EPILOGUE

It is beautiful that our lives coincided for so long.
—Simone de Beauvoir

Between us it was a question of an essential love.
—Jean-Paul Sartre

Claire pushed on her glasses, the line through the center dividing the lenses in two. The bifocals improved her vision for distance while allowing her to read the speedometer. She was in a hurry to get home. She'd tried not to exceed the speed limit; HurryUp had never sounded so appropriate.

Placing her high heels on the leather seat next to her, she slipped on her Belgian driving shoes, the ones with the rubber bubbles on the soles. Billy had gotten them for her with the inducement, "Gram, *anybody* hip is wearing these." She loved being in the driver's seat by herself and had sent the chauffeur home. She figured she'd have enough attendants buzzing around as soon as she began the new job. After she was sworn in she'd be driven everywhere. Probably have those bothersome bodyguards with her as well. She couldn't wait to tell *him* the news. She wanted to be the first and hoped it hadn't been announced on television yet.

She wondered how her critics would respond to the new UN ambassador's resident houseguest. Ambassador-to-be, Claire Harrison smiled to herself.

As she crossed into Virginia and barreled on toward Middleburg, she noticed she'd picked up a police car. Dammit. Couldn't
they see that her license plate was CALIFORNIA 1? She'd thought
she was only ten miles over the limit. The whirling blue light
pulled her over and both state troopers got out. Claire could see
her reflection in Office Beck's badge. And she could see herself
more clearly in Officer Dey's Ray-Bans.

"I'm sorry, boys. I didn't—"

"Excuse us, Senator Harrison. We were just being neighborly.
Both of us just wanted to congratulate you on your ambassador-
ship. Guy here heard it over his radio. We just wanted to wish
you luck."

"And warn you to be careful of those Russkies at the UN." Guy
tipped his hat to the popular senator.

"Well, that's really lovely of you boys."

"Will you be wanting an escort or anything, Senator . . .
Ambass—aw, geez, you'll always be Senator to us."

"And home will always be HurryUp in Virginia." She shook
their hands, and then turned back to the road, and sped along.
She was anxious to share her news with only one man.

She walked up behind him. His thick white hair was neatly
combed, all except for the still-stubborn forelock in front. He was
working on his latest book on the Middle East, sitting on the
back veranda off his room. It overlooked the man-made lake
they'd put in in late September. They called it Lake Como, just
for fun.

She watched him lovingly for a moment before she slipped behind him, wrapping her arms around his neck and planting a kiss
on top of his luxurious head of cloud-colored hair.

"Hello, darling. I'm home."

"I heard your car drive up. Well, am I sleeping with an
Honorable woman or not?"

"I'm Honorable. The Honorable Ambassador Harrison to you."

"Now there are two Ambassador Harrisons in this house. It's going to get confusing around here."

"It's always been confusing." She smiled. But it had always been Harrison.

"I don't suppose you'd agree to marry me at last?"

Claire was close enough to him to smell her favorite cologne, a combination of English soaps, tweed, and his perspiration. "I'm already a Harrison. Who would I be then? Ambassador Harrison Harrison?"

From where she stood she could see his velvet slippers with little embroidered foxes at the foot of her bed. "We don't need marriage, darling. It would only confuse the grandchildren, who are *your* great-grandchildren."

"I'd like to legitimize you, my dear."

"Why mess with success, my love?"

"Why indeed?"

He must have been expecting her Senate confirmation. There was a gift box in the corner of her chair.

"Presents?" Her eyes turned the loveliest amethyst color when she was pleased.

"More like a medal."

"Ooh, the Purple Heart. I've earned it."

"No, a special medal. Only you could wear it."

First the ribbon, then the pale blue box, then the tissue paper, and finally the gray velvet case. She smiled at him as she snapped open the lid, prepared to like whatever he had selected.

"A leaping lizard! In diamonds."

"Don't get cute, Ambassador, or I won't counsel you on foreign diplomacy."

"We make quite an astonishing team, don't we, my love?"

"Would you like me to pin on your chameleon?"

Claire moved closer to Harrison, just a breath away, in response. She handed him the chameleon and lifted her left shoulder toward him.

He smiled as he pushed his fingers under her jacket.

"I tried to convince Tiffany's to design one that changes colors. They added a yellow diamond here and emeralds for eyes. A blue diamond on the tail—quite rare, I'm told. Evidently it was the best they could do."

"It's charming. So this is what I am, is it?"

"If we don't know what we are, surely the people who love us do."

"How beautiful."

"The brooch or the sentiment?"

"You, my dear."

And she kissed the man, the only man she had ever loved.

It had been a lifetime of waiting, but the man who had long ago captured Claire's heart now shared her bed, her days, and her future. They had survived the stormiest of seas, both apart and together. And both of them knew they were much better, even stronger, in one another's arms.